The Perilous Journey of Gavin the Great

The Perilous Journey of Gavin the Great

A Fable
by Don Gutteridge

With afterword by Brian T. W. Way

First Edition

 Wet Ink Books
www.WetInkBooks.com
WetInkBooks@gmail.com

The Perilous Journey of Gavin the Great
by Don Gutteridge

Cover Design – Richard M. Grove
Layout and Design – Richard M. Grove
Cover Image – stained-glass image by Zagory – Shutterstock, used by permission

Typeset in Garamond
Printed and bound in Canada
Distributed in USA by Ingram,
        – to set up an account – 1-800-937-0152

Library and Archives Canada Cataloguing in Publication

Title: The perilous journey of Gavin the Great : a fable / by Don Gutteridge ; with afterword by Brian T.W. Way.
Names: Gutteridge, Don, 1937- author. | Way, Brian T. W. (Brian Thomas Wesley), 1951- writer of afterword.
Description: Previously published: Ottawa: Borealis Press, 2010.
Identifiers: Canadiana 20220471045 | ISBN 9781989786772 (softcover)
Classification: LCC PS8513.U85 P37 2022 | DDC C813/.54—dc23

This one is for
my grandchildren:
Tim, James,
Kevin, Katie and Rebecca
and for Tom in loving memory.

Table of Contents

Book One: Deadwood

Book II: Everdark

Book One

Deadwood

Chapter 1

A Flood

LONG, LONG AGO NEAR THE BEGINNING OF TIME
(or, as those few hardy survivors of Earthwood might
have put it to their grandchildren, at the end of one time
and the beginning of another), the spring rains that came
without fail and fell without favour upon woodland,
shore, meadow and waterway decided for no discernible
reason not to stop. Oh, there was much speculation
among the many-named creatures who scampered or
slithered, darted or lumbered, clambered or burrowed,
stalked or cowered among the benign boughs and mossy
underpaths of the forests that Gollah had created
principally for the benefit of the Chosen Ones – whom
He had dubbed "woods-creatures" to distinguish them
honourably from the lesser beasts and beings. (Or so it
was said by those who ought to have known.) Shivering
under a damp canopy of branches or huddled along the
soggy corridors of a burrow, while rains poured down
upon the greening of sprout and shoot and leaflet as if
determined to murder what they had just persuaded to be
born, the woods-creatures ruminated thus:

The raccoons, who judged themselves to be the
cleverest of all earth's beings, suggested to anyone who

would listen – or anyone who could hear them above the din of rain-rattled twig and seething stream – that it was undeniably due to the after-effects of the Great Burning. After all, the fires they had seen erupting like exploded suns across the night-sky till the very stars trembled and went out and the wintriest of snows sizzled and steamed in mid-descent – such conflagration would need much rain to be brought to its senses and, as RA-Mosah (the eldest and wisest of the wisdom-dispensing clan) perpetually preached: "Dame Nature, who is herself but another manifestation of Gollah's all-seeing purpose, must right herself so that all things be kept in precise balance like the perfect halves of an apple or a walnut split by a coon's cunning." The rains will stop, the elder-coons assured a pair of droop-winged blackbirds and one drenched jackrabbit who happened to be within earshot, the rains will stop when they must, and not one milli-moment before.

The cottontails, on the other hand, who kept their ridiculously oversized ears close to the ground, insisted in their chattering, all-talk-at-once way that the thundering rumble (which had preceded the Great Burning and brought every animal upright and rigid with terror) had in truth not yet completed its dire reverberation, and was for those of sensitive ear and tender footpad still horrifically audible, and therefore one should not be concerned about a little surplus rain or the grass being a tad juicier than usual.

The mice, ever nervous and thrice superstitious, were inclined to blame it all on the intemperate greed of foxes and ferrets who last Fruitfall had helped themselves to more than their allotted share of rodent-pie and then further displeased the All-Knowing One by boasting of their obscene excesses. The upshot being the all Gollah's creatures were now being made to suffer for the transgressions of a few. How else could the denizens of Earthwood be reminded of their place in the order of things that was never to be challenged or changed? "We may be lowly, despised tunnellers of the underearth," an upstart mouseling named Bucktooth proclaimed from the crest of a flooded anthill, "but we know our place and do our duty, without complaint or braggadocio."

So bright had the Great Burning been, especially in the suddenness of its first burst somewhere over the house-habitats of the Tallwalkers who lived, thank Gollah, far to the south and preferred to stay there, that the moles of Earthwood rose out of their cozy vestibules up into the illuminated air like a chorus of blind cherubim and announced that at last they could see the light so long denied them. Even Owl, who was called Minervah by all who revered her and no less so after she had been struck sightless by the cruel dazzle of a Tallwalker's firestick, even Minervah had blinked and let the blast of brilliance shudder through her. But of the rains that refused to stop or what they might portend, she had nothing to say, or, if she did, it was too terrible to tell. And the moles, drenched but still blind, hunkered back in their holes and tried to find an undamp chamber where they could brood and indulge their disappointment.

The rains continued in spite of creature-talk, prophecy, good reason or, in the end, desperate petition to Gollah or any of the lesser gods who might be in a more merciful mood. So strenuous was the rain's falling that Serpentine Ridge itself became a blur, then a blotch, then a blank. The sinuous, barren parapet of rock and pitiless stone that had spawned the sun every morning of their lives and the lives of the dear dead-ones; whose

Ghosties and Phantasma (the very stuff of animal dreams and sleep-stirrings in the ever-dark), kept the Warlows, Bandahs and fanged Karkajim from devouring utterly the wise and foolish alike; whose grim, granite-rim defined for good or ill the eastern border of the known world — was no longer visible! Had the rains washed it away? Drowned the sun or driven it, horrified, in some other direction? Surely there could be no flicker of its flame left anywhere? Surely whatever transgressions had been made against Gollah's law were now fully punished? Surely Gollah would not be so spiteful as to destroy what He Himself had made and blessed and — through the generosity of His soul-mate, Dame Nature herself — encouraged to flourish from season to season in the great circle of Ever-Time?

Thus reasoned the Chosen Ones of Earthwood in the midst of trepidation and hope. But finally the hour arrived — it could have been high-sun or mid-dark, no-one could tell for certain — when reason itself went under. And instinct, older than Gollah and deeper than the world, took command.

* * *

The moles spluttered and paddled out of the flooded ground, nosing dew-worms and root-grubs, flaccid and slimy, before them. Leaderless, panicked, in tumbling hundreds they rippled over the forest floor, whose drenched mosses and runnels of rain left no place to settle or pause. Whether they knew it or not, the whole jumbled troop of them was heading east. Towards high ground. Towards Serpentine Ridge.

"They'll soon be eaten," Hubert, the brightest and most admired of last season's litter of cottontails, informed Renée, who was herself not far from producing her own brood.

"Well, what can you expect of moles?" sighed Cuspid, the young beaver, to his twin-sister as he watched her, with pride and brotherly affection, wedge an unco-operative cedar-twig into the dam they were dutifully repairing even as the floodwaters began rolling over its high, never-before-breached rampart. "You don't need eyes or a brain to snout your way through life."

Paddle-Whee giggled, and dropped a birch-branch. The torrent behind her spun it away and whistled it past the humped lodge where Mama and Papa stood stalwart and brave against every threat.

"Let the four-legged groundlings run like rats to their doom," one of the recently-arrived robins smirked to a nearby flock of starlings. "When the rains reach the top of the tallest tree, then we feathered folk might think about worrying. Gollah gave us wings to soar above His earth and all its lesser creatures." That not one winged-and-superior being had ventured up into the teeming murk of the air for days was not, out of politeness, mentioned. Nor was the question of how berry-bereft bushes and uncocooned larvae and wormless soil and flood-stunned grasses and leafless trees would provide sustenance enough to energize flight and quicken the eggs now withering within. Nor could anyone recall hearing a chirrup or a chick-a-dee-dee-dee for days and days. And Baldur, the great bachelor eagle, grateful for the liberal provender of mouse and mole over the long annuals of his life, had swung his wide wings into motion and bullied his way upwards to see if indeed Serpentine Ridge had been obliterated and whether the rains extended as far as the Tallwalker colonies to the south or the Lake of Waters Unending to the west or, improbably, to the borderless realms of North Holy where Gollah and the other gods were thought to dwell and contend. But barely had he made it above the treetops, shorn now of those few virgin leaves that had dared the Rootburst air, when the wind-whipped rain tormented his lofting feathers into leaden petals, and he sagged and bent and flapped crookedly landward.

But it was when the groundhogs and rabbits and, incredibly, the water-loving muskrats surged out of burrow and nether-den and, saying no word to friend or foe, stampeded eastward – to the Ridge and certain death – that RA-Mosah summoned the Council of Elders to emergency session, something he had not done since that long-ago day when the Tallwalkers had rampaged through Earthwood as if they had owned it, discharging their death-dealing firesticks and dragging behind them, bloody and bone-shattered, every whitetail doe and buck the forest had to give. Only the fawns and a few yearlings survived – to perish in the brutal cold of a dark, dark winter. No deer had since been seen. Nor had the Tallwalkers bothered to return.

RA-Mosah gazed thoughtfully around the ancient High Ring of sacred pines, the holiest precinct in all of Earthwood, for the raccoons and for those creatures who held their wisdom and canniness in awe. The elders had assumed the upper branches, as their age and sagacity warranted; the rest of the clan coon were squeezed, family by family, onto the stoutest branches farther down. Below them the watery ground swirled and seethed. The sanctified air enclosed by the High Ring shimmered before them like melting ice. Above the steady, reassuring words of their RA, the roar of the storm uttered its own, incomprehensible, speech.

"Elders, friends and children," he intoned as if the sun were still shining and beaver-meadows greening again, "we have no cause to abandon reason, the gift of the mothers and fathers who have lived before us, have seen and endured much, and loved us enough to try and make us as wise as any woods-creature is allowed." RA-Mosah always looked as if he were staring into some magical spot just behind the sun, but Gavin – the oldest of the three grandsons, the sons of Uthra, who sat erect and solemn just below and opposite their father – was certain that the seer's eye was cast in his direction only and was blessing him in some important but still-secret way. His brothers, who had not ceased to mourn their mother's death, huddled against him and paid little heed to the words of RA-Mosah.

"Panic is the mundane staple of the tunnellers, the diggers and the nether-nosers placed here in Earthwood by Gollah to be the fodder of hawks and coyotes. If there must be a flood – and we can be certain that Gollah Himself has brought it into being for His own purposes and will, when He is satisfied, bring it to a just conclusion – then it is surely fitting that the lowliest and meanest of creatures should panic and flee its fury, while we remain firm in our faith that the forest itself is meant to be and is indeed the flower of all Gollah's handiwork. It will survive. And as the principal wardens and watchmen of His glorious creation, we will survive with it. Our wisdom and steadfastness will be needed more than ever when the ruins are to be rebuilt, and the havoc turned back to harmony."

Oh, how RA-Mosah could speak! Gavin's heart trembled in his breast as if it had become words crying to be spoken. He clutched to his side the perfect little leather-pouch that Papa had given him just before stepping up beside grandfather-RA. Papa had smiled, as he habitually did when looking upon the wonder of his sons, but something like fear had fluttered in the air between them.

It was Uthra's turn to speak. Just then a flurry of blackbirds attempted to negotiate the space provided by the High-Ring pines, and almost made it to the eastern edge when their wings, furious with the wet weight of the wind, collapsed without warning, and they plummeted – askew, bewildered and broken – into the dark surge of the ground.

Ignoring them, Papa spoke: "As long as there are trees left upright and last fall's dried fruits unblemished on them, we shall have food aplenty and makeshift shelter enough to ride out the tempest. I too have read the sacred and ancient texts of The Book of Coon-Craft and Animal Cunning – " (he did not confess, as he had to Gavin, that he alone had perused the profane texts of the Tallwalkers and mastered their Gibberlish) "and I tell you that such plagues as this have been visited upon the world many times in the days before Earthwood was deemed to be the chosen ground of the great Gollah. Locusts and fire and flood have been sent to test those favoured too much perhaps by the All-Knowing, to tempt them beyond endurance, to make them go mad with the very reasoning He gave them to ensure their sanity."

Trisbert, who was half again as big as Gavin, gripped his older brother's paw as if he wished to lock onto it forever. Cuyler – tiny, sinewed, hardly weaned – buried a cold nose into Gavin's thick coat, and fidgeted.

"Do those foolish enough to think the heights of Serpentine Ridge will save them really believe that the roots of these mighty pines will suddenly jump out of the bedrock and skitter away, trunk and branch and everlasting needle? Are these roots not wrapped around the granite plates Gollah laid down to spread his seed-breathing soil upon? Has this needled limb I have my claws around ever been any colour but a living green? Since the very day it was created?"

The rain-soaked wind lashed at the High-Ring pines, bending the evergreen bitterly, howling against the words of belief flung against it. The branches, as promised, did not break. Not one needle was intimidated to abandon its post. But somewhere nearby a creek was transforming itself into a river, renegade and unrepentant.

RA-Mosah himself took up the animals' burden again. "Let us join hands and pray to Gollah. Let us swear to remain firm and reasoned and faithful to our purpose in Earthwood so long as Gollah grants us air to breathe, trees to harbour us, roots to hold the – "

RA-Mosah seemed to be leaning sideways, improbably tilting away from the topmost branch of the High Ring. His mouth hung open, stopped in mid-sentence, as if startled by something it had just said. The trees beside him seemed to be losing their bearings. The entire High Ring of pines began to waver and bob. Trees bounced against their neighbours. A hundred raccoons clung fiercely to the one branch that held them above whatever roiled below them.

Then RA-Mosah, Uthra, and the brotherhood of elders slowly sank away into ordinary forest until, with a scream like skin being flensed from vivid flesh, the roots that anchored everything to everything else gave way. They reared up into the most holy of spaces like crazed octopi, then followed trunk, branch and scattered needle into oblivion.

Not a cry, not a whimper, not a gasp of astonishment or a goodbye (if such had been offered) was heard above the roar as the waters of the world – in vengeance, spite, jest, indifference (who could say?) – eradicated the trees of Earthwood and tossed them topsy-turvy upon the flood that was surely, unstoppably, turning itself into a sea.

* * *

Whether it was instinct or reason, or some combination of these ever-contending elements, or some other motive too fresh and overwhelming to be given a name, all those woods-creatures and their lesser vassals who had not been drowned outright when the first wall of water struck, took to their legs and aimed them at Serpentine Ridge. Better to be chomped in half by a Three-Toed Bandah or benignly frightened to death in an instant by a Ghostie or Warlaw! No such thought was spoken aloud, however. Not even among members of family or clan, who tried desperately to stay close to their kin as the rain slashed sideways at them, blurred their vision and slickened fur or feather, while the rising riptide behind them licked at their tails and drove black panic deeper into belly and brain.

Soon there was not a creature who was not alone, though the undergrowth and moss-beds seethed and shuddered with a thousand of their kind in full flight. Fox tripped over Mouse and took no notice. Rabbit stumbled on Weasel, righted himself and carried on. Raccoon tangled with Coyote in a maze of leg and fur without a hiss or yelp. Squirrel felt the skim of Hawk's talons whisking above him and beyond. Porcupine bellyflopped upon Mole who did not mind. And did not mind again when Beaver did the same.

Still the rains did not relent, determined it seemed to swallow the whole of Earthwood till not even the tiniest tip would peep above it like a hopeful oasis or reminder of what had been and might be once more. No-one could see Serpentine Ridge. No-one could see an inch in front or beside. But the ground under paw and pad and snake-belly, beslimed and insubstantial, was rising, was lifting them upwards with each terrified step. Steeper and steeper. Grassier and grassier. Rockier and rockier. Surely this was the eyrie of monstrous birds and Three-toed Bandahs and Ghosties who feasted on obese clouds. But no such images, so common in the dreams of ordinary animals, occurred to them now: their panic was supreme. The heights of Serpentine Ridge, perilous and unknowable, now beckoned them, held out to them a last, frail hope.

Not all of Gollah's creatures reached even the first outcrop of rock, black and treacherous in the gloom above. Those who were small of limb soon scampered themselves into exhaustion and lay down as if preparing for some exotic, underwater sleep. Those whose heartbeat was frantic and tuned to quick escape soon felt the blood thicken and swell till it burst its chambers, and did not blink when the deluge closed over them. Others, more thoughtful perhaps than their cousins, simply arched forward onto a grassy foothill and gave up. And some, too clever by half and knowing less about water than they professed, clung to the flotsam of disgorged trees and let the flood take them where it wished.

The brave or naïve few who did reach the dizzy, twisting summit of the Ridge (they knew they were there only when their front feet suddenly pitched downwards) paused in solitary relief, slumped against a pitiless boulder or stunted root for balance, and waited. The sound of their own breathing and the roar of the tempest was all they knew until a ripple of wavelets whispered at their feet, at the knee-joint, at the vulnerable belly. With hope exhausted and courage mocked, who could blame them for sliding down into the waiting ooze – eyes shut and jaws wide open? Was Gollah's name the last word in their mouths?

So blinding and impenetrable had the rain become that the shadows flitting along the high crest of Serpentine Ridge might have been the last and boldest of Earthwood's elite or merely the phantoms of those already succumbed – travelling towards the abode of the gods who seemed to have abandoned them, towards mysterious North Holy where water, sky and land came together so harmoniously they no longer mattered. The Ridge rose with them, and the grim flood followed.

Then, as it had been foretold but not believed, water, rock and air met in sudden and final perfection. Earthwood was no more.

Chapter 2

Adderly

BEFORE HE REMEMBERED HE WAS NO LONGER A PUP in his parents' nest, Gavin heard himself calling out, "Papa! Papa!" When no-one from a neighbouring branch replied, he sighed in relief. How embarrassed he would have been if Papa, rune-master and the one who would lead them when the spirit of RA-Mosah faded finally, had been wakened by his childish cry. After all, it had only been a nightmare, induced no doubt by Ghosties and Warlows drifting down from the Ridge under cover of darkness to taunt and tempt and terrorize the impressionable young. (Which is why the wise raccoon sleeps during the day.) Some day he would dream the real dreams of RA-Mosah and Papa. He shivered and scrunched down into the furry coat that Gollah had given to every raccoon.

But what a nightmare it had been! He shuddered at the memory of it: torrential rains and tidal waves and woodscreatures in terrified flight. The very trees that held Earthwood intact giving up their roots, collapsing on the waters like Tallwalkers struck by one of their own thundersticks! How similar it had been to the vengeful flood Papa had secretly told him about, the one that long ago had engulfed the wicked world of the humanoids. And then, scariest of all, had been the spectre of Serpentine Ridge looming up before the fleeing, half-drowned hordes of animal clans, tribes and families.

Oddly, for he had the sensation of having slept long and deeply, Gavin felt very tired. The hollow of his bones ached. But he would not return to sleep. Such a nightmare would need time to untangle itself and a full day's sun to burn it away forever. Curious, he glanced up to look for the first or last glimmer of light, for it was either dusk or dawn and he had somehow been asleep for much longer than a day: if nothing else, the growl of an empty stomach told him so. And he felt also something of the profound drowsiness that settled into a raccoon's blood during the season of snow, when so many of Earthwood's inhabitants rested, fasted, and waited for Gollah to invite the sun back from its southern journey.

Gavin peered left, then right. He stared straight up towards the blue or black of sky. Someone, he thought, has slipped a white veil over me while I've been sleeping. Cuyler, most likely, playing one of his juvenile tricks. Still not fully awake, Gavin slapped lazily at the diaphanous wisps that seemed to be floating about a leg-length beyond his nose in the most tantalizing – nay, irritating – manner. His paw sailed right through whatever-it-was. Surely it couldn't be the skirts of a Ghostie? The petticoats of some Warlow escaped from his nightmare?

He opened both eyes wide, stretched out his forelegs, and sat up. His hind-claws dug into wood, solid wood. Yes, he was on a limb, a sturdy one – on his nap-tree perhaps. His hunger was genuine. And he really was awake, sitting secure on a high branch in Earthwood, his father and brothers no doubt equally secure on their own favourite branch nearby. What, then, was this silky drapery tickling his nostrils and cloaking the sun or moon somewhere in its folds?

Fog. It had to be. He had seen such stuff hanging above the stretch of Gullwing Sands at the far western edge of Earthwood that time when he had been permitted to join Papa in his search for Mama. Once in a while, he recalled now, such mist would sift through the pine-tree tops, dulling the sun above it for a few moments or transforming it into a red, shimmering disk. But never for very long: the forest was too thick and the sun too potent.

Somewhere behind this unexpected, upstart fog, Gavin was certain he could detect a wavering sort of light. Yes, it was definitely daytime, though morning, high-sun or later he could not tell. But the sun was still the sun, proud and unmovable on its appointed route. Well then, it was time to wake his brothers and have a closer look at this strange new phenomenon. He was about to call softly to little Cuyler, whose waking shenanigans never failed to rouse the sound-sleeping Trisbert, when he realized with a start that the "branch" he had been lying on was actually the trunk of a large, leafless tree, an elm by the smell and feel of the bark. And this trunk, which had provided him such a comfortable perch (if you didn't count the attendant nightmare), did not seem to be in its customary upright position; rather, it was, oddly and alas, sprawled horizontally, with its branches and twigs (at least those that Gavin could discern through the intervening mist) jutting skyward. Had he foolishly fallen asleep on a dead tree-trunk no farther than a wolf's paw could reach above the forest floor? But this tree was not quite dead. Rotting, baby-fisted leaf-buds winked up at him.

Cautiously, as some cold coil of fear tightened inside him, Gavin sniffed the windless air for the seasonal scents of Rootburst or Blossomflower: for the tang of sap oozing outward; for the musky odour of fungus, bulb and tuber; for the high sweetness of grasses reviving in hot sunshine. But the only smell here was the dank slipperiness of the fog and the rough aroma of elm-bark. He tugged at one of the buds: it crumbled in his paw. He cocked an ear for birdsong, the kind that shook Driftdeep out of your sleep with its melodic tinkling. Not a sound could he hear, strange or familiar.

"Papa!" he cried out, caring not that he was too grownup to do so. "Where are you?" The muffling fog caught his question, and did not answer.

Gavin knew he was not brave – not like Trisbert, who was a minute younger but half again as big – but he had been assured by Papa and grandfather Mosah through nod and wink that he was clever, with a cleverness well beyond that quantity already assigned by Gollah to the species chosen to hold dominion over the creatures of Earthwood. It was time to bring his brain into play, he knew, but the thumping of his heart in its hollow was so buffeting the thoughts inside his head that he could not tie two of them together for more than an eyeblink.

Sucking in several large breaths of foggy air, Gavin sat perfectly still and waited for his fear to subside. Soon, and with some relief, he heard his mind speaking its own words, as it had done for as long as he could remember. ("Every coon has more than one voice to plead or whine or mutter through the night with," RA-Mosah had told him solemnly, "though very few have the patience to listen or possess the gift of heeding the other voices Gollah gave us. But you, son of my son, are a listener, and you may indeed have the gift of interpretation, as Time will tell.")

So you've acted stupidly and fallen asleep on a fallen tree-trunk, Gavin thought. So what of that? Many a tree has been split asunder by lightning in the necessary storms of Snowmelt and Rootburst, and many a raccoon has traded wisdom for the occasional foolishness. True, there never has been such a fog as this in the forest, but then you have lived in it but the few scant annuals of your puppyhood. Get up off your ringtail and get your questions answered: you don't expect answers to float into your brain out of the fog on their own account, do you?

As if in fact the fog had decided to offer some assistance anyway, a familiar sound issued out of it: the rumbling, imperturbable snore of Trisbert. And, Gollah be praised, no more than a branch or two away. Now here was the obvious answer to Gavin's most pressing concern: sometime in the night (or day), this elm, undoubtedly one of several his family used for slumber in their privileged part of the forest, had been felled by lightning. And, still sleeping the comatose sleep of the snowy season, no-one had yet noticed, in part because the undulating mist had blurred the borders of day and night. Moreover, like most animals faced with some mysterious alteration in the elemental routine of their lives, they had just hunkered down in the safety of sleep to wait things out.

Gavin picked his way among the twisted limbs of the stricken tree towards the seesaw drone of Trisbert's snoring. He smiled to himself: his brother loved sleeping almost as much as he loved eating. It took an intrepid soul to disturb him at either pleasure. And what a surprise he would get when he discovered that up wasn't really up! As Gavin could see only one or two paces in front of him, he continued to edge cautiously, step by step, using the sound ahead of him as his guide. Even so, he almost stumbled off the elm's trunk when one claw skidded on a slippery knot. Instinctively he reached out with a forepaw and grasped the nearest branch, a sturdy black one that bore his whole weight easily.

"Don't you realize it's rude to use other people's bodies as a walking stick?" said the branch in a most unfriendly manner.

Gavin let go of the branch, too astonished to reply or be afraid. The branch curled and uncurled itself as if it were free to go wherever it pleased. "I always thought raccoons had more courtesy," it complained in a low, ruminative tone, its reprimand coming from somewhere below the fog-shrouded trunk. "Bossy, mind you, and big for their boots, but unfailingly polite – to a fault."

I'm still in my nightmare, was Gavin's thought, and he shuddered. He was surprised to hear himself say, to a branch, "Well, then, I am sorry if I've offended you. I was merely trying to find my brother and wake him up."

"Oh," said the branch, as the end of it with the voice rose up through the mist into clear view, "is it the season of Rootburst, then?"

If he had not been afraid of being discourteous, Gavin would have had a good laugh, for he now realized he was looking straight into the red, beady eyes of a full-grown fox-snake. "That is precisely what I was hoping to find out," he said, then thrust out a paw. "I am Gavin, son of Uthra, RA-to-be."

"You'll pardon me if I don't shake hands with you," said the branch-become-snake with gloomy humour. "I am Adderly, son of Adderly. But if it isn't the season of Rootburst, then there's no purpose to my lounging about here conversing with one of the lesser raccoons." His vermilion tongue flickered like a flame doing its own private dance. "I ought to be back in my den having a good dream." He swayed back into the fog as if to take his leave. "That is, of course, if one knew where one had left his den."

"Perhaps this tree fell on it when it came down in the storm," Gavin said helpfully.

"Perhaps. But I had just returned from a trip to the ground when you so immoderately clasped me by the belly, and I regret to have to tell you that there is little ground of any sort down there. Certainly not enough to make the kind of den an Adderly of my pedigree deserves."

Gavin peered over the edge of the trunk. There was no ground visible. The fog, visible everywhere, could, for all he knew, just as easily be a cloud, and he and Adderly and the snores of Trisbert could just as well be floating miles above Earthwood. He shivered, and for a moment fear stood upright in his eyes.

"Nothing down there but water and mud," said Adderly as he settled his coils comfortably along the trunk and several nearby branches. "But there's no need to be afraid. The thing to do is go back to sleep and wait for the next season to arrive." To emphasize the point he gave a huge yawn.

"I'm not afraid," Gavin said quickly, more to calm himself than contradict the serpent. But Adderly had already taken his own advice. At least he doesn't snore, Gavin thought as he stepped carefully over Adderly's numerous loops and, less certain now where he was or what he might find next, he continued on his way towards the raspings of Trisbert.

The familiar figure of his brother and litter-mate materialized hazily before him. It was no surprise to find Trisbert's large and fleshy body curled in upon itself like a hibernating bear. He was firmly wedged between the tree-trunk and a pair of stout branches. His eyes were squeezed shut in the bandit-mask that every raccoon wore proudly, his lower jaw slack with contented sleep. It seemed a shame to rouse him, but Gavin was suddenly sure that the rains had been no bad dream. The eternal trees of Earthwood had indeed collapsed before the torrential might of the great flood. He and Trisbert were clinging to one of them at this moment. They seemed to have survived. But had the others? Any others?

"Go away, Gav," Trisbert muttered about half-a-blink before Gavin's paw nudged his shoulder. "Wake me up when the sun goes down."

"There doesn't seem to be any sun," Gavin said gently into his brother's ear. "And I don't think we'll be fishing in Ambling Creek tonight."

Trisbert grumbled something unintelligible, snuggled down into his cowl, and gave out several theatrical but unconvincing snores.

Ever patient, Gavin waited, and tried not to think the thoughts that nibbled where they were not wanted.

Trisbert's eyes popped open. He heaved a huge sigh. "Now you've gone and done it," he said. "All that chatter about fish has made me hungry."

Gavin wondered whether fish could drown. Whatever havoc had been wrought upon Earthwood, the survivors would have to find food – somewhere.

Trisbert began to stretch out his powerful limbs one by one. "Hey," he said, "who threw the white stuff all over us?" He started to swat at it in a lazy sort of way, but he was chuckling all the while. It took a lot to disrupt his good-natured, casual approach to the world. "Are we in a spider-web or a caterpillar's tent?"

"It's fog or ground-mist," Gavin said. "Something dreadful has happened to us, to everyone in Earthwood. Don't you remember the rains? RA-Mosah and Papa speaking in the High Ring and – "

"I thought I was havin' a bad dream," Trisbert said, "from eatin' too much mullet." But he did not laugh. He turned as if to climb farther up the elm and have a good gander at their situation, as clever raccoons invariably did. "Something funny's happened to this tree," he said. "We've been climbin' up sideways."

Gavin smiled as best he could. "I'm now of the opinion," he said, "that we've been floating for some time on this uprooted, near-dead tree on top of the waves that rolled over the Realm of Ringtail and the whole of Earthwood."

"Oh," Trisbert said, looking about with half-hearted concern. "For how long?"

"I don't know. The last thing I can remember is dropping to my knees in utter exhaustion somewhere along the northern crest of Serpentine Ridge. And hearing your voice begging and cursing me to hurry."

"Gollah be darned!" Trisbert snorted. (No amount of urging or threat from Papa could curb Trisbert's delight in the use of mild oaths to make the points he did not have better words to.) He sat back on his haunches and peered into the fog as if its tortuous swirls might suddenly take shape and tell all. "Cuyler was on my shoulders," he said. "He thought we were on a great adventure."

"Maybe we are," Gavin said.

* * *

Trisbert, of course, was all for leaping off their only lifeline and thrashing about in the murk and muck of wherever-they-were until their baby brother, and every other raccoon of their acquaintance, was found. However, three or four futile attempts to intimidate the fog with his fists and Gavin's pointed remark ("We can't find what we can't see") soon persuaded him to remain where he was.

"But what can we do?" he spluttered. "We can't just sit here like bumps on a log when Papa and Grandpapa and little Cuyler are somewhere out there waitin' for us to help them."

Gavin placed a gentle paw on Trisbert's shoulder. "We don't even know if they are out there waiting," he said as calmly as he could. "We don't know for sure if we are even in Earthwood."

"But we have to be," Trisbert replied without much conviction. "We hadn't got to the north end of the Ridge before the water – " Trisbert stopped in mid-sentence. "It isn't funny," he said sharply.

"I wasn't laughing," Gavin said, but he was already turned in the direction of the giggle, scanning the fog-draped twigs of the thick limb next to him that jutted straight out into nowhere like a gangplank over a treacherous ocean. "But somebody we know was!"

Another giggle, louder and more rippling than the first, bubbled up into the fog, as if someone had found his own joke irresistibly hilarious and had begun to laugh before the punch-line. "Don't move, Cuyler!" Gavin cried. "Stay right where you are. I'm coming along this branch to get you."

"I had the craziest dream, Gav," said the voice of little Cuyler in a sleepy, contented sort of drawl. "I just had to laugh, and I woke myself up."

"You can tell me all about it," Gavin said as he eased back twig after twig and inched his way along the branch.

"Hey, I feel like I'm wrong side up," Cuyler said, no more than a pace away. "Somebody lumpy and fat and related to me must be leaning on my nap-tree."

"Our nap-tree fell over," Gavin said, trying his best to sound casual. The figure of a small raccoon was suddenly visible, perilously close to the outer edge of the elm. "Nothing serious, but you ought not to move too sprightly," Gavin added in his usual older-brother tone. "It's a trifle damp below."

"Don't be such a scaredy-cat," Cuyler said, rousing himself for a challenge. As Gavin reached out to grasp him, Cuyler did a dainty, one-pawed pirouette on a swaying twig, followed by a two-pawed trapeze-arc that took him under and past his startled brother and brought him, teetering but safe, up onto the big branch directly opposite. The fog seemed to have thinned a bit, for Gavin could now see Cuyler's grinning, mischievous face as clearly as if it were yesterday and nothing catastrophic had happened.

"Where is everybody?"

"We don't know for sure," Gavin said as he motioned for Cuyler to move towards the trunk of the elm. "It's the fog."

Cuyler was doing his tightrope act along a narrow limb, pretending as always to lose his balance before righting himself at the last possible moment, then darting a "gotcha!" look in Gavin's direction.

"About that dream . . ." Gavin said.

* * *

The three sons of Uthra crouched together on an anonymous tree-limb and stared out at the slowly dissolving mist. Cuyler had been told only that a storm had uprooted their nest and inconvenienced the proceedings of the High Ring. "When the fog clears, we'll find the others," he had been reassured, "or they'll find us." But now that the mists were, it appeared, beginning to thin and expose the true extent of the calamity, Gavin was not at all certain of what he could say, or do. ("You are the eldest, and an elder-son," Papa had said to him more than once, "and the brightest. We coons have supervised Earthwood on Gollah's behalf for time out of mind, living by our wits whenever we can. If anything happens to me, you are to take care of Cuyler, then look to your duty as a woods-creature." Gavin had considered reminding Papa that he was but a minute older than Trisbert, but decided not to press the point.)

What they now gazed out upon, in awe and not a little trepidation, was a scene of utter desolation. In the ambit of the twenty paces or so now visible, they beheld a jumble of uprooted trees, tossed and twisted every which way, as if the wind and rain had come from all directions at once and couldn't decide which way to hurl whatever stood in their path. And as the tattered remnants of fog dripped over them, like rags on skeletons, the ground below – which ought to have harboured seed and sprout and bulb and acorn and saturated root – was now a swampy mélange of mud and sunless pools of dead water. Nothing twitched or swam, cawed or buzzed.

"Hey," Trisbert said when no-one else ventured to speak, "Cuyler looks a mite bigger to me."

"And you look like you've spent your day-nap chanking bumbleberries," Cuyler said with a wee chuckle. "As usual."

"No, I mean it," Trisbert said. "You've grown a – "

" – paw's-width or two," Gavin said, stepping back to observe Cuyler more keenly.

"Not possible," Trisbert said, sorry to have brought the matter up: he was forever of the opinion that too much thinking invariably led to confusions and unnecessary trouble.

"Of course it is," Cuyler chipped in. "You two never take any notice of me until you have to."

"Well, I don't know how anyone could not notice you," Trisbert grumbled.

"Anyway, why are we sitting here feeling sorry for ourselves?" Cuyler said. "Let's head out there and find the others." He took a step towards the edge of the trunk.

Gavin touched his elbow. "We will," he said. "But we can't go down there, or anywhere, until we know where here is."

"Here is here," Trisbert said, "ain't it?"

"Not always," Gavin said, keeping a firm hold on Cuyler. "Do you realize that every tree we can see is a cedar, except the elm we're standing on?"

"And there aren't any cedars in the Realm of Ringtail," Cuyler said triumphantly. "So that means – "

"Not possible," Trisbert grunted. "This is one of our nap-trees. I'd know its smell anywhere."

"So that means we must be on the fringe of Webmarsh," Cuyler said rudely. " We've sailed all the way up to the northern tip of Earthwood — on this old log. Wow! What a tale we'll have to — "

"I think you're right," Gavin said, scanning the farthest reach of the stubbornly retreating fog and seeing nothing but withered and rusty clumps of cedar. "Which means we'll have to head south. But until the sun decides to show itself or the stars surprise us, we won't know up from down. Sometimes the best thing to do is to do nothing."

"Nonsense," said Cuyler, who had indeed sprouted an inch or two in some mysterious way. (How long had they been drifting, comatose, on this makeshift craft?) "At least we can see if that swamp down there can hold a coon's weight." And so saying, Cuyler leapt instantly outward and landed nimbly on all fours.

"See," he called back up to his naysaying brothers, "it's just a little sticky mud." And to prove his point he began a kind of jig on his hind-legs. "I'm gonna waltz around this nap-tree and see what I can see."

"We better go," Trisbert said.

"All right," Gavin said, still skeptical, and they climbed down to the ground, where they promptly sank up to their knee-joints in the ooze.

Cuyler was already dancing backwards away from them. Suddenly his left hind-paw went down and refused to come back up. "Hit a gooey spot!" he shouted, and started to use both of his forepaws to try and pull his rear foot free.

"Lean forward and ease yourself out," Gavin called. "Don't flail about or you'll — "

But Cuyler was already flailing about, and laughing as if he were in the midst of a practical joke being played by his envious brothers. "Takes more than a patch of gumbo to stump a coon!"

Moments later the laughter stopped. All four legs had vanished into the muck: Cuyler was caught like a fly in pine-sap. "Okay, fellas," he said, "I guess I could use a little muscle to get me moving again."

Trisbert lumbered forward. And stalled. "Let go of my tail!" he yelled back at Gavin.

"You'll go down with him, Bertie!" he said as loudly as he dared. "And twice as fast."

Sensing the mud already halfway up his legs, Trisbert turned back.

"Help me, Tris, I'm going under!"

The deadly slime was rising rapidly – or seemed to be – up Cuyler's breast, and he was tilting his snout skyward in a futile attempt to save himself from drowning. One forepaw waved gamely in the air.

"Rip off the biggest branch you can find," Gavin said to Trisbert. "Quickly!"

With his heart pounding even faster than his brain was spinning, Trisbert lurched sideways and clawed at the nearest elm-branch. Using his enormous strength, he began to rip it away from the mother-limb. Meanwhile Gavin stretched himself prone along the slick surface of the muck as if it were ice (his nostrils prickled with the scents of decay and putrefaction) and waited for Trisbert to toss him the branch that might save from certain death the brother he was now responsible for.

"I'm going down!" Cuyler said, intending to shout but failing to raise his last words above a whisper or to shape a silent plea to Gollah to take into account his youth and its courageous folly. The ooze was licking at his lips, tasting him, mocking him. Even as it slithered through his clenched teeth, he kept his paw in the air, the baby-fist of it either a final gesture of defiance or a wordless farewell.

With a protesting shriek the elm-branch was torn away and flung towards Gavin, who, in turning his eye back to make sure he caught it, could not see whether it was already too late. But the look of horror upon Trisbert's face conveyed the dreadful news. The branch sagged in Gavin's hand, as defeated as he was.

"By the gray locks of Gollah!" Trisbert cried suddenly, and his eyes lit up as if he had just seen a Ghostie. But there was a joy in them that no Ghostie could have engendered. Gavin rolled over and stared at the scene before him in disbelief. Then elation.

A branch, not the one Trisbert had manfully secured, had stretched itself out, magically, from the elm-trunk across the open expanse of mud and then insinuated itself into Cuyler's fist. It was now tugging, or being tugged by, the drowned creature who was, hair by hair, rising, or being raised, out of the murderous cesspool. With a slurp and a swoosh Cuyler was abruptly freed – slimed and disfigured but spitting and wriggling – then swung along with his rescuing limb to the terra firma of the tree-trunk.

"It's well nigh impossible for a peaceable person to take a nap when the world's so full of foolish raccoons," grumped Adderly, before settling back down into the rumple of his coils.

Chapter 3

A Mated Pair

WHILE ADDERLY DOZED in the warm, ever-brightening air, Gavin and Trisbert did their best to clean the mud out of Cuyler's nostrils, mouth and eye-pouches, and scrape at least some of it away from his once-lustrous raccoon coat.

"Tris is rubbing it into my eyes," Cuyler complained. "You do it, Gav."

"Well, if you'd quit squirmin'," Trisbert said, "and if you hadn't been so stupid in the first place – "

"I think it best if we all wait for the sun to come out," Gavin said, giving his brother's soggy, soiled tail a pathetic shake. "The sun has to be out there somewhere burning off this fog."

Trisbert chuckled in his slow, throaty way: "Well, don't you look like a drowned muskrat!"

"At least I'm not scared of my own shadow – "

Gavin ignored these remarks as he moved deliberately and thoughtfully down towards the base of the elm-trunk. He noticed that many of its branches had been torn off in the fury of the storm as tree had battered and churned against tree. A few paces ahead he could now see the elm's roots sticking up into the air like hair on the neck of a terrified animal. A little later he heard his brothers come up beside him.

No-one spoke for some time.

"If we were saved by hangin' on to this nap-tree," Trisbert mused, "then lots of other creatures could've done the same."

"And Papa and RA-Mosah were on the biggest tree in the High Ring, weren't they?" Cuyler pointed out hopefully.

Gavin was still surveying the shredded and maimed branches of the tree that had miraculously saved them, and remembering the pitiless roil of wave and wind.

"So all we got to do is go looking for them or – "

"Wait here for them to find us," Trisbert said.

Gavin turned to face his brothers. "Yes," he said, "Papa and Grandpapa are probably on their way here this very moment."

"And it's awfully warm, don't you think?" Cuyler said.

"Feels like the middle of Blossomflower to me," Trisbert said. "Things'll start growin' again, eh, Gav?"

Gavin decided not to mention the eerie absence of birdsong, bee-buzz, swamp-croak, or the wing-hum of the million insects that ushered in the seasons of Blossomflower and Greendaze. Instead, he said, "While we're waiting for the sun to show us exactly where we are and dry up enough of that slop down there to let us venture forth, we need to think about finding us some food and making sure that Adderly and we three are the only ones on this tree."

"I don't fancy a water-logged mouse," Trisbert said gloomily.

"Well, there's got to be a winterberry bush or two in all this tangle," Cuyler announced, choosing not to remark on Trisbert's gratuitous reference to "water-logged." He hopped from branch to branch like a famished opossum.

"You'd think he'd learn his lesson," Trisbert said to Gavin. "Come back here!" he shouted uselessly at his delinquent brother, who was growing smaller by the second. "Do something, Gav!"

"Maybe all that clambering will help him dry off," Gavin said.

So they watched in silence, and not a little apprehension, as Cuyler bounced and sallied back towards them. He was carrying the remnant of a cranberry bush, last year's fruit gleaming in the misty light as if it were manna from Gollah.

* * *

When the last berry had been meted out and its juice licked clean of lips and teeth, Cuyler said with a glance at Trisbert's bulging belly, "Now we can get on with the really important things."

"I feel more like a snooze,' Trisbert said.

"Do you really think anyone else could be here?" Cuyler said, looking about restlessly, as if trying to decide in which direction he ought to begin the necessary search.

"Not likely," Gavin admitted. "We've made enough noise to attract a pack of wolves and a horde of coyotes."

Cuyler smiled, as he was meant to, but the mere mention of such predators – reputed to show no mercy towards any coon young and careless enough or too old to outrun them – made him shiver. Not that he had seen or even heard a wolf in full cry. Long ago, Papa had told them many times in the many ways of his stories that wolves and coyotes had prowled the domain of Earthwood and wreaked havoc among the lesser creatures. Raccoons, of course, were too nimble in their cunning and night-vision to be simple prey, but were nonetheless happy when, in the time of RA-Mosah's grandfather, a dozen Tallwalkers appeared on the shining blackpath (now beset with weeds and frost-rot) that paralleled the southern edge of Earthwood, abandoned their doomsmobiles and marched north into the bush. The horrible cawing of their firesticks could be heard everywhere, from Gullwing Sands on the west to Serpentine Ridge on the east, from treetop to deepest burrow. It was reported that the Tallwalkers had tame wolves and foxes to do their bidding as they tracked and exposed to bloody, undignified death every white-tail doe and stag in the forest. Then they dragged the trussed carcases out of Earthwood forever and roared southward with their cargo of deer-flesh. Oh, Papa had said in a voice most solemn, how the wolves had howled out their hunger and the coyotes yodelled their despair. But there was no-one to answer their piteous pleas: no new fawn dropped from its mother's womb that season, or ever again. And no-one, not even the sagest of coons or most prophetic of owls, knew what night it was when Wolf and Coyote slipped out of Earthwood, starving and bewildered, to take their chances on Serpentine Ridge and the hope of fresh prey in the Forest of Everdark on the far side of it. Even now, Papa's story could make Cuyler shudder.

"Halloo out there!" he called in his boyish but exuberant voice. No echo was returned from the muffling patches of fog that clung to the tangle of capsized trees and shrubs all around him. And no reply.

"As I thought," Gavin said. "We're on our own."

"Just you and me," Cuyler tittered, then elbowed Trisbert between snores.

Trisbert lifted an eyelid. "What's that noise?" he said.

"What noise?" Gavin said.

"You've been dreaming," Cuyler said.

"But I can feel it," Trisbert said, coming awake reluctantly. "Like a shiverin' in my bones. Some fool's poundin' on something hollow."

No-one moved a muscle. Moments later, all three of them could hear a low, steady, thrumming sound: hollow and regular in its repetitions.

"This way," Gavin said quietly and led his brothers towards the base of the elm's trunk. The drumming grew louder and more frenzied. And seemed to be coming from somewhere under them.

"The trunk's hollow down here," Gavin said. "Someone's inside it, trying to get out perhaps." He peered around a rather lumpy limb that had been shattered close to the trunk. "And here's the entrance," he said, "or the exit."

"I'd better handle this," Trisbert said. He pushed his bulk past Gavin and stood astride a round hole that had been worn smooth by hundreds of comings and goings over many seasons. "Come out of there, whoever you are, right now!" Trisbert boomed so loudly that little Cuyler flinched and then had to pretend to stumble in case Gavin should be watching.

Two lengthy brown ears rose slowly up into view, followed by a pair of startled eyes and one set of whiskers that did nothing to disguise the exaggerated teeth they bracketed.

"Well, there's no need to screech like a lunatic owl," said the rabbit as soon as he had gotten all four feet planted on the horizontal and taken the measure of the intruder. "The missus is very sensitive to loud noises, especially in her present condition." He sat back on his fluffy white tail as if it were a convenient stool and glared at Trisbert. "Did you not hear my message?"

With mouth agape, Trisbert could only shake his head.

"I drummed it out as clear as a gull's cry," the rabbit said in a most critical and uncalled-for tone. "I don't see how you could have missed it. My good dame is in considerable distress, as you may well imagine if you'd been buffeted about as we have been on this highly unsuitable and less-than-seaworthy vessel."

"And who in the name of Zeebub's horns are you?" Trisbert was able to splutter at last, just as Gavin and Cuyler succeeded in bunting him sideways enough to press by him and present themselves.

"I am known throughout Earthwood and beyond as Hew-bare de Cottontail," the stranger announced, putting careful stress upon the fine twin syllables of his given name. "And this," he added as he raised up out of the elm's hollow by a single paw a diminutive, more delicate version of himself, "is Re-nay."

"Pleased to meet you," Renée said with a bashful blink of her comely lashes.

Gavin stepped forward and introduced himself and his brothers. "There's no need to be afraid," Gavin said when Hubert held back and kept a good part of his finely-furred torso in front of his missus.

"It is not myself I am afraid for," Hubert said, "but Renée is enceinte and I am obliged to take no chances, despite the oddity of the circumstances in which we find ourselves."

"On-what?" Trisbert asked.

"I see you do not comprehend the ancient cottontail tongue," Hubert said to the puzzled raccoons. "Pardonnez-moi, but I meant to inform you that my wife and helpmate is with child, and thus to appeal to the sense of compassion and fair play your kind is renowned for throughout Earthwood – "

"– and beyond," Renée appended sweetly.

In fact, raccoons were known occasionally to feast upon small rabbits unable to outrun them, but such outrages now seemed far away and without substance, here in this exotic, fog-haunted landscape upon which they had been randomly tossed and, in all likelihood, abandoned. For a long moment no-one spoke or felt the need to speak: there was something in the silence, in the strangeness all about them that needed listening to.

At last Gavin said, "As soon as the sun breaks through the fog and we can tell east from west, we intend to venture out to look for food and for our families, who may well be scattered across the many leagues of Earthwood or even upon the slopes of the Ridge itself. You are welcome to accompany us."

"Most gracious of you, monsieur," Hubert replied, "but I could not contemplate even the merest stroll or promenade for Madame, whose time I fear is fast approaching and – "

"Hubert and I will be most pleased to join you," Renée said softly but firmly from behind her mate's left haunch. "We are strong runners and our hearing is most acute."

"But cherie, my poppet – "

"And Hubert can drum out any message you think necessary to send, can't you, mon cher?"

Trisbert was about to point out that no raccoon would stoop so low as to accept or require assistance from a mere rabbit when he was forestalled by a sharp cry from Cuyler, who had taken the opportunity to reconnoitre some nearby branches.

"What is it?" Gavin said.

"Let me at it!" Trisbert cried.

Cuyler giggled. "I'm all right, big brother. I've found something hanging on one of the twigs out here, that's all."

"Something to eat?

"I'm afraid not, Tris. It's a leather thing. A Tallwalker's pouch."

Gavin let out a whoop that frightened Hubert de Cottontail, whose fright was immediately transferred to his spouse who otherwise would have thought nothing of it.

"Papa's books and papers!" Gavin shouted. "They've come with us!"

"Good gracious," said Hubert as soon as his breath returned, "you might have saved such obstreperous celebration for something of value or practical application."

"Like food," Trisbert sighed.

But Gavin just smiled, and kept on smiling.

* * *

Gavin remembered that Papa, RA-elect and successor to RA-Mosah, had removed from its leather-pouch the sacred Book of Coon-Craft and Animal Cunning, and had then handed the supple cowhide case with its sturdy shoulder straps and crisp buckles to his eldest son, before he himself had crossed the Ring and ascended the High-Ring tree to take his place beside RA-Mosah. (Gavin did not have to be told to guard the other books and documents with his life, not because they were sacred to the clan coon but because they were to be kept as secret as they were dangerous. Only Papa, and now Gavin to whom Papa had just begun to entrust his dark secret and its encrypted codes, knew of their existence and guessed at the power of the words petrified upon their pages.) From the beginning of creature-time, that is from the first germination of Earthwood, Gollah had decreed that there should be but one written code for all woods-creatures, that it should be kept and passed down from RA to RA, that its blank parchment pages (bequeathed to the clan coon and stored in the bole of the High-Ring tree) should over the seasons and annuals be inked with the wisdom and folklore and heroics of all Gollah's creatures. But to the great RA alone was given the guardianship of the scared tome itself, and to him or her alone was entrusted the raccoon-script and alphabet in which all record would be inscribed. These holy tasks were to be handed down to, and nurtured by, the future elder-sons and elder-daughters of the clan. All truth, all wisdom and all history were to be contained therein and added to by each succeeding generation until every vacant page was filled and overflowing. All else was heresy or blasphemy, a form of insurrection against Gollah Himself.

"Is The Book in there?" Cuyler whispered in his former puppy-voice.

"Of course it is; that's the sacred pouch," Trisbert said and, not having been anointed an elder-son by virtue of his sloth body and ordinary brain, promptly turned to the more pressing business of the retreating mist.

"What book?" Hubert de Cottontail cried and, to be on the safe side, he covered Madame's eyes with his right forepaw.

"The Book of Coon-Craft," Cuyler said in a hushed tone.

Hubert slapped his other forepaw over his own eyes like a soldier saluting a general.

But Hubert had little to fear: The Book of Coon-Craft was not in its sacred pouch. Even now Gavin could close his eyes and picture its slim, voluptuous leaves riffling silkily as Papa had thumbed it proudly and patiently, waiting at the side of RA-Mosah for his turn to speak some words of comfort from the High-Ring tree, while the rains that refused to cease or desist lashed the trembling forest and swept everything away: family and clan, history, and the tales that sanctify it.

Gavin drew one of the loose buckles taut, and dredged up a smile for those watching him warily. "Yes, the sacred text is safe," he lied, then compounded the lie by adding, "Thank Gollah for that."

"I trust that you will keep it secured in its pouch," Hubert said. "We don't want any unforeseen accidents to happen in regard to unlawful persons catching sight of it, however unintended such a sighting (or however delicate such a sighting person) might prove to be." And he winked in the general direction of Madame Renée, as if too direct a glance might prove fatal in the circumstances.

Gavin threw the pouch over his shoulder with a careless shrug (though he thought he could feel along his spine the illicit vibrations of the Tallwalkers' untranslatable script, the Gibberlish tongue that Papa had mysteriously decoded and was preparing to teach his elder-son).

"It's time we got ourselves down off this dead tree," Gavin said.

* * *

The six woods-creatures stood (or lay) on a muddy patch of ground near the elm-trunk and gazed at the brightest spot they could find in the mist around them, knowing instinctively that the sun had to be somewhere just behind it, burning and purging as it ought to. Any thought that they might be the last remaining creatures alive was lost in the surge of hope offered by the certainty of the sun's survival and what that boded. In fact, before their collective gaze the fog was receding, rapidly now, and though no-one said so aloud, the murderous rains had definitely ceased.

"There it is!" Cuyler shouted.

But the others had seen it for themselves, and were too awed or happy to speak. Through an irregular rent in the mist, a scarlet sphere boiled and fumed low against some far horizon. The tattered fog was fleeing in the face of such awesome power.

Adderly was the first to move: he twisted luxuriously until his pale belly was completely exposed to the sudden radiance of light and heat.

"We are saved, Madame," Hubert sighed in Renée's ample ear.

"And now we know where we are," Trisbert said, looking at Gavin. "Don't we?"

Gavin nodded, but his eye had quickly moved from the miracle of the sun's revival to the landscape that it now illuminated in stark outline and bleak shading. Devastation was everywhere, and everywhere it was complete. As far as one could now see (and only a few scarf-like remnants of mist still clung to low-lying hollows or what appeared to be a black smudge of cloud at the horizon-line), not a tree in Earthwood was left standing, nor any shrub or bush. The grasses, mosses, and other ground-cover foliage had been drowned or wiped clean from the soil they had once held together. Brownish clots of dead root and suffocated shoots could be seen here and there in the gray murk. The resurrected sun would only scorch them further.

"That's the Ridge, isn't it, Gav?" Cuyler said, all legs and fidgeting again.

Gavin stared for a long moment at the dark border underlining the sun, which had now become too bright to be looked at directly. "Yes," he said. "The sun must be rising above it, as it always has. Which would explain why the fog has been burnt off."

"A new day has dawned, Madame," Hubert said, and squeezed his lady's paw.

"And you were right, Gav," Trisbert said. "We must've landed somewhere up north, near Webmarsh."

"Yes," Gavin said, "at least we know where we are."

No-one felt much like speculating how they had managed to cling to a nap-tree in a raging gale long enough to be deposited neatly (and unconscious?) some fifty leagues or more away from where they'd started. Or how many days of sunrise and sunfall it had taken for the enshrouding fog to be burned away.

* * *

It would be a long and arduous trek to the Realm of Ringtail, with only the slim chance of an uprooted berry-bush or occasional tuft of bleached grass to still the hunger that would be engendered by travel across a muddy and mangled terrain. But no other choice offered itself. By keeping the Ridge on their left, they could walk parallel to it and be as certain of coming home as if they had a Tallwalkers' compass-contraption to guide them.

The first challenge facing Gavin – who, as the only elder-son amongst them, was made leader by tacit consent or default – was to establish the order of their marching-in-column. Hubert volunteered to be first in line because, as he said, cottontails were nimble of movement and generous of foot and had the keenest ears of any woods-creature (and the most shapely, he had added in deference to Renée, who blushed nicely), but then he suddenly remembered that Madame would have to trail in his footsteps, thus making her vulnerable should any trouble assert itself at the front of the line. Trisbert resolved matters by offering to bring up the rear and keep Renée and her unborn brood carefully protected by his intimi-dating bulk and his (as yet untested) courage. Hubert scrutinized the large raccoon as if he were trying to determine whether or not he would, despite any promises made, be tempted to gorge himself on a newborn rabbit or two, should such decide to enter the world without warning. Then he sighed, on principle, and consented to the arrangement. Gavin and Cuyler made up the middle of the line, while Adderly, who found the sun alternately sleep-inducing and revivifying, was left to follow them at whatever pace he could manage.

The broad but light-stepping pads of Hubert's paws soon proved invaluable as the animals ventured out upon the sad ruins of their territory. Hubert seemed to have a sixth sense about whether the gumbo he hopped on would hold his weight or not and, when he did infrequently land in the kind of quicksand that had almost swallowed Cuyler, he was able to leap sideways or quarterwise to safer ground before anything other than a paw began to sink. Without him, Gavin realized, they would have had to remain on the rotting elm-trunk (who knew for how long or with what consequences), or else soon be sucked down to a grotesque death in the mud around it.

Several times they paused to munch on a few wizened berries or shrivelled tuber-root, or to take a repulsive but necessary drink of stagnant water. But they were on the move. They knew where they were going. Being woods-creatures, they understood that whatever energy was left in the layers of their flesh would be needed for walking on the ever-alert that kept them a split second ahead of any predator. No word was given or received. They simply walked, wrapped in their own silence. Even Cuyler's initial quick-step soon subsided to a steady, animal trudge.

It was while they were stopped for a drink that Trisbert craned his thick neck about and brushed a puzzled paw over his eye-mask as if it had suddenly squeezed itself shut. "Hey," he said, "either I'm goin' blind or it's gettin' dark."

"I think Tris is right, Gav. It is getting dark," Cuyler said.

"And colder," Adderly yawned.

"Not possible," Trisbert said with a desperate glance at Gavin, "is it?"

Slowly they all turned towards the Ridge that lay on their left, at the eastern edge of Earthwood, where Gopllah had placed it to keep them safe from whatever Zeebubian horrors lay beyond it. The sun was still a reddening disk, but only the upper half of it was now visible. Even as they watched, in confusion and growing anxiety, it sank in slow but inexorable degrees behind the jagged crest of Serpentine Ridge.

"Mon Dieu!" Hubert said. "The sun has always gone down in the west – at least as long as I have been alive to observe it. Is that not so, Madame?"

"Oui, my love," said Madame.

"What does it mean?" Trisbert said to Gavin, who was still gazing incredulously "eastward."

"Has the world turned upside down?" Cuyler cried, as if he were finally on the verge of some adventure worth his attention.

"Now, now," Hubert remonstrated, "there are persons present who might be disconcerted by such bizarre speculation."

"It means we have been walking northward," Gavin said quietly. "The sun is going down the way it always has – in the west."

"Not possible," Trisbert said. "We'd have to be — "

"On the other side of the Ridge!" Cuyler shouted.

Hubert clamped a paw over Madame's shapely ears, but he never took his eyes off Gavin.

"Then . . . we're not anywhere in Earthwood at all . . ." Trisbert said. "We must be — "

"Yes," Gavin said. "We're somewhere in the Forest of Everdark."

Chapter 4

Tallwalker

NO OTHER NEWS COULD HAVE DEALT SUCH A BLOW to the stalwart little band of survivors. The Forest of Everdark, mercifully sealed off from Earthwood by the rampart of phantom-haunted granite and limestone known as Serpentine Ridge (oh, Gollah be praised!), was reputed to be the killing ground of wolves and coyotes, cougars and karkajim, eagles more terrible than pterodactyls, and grizzlies that tore each other to pieces for sport. Its trees – giant firs, soaring redwoods, mountainous pines – were so tall and smothering that no sunlight reached the forest floor, where fern and ivy and hugging vine grew not in the clotted forever-dark. And the roots that held these towering obelisks were said to be curled tight around the bedrock below, like the elongated toes of the demon Zeebub himself.

"We'll discuss our situation in the morning," Gavin said, surprised by the calm in his voice. "It'll be pitch black in a few moments, and we need to find some shelter for the night."

Shelter from what, Gavin did not say, but each member of the troupe had his own opinion on that score.

"But we can see quite well," Cuyler said, speaking for the raccoons. "I'm for pushing ahead. We've got to find food or – "

"Some of us have not been blessed with the advantage of night-vision," Hubert said sharply. "And your brother has given my lady a most unpardonable shock."

"I'm perfectly fine, mon cher," Renée said bravely but nonetheless wearily. "All we have to do is follow Monsieur Gavin."

"It's up to you, Gav," Trisbert said when his brother turned an inquiring eye in his direction. "You're the elder-son."

Gavin pressed a paw against the leather-pouch at his side, and wished fervently that The Book of Coon-Craft and Animal Cunning were there instead of the forbidden scriptures his father had discovered and kept to himself. In The Book (as it was known throughout Earthwood) resided all the lore and canniness of their clan's long and illustrious history. Along with a dozen other elder-sons and a pair of elder-daughters, Gavin had joined the Ring-elders to be schooled in the magic of coon-script and taught the sayings that would guide them when it came their turn to superintend Gollah's plan for the well-being of Earthwood. And one of them, of course, would eventually be chosen RA-elect and (like Papa) be given unlimited access to The Book itself. Up till now, they had had to be contented with reading (as practice in decoding the script) only the Tale of Beginnings (chapter the first) and selected proverbs deemed suitable for tender minds. Would these few snippets of wisdom be of any help here and now? And if they could somehow navigate the terrors of Everdark and the phantoms of the Ridge, what then? What might they find in Earthwood? What if The Book had indeed been swept away with Papa and RA-Mosah, its parchment leaves scattered, the ink of its telling blurred and untranslatable, the very slate of animal memory wiped clean?

"We all need to rest," Gavin said.

"Look!" Cuyler chirped, capering ahead, "there's the perfect spot!"

And so it was. One of the resident firs of Everdark – whose ruined trees, they were now compelled to notice, were gargantuan and undeniably foreign – lay on its back with a huge hollow gouged out of its massive bole, as roomy as a bat-cave. Without exchanging a word (not counting the comforting whisper of Monsieur to Madame), the weary troupe squeezed into the concavity, shuffled about briefly, shivered as if the oncoming dark were cold (it wasn't), and closed their eyes.

"Do you think Papa and Grandpapa are out there somewhere looking for us, Gav?" Cuyler said.

Gavin had no answer.

* * *

Trisbert was having his favourite dream: he was standing knee-deep in Ambling Creek with its pure waters rippling and racing under him and a moon as bright as Mama's face smiling down upon him, and every time he stretched out a forepaw a plump and compliant trout would leap starward and attach itself, until he became so stuffed and sated he could no longer stand on two or four feet and simply lolled over and lay a-slumber in the cooling currents. Aah, if he could just reach out for one last, willing morsel, he could sleep forever and –

"Oww!"

Trisbert's cry brought everyone instantly awake.

"What is it?" Gavin said groggily, squinting into the sudden sunlight of just-morning.

"I've been stabbed!"

"Where? Where?" Cuyler cried as he untangled himself from Trisbert's tail and sprang upright, fists and claws at the ready.

"In the rump," Trisbert moaned and, still drugged from sleep, rolled over and away from the offending point.

Sure enough, a sharp, quill-like spear had imbedded itself in the raccoon's hind-quarter.

Everyone leaped into action at once, but as it was not particularly well co-ordinated, it produced a less than satisfactory result. Hubert threw his body across that of his good lady in an effort to shield her from the next missile – if and when it should come – but as she herself was in the midst of squeezing farther into the sheltering tree, he missed her entirely and wound up protecting a patch of desiccated moss. Cuyler hopped onto a nearby limb and scanned the horizon for any sign of bowman or spear-carrier, caring not that he made himself a visible (if jiggeting) target. Gavin stepped cautiously out of the "cave" and appeared to be appraising the landscape or thinking fiercely. Adderly had begun to waken and wonder what the fuss was about, while Trisbert seemed more interested in removing the present dart from his flank than worrying about the possibility of a second assault.

"Pardon my obtrusion, but if you coon-creatures had the courtesy to watch whom you use for a rump-pillow, you wouldn't find yourselves quilled."

The voice, raspy and irritable, came from somewhere under the tree-trunk. Everyone stopped doing whatever heroic action they were doing, and stared at the hollow out of which the voice and its reprimand had come.

"I retaliate: those foolish enough to depose on pin-cushions are bound to be pricked awake. That's all I have to say on that subject."

To the evident relief of the others, Gavin smiled and approached the voice. He bent over, reached slowly into a shadowy recess of the tree-trunk, and with one claw made a kind of plucking gesture.

"Hey, that's my propriety you're twanging!"

"It's all right," Gavin said affably. "We're friends. Come out and join us."

Several moments later they heard a ragged, shuffling noise, as if some awkward body or bodies were being manoeuvred in too small a compartment. At last a snout, a brace of beady eyes and a spiked head emerged, blinking and wary.

"A porcupine!" Trisbert cried in disgust as he held up the offending quill for all present to see, and condemn.

"Quiver's the name," said the newcomer, bristling with some indignation whose cause was not apparent to any of the welcoming party. "Anybody got a problem with that?"

* * *

Quiver's story, given grudgingly and succinctly, was not unlike their own. Thinking that the rains over Earthwood would end sooner or later (later had been his own unsolicited opinion), he had gathered a week's supply of tender morsels and crawled into a hollow log to munch and doze. Mrs. Quiver had done likewise but, alas, had decided upon a roomier (and less seaworthy) log within hailing distance of her faithful mate. He had, he said, been napping between snacks when he suddenly woke to find himself pitching and yawing as if he were captive in the belly of a giant fish-creature that was itself being pummelled by wind and wave. When even the darkness disappeared around him, he was certain he was now dead, and waiting to wake up in North Holy or, Gollah forbid, the bleak dungeons of Zeebub.

The rest of the tale they already knew. Gavin then related their own story, and invited Quiver to join them in their search for Earthwood.

"We're saturated in the Forest of Everdark, you say?" Quiver said, trundling a few paces into the open and gazing about in bewilderment.

"I know it doesn't look like it," Gavin said, "but we have to be. The morning sun is behind us, even now. And there to the west of us is Serpentine Ridge. The storm must have carried some of us over the crest of the Ridge and deposited us here in the ruins of Everdark. How much time has passed since all of this happened, we cannot tell for sure."

Quiver sank his razor-sharp teeth into a convenient branch of the big tree, the tender end that his kind preferred. The others watched as he ground and crunched, paused like a gourmet, then ground and crunched again with more precise purpose. Finally he spat everything out in a furious burst.

"Dead," he pronounced. "Decreased! Not an ounce of juice or neuterment left."

No-one said a word. As if connected by the same urgent thought, though, they all stared about them at the devastated tumble of tree and shrub, at the root-drowned grasses and graying mosses.

"I believe we've been here, or somewhere, longer than we think," Gavin said for the others, who were merely thinking it.

"What'll we eat, then?" Hubert said quietly. "My lady requires nourishment, as all in her condition do."

"As any of us do," Trisbert reminded him.

"As I see it, " Gavin said, "we have two choices at present. We can walk eastward towards the morning sun over there in hopes of coming to the Lake of Waters Unending, where we may, if we're lucky, find fish and – "

"Fish are of no use to Madame," said Hubert.

"Nor me," Quiver added.

" – and possibly waterplants or shore grasses," Gavin continued with admirable patience.

"But the Lake is on the west side of Earthwood," Trisbert said reluctantly. "At home, it's where the sun sinks every night."

"Or used to," Hubert said.

"The same or a similar lake lies east of Everdark," Gavin said solemnly, and for a moment he was not certain how he knew that to be so.

"Yes, I see," Trisbert, who didn't, said.

"See what?" Hubert demanded. "You raccoons are confusing my lady, and causing her much unnecessary agitation."

"I'm perfectly unagitated," his lady replied. "You are forgetting that, among raccoons, our Gavin was selected to be an elder-son and, if I am not mistaken, privy to the secrets of The Book."

All eyes, including those of Adderly who was at last fully awake and not unintrigued by his situation, were turned upon Renée de Cottontail in astonishment: at either the length of her speech or the pertinence of its content, or both. In any event, the same astonished eyes now swivelled back to Gavin, then to the leather-pouch strapped to his back and the bulge of the book it must contain. Gavin could read the resurgent hope in their look, and his stomach went queasy. They were convinced now that he possessed The Book of Coon-Craft and, more daunting to him, they assumed he had the gift of interpretation, the RA-magic to work the miracle they would need to survive and find their way home.

He paused and swallowed hard (which his apostles took as a sign of confidence), then said, "We can head east in the hope of finding fresh water and food, or we can walk due west, away from the morning sun and into our own shadows towards the Ridge – and the home ground that awaits us on the other side."

No-one even glanced in that direction, despite the fact that Earthwood beckoned them in the western distance. The very thought of scaling the Ridge, with its Warlaws and Ghosties (should they happen against the odds to get there across this watery wasteland), was enough to make the decision for them. But Gavin himself, elder-son and perhaps even a RA-elect, was staring at the Ridge as it rose stealthily out of the early ground-mist and began to dominate the western horizon. But it was what he could just now see taking shape below the jagged outline of the Ridge that arrested his attention: a darker patchwork of trees, all of them upright.

"I believe that not all of the Forest of Everdark has been inundated by the flood," he announced to the startled troupe. "Look there. Some trees are still standing. Close to the Ridge, I think. Their roots must've been too deep in the rock to be torn up or drowned."

"But that means wolves," Trisbert said," with an apologetic nods towards Renée.

"And coyotes and foxes and grizzlies," Cuyler said excitedly.

"Maybe so," Gavin said. "But more likely it means live twigs and branches and grass: food."

"We'll be food for the foxes, you mean," Hubert said.

"Well, I can see the forest," Gavin said. "I can't see the Lake of Waters Unending."

"I suggest we take a vote," Hubert said.

"I confer," Quiver said. "But I don't see why the snake should have a say."

"Well, I'm going with my brother," Trisbert said.

"Me, too," Cuyler added.

The dispute might well have continued, with unpredictable consequences, had not the argument that Hubert was about to put forward been rudely pre-empted by a loud cracking sound, like the snapping of a dead branch — followed immediately by the surprised look upon the cottontail's face.

Into the stunned silence that followed, Hubert clutched his shoulder and sighed, "I've been hit."

* * *

While everyone else seemed to scatter in quest of a hiding place or any sort of temporary cover among the pathetic hummocks and skeletal shrubs around them, Gavin dropped beside the stricken Hubert and his agitated helpmate. A red welt oozed up out of Hubert's left shoulder and throbbed in the morning sunlight.

Hubert tried to raise himself, but Gavin held him down firmly and motioned Renée to stay low.

"It's only a graze," Hubert said shakily. "No more harm done than a tangle with a thorn-bush." Whether this bit of bravado were directed at him or Renée, Gavin was not certain, but it seemed to be an accurate summation of Hubert's condition.

Behind them Gavin could hear the desperate scurrying of his companions, more frightened of the Tallwalker's firestick — if indeed that was the source of Hubert's injury — than they were of the predators Gollah had in his infinite wisdom prepared them to fear and accept. Not that anyone now living had actually seen a Tallwalker or experienced the thunderclap of their killing-sticks. Papa himself had been but a lad when the last of the Tallwalkers had come looking in vain for deer, and few woods-creatures had ever seen them whizzing madly in their doomsmobiles along the blackpath that marked the southernmost border of Earthwood (and lived to tell about it) — even before the Great Burning. For reasons that Gollah Himself might not know, the Tallwalkers had lost interest in Earthwood and in the Lake of Waters Unending, where the blackpath ended abruptly at Gullwing Sands. But the stories told of their cruelties and murderous follies, their mindless zeal for speed, their callous abandonment of creatures maimed and dying in the ditches beside the blackpath (though merciful Gollah dispatched vulture and crow to pick them pure again) — such tales were iterated in the dark by well-meaning elders or embellished by blind Minervah to anyone brave enough to listen.

Gavin felt the sturdy weight of Trisbert's body lean against him. "I didn't mean to run, Gav. Honest. But I never heard a firestick go off before."

"I wasn't scared, Gav," Cuyler said from somewhere in back of Trisbert. "Is the cottontail dead?"

"The cottontail is very much alive," Hubert said, "but such thoughtless remarks might well prove fatal to Madame."

Madame lay quietly trembling beside her trembling mate. "Is it really a Tallwalker?" she asked Gavin.

Gavin was staring at the eastern horizon, whence the crack of the firestick had come and where a steaming sun lolled, bloated and unblinking, and exaggerated the stark silhouettes of deformed shrubs and the grotesque roots of trees. But nothing out there seemed to be moving or upright. Nevertheless, Gavin felt the first shudder of fear in his belly, the kind that strikes and grips at the moment between the nightmare and wakening. He tried to think, to use the mother-wit that was Gollah's gift to the clan coon, but his mind was a blank. His fear had no sound or shape, not even when a hump of shadow thirty or forty paces away slowly uncrumpled itself, hunched upwards, and then thinned out as legs, arms and a shaggy head separated themselves and took the unmistakable form of a Tallwalker. One of its limbs — Tallwalkers used only two of them for locomotion — suddenly split in half: the skinnier half was long and rounded and too stiff to be any kind of appendage.

"It's one of them, isn't it?" Cuyler whispered from a dry throat.

"And that's a blunderstick!" added Quiver, who had come up to the group to lend support to its vulnerable rear.

"Mind your language," Hubert said, trying to keep the tremor out of his voice and somewhat reassured by Madame's paw on his shoulder just below the welt that was still throbbing.

"He's seen us, Gav," Trisbert said.

"And he's lifting up the firestick!" Cuyler cried.

"I say we make a run for it," Hubert suggested. "That's why Gollah gave us four legs."

"Oh, dear, I'm not sure how fast I could run," Renée said softly. "I'm feeling remarkably heavy at the moment – "

"Good Gollah, what can we do? What can we do?" shouted Hubert, leaping up and dancing in circles.

"You can stop shouting for a start," Quiver said.

"I'll dash off this way," Cuyler said, pointing to the south, "and zigzag my way in front of him, while you fellas sneak off the other way. I'm not scared of any ol' two-footed Tallwalker."

Nonetheless, Cuyler made only a token effort to break loose from Trisbert's firm hold on him. "What should we do, Gav?" Trisbert said.

But Gavin said nothing, not even when the black figure took its first threatening step in their direction, then a second one. Trisbert stepped up beside his brother. Still Gavin continued to stare at the advancing Tallwalker, who looked now as if he were one of

Zeebub's demons marching straight out of the sun's molten fire, dripping flame with every lurch of his charred stick-body.

"Gav?"

No-one behind them could speak, not even to mumble a prayer: they were transfixed. Terror had taken their breath.

The Tallwalker's eyes – or perhaps just the sockets – could now be seen, white and wobbling against the shadowed oval of his face. He appeared to be crossing uneven ground, for he stumbled often and caught himself just before toppling. The firestick was not raised, but he knew exactly where he was going and what awaited his arrival. Of that Gavin had no doubt.

"Three more paces and I'll rush him," Trisbert said, and edged in front of Gavin. "Even if the firestick hits me, I'll get a claw into him and when I do, nothing'll get it out of him."

At some point during the Tallwalker's approach, Gavin's fear had abated enough for his brain to start functioning again, and even though his blood still ran cold around his heart and his bowels heaved and he dare not speak without betraying his general state of alarm, his stare at the Tallwalker quickly became a study – a scrutiny – of its steady advance.

Gavin touched his brother's elbow, and shook his head. Still unable to speak, he aimed a paw towards the Tallwalker, who was now no more than ten paces away, weaving and tottering towards them.

"He won't get this far," Gavin was able to say at last. "And I don't think he can set off that firestick."

The others, including Adderly who was now wide awake, rose up from their resigned crouches and followed Gavin's gaze. The Tallwalker staggered, steadied, and staggered again. Even the most frightened of the woods-creatures (and it would have been difficult to say who that might have been) could see that the ground before them was perfectly flat and most suitable for stalking one's prey unimpeded. The Tallwalker did not think so apparently, because upon his next stagger he did not right himself, but rather sidled to his knees, and saved his face from slapping the ground only by flinging out both hands, palm-first. The firestick rolled harmlessly away. For a second, neither predator nor prey had the wherewithal to move. Then the Tallwalker slowly, agonizingly, raised his head, fringed with a shock of dishevelled hair the colour of tiger-lilies in Webmarsh, and peered vaguely towards the mesmerized creatures not eight paces in front of him.

"We can go now," Gavin said. "That way. Away from the sun."

"But Everdark's over there," Hubert objected.

"And Tallwalker came out of the morning sun," Gavin said.

"No need for talkin'," Trisbert said, helping Renée to her overburdened feet. "We go where Gav says we go."

* * *

With some haste but no panic, the brave little troupe followed their leader-elect westward, weaving in and out of the meagre brush as often as possible, in the time-worn manner of untrackable raccoons, in order to discourage Tallwalker from their trail — should his hunger become more biting than his exhaustion. ("But I'm sure we have nothing to fear from him or his firestick," Gavin proclaimed.)

Hubert de Cottontail was just about to admit to all and sundry that in their collective wisdom animals always know instinctively whom to choose as their leader, when the boom of a firestick sounded and echoed somewhere close behind them.

"You can't expect Gavin to be right all the time!" Cuyler called out vainly to the naysayers who were busy scampering, hopping or slithering in full, panicked stampede. The sun reared and followed after them.

Never had Gavin felt less like an elder-son or, Gollah forbid, a RA-to-be.

Chapter 5

Flight

THE VARIOUS MEMBERS OF GAVIN'S TROUPE took flight in a westwardly way, not because they wished to draw one pace closer to Everdark's forest but because the carnivore with the firestick was, they assumed, in hot pursuit from his easterly lair. Which meant that they had to keep their shadows, exaggerated by the morning sun, in front of them, so that the exact state of their terror and disarray was ceaselessly projected before their eyes. Nor could it be said that they fled as a group, and certainly not as a cohort with a captain to guide and comfort. Now and again when Hubert paused in his three-legged lope in order to prevent his heart from beating itself to death or to make sure his panting mate did likewise, he would utter the eerie, squeezed squeal that rabbits usually reserve for their next-to-last breath, after which he would listen hard with both of his big (ungrazed) ears. And now and again he would detect a raccoon cry not too far away to his left or right, or a shrill complaining noise a little ways behind or a deep grumbling sound zigzagging somewhere ahead.

"It's all right, cherie, we're not alone," he would say whenever he dared, and Madame would answer, with the forbearance of those creatures destined to be the prey of others, "Not yet, mon amour."

Sometime just after the sun caught up to them and their panicked shadows shrivelled before them, one by one they stopped: in temporary exhaustion, with barely enough strength to call out to one another and stumble together into a muddy depression whose only camouflage was two twisted and barren barberry bushes.

"Maybe he's given up," Cuyler said, too tired to sound hopeful.

"In my considerate opinion," Quiver said, shaking the muck out of his quills, "we have heard no boom-noise for some time now."

"Ouch!" cried Trisbert, and all eyes swivelled around to the east.

"Pardon my obtrusion," Quiver sighed, and the others would have laughed with relief if they had had the energy to.

"My underparts are very attuned to thumpings on the earth," Adderly said, "and I've detected no two-footed clumping since we passed that big dead tree back there."

There was a pause as the refugees let this good news sink in, and once again waited for instruction from their leader.

Gavin's tender feet were sore, his furred flanks were scratched by thorns and sharp twigs, his ringtail – the badge of coon-honour – was nested with burrs, and his throat raged in its thirst. But he was no worse off, he thought, than any of the others. Unable to summon any words of consolation, he said the only thing, however harsh, that made sense: "We have to put as much distance as we can between us and the Tallwalker's firestick. Our paw-prints are visible in the mud, and even without the sense of smell that Gollah gave only to animals, the Tallwalker will know where we've come. He may be crawling as if his hands were feet, but he will come for us just the same. He has to."

"But Madame is starving," Hubert objected mildly, "and think of the little ones soon to be dependent upon her."

"I have depicted nothing edible," Quiver added, "not a green twig or a morsel of bark with even the scent of sap in it."

"I do believe we are the only living things, but for the Tallwalker, left in . . . in wherever-we-are," Adderly said gloomily (but, of course, he had only one tone of voice for all occasions).

"And the water has a strange taste to it," Cuyler said. "It made me more thirsty, so I spit it out."

"If we don't maintain food and water soon," Quiver said, "it won't matter whether the Tallwalker catches up to us or not."

"Maybe we'll be too stringy and dried-out to eat," Cuyler said, but nobody laughed.

"Quiver's right, Gav," Trisbert said.

"Then we've got to stop and fight him," Cuyler said.

"We could lure him into some kind of trap," Trisbert suggested.

"We'd need someone to act as bait," Cuyler said, growing excited enough to alarm the cottontails, who quickly deduced who might be candidates for that job.

"Then I'd flail him from behind with my behind," Quiver said, "till he cried for mercy!"

"While I got a pawful of claws into his throat," Trisbert said.

"And Adderly wrapped a coil 'round his middle," Cuyler said.

"What do you say, Gav?"

Everyone, even those doomed to be bait, turned a hopeful eye towards Gavin. After all, raccoons had cleverness, and here was one of their elder-sons who had, even so young, been privy to some of the divine stratagems of The Book itself.

"We'll rest for a little while longer," was Gavin's inspired advice, "then we'll continue westward. We won't go in panic but as swiftly as we can manage, and we'll stay together. We'll drink what we can and try to forget about food. If anyone falters, he'll be carried."

No-one spoke for a moment.

"You're not forgettin' that it's Everdark we're headin' for," Trisbert said carefully. "I can see it up ahead, that greenish blob, an' the black blob above it must be Serpentine Ridge."

"Is it better to be ripped apart – alive – by the wolves of Everdark or shot dead by the Tallwalker?" Hubert inquired with a paw over each of Renée's ears.

"Indeed," Quiver said, "we should pause and agitate this matter most attentively. I am not fond of vivisuction."

Gavin said: "Everdark may be forbidding and most assuredly it is dangerous. But it is a forest. Those tiny points we can see clearly at the top of the green blob are trees, the tops of trees, trees upright with ripe branches and sap-swollen leaves, and all the creatures that live in the shadow and trust of trees: mice, worms, mosses,

grasses dripping with juices, streams burbling with trout
– "

"Please," Hubert moaned as he rubbed the cavity
below his breast.

"At least if we have to die, it'll be on a full stomach,"
Trisbert said.

"Then lead the way, mon capitaine," Hubert said.

Gavin blushed, but did as he was bidden.

* * *

Much time passed. The sun overtook the fleeing woods-
creatures and began to hover before them, mocking in its
false promise of the heat-blessed seasons of
Blossomflower and Greendaze. They kept a steady but
manageable pace: Gavin ahead, Adderly sinuous in the
rear. Still, Renée had to be assisted by Hubert, and when
Hubert's flayed shoulder grew too painful, Trisbert
assisted him while Quiver, careful to keep his quills at
ease, lent a shoulder to Madame. For a time, Cuyler clung
to Adderly's neck, pretending to be enjoying the ride by
hollering a fatigued "whee!" every few paces. The
wasteland around them was unchanging. No tree remained
vertical. Every branch was dead to its pith, and splintered
whenever a hungering tooth struck it. The pools of
standing water were saline and void of fish or weed,
spore or larvae. Where the hot sun had penetrated, the
earth had cracked like old skin, and no grub wriggled up
to taste the light.

However, the sinking sun did illuminate the objects
that lay ahead of them along the western horizon. And
although it may have seemed to the band of starvelings
inching towards it to be days or seasons away, they were

advancing, tread by weary tread, ever closer to it. As the sun in its slow plummet neared the crest of the Ridge, the rippled mass below it became a richer and leafier green. Its jagged upper fringe was distinctly pointed in the manner of pine and spruce and fir: the Forest of Everdark! If it were an hallucination raised by hunger, then it was a welcome one, and drew these famished survivors towards it as a bright flame entices a moth out of its home-darkness.

Desperate not to think about food or what, besides sustenance, they might discover should they live long enough to reach Everdark, Gavin found himself remembering things he had long ago decided to delete forever from his memory . . .

Mama and her sister Rootha had not returned home by daylight from their berry-foraging down near the southern border of Earthwood. Here alongside the Tallwalkers' blackpath (now gnarled and weed-infested), the red plumpberries ripened in profuse numbers every spring at the beginning of Meadowbloom. And every annual, before the other berry-eating animals or birds found their way to this sweet harvest, Mama and Rootha (Aunt Rootha to Gavin and his brothers) arrived just as the first berries, low on the bush, were tingeing themselves red. Using a discarded eagle's nest as a hamper, they would fill it to the brim to bring home, and then settle down to gorge themselves as a reward for their thoughtfulness. On this day, however, when high-sun came and went and the sisters still had not returned, Papa set out to find them. "Come with me, Gavin," Papa said. "I'll come, too," Trisbert said, flexing his new muscles. Papa reflected a moment before saying, "Not today, Bertie. Gavin is the elder-son; there are things he knows or must come to know."

So Gavin, trembling all over for more than one reason, and Papa, silent and solemn, set out for the berry patches along the abandoned blackpath. They had no difficulty in spotting the place where Mama and Aunt Rootha had begun stripping fruit from the lowest branches of the berry-bushes. Cautiously, they followed this "trail" westward. Beside them on their left, the hot asphalt of the blackpath simmered in the afternoon sun. They halted often to listen, but the only sounds were a crow cawing far away, the rustle of leaves overhead, and the pounding of their hearts as they came to the last of the stripped bushes. There beside it lay the overturned hamper, the spilled plumpberries already wizening.

"Fur," Gavin whispered before his throat seized shut. Papa had espied it also, a wisp of gray coon-fur swaying on a branch in the breeze like a miniature pennant. He stepped resolutely into the shrubbery at the edge of the woods. "Don't look!" he cried, but it was too late. A single, half-second glimpse was all Gavin needed to remember forever the image of his mother tilted on the grass below a hawthorn, four legs still, most of the face blown away but for one eye. Gavin was the one to spot the trail of blood. Inspecting it closely, Papa said, "Somehow she must have managed to crawl away from the pathside and die here – alone." Gavin could hear the strength in Papa's voice and knew why he had been chosen RA-to-be by the elders of the High Ring. "And away from the evil gaze of the Tallwalker who shot her," Papa added.

Keeping his own gaze well averted from the hawthorn tree, Gavin said, "But where's Aunt Rootha?" Papa shook his silver-gray head as if to clear his mind of the sorrowful thoughts in it and then, nose down, followed the dried bloodlets and lingering scent of his dear, dead mate as they wound through the underbrush and eventually led Gavin and Papa back onto the gravelled edge of the blackpath. Papa sniffed at the oozing tar. "Look here, son, these are the faint paw-prints of a Tallwalker. A very heavy one. Running or staggering." "But no-one has seen a Tallwalker since long before the Great Burning," Gavin said. "RA-Mosah told us that their destruction was foretold at the beginning of The Book." "So it was," Papa said, moving westward along the gravel shoulder. "They are the lesser beings and pawns of Zeebub. But how and when they are to perish is not exactly known. Whatever may come to be, this one has killed your mother — and your aunt." They both stared at the pool of blood congealing at the pathside. No telltale droplets led hopefully towards the safety of the woods. "He's picked her up and taken her away," Papa said. Gavin's sorrow suddenly overwhelmed him despite his determination to be brave and worthy. "What will we tell baby Cuyler?" he sobbed.

Papa did not reply. He moved back towards the place beneath the hawthorn tree. Gavin followed, ashamed and stricken. Part of his world had come apart without warning or explanation. "I'll ask Trisbert and some of the elders to come for your mother's body," Papa said. "Bring the hamper of berries, will you, son?"

But it was on their journey home that further shock waves, as great as Mama's death and Aunt Rootha's disappearance, were hurled at Gavin the elder-son. Something in the fact or nature of Mama's death prompted Papa to begin talking in ways he had never done before. It was as if he were talking to himself yet aware, and not displeased, that Gavin was there to overhear what could be said once only:

"I have seen a Tallwalker up close; I stared into his eyes as he was dying. The look he gave me will be with me till the day I die. He was not far from where we found Rootha's blood today, though this story happened some time ago. My brother Sylva and I were young rascals in those days before I settled down." (Gavin's "But who is Sylva? I have no uncle by that name!" died on his lips.) "How often we disobeyed Papa Mosah to sneak down to the blackpath and watch the doomsmobiles whiz by, their occupants' faces a white blur. Sylva was bolder than I. At night he would dash out onto the blackpath as if he were about to cross over into terra incognita on the other side, then turn to stare down the two big sun-things of the doomsmobile, as if frozen to the spot, then leap adroitly to safety even as the mechanical creature swerved to finish the assassination, and Sylva's laughter would boom into the night and we would both tumble onto the grass with the hilarity of it all. Sylva was also bigger than me, more like Trisbert than you or Cuyler, and he was handsome – except for the blob where his left eye used to be. But the story of how he lost that eye was so full of derring-do and adventure that the young maiden-coons found him more appealing than ever.

"One night when he was teasing a doomsmobile, the contraption suddenly stopped and two Tallwalkers with firesticks jumped out and pursued him into Earthwood with the aid of a giant wolf-dog. Naturally this pleased Sylva, who led the would-be hunters a merry chase, backtracking on his own scent and criss-crossing streams and travelling treeward from top-branch to top-branch for a change of pace, until the wolf-dog collapsed in exhaustion and pique not a stone's throw from its prey, and the hunters boomed their firesticks upwards in disgust and trudged away. However, one of the missiles shattered a branch beside Sylva and a splinter struck him in the eye, putting it out forever and forever making him romantic and fascinating to all twin-eyed maidens (and to himself, I must admit).

"A little later, in the season of Fruitfall, Sylva and I were back at the blackpath one evening when we heard an awful screeching sound and then a terrific crash. We arrived at the scene to find a doomsmobile smoking and twisted about the trunk of an oak tree near the path. There was one Tallwalker in it. His head was slumped crookedly against the wheel-thing, his neck broken as cleanly as if a Karkajim had got him. But his eyes were alive for the moment it took me to peer in at him. Then Sylva called out and when I looked back in, the Tallwalker was dead. Sylva was rummaging about behind us in the doomsmobile, smelling food no doubt and very excited. This was forbidden territory: he was in his element. He came out with several cloth sacks that bulged with jars and packages. In his haste he spilled several other objects out onto the gravel. In the morbid light of the moon I could see they were books.

"While Sylva was clawing his way into the foodstuff and yipping with delight, I picked up one of the books and stared at it in awe, then in consternation. For RA-Mosah and RA-Jacib before him had told us time and time again that Gollah had given the powers of pure speech and true writing only to his chosen woods-creature, the raccoon, and that the offspring of Zeebub, like the pathetic Tallwalkers who toddle on two feet and murder each other for sport, were given only Gibberlish to babble their inanities to one another but no-one else. I decided to keep the book, to study it when I got home, in secret, until I came to some understanding of how this strangeness could be.

"Just then, though, the suns of another doomsmobile struck us both in the midst of our separate activities. Instinctively I rolled away into the pathside grass, got up, and scampered into cover, expecting to hear Sylva panting and chortling behind me. What I did hear was a screech, a thump, a cry, the commotions of Tallwalker babble-talk, and boot-thumps. I waited, alone and terrified, until the sun came up, then ventured back to the blackpath. Despite my childish fears, there was nothing horrific to be seen. The wrecked doomsmobile was gone, and the dead one in it. Having run over poor Sylva, the others had taken his body with them to do Gollah knows what with its flesh and fur. Before I slunk home to relate the awful news, I picked up the Tallwalker's book. It was torn, with many pages missing. But the remaining pages had words written on them, and though it took me many seasons and annuals, somehow I began to understand them, as if they were part of a language I had once known and forgotten – though that is, of course, impossible."

It was just as they were entering the Realm of Ringtail that Papa dropped the bombshell. "RA-Mosah, your grandfather, always blamed me for Sylva's shameful and untimely death. It took him many seasons to admit that I had the ability and character to be nominated an elder-son. Yes, Gavin, Sylva was older than me by an eyeblink or two: he was the firstborn son and favourite of RA-Mosah, and destined to become his successor. He would have been the greatest RA of our clan and added his glorious chapter to the neverending Book of Coon-Craft. And he would have been your uncle . . "

And, of course, it was only during the past annual that Gavin himself had been allowed to sit beside Papa, alone in one of the High-Ring trees, as he murmur-read a few of the weird and captivating tales apparently penned by the Tallwalkers in what Papa called Gibberlish – while Gavin peered over his arm and tried to unscramble its eccentric letters. The title of the book, Papa said, was Tales of Arthro. And it was the only book in the leather-pouch that swayed upon Gavin's back with every step he now took westward towards Everdark. In all likelihood it was the last book left in the world.

Well, for the nonce, no-one but Gavin need know. Keeping secrets, Gavin mused, seemed to be one of the burdens thrust upon those who, willingly or not, aspired to RA-ship. But if they didn't soon find food, none of this would matter a tittle.

"Over there," Trisbert gasped. "Them bushes: there's green on them!"

* * *

The animals needed no guide or captain to suggest that they put aside their bone-weariness and make haste towards the object of Trisbert's excitement. They could see, smell and taste the green haze that shimmered, mirage-like, thirty paces in front of them. That it might be an hallucination brought on by their desperate plight and their deep desire to survive (the first commandment of Gollah) did not occur to them and, if it had, would not have slowed them one whit. As they drew raggedly near the greenery, Gavin held up a paw and the others dutifully stopped behind him.

"It's not a mirage," he said. "It looks like a small valley or coulee. There are things still growing or not yet dead. I can even smell water running."

"Thank Gollah," Hubert sighed amidst a general round of hosannas.

"You don't suppose this is where the Tallwalker hangs out, do you?" Trisbert said slowly.

"Ever the optimist, aren't we?" Hubert said.

"I'll sneak down there and have a peak," Cuyler said as cheerily as his exhaustion would permit.

"I don't care if the place is crawling with Tallwalkers," Quiver declared. "I intend to die with my stomach full. I could consommé the handle of a firestick."

"No-one's been here for a long, long time," Gavin said. "There's not a humanoid or creature track anywhere that I can see, and no body scents."

To confirm this, and despite the temptation of everyone to simply dash forward and accept whatever fate awaited them, Adderly and Trisbert set out to reconnoitre the perimeter of the apparent oasis. Meanwhile, Gavin slipped silently up to the edge of the valley just ahead of him to get a better idea of the terrain and assess the level of hope he should allow himself. How had such a place, small though it be (he could now see Trisbert at the far end of the oval-shaped depression no more than a hundred or so paces away), have avoided the devastation that had seemed until now total and irreversible? This valley – a dale, really, set among half a dozen hummocks – had once been surrounded by a ring of sturdy cedars. These were now, of course, capsized, shredded and scattered willy-nilly; but they had likely protected the shrubs and bushes and grasses – winking greenly below him – from the worst blasts of wind and ruinous rain. Even so, the rolling flood – the tidal wave – that followed should have swamped all vegetation – root, shoot and seed – as it had everywhere else, drowning even the worms and the earth that harboured them.

It was then that Gavin saw what he had earlier sensed: a swift-running creek, dancing through the grassy bottomland of the dale and vanishing into a tangle of boulders. An underground stream, funnelling spring-water from one part of the earth to another, perhaps as far as the Lake of Waters Unending? A miracle, no doubt. Perhaps Gollah was watching over them after all. If not Gollah, then who?

"You were right, Gav," Trisbert announced as he and Adderly returned from their circular inspection. "Nobody's been here since the flood."

"Let's go, then," Quiver said. "I'm famwiched."

"Uh, my mistress will require some assistance," Hubert said, leaning discreetly on Renée's shoulder.

Trisbert came over, gave a paw to Hubert, and helped him navigate beside the others towards the Valley of Last Hope (as Gavin named and recorded it much, much later). Renée followed, needing no assistance but keeping a close watch on her injured mate.

* * *

Two days passed without incident. Two glorious days in which the intrepid members of the troupe fed (variously) on tender branch, sweet couch-grass, ripened plumpberry, swollen brook trout, and astonished frog. They replenished their attenuated flesh and, gradually, their frayed spirits. But with Cuyler and Trisbert taking turns patrolling the perimeter of the valley and reporting no sign of the Tallwalker by the end of the second day, even Hubert, whose wound had healed nicely, began to allow his lady to relax.

"If we had to, we could stay here forever," Cuyler mused aloud to the others as they once again gathered at nightfall for mutual comfort, protection, and quiet conversation. During the day the different species went their different ways, as they were meant to do (raccoons, being adaptable, gave up their night-wandering for the sake of the group). In the evening, though, they seemed relieved to relinquish their own specific behaviours for a chance to socialize merely as woods-creatures. What would Gollah think?

"At least until Madame has given birth to a new generation of cottontails," Hubert said, chewing contentedly on a stem of timothy.

There was a deep pause in the conversation.

"I'm afraid that forever wouldn't be very long for the rest of us," Quiver said sadly.

Thoughts of Earthwood and those siblings and mates and potential mates struck each of the animals simultaneously. Even Hubert wondered to himself what the world would be like peopled only by rabbits: free of fox and weasel but also devoid of birdsong and cricket-music and the genial chatter of field mice and the wise councils of raccoons in their high-and-mighty Ring.

"We can't just forget about Papa and RA-Mosah and the others, can we, Gav? If we came through alive, who knows how many others did the same?"

"I have no intention of abandoning the search for Earthwood, Cuy," Gavin said, surprised at the conviction he was able to put behind the words. "Whatever is left of home on the west side of the Ridge, we must find and face it."

"Well, we should be grateful for this place, I suppose," said Quiver, "and the fact that the Tallwalker has not tracked us here."

"I for one," rumbled Adderly, "would appreciate some dietary supplement to frogs: a juicy mouse, for instance."

"I must tell you all," Gavin said, suddenly grave, "that we couldn't stay here for long anyway. I've been studying the creek. At the east end of the valley where the spring feeds it, it is running dry. I can see more stones showing through the water each morning. It may soon dry up altogether. And the sun above us is hotter than I've ever felt it, even in the season of Skysun."

"What are you replying?" Quiver said anxiously.

"I'm not certain that the seasons here are the same as they've been since the beginning of time. I'm not sure the green things we've been enjoying will re-create themselves. Like us, they may be the last of their kind."

"I never knew raccoons to be so morose," Adderly muttered.

"And inconsiderate of the feelings of the tenderer sex," Hubert added.

"Oh, my!" Renée cried in a voice not at all tender.

"Oh my, oh my, oh my!" echoed Hubert.

"It's not that," Renée said, and she pointed upwards to where Trisbert, their sentry, was scuttling noisily through the first shadows of the night.

Gavin and Cuyler met Trisbert halfway up the slope.

"What is it, Bertie?"

"Something's out there!" Trisbert said. "Comin' our way."

"Tallwalker!" Cuyler cried, and Hubert's groan reached him from the valley below.

"No," Trisbert said, catching his breath. "Come an' look. There's just enough light left up there to see its outline, and it's not a Tallwalker."

"He could be crawling," Gavin suggested, remembering what he had observed two days ago.

"Not unless he's grown a tail," Trisbert said.

With that startling but not unwelcome news (had another woods-creature survived here east of Everdark?), the brothers ran up to the crest of the valley and, crouching low, peered eastward in the direction from which they had come to this place. Against the last glimmer of light from the west, they beheld a four-footed, bushy-tailed figure, in silhouette only but unmistakably an animal. And one who was limping badly – panicked and near the end of its tether. They recognized the signs only too well.

Gavin stood up.

"It could be a wolf or coyote from Everdark!" Trisbert hissed as he tried to pull Gavin back down beside him.

"And he could be one of our own," Gavin said, "with some news of Earthwood."

"I'm ready for him, whoever he is," Cuyler said, showing his teeth.

The staggering figure now spotted Gavin, and was aiming itself towards him. At every second or third step, it went down to its knees. They could hear it wheezing and coughing as it struggled up onto three feet and, dragging its left hind-leg like a dead branch, plunged ahead once again.

"It's a fox," Trisbert said. "I'd know that cough anywhere."

"Yes," Gavin said. "But I don't think it'll be feasting on raccoon or anything else for some time. Come on, follow me."

When they reached the fox, which had fallen and found itself unable to rise again, Gavin and Trisbert lifted it gently up into their strong double-embrace.

"I'm Wylee," the fox gasped. "I won't hurt you."

"We know," Gavin said. "But there's other food just ahead. Hang on, if you can."

"That's a horrible gash you've got on your leg," Trisbert said. Then, almost afraid to ask, he said, "How did you get it?"

"Tallwalker," Wylee said, his dulled eyes brightening. "Shot me . . . back there . . . not far."

Chapter 6

A Strange Covenant

EVEN IN THE MOONLIGHT that mellowed and bejewelled everything it touched, a fox – starved, bleeding, hollow-eyed though he be – could not be rendered less threatening or more welcome. For Fox was a lone and unpredictable assassin. It would devour whatever was insignificant enough to be bullied, living or dead. Its cunning was exceeded only by its cowardice. It was Gollah's renegade, with the blood of Zeebub in its veins. A collective shudder went through the band of survivors when Wylee was laid down in the midst of their evening circle by Gavin and Trisbert.

"You can't bring a fox in here," Hubert spluttered before placing his body in front of Renée, who promptly stepped aside for a closer gander at the newcomer.

"Really, Gavin," said Quiver with a sudden bristling of quills. "I must recur with the rabbit and demonstrate most forcefully with you for showing such poor judgement."

"I have never been fond of foxes," Adderly said.

"He's in no shape to hurt anybody," Trisbert said and, indeed, at that moment it appeared that Wylee might never frighten anyone again, for his long tongue slid sideways out of his slack jaws, and the dull glint in his eye darkened and began to film over as if an eyelid had come down to shield it from shame.

"Well, then, drag his carcase out of here and let him go peaceably back to his maker," Hubert suggested.

"He didn't get that wound from any thorn-tree," Quiver observed.

"He's been shot," Trisbert said.

"Then the Tallwalker's found us!" Hubert cried. "Why are we sitting here waiting for him?"

Everyone now turned to Gavin, who had said nothing so far but had perhaps been too busy examining the shattered hind-leg of the fox and stroking the matted fur at the base of his neck.

"We can't leave him," Gavin said. "After all, he's an animal and a woods-creature. Like us, for reasons we don't yet understand, he has been allowed to survive the flood."

"But he's going to die anyway," Hubert protested mildly.

"His demise is inenviable," Quiver said.

"In The Book Gollah commands that no creature of His should die without good reason," Gavin said, recalling one of RA-Mosah's earliest lessons among the pupils of the elder-school.

Glancing at his mate's ripening abdomen, Hubert said, "The preservation of our lives and of those yet-to-be-born surely constitutes the very best of reasons."

Just then Cuyler came down from his watch at the top of valley. "No sign of any Tallwalker," he announced rather regretfully. "The moon's gone under for the night. He won't be able to track us here."

"Good," Gavin said above a sudden outbreak of whimpering from the fox. "That gives us the rest of the night to get organized and decide what to do next. Go back up and keep patrolling, Cuy."

Cuyler scampered off to his sentry duties.

"What we have to do is oblivious," Quiver said. "Stuff our stomachs with food and then head out of this place. Even a nose-dead Tallwalker can follow a trail of vulpious blood-drops."

"I say we do what our leader tells us to do," Trisbert said, and moved his imposing bulk next to his brother.

Gavin said: "I'm only your leader because you chose me so."

"But you're a raccoon," Hubert protested, "an elder-son. Your Papa was RA-to-be."

"And you've got The Book of Coon-Craft in that leather-pouch," Quiver added for good measure.

"It is possible that we might be safer if we split up and went our separate clannish ways," Gavin said gravely.

This remark was greeted with a chorus of "no's!"

"Gavin's our leader, then," Trisbert said. "An' we stick together."

Gavin sighed. One paw unconsciously stroked Papa's leather-pouch, slung now at his side. Alas, no wisdom of the animal ages was written on the pages inside it. For all Gavin knew, what remained of coon-craft and creature cunning was whatever he himself could remember – from The Book (now lost forever) and from the lips of Papa and RA-Mosah (now lost, possibly forever). Could he be a leader and not tell the truth? But revealing the fact that with the destruction of The Book they had erased their own history and severed their only connection with Gollah the Great protector – that would be an act of supreme cruelty. The animals would surely give up and, like true woods-creatures, resign themselves to their fate.

"So be it," Gavin heard himself say.

"Then tell us what to do," Hubert said. "Renée is nearing her time."

"If I am to be your leader," Gavin said, "then I insist that we agree to three principles. First: we stay together no matter what happens. Two: we fully support one another, whatever our personal feelings might be. Three: we suspend Gollah's laws of nature until we have found Earthwood again. And that means, for a start, that we tend to the wounds of Wylee the fox and include him as a member of our troupe."

No-one spoke. Defying Gollah's immutable law was too blasphemous a thought to be uttered in mere words. But their leader-elect took silence as consent.

Renée stepped out from behind her mate and said, "The fox's wound is still bleeding. I've pulled out some of my fur to help stanch the flow."

A wave of embarrassment, perhaps even shame, rippled through the other animals.

"I'll chew off a branch and make a splint for the broken leg," Quiver said.

"There's some pliable vine down by the creek," Hubert said. "I can fetch it to fasten the splint onto the leg."

"I'll bring some water in a clamshell," Trisbert said.

Gavin smiled. He knelt beside the fox and held its head gently between his front paws. Gollah had bestowed a dexterity of finger upon his chosen clan and they had used it to good purpose, including of course the nimble turning of the pages of The Book.

Wylee's eyes drew painfully open. "Thank you," he said. And then: "I won't hurt you . . ."

Just then Cuyler could be heard skittering down towards them. Everyone stiffened, braced for bad news.

"It's all right," he said, and it was clear that he was laughing as he spoke. "I decided to go exploring – "

"You'd no business diverting your post!" Quiver snapped.

"Coons can see better in the dark than in daylight," Cuyler replied.

"What'd you find?" Trisbert asked.

"I picked up Tallwaker's scent and his ugly hoofprints. He didn't get anywhere near us. The tracks turn off and go towards North Holy. I followed them for a long ways. They sort of wobble a bit but, direction-wise, they're straight as a tree-trunk. I'm sure he's heading for some place he knows." Cuyler puffed out his pup's chest and said, "He won't be bothering us for a while."

"Thank Gollah," Hubert sighed.

"Thank Gavin," Trisbert said.

* * *

While the hearts of the survivors were warmed somewhat by Cuyler's news and more than somewhat by their unexpected kindness towards a fellow creature-in-distress, the night around them grew cold and dank. A chill wind arose and blew hard from the north. The stars were smothered by cloud. It felt like a Witherstalk night even though the sun that day had burned with the fury of Skysun. But when the rain came just before dawn, it was as warm and mistful as as a morning in Greendaze.

Wylee was kept dry under a leafy hawthorn, while Trisbert laid his long body close by for warmth and moral support. Gavin and Cuyler took turns at the watch above. By the time the sun boiled up out of the Lake of Waters Unending somewhere in the eastern distance, the rain had ceased, and the cloud with it.

Cuyler came down to the group, who had not yet scattered for their daytime foraging but were, rather, huddled near the injured interloper and waiting, it seemed, for him to awaken and pronounce himself both grateful and harmless.

"Well?" Gavin said.

"Just as you thought," Cuyler said. "There isn't a paw-print or a claw-scratch to be seen. The rain's washed them clean away."

"I trust that includes slither-marks," said Adderly.

"So Tallwalker won't be able to trace his own tracks back here," Trisbert said. "Which means we're safe, for a while."

Gavin nodded assent, which pleased the others more than it should have. "But," he said gently, "we don't know for certain whether Wylee was shot by the same Tallwalker that shot Hubert."

This dreadful prospect was greeted with silence.

Finally Quiver said, "But what does this mean?"

"It means we have to keep a constant watch," Gavin said.

Taking his cue, Cuyler dashed back up to his post.

"It means trouble," Adderly said. "But then there's always trouble."

"And what can we do when one of them does find this place?" Hubert said. "Or more than one of them!"

"What place?"

Every head swivelled around to the sound of the new voice.

Wylee stared out at them from a pair of bewildered eyes, certain that he had died and awakened in one of Zeebub's tormenting dens where he would be nibbled fleshless by the very creatures he'd spent his life terrifying. But he was too tired to move. It was an agony merely to blink.

"It's all right," Gavin said. "You're among friends."

* * *

For the next two days the survivors fattened themselves on the provender of the Valley of Last Hope. Its perimeter was ceaselessly patrolled, but nothing was seen beyond it except the barren mud-flats and the wreckage of trees. Only the wind moved, in a sky emptied of wingbeat and insect-hum. Hubert noted, but did not report, that the grass he and Renée dined upon was overripe and that there was no young grass springing up under it, while its seeds lay inert upon the ground. Trisbert feasted upon trout until he grew almost wall-eyed, but mentioned to Gavin that he had observed not a solitary fingerling anywhere in the creek. The crabapple and plumpberry were suffused with sweetness but carried no seed in their core. Quiver munched luxuriously on sap-softened branches that bore no sign of rejuvenating sprout or nodule. On the third day following Wylee's arrival, Adderly ate the last of the bullfrogs.

Gavin was pleased with the splint holding Wylee's injured leg firmly in place. He realized that the loss of blood had left the fox very weak, and that food was an immediate necessity. As Wylee was in a near-coma most of the time, Gavin would wait patiently, frog in hand, until Wylee opened his eyes to glance at the world and heave a resigned sigh. Then he would force the tidbits of frog into the resisting jaws (foxes ate frog only in extremity).

Towards the end of the third day, the animals, as their kind so often did, came to a conclusion simultaneously and collectively. Gavin was not surprised to see them gather about him, then sit quietly as dusk began its descent upon the valley. Even Cuyler left his post to join them.

"Yes, friends, I know . . . " Gavin began. "We cannot stay here much longer. We have eaten what we can of the fruits of this oasis. But like the land out there, it too is sterile. The only growing, living things lie leagues away to the west, in the Forest of Everdark. Between us and Everdark, in all likelihood, stand one or more Tallwalkers – with firesticks."

"And I have the leg to prove it!" Wylee cried as he hobbled into the improvised circle.

A cautious round of friendly greetings followed, with astonished comment on the fox's miraculous and abrupt recovery from mortal danger. Indeed, although still limping dramatically, Wylee appeared sprightly and bright-eyed, like one who has come awake not from a nightmare but from a revivifying dream. The sharp look in the eye was not wholeheartedly welcomed by those who had made it possible. But Wylee smiled most amiably and he bespoke in softened tones his gratitude and amazement at what had been done for him.

"You are welcome to our council," Gavin said when the initial fuss had died down. "But first I must outline for you the tenets of behaviour we have all agreed upon, and narrate what has happened to us so far."

Thus, while Wylee listened (and managed despite his humble demeanour to discomfit Hubert and Renée with an occasional gourmandizing glance), Gavin outlined the strange covenant and code of conduct they had sworn to uphold (Wylee's eyebrows arched and interrupted his grin for a half-second). Next he gave him a brief account of the events since they had discovered themselves alive and befuddled somewhere east of Serpentine Ridge and the grim forest below it. Gavin then invited Wylee to tell his own story.

"With pleasure," Wylee enthused, and would have leapt centre-stage if his splint-stiffened leg had permitted. "When the rains came," he began, " we foxes retreated to the warmth of our dens, not because we fear any beast or the worst of Gollah's angered elements, but merely because we prefer dry comfort to sodden bravado. Of course, not even the canniest of our clan could have predicted the flood or the inconvenience of topsy-turvy trees or rivers without the courtesy of banks. After a while, hunger made me a little curious and, being a bachelor still with a choice of willing mates among the unattached vixens, I felt bold enough to venture forth to reconnoitre a meal and present it as a token of esteem to one of them. I soon found that the rains had grounded innumerable fowl – grouse, partridge, tender pheasant –

rendering their wings flightless, and I felt almost sorry for dispatching them so readily, except that in such circumstance their death as my dinner was a more dignified end than drowning in their own squelched feathers. Most gave up with a grateful squawk."

Several of the herbivores in the audience failed to appreciate this latter point.

"I was on route home, sated and freighted with quail and such – prize enough for any bride – when the trees around me began to tilt and sway and then, incredibly, abandon their roots and the earth that anchored them. With the grace and alacrity of my breed I dodged falling branches and splintered trunks and catapulted limbs, but in doing so I momentarily lost my way. Which was all it took to become hopelessly lost, as within an eyeblink no familiar landmark was left standing. Naturally I did not succumb to the panic of those around me, who, it became piteously clear, had decided to race like lemmings towards Serpentine Ridge in the foolish hope of drowning in a high place instead of a low one.

"But we foxes use our brains for more than butting heads or keeping our ears from colliding. If Earthwood, as it seemed, was being transformed from a forest into a sea, then our only salvation lay in something that preferred water to land. What floats? I asked myself rhetorically. Wood. What kind of wood floats best? Hollowed wood. And where does one customarily find such wood? Why, in the older portion of Earthwood where industrious raccoons and squirrels had already dug out the pith and rot of elderly trees to keep themselves cozy against the snows of Driftdeep. And so like the wise reynards before me, I swam against the tide of unthinking creatures, not towards the dubious safety of the Ridge but back towards the Realm of Ringtail, where

I soon met, a-bob the tormented waves, a bountiful and bouncing and watertight log of considerable girth and, I am certain, of some erstwhile significance among the clan coon."

Here Wylee paused to scratch his trussed hind-leg and, incidentally, to gauge the effect of this last remark upon the masked members of his audience.

"One of our hibernation trees," Gavin said.

"Empty?" Trisbert asked, holding his breath.

"Alas, 'twas so," Wylee sighed, "though it soon welcomed me in as if I were a Chosen One."

"Did you see any sign of raccoons or their . . . accoutrements?" Gavin said.

Wylee did not answer right away. He appeared to be either consulting his memory or considering prudently what words he ought to deploy next. "Just as I was plugging the entrance-hole to my seaworthy craft, I did notice out of the corner of one eye an enormous pine-tree spinning crazily past. Its branches were gruesomely sundered and the floodwaters were tossing it like milkweed in a tornado, and I heard – but did not see the source of – a wailing and a keening very like the cries of raccoons in distress . . . "

"One of the High-Ring trees," Trisbert said.

Cuyler stifled a sob.

"Thank you for telling us," Gavin said. "All of us here have been separated from those we love. That is why we are determined to return to Earthwood. There may have been many survivors besides us."

"Indeed," Wylee replied, eager to be more cheerful and to re-establish the gist of his narrative. "Though I fear only the bravest and the best could have done so. At any rate, to resume my tale: I found myself inside a dark and bumptious den of wood. I had no notion of how long I lay there or how far I was flung and shaken, for after a while I found myself falling asleep, not out of hunger and certainly not out of despair, but as if Gollah had deemed it necessary for my miraculous survival. I had no dream. I woke up and climbed out into this despoiled landscape, most likely about the same time as you did. I was hungry but not starved, anxious but not scared."

"When did you first observate the Tallwalker?" Quiver asked.

"A little while before I arrived here. I saw him first, naturally. No-one spies a fox before the fox spies him."

Hubert considered an objection here, but thought better of it.

"I noticed that he carried a pouch strapped to his side, the sort of straw-thing they often keep food in, so I decided to track him and, should he pause to sleep, boldly approach and silently purloin anything edible from his person. I even contemplated lugging the firestick off and burying it."

"I prefer, then," Quiver said, "that he did not in fact fall into slumberment?"

Wylee gave Quiver a long look, then said, "That he did not, though he appeared to my hunt-hardened eyes to be exhausted, so much so that he fell to his knees and lay his head upon them. Alas, in doing so, he inadvertently directed his gaze towards the stump I was using for cover. Naturally I made no impetuous gesture of retreat, but part of my tail must have remained visible, for he suddenly leaped upward with a humanoid grunt and the firestick in his hands burst into flame, again and again.

One of its missiles must have ricocheted off a boulder and struck my hind-leg. As quick as that, the stalker became the stalked. However, by sprinting on three legs only and exercising my superior intelligence, I was easily able to outrun my pursuer. Alas, the loss of blood from my wounded leg eventually slowed me down, and the fiend caught up with me. I had resigned myself to an ignominious death at the hands of Zeebub's agent, when I looked up and was astounded to behold a pair of friendly eyes in a coon's mask. The rest of the tale you already know."

"Thank you for telling it," Gavin said. "It must have been difficult to relive such appalling events."

"Yes, a very repelling saga," Quiver said.

"You brought a tear to my eye, mon ami," Renée said.

"Reptiles do not weep," Adderly said. "We don't see the point."

"Enough yarn-spinning," Trisbert said brusquely. "We're here to listen to our leader."

"Indeed, indeed," Wylee said, "and a thousand pardons for my interruption of your . . our most urgent business." When he smiled – a grin really – his scarlet tongue flopped here and there as if it were seeking some means of escape.

Gavin decided to step up onto a nearby boulder so that he could command the high ground, as it were, and perhaps enhance an authority he was sure he did not deserve. Nonetheless, he was pleased to see that everyone was staring solemnly up at him in mute expectation. They were also, he was aware, watching the leather-pouch swinging gently on his back – in the certain belief that their leader had said little to them for two days because he was spending his quiet hours in contemplation of the runes and sayings in The Book. Somewhere in its inscrutable script, they were sure, lay the secret not only to their survival but also to the divine purpose behind it. In truth, Gavin had not opened the pouch at all: of what use were the blasphemous Tales of Arthro? Well, let them believe a little while longer. Faith was all they had left, besides a blind determination to live and live on.

"I have given much thought to our plight," Gavin began, doing his best to make his voice sound as swelling and oracular as RA-Mosah or Papa in the High-Ring tree. "It is only a matter of time, a day or two at most, before one of the Tallwalkers discovers this valley and its food supply. We have taken what we can of its bounty, but it will soon have no more to give. On the other hand, our only chance for true survival is to travel west until we reach Everdark — "

"I think you meant to say that the trout supply is dangerously low."

The interjection came from Wylee. The others turned to him, open-mouthed, then swung their gaze back up to Gavin.

Gavin stuttered: "Well, that is so. The frogs are entirely gone. But I admit that there is much grass left and many days-worth of tender branches. But that means that there will be sustenance here only for the cottontails and porcupine. The raccoons, snake and fox would be out of luck."

"And out of breakfast," Adderly added.

"Nevertheless," Hubert said very slowly, "Wylee has a point. I would find it difficult beyond measure to insist that my delicate Renée depart a place where she, and her little-ones-to-come, could feed for several seasons and find sufficient cover to elude the no-nosed Tallwalker."

Hubert's remark caused a stir among the others, who began muttering half-formed, treasonous thoughts.

"When you chose me leader – " Gavin shouted to no avail.

"Shut up an' listen!" Trisbert commanded in his most bullying tone.

They did, though the grin on Wylee's face never faltered.

" – you agreed that we would face all dangers together and that we would support one another unconditionally. Here is the very first test of our resolve, but I assure you it will not be the last or the most challenging. Much worse is to come. Are we to fail in our purpose at the very outset? Does the hope of regaining Earthwood and doing the bidding of Gollah Himself not override all other consideration?" Gavin blushed at this unsanctioned reference to Gollah and His will, but the others apparently did not notice, for all but Wylee hung their heads in shame.

"Are we together, then?" Gavin asked, and was relieved to hear the collective "yes."

"I was merely raising a point for debate," Wylee said affably. "After all, there is no more food in this valley for a fox than there is for a coon or a snake. It is in my own interest to leave this place, a manoeuvre our leader was no doubt about to suggest."

Trisbert made a threatening gesture towards the upstart, but Gavin caught his brother's eye, then said, "We have always encouraged and thrived on debate. Our RAs, as The Book records," and here he shamelessly tapped the leather-pouch, "make their final and irrevocable judgements only after everyone in the High Ring has had his say. And the RA is chosen by the elders from amongst the elder-sons and elder-daughters."

"What you mean, of course," Wylee grinned most genially, "is that the raccoons have their say. I for one have never been invited to a colloquium of the High Ring."

"One more crack like that and I'll bust your other leg," Trisbert snarled.

"Here, we are all members of the Ring," Gavin said to Wylee. "Until we reach Earthwood and the world is restored to us, we are animals only, Gollah's woods-creatures. You have as much right to your say as Renée or her young ones when they come."

"And you've already had your say!" Trisbert informed the fox.

Gavin gathered his tattered dignity about him and continued: "We will leave here tonight. We will travel only in the dark. We will seek cover and sleep through the day. Adderly will bring up the rear and sweep away our tracks. Cuyler will move out from time to time and set false trails in the ancient manner of the raccoon – "

Little of Gavin's plan was heard after his remark about night-travel, especially among those who feared the dark and its ghostly dangers. Among the mutterings of discontent, Wylee was heard to say, "Typical coon-thinking."

Gavin waited until he (or Trisbert with his fierce glare) had got their full attention again before he went on: "It is indeed typical coon-thinking. Bertie, Cuy and I have superb night-vision. We will lead and protect our flanks. The Tallwalkers, our only enemy in this wasteland, cannot see in the dark, nor can they smell or hear with animal acuity. Since we will have no sustenance but what we have added to our bones these past few days, travelling in the cool of the night will expend less energy than in the swelter of the days here. If Gollah wills it, we could reach Everdark with three day's march."

The dissent turned quickly to admiration and approval. Trisbert beamed. Cuyler puffed out his tiny breast. Adderly rehearsed a spoor-sweeping swing of his mighty tail.

"And if we don't?" Wylee said as the hubbub subsided.

"Then we shall perish," Gavin said calmly, "together, in the comfort of fellow creatures and the certainty that Gollah foreordained it so." Gavin fervently prayed that at this moment Gollah was busy elsewhere.

"Why not simply state that we'll starve to death?" Wylee said.

"Pul-leez!" Hubert cried. "Bite your canine tongue!" And he shuddered for them all: starvation was an animal fate as terrible as it was common.

"I didn't think I needed to state the obvious," Gavin said with a great effort to control his temper.

Ignoring this sheathed barb, Wylee carried on: "What I suggest, and feel to be equally obvious, is that, should we reach a point of extreme necessity – and that must be admitted as a possibility before we assent to our leader's scheme – our agreement to suspend the laws of Dame Nature ought to be summarily rescinded. After all, survival – individual and species survival – is the deepest instinct we possess."

"What are you implying?" Hubert snapped.

"Yes, exonerate yourself," Quiver demanded.

"What I mean is what Gollah has written on the sky every day of our lives: those deemed eternally to be prey and flesh-fodder must submit to those deemed eternally to be predators." And here he aimed a gluttonous smirk at the cottontails.

Wylee's proclamation was greeted with consternation all round.

"Peace! Peace, my fellow creatures," Wylee shouted them down. "I have agreed to uphold your covenant, and I will. Moreover, you have saved my life and I shall never forget such an act of charity and self-sacrifice. In addition, I am crippled and couldn't outrun a mouse. I was speaking hypothetically. If we don't work together to reach Everdark, whatever benefit that grim abode might hold for us, we will all starve. I was merely indicating the natural and inevitable sequence in which that catastrophe will visit us as individuals."

These assurances did not have the pacifying effect intended.

"Your comments don't sound hypodermical to me!" Quiver cried.

Again, Gavin shouted into the uproar: "Under no circumstances will one of us feed upon another member of this company or upon any survivor of Earthwood who might be fortunate enough to join us. Consider this, fox: thus far, Hubert and Renée are the only mated pair of animals we know to have survived the flood. If you or any predator were to eat either of them or their offspring, whatever the temptation, there would be no more rabbits — ever. You would be sealing your own fate, and the future of Earthwood itself."

Wylee had no rejoinder. Even his grin faded, just a touch.

And so it was that Gavin and his troubled troupe set out under a moonless, black canopy – travelling, it would seem, through one darkness towards another.

Chapter 7

New Arrivals

FOR TWO NIGHTS AND TWO DAYS Gavin's plan worked to perfection. As soon as the moon went down, Gavin stepped to the fore and, sighting the North-Holy star and keeping it a-wink at the corner of his right eye, guided his followers unerringly westward. Meanwhile Trisbert, stout of stature and of heart, patrolled both flanks with the perseverance and zeal of a lynx on the prowl. Adderly swept away all evidence of their passing with the prodigious lashing of his tail. The others, suppressing their fear of the dark as best they could, kept pace with their leader, and trusted, as much as they could, in the night-vision and animal cunning of the coon. No-one spoke, for even a cough could carry far into the pricked ears of the enemy. And what was there to be said anyway?

Quite often Hubert or Quiver had to support Wylee when his strength gave out and he toppled over with a smothered grunt. Left to their own devices, they might well have abandoned him to the fate they thought he deserved but, each time, Gavin would halt and simply wait – unmoving and stern-faced ahead of them – until he heard once more the thump of Wylee's splint against the ground.

Cuyler gloried in his role as scout and outrider. Whenever they came to a fallen tree of any size, he would vault onto the trunk, trot to the far reaches of root or branch-tip, swing elegantly onto the muddy earth and, depending on the strategy selected, land with four-footed weight or butterfly delicacy.

Most often he chose to blaze a false trail, sometimes for a league or more, stopping it abruptly and then, on feather-feet, flitting back over it till another collapsed tree or sequence of log-and-brush permitted a lateral (and baffling) exit. This was the easy part, instinctive to raccoons, even young and impetuous ones. Much harder was finding his way back to the troupe, in a circuitous and clandestine manner, before the unseasonable sun seethed up behind him and exposed him and his stratagems to any predator's eyes. He too kept a watch upon the North-Holy star and guided his westerly return by its opal glow until he could detect, with his keen ear, the faint but familiar footfalls of his brothers. Even then he kept his route roundabout (occasionally paddling across a foul-smelling pond) until he was able, at last and to the constant irritation and relief of the troupe, leap from the cover of a brush-pile into their startled midst.

"You could give a certain person a heart attack doing that," Hubert would cry, and then look to that certain person to assure himself that such a dire consequence were not proven.

"Or cause a creature-companion to trip on his disabled limb!"

"Or prick yourself axe-i-dentally on someone's quill!"

"Good work," Gavin would say without fail.

"Were you worried?" Cuyler would ask.

"I'm always worried."

* * *

By day they hunkered down in some low-lying brush and feigned sleep, except for the raccoons of course, who managed to doze fitfully. It was not that there were noises to disturb this daylight slumber, but rather the opposite: an eerie silence everywhere around them, above and below. The sun that boiled soundlessly in a cloudless sky should have quickened the air with wingbeat and bee-buzz, stirred the soil to some fertile heaving, and driven worm and grub to writhe towards cooler places under living root. But it was clear, even by starlight, that the terrain they were traversing was becoming more, not less, wasted.

It was sometime during the windless chill of the second night's trek that hunger once again began to whisper its insidious treasons, making each additional step more ponderous, shortening the stride (or slither), and weakening the will. But they were animals, proud woods-creatures, and hunger was often their lot. No complaint was made, though Hubert was quick to note Wylee's sidelong appraisal of his mate's profile, particularly her more pendant nether-parts. At dawn they slumped exhausted in their tracks, barely able to scratch out shallow hiding-holes in the earth beneath the brush-pile Gavin had wearily chosen for them.

One by one, after another sleepless day disrupted only by pangs of hunger and the hallucinatory dreams it induced, the members of Gavin's troupe (as they now thought of themselves) raised their heads and peered, with hope or despair, at the setting sun as it touched the jagged rim of the Ridge, reddened, and bled happily upon its host before vanishing without a trace.

"We are getting closer," Gavin said in what he took to be a cheerful voice. "I could make out the greenish spikes of spruce and fir just as the last light faded."

Even if they were the haunts of giant wolves and marauding bears! Or, more likely, the refuge of wailing banshees driven down from the Ridge into Everdark by the great storm. Death by ripped throat or phantom fright: some choice!

"We could reach the edge of the forest by sun-up," Gavin added.

"If we had employed some of the daylight for travelling, we'd be there by now," Wylee said, conveniently forgetting his own nocturnal preferences.

"Or maybe we'd have had time to put a splint on your other hind-leg," Gavin said sharply.

"We need food and fresh water more than we need sleep," Wylee persisted.

"Without Gavin we wouldn't be this far," Trisbert growled and, as if to underline his warning, he let go of Wylee's shoulder and watched him teeter awkwardly on his crippled limb.

Suddenly Hubert cried, "What is it, cherie?"

"I feel a twinge," Renée said calmly. "Down here."

"Then we'd better be on our way," said their leader, ignoring the bright, gibbous moon still far above the horizon.

* * *

The moonlight not only cast their silhouettes high, visible and vulnerable, it also made grotesque shadows out of every bush, root-cluster and desiccated tree in their path. Visions of what they had tried to forget from their most heinous nighmares loomed up before them, stark and indelible: the jinns of Everdark come to prove themselves palpable. Someone's teeth began to chatter and would not stop. Cuyler made no attempt to play the mischievous scout. Quiver and Trisbert each took a shoulder and carried Wylee along with them, while Adderly moved fretfully among his comrades. There seemed little need to protect either flank or rear: they were helpless targets for any Tallwalker they might blunder into. And yet despite the steady, brave walking of more than half-a-night, they were pursued by a moon that refused to go down, that stood garish and mocking above them. After a while, only Gavin dared to glance skyward, and then only when he had to.

Soon the famine in the belly was not merely keen but debilitating. Everdark had to be reached by daylight – or shortly thereafter. More than one of the animals recalled the fox's proposal regarding their behaviour if the situation became hopeless, and quickened his pace. And even though each of them expected at every laboured step to hear the crash of two-heeled footfalls from the lurking shadow or the crack of a firestick against the silence, when the latter calamity actually occurred, no-one flinched or felt the somersault of his heart.

By the time the second shot rang out, however, somewhere to the north or south of them, absolute panic had set in. Eight silhouettes froze. And remained so. You could not flee what you could not see. Just ahead lay a labyrinth of shadowed root and branch: camouflage or a Ghostie's lair?

Finally Gavin straightened up, both ears pricked, head swivelling slowly. "I hear animal thumpings," he said.

"That way." He pointed to the north. "Fleeing the Tallwalker."

After pressing one floppy ear against Renée's stomach, Hubert squatted low and said, "Yes: animals in full flight."

"What'll we do?" Quiver said, all a-quiver.

"Can you tell how far away they are?" Gavin asked, "or what direction they're running in?"

Renée, who had just joined her protector on the ground, said, " They're coming this way."

"Don't leave me!" Wylee cried in a wee pup's voice.

"Not a chance," Trisbert said, then, partly to relieve the unbearable tension, added, "We'll need someone to chew on when we really get desperate."

"Into that brush-pile," Gavin commanded. "It's our only hope." The idea of leaving whoever was being pursued out there to the savagery of the Tallwalkers was repugnant to him, but he had sworn to lead his own troupe to safety, and that duty overrode all others. They had not been seen, nor were they likely to be. Without realizing it, those doomed creatures out there had acted as a warning and given Gavin a few precious moments in which to devise a means for his company to stay out of harm's way. They won't die for nothing, was his consoling thought.

"I'll go in first," he announced when no-one, not even the redoubtable Trisbert, made a move to seek immediate cover. "It's only a bunch of shadows."

But shadows, as every spooked day-creature knew, were cast by the invisible shapes and spectres which they embodied, and which manipulated them to unspeakable purpose. Accustomed to the play of moonlight in the night-forest, Gavin strode manfully into the maze of rotting branches, flapped his paws about as if brushing bees from a honeycomb, and called out softly, "Come on. There's lots of warm sand here to burrow into. And a hollowed-out stump with a bit of rainwater inside. We can huddle in here together until the ruckus dies down."

Reluctantly, and too weary to do anything else, the others squeezed their eyes tight and entered the site of their nightmares. They shuffled close to the comfort of the nearest breathing body — furred, scaled or quilled — and wriggled down into the tentacled grip of shadows. Renée was considering mentioning a further twinge when she heard Quiver whisper beside her: "Pardon my obtrusion, mes dames."

For several suspended moments nothing seemed to be happening. No firestick flashed or boomed. No rumpus of paw or pad in flight. Had the missiles from the firestick already found their target? Had the hunger and sadism of the Tallwalker been satisfied? If so, for how long?

Three more shots shattered the silence in rapid succession. The ground suddenly reverberated with the pounding of feet, animal and otherwise.

"Oh my," Renée sighed, "They're coming this way."

"What'll we do? What'll we do?" Hubert babbled.

"We'll keep quiet," Gavin said, "and stay absolutely still. Not a twitch."

Wylee was about to comment on the folly of this suggestion when the sound of footfalls became loud enough to be heard on the moon and so close to the brush-pile that the thudding feet themselves were visible, and then the moonlit figures attached to them!

Hubert stood up on his hind-legs and shrilled, "Don't come in here! For the love of Gollah!"

Neither love nor hate applied in this circumstance, however, and seconds later the branches about him flew apart, and several furred bodies plummeted to the ground and lay motionless in the shadows there.

"Get up! Get out!" Hubert screamed, caring not who heard him. "You'll lead the Tallwalker straight to us!"

With a firm but gentle paw, Gavin eased Hubert back onto all fours. "Crawl to the edge of the brush," he whispered to Trisbert, "and keep a close watch."

Weakened though he was by hunger and thirst, Trisbert dredged up a smile: "I was hopin' you'd say that."

"We can take him," Cuyler said. "I'll go for the firestick."

"He's not here yet," Gavin said.

At that moment a cloud as big as a dozen ring-trees passed over the moon, extinguishing all light but the ineffectual flickering of the stars.

"And won't be for a while," he added. "He won't be able to see his own fingers on the firestick."

"That's odd," Trisbert grinned. "I can see perfectly well." And he and Cuyler slipped eagerly away to stand sentry.

Gavin turned now to the slumped bodies in their midst. Hubert, Renée, Quiver and Wylee were staring at them in a vain attempt to discern both their breed and the degree of their wretchedness. Adderly seemed uninterested.

"I can't see who these creatures are," Wylee complained, "and they haven't the decency to rouse themselves and enlighten us. Whose foolish idea was it anyway to have us traipse about in the pitch dark?"

Renée placed a motherly paw on what she hoped was a shoulder. "It's all right," she said. "We're friends." Then she gave a little cry and leapt back. "Blood," she gasped.

"Let them die in peace, cherie," Hubert said, not too unkindly. "You mustn't receive any further shocks."

"Give them a prick with one of your quills," Wylee suggested to Quiver.

Meanwhile, Gavin had knelt beside the nearest of the three bodies – all of them breathing – and was studying them carefully. "He looked up at the others. "I know them," he said solemnly. "And they know us."

* * *

When Cuyler came back to inform Gavin that they could neither hear nor see any sign of the Tallwalker, the three newest refugees were sitting up and blinking warily at the figures crowded around them. Gavin signalled for Cuyler to resume his watch, then turned his attention to the scene before him. "This fellow is Jocko, if I remember rightly," he said.

The large jackrabbit – for such he was despite the ragged, thorn-tormented fur and drooping ears and bloodied snout – nodded, tried to speak, failed, and then pursed his bruised lips into the semblance of a friendly smile.

"And these are members of the clan beaver: twin brother and sister, I believe," Gavin said. "Cuspid and Paddle-Whee, isn't it?"

A young beaver teetered towards Gavin and held out a
paw. His sleek fur was begrimed and matted with burrs
and his amiable eye was glazed with fatigue. "I am
Cuspid, son of Birchbig and Diver." Beside him, Paddle-
Whee started to hold out a paw, then quickly drew back.

A gasp of horror shuddered through the group, and
several recoiled as if they had seen a Ghostie or loosed
Warlaw: where the beaver's left forepaw should have been
was nothing but a bloody stump.

"I'm sorry," she said. "I didn't mean to frighten you."

"Please, tend to my sister," Cuspid said to Gavin.
"She's been hurt, terribly."

But Renée had already moved to Paddle-Whee's side,
raised her truncated limb, and was licking it ever so
gently with her antiseptic tongue. The others watched
with a mixture of fascination and revulsion: they had
never seen such unnatural behaviour between members of
clans designated by Gollah to maintain forever their
separate habits and instincts: how else would the world
work? Too weak to resist or comment, Paddle-Whee lay
down and let herself be nursed. Hubert was sure he saw
the fox slavering at the scent of blood.

"It was healed over," Cuspid explained, "but when the
Tallwalker discovered us, we had to run for our lives and – "

Jocko, who had been struggling to find sufficient
breath to speak and finally did, interrupted Cuspid with a
faint but candid query: "What happened to the mice?"

"Mice!" Wylee yipped.

"Yes, a whole family of them," Cuspid said. "The
Tallwalker had been digging at their pathetic little burrow
under a brush-pile when we stumbled upon him and

offered him the chance at a bigger meal. We all took off at the same time."

"And flushed me out, too," Jocko sighed. "Though I'm sure it couldn't be helped."

"Nothing can be helped," Adderly said in his matter-of-fact, gloomy way.

Just then Trisbert and Cuyler arrived. "Cuy disobeyed me and went out to look for the Tallwalker."

Cuyler beamed, and seized the opportunity to report his news. "And there's no sign of him. But he did leave his clumping hoofprints for anybody to find, and they're headed north, well away from us!"

A restrained cheer went up from those woods-creatures who had the strength to use their voices.

"We're safe, then," Hubert said, "should the missus have any more serious twinges."

"I'd better go back and stand watch," Cuyler said, "just in case." And off he went.

"I don't know how you define safe," Wylee said to Hubert. "Here we are almost starved to death. Not one of us has more than a quarter-day's walk left in his body. There's a maniac of a Tallwalker out there not a league away, plotting our death and devourment. And to top it all off, three more pathetic woods-creatures have the temerity to plop themselves defenceless in our midst."

"We're not all defenceless," Trisbert said, showing his claws. "Some of us know how to fight, and have the courage to do it."

"Don't carry on so," Wylee grinned. "No insult intended. I was just trying to be frank."

"You're both right," Gavin said. "We may well have to fight. But it won't be each other. And our safety here is precarious at best."

"And we must have food and water, immediately," Hubert reminded him.

Again they all turned to their leader and to the leather-pouch at his side, as if some wizardry of coon-cunning were still possible.

"We can't do anything until our guests have had time to recover from their ordeal," Gavin said, "and I've had a chance to inform them of the special covenant we've all agreed to."

"Talk, talk, talk," Wylee muttered.

Cuyler popped up before them: "All clear. And the moon seems to have disappeared for good."

"Nice work," Gavin said.

"And look what I've brought with me,' Cuyler giggled.

Into the pallid starlight tottered two field-mice and three of their recent offspring.

* * *

When the hubbub had subsided somewhat, Gavin, with Trisbert's assistance, called his suddenly expanded troupe to strict attention.

"You are survivors of Earthwood?" he said to the male mouse.

"We are. I am Bucktooth and this is my mate, Petite. Pardon me for weeping, but two of our dear ones are already dead, and these wee souls are horribly maimed."

With that he burst fully into tears and was soon joined by the mother of his babies.

While Bucktooth and Petite were as emaciated and bedraggled as the creatures surrounding them, the newly-born mice, whom they had been half-carrying and half-dragging for most of the night, were obviously near death. Their tiny eyes had opened upon the world but, finding little to delight or inspire, had closed again. Along their furless flanks were ribbons of blood where the ground or brush had struck without mercy. That they had just made the predicament of their fellow creatures infinitely more complicated did not seem to concern them.

But it concerned others in the troupe.

"What on earth will we do now?" Hubert said, wanting to be stern with the thoughtlessness of these hapless rodents but unable to stop himself from staring at the little ones and thinking of other progeny who were present if not yet visible.

"I hate to be uncharitable," Quiver said, "but I don't see how we can invite every ragtag survivor of the Earthwood apostrophe to become a member of our coven."

"How many crippled and wounded can we be expected to carry?" Adderly said.

"I can carry my sister," Cuspid offered.

"It won't matter a fig one way or another," Wylee said. "We're too starved to walk another league. And with all this falderal and dithering, we've already lost half-a-night's travel. Perhaps the time has come – "

"Shut up, everybody! Gavin wants to speak." Trisbert barked.

Gavin certainly would have spoken before Trisbert's intervention if he had had any notion of what to say. The desperateness of their situation had been vividly outlined by the others. Gavin was suddenly assailed by doubts. Should they not have travelled by night and day? And paused only for brief rests? (No-one had slept much anyway, and the interminable days of waiting and worry had perhaps done more to demoralize than revive.) So, precious leagues had been lost, leaving the Forest of Everdark still impossibly distant. His proposal to act collectively and in defiance of Gollah's natural law seemed brilliant when they had been seven healthy animals. But now? Now they were a crippled fox, jealous of authority; two cottontails, one of them wounded and one of them about to give birth to a dozen hairless blobs; a legless beaver; and a pair of grieving mice who would be winded before Jocko had taken six hops. Yet they were all woods-creatures. Did he have the right to pick and choose who among his fellows should have the opportunity to survive, slim though it was?

"They're waitin', Gav," Trisbert whispered anxiously.

Gavin spoke into the near-darkness: "I submit to you that we do nothing for the next little while – "

Murmurs of astonishment and discontent.

" – for two compelling reasons. First we all need to rest, tend our hurts, and gather spiritual strength for the last and most dangerous leg of our journey. Since we must find food and water, we have no choice but to travel in the daylight."

"Some of us could have told you that in the first place," Wylee said.

"Secondly," continued Gavin, "I require some time to study The Book." Here he brazenly stroked the leather that concealed the bogus text. "We will need a plan of action that meets with Gollah's approval and that is consistent with the wise, and some say magical, sayings herein."

Reference to Gollah and the possibility of some supernatural intervention was precisely what many of his listeners wished to hear. Sometime in the last little while most of them had given up all hope in their own ability to save themselves.

"In the meantime," Gavin heard himself say, "we will listen to the stories our guests have to tell us – about their survival and what they can remember of the catastrophe in Earthwood."

"What!" Wylee cried, turning boldly to the others. "Are you suggesting that we sit passively here and listen to some half-baked tales of narrow escape, when our lives depend upon what we do in the next few moments?"

"Wylee has a point," Hubert said reluctantly.

Gavin undid one of the straps on the leather-pouch. He suddenly recalled one of Papa's sayings – whether it had come from The Book of Coon-Craft or the shrivelled pages of the Tallwalker's Tales of Arthro he did not know. "Gollah tells us," he intoned, "that stories are a kind of sustenance, as necessary to us as flesh or fodder. We may well starve to death before another night is come; we may find ourselves eaten by fiends on two feet: these matters are in Gollah's hands. But we will not die starved of the stories we are destined to tell."

No word was offered in dissent.

"Who would like to begin?"

Chapter 8

More Sad Tales

"HERE IS OUR TALE," CUSPID SAID. "We were all busy in Beaver Pond – Mama, Papa, my brothers, Paddle-Whee and I – repairing breaches in our dam while the rains poured down upon us and the pond-waters rose alarmingly inside our family lodge. Suddenly, the tree whose branches we had just been gnawing off seemed to leap upwards in a hurricano of wind and rain, and began tossing themselves every which way. We thought that Gollah Himself must be going mad with rage. Elms and birches and mighty pines began to bounce and roll and seethe around us. Then the dam exploded in our faces and a wall of water swept us away before we could cry havoc or find a word for goodbye. The last we saw of dear Mama and Papa, they were twisting and gasping in a tangle of trunks and broken branches."

Cuspid glanced at Paddle-Whee, who smiled wanly and urged him to continue.

"By fate or chance, my sister and I found ourselves clinging to the same shattered cedar. Terrified, certain that we would be drowned or battered to death, we sank our powerful teeth into the bark of the tree, and held on. Somehow, despite many close calls, we managed to avoid the flailing trunks and thrashing whirlpools, and were amazed not only to be alive, while others of every tribe and clan were perishing around us, but to realize that the floodwaters were rising rapidly and stupendously. We could see, when we dared to open our eyes, the steep sides of Serpentine Ridge and the riptide roiling up towards its high, rocky spine. And just ahead of it, a jumble of terrified creatures in helter-skelter flight. I looked at Paddle-Whee and saw in her sharp glance that we were to stay where we were: in a flood the beaver is safer afloat than ashore, whatever the weather. A few others, we noticed from time to time, had made a similar decision."

"Did you see any racoons?" Cuyler said.

Cuspid looked to Paddle-Whee. She nodded. "Yes, we did," he said.

"RA-Mosah? Any of the members of the High Ring?" Trisbert said.

"Yes. We saw, clinging to the wreckage of a pine that perhaps had once been a majestic ring-tree, Grayfur and his mate, Sleekcoat."

"No-one else?"

"They were cradling a youngster between them. Tee-Jenn, I think she was called."

Gavin had been half-turned in the dark so as to be listening to the tales he had slyly ordered up, while at the same time making a great show of "reading" one of the "sacred" texts he had eased partway out of its satchel. But hearing the name Tee-Jenn jolted him upright and fully around to face the storytellers. Grayfur was a respected elder in the Ring, and his only child was an elder-daughter who attended study sessions with the dozen or so elder-children under the tutelage of RA-to-be Uthra or the great RA-Mosah. And although Gavin himself was still a full annual of seasons away from choosing a mate (or being chosen one), his heart had skipped a beat or two on more than one occasion at the sound of her voice or the dart of one of her frequent, sidelong glances. How many others, he now wondered, had clung to root-and-branch rather than risk the doomed climb to the ridge-crest where all who sought its safety had been washed away like flotsam? Was it still possible, against all odds, that Papa lived? Hope was a hard opponent to wrestle down.

"And so," Cuspid was saying (or whistling through the impressive impediment of his incisors), "we rose with the tidal wave itself to the very top of the Ridge, and watched in horror as thousands of our companion creatures in their sundry clans were swallowed up and silenced forever."

"The wave must have rolled on down the eastern side, then," Gavin said, "and into the Forest of Everdark."

"That would seem to be elemental," Quiver said. "Where else could it go?"

Cuspid squinted thoughtfully. Paddle-Whee shrugged.

"What goes up customarily comes down," Wylee offered.

"That's just it," Paddle-Whee said, "we don't know whether we did or didn't."

"That's right," Cuspid said. "We bobbed under for a few moments, as we had several times before that, but I don't remember surfacing again. Nor does my sister. It was as if we were drifting into a dream or, according to beaver-lore, slipping out of breath into the painless oblivion of the drowned."

"When we woke up two days ago," Paddle-Whee said, "we were still clinging to the cedar. But we felt as if we'd been asleep for a long time and, of course, did not know where we were, or how far we'd come, or how."

"All of our cold-season fat was gone, and our extra fur. We set out immediately in quest of a pond or stream or anything edible. As you know, we found nothing but brackish pools of dead water. On the second day Paddle-Whee spotted what might have been a living pond and dashed on ahead (she's the quickest and strongest of our clan). When I heard her scream, my heart froze: it was a death-cry. When I reached her, I discovered she had been savagely attacked by one of those iron paws the Tallwalkers use to capture us."

The assembly shuddered as one. Wylee fingered his splinted leg.

"Her left forepaw was clamped cruel and secure. These teeth that have felled the hardest maple could not pull those iron claws apart. The pain was unendurable, and Paddle-Whee had fainted. When she awoke, still pinioned, she begged me to put an end to her agony."

Renée began to weep.

"I do not find this story to be edifying," Hubert said to Gavin.

"You do not need to exaggerate how you freed her," Quiver said.

But the evidence was there before them: in the bloody, gnawed stump of the storyteller's sister. Which one of them had done the gnawing, they did not care to know.

"The Tallwalker came at sun-up to check his killing contraption. We fled as best we could. He tracked us until it grew dark. And even though my sister could barely hobble on three paws, for some strange reason he was never able to gain a pace on us. The rest of the story you already know."

While Gavin was as shocked and saddened as the others at these depictions, his mind raced ahead to several related thoughts. If a number of animals had clung to trees or had hidden out in hollow logs and, like the beavers, floated over the Ridge and somehow, much later, awoke here somewhere east of Everdark, then perhaps there were many others of their kind to be found not far away – searching, as they were, for food and fellow survivors. Moreover, since it appeared that part of the Forest itself had survived inundation (those were green trees they had been travelling towards these past two days and nights), was it not possible that some of those life-preserving rafts had settled on or near Everdark? Would they find not only food and danger there but also a host of revived woods-creatures? This latter notion, however, left Gavin feeling suddenly empty and heartsick. They were so close to reaching Everdark, yet, exhausted and starving, were impossibly far. At dawn they would have no choice but to draw upon their last reserves and trek though the searing heat over exposed ground without defences of any kind. He had no other plan because there was none to be had.

Jocko, who had recuperated amazingly, was already well into his tale: "And, my goodness Gollah, but I did begin to think there might be a tad too much rain, even for Rootburst. But I was still a young and eligible bachelor, and able to roam the beaver meadows and grassy fringes of Earthwood at will to fetch myself a juicy dinner, while less endowed creatures were wasting their breath to curse the weather. We hares (a name we prefer to jackrabbit) travel free and independent. We don't feel the need for the cloying company of other furred bodies (as does a cousin species whom I shall not name out of common courtesy). So it is we are not given to gossip or idle speculation, and that is why I found myself bounding merrily along through puddle and rivulet towards a favourite field where a young doe called Sprightleg was waiting for me to proclaim her my betrothed. My goodness Gollah, but I never reached that field or my inamorata."

Jocko paused here to catch his breath or let the pathos of the scene take hold of his audience. Someone eventually sniffled, and Jocko took that as a cue to say, "Oh, please do not despair. We hares are inveterately cheerful. It comes from travelling alone so much: when we do on occasion decide to be sociable, we are eager to dwell only upon the happy circumstances Gollah has provided. The rest cannot be helped, eh?"

"Nothing can be helped," Adderly said in what he took to be a cheerful tone.

"Your conjugational efforts were thwarted, then?" Quiver prompted.

"Oh, goodness Gollah, yes. I wasn't ten hare-bounds from our trysting place when the sky fell in. And as everyone knows, hares of every hue take no delight in swimming. But there I was, swept away from my beloved on the crest of a wave in the middle of a river that had been, moments before, a perfectly well-tramped ravine. By the time my feet next hit solid ground, I found they were buffeting me up a very steep slope that could only have been the treacherous approach to Serpentine Ridge."

"This is getting to be a familiar story," Wylee complained. "And a dull one. Do get on with it. I'd sooner starve than be bored to death."

"Now that's not a very cheerful thing to say," Jocko said.

"It wasn't meant to be."

While Jocko took no permanent offence, he did speed up his delivery, and the animals quickly learned that he had been saved from certain drowning, when the flood-tide crested on the Ridge, by a large log that bobbed up under him, knocked him sideways and then, as it were, cradled him in one of its hollowed-out crannies. All ears, including the fox's, pricked up when he began to tell about his waking up, like the others, but, unlike the others, noting that there was only an uprooted hawthorn tree between him and a Tallwalker!

"Gracious Gollah, friends, don't be alarmed. He was asleep on the ground. I could hear him snoring, raucous as a moose. And being very hungry, as you can imagine, and observing not a shred of grass or leaf anywhere, I loped soundlessly (as only we hares can) over to where he lay on his face amongst a pile of Tallwalker rubble and – "

"Oh, I hope you didn't touch him," Quiver cried. "He could've been contiguous!"

"Not likely. The stench was unbearable. But I knew from tales my pappy told me that the Tallwalkers he observed along the blackpath at the edge of Earthwood usually carried food in the softsacks on their back."

Gavin gave up all pretence of consulting the "word of Gollah" and turned to give his undivided attention to Jocko's story. The mice, Bucktooth and Petite, who had been too preoccupied with the fate of their battered offspring to listen to the stories so far, suddenly paused and peered up, with their keen night-vision, at the still-smiling jackrabbit.

"I couldn't see his face as it was covered with hair. Only his hands showed out of their coverings, and they seemed horribly misshapen. I am certain now that the Tallwalkers are the spawn of Zeebub, his ogre-sons. The firestick lay nearby, but I took little notice as I boldly opened the softsack – "

"You wouldn't congest Tallwalker vitals!" Quiver said.

"The sack held part of a mouldy carrot and a sliver of blackened turnip. That's all."

Gavin was listening closely, but made no comment.

"I was preparing to ingest this pathetic fare when the monster groaned and swung his hairy head around. I didn't stay to look him in the eye. I bounded away in the time-honoured manner of hares, putting several clumps of tree between me and the firestick that started popping behind me. The humanoid pursued me until the sun vanished, unaware of course that I was toying with him to keep myself cheerful and forgetful of my hunger for a while. When it got dark, I rested a bit, but I was rudely awakened by two hairy lumps thudding into my slumber (pardon my candour, I didn't know at the time that those lumps were Cuspid and Paddle-Whee). The firestick was popping away again. I could see its flames snap in the darkness. My goodness Gollah, the rest was panic and flight till we tumbled together into your midst."

"You left out the part where one of your boundings landed on a family of mice, also in panic and flight." Bucktooth stood on his hind-legs in order to be better seen and heard.

"Surely we don't have to listen to a mouse's tale," Wylee moaned. "Gollah put them in Earthwood for one purpose only, and it wasn't to entertain carnivores with tiny, inconsequential sagas."

Desperate now to put off the inevitable, Gavin said, "Kindly tell us your story, Bucktooth."

Wylee stared for a long moment at Gavin's leather-pouch, then peered up at him in puzzlement. Gavin looked away.

Bucktooth narrated his tale in a wee squeak of a voice, but it was nonetheless harrowing, and touched several of the listeners deeply. He and his mate, who had been pregnant, lived along the fringe of the blackpath. For shelter they sometimes crouched under an overturned wooden bowl long abandoned by some careless Tallwalker. It was especially useful whenever they felt the shudder of a hawk's shadow upon them. Old Minervah the owl lived in a horse-chestnut nearby, Bucktooth told them, but she was too blind to spot a quick-witted mouse. They saw her flapping up into the storm just after the flood struck. They themselves flipped the bowl over and, Gollah be praised, it did not capsize when they tumbled in.

Like the others, they had bobbed about until they too floated up (and over?) Serpentine Ridge, and woke sometime later on dry land. However, and mysteriously, they were now seven (Petite did not recall giving birth) – seven mice in a feeding-bowl. Expecting to be preyed upon instantly, they began burrowing into the muck, where for a day or so Petite was able to nurse her five sucklings, until her milk dried up. Bucktooth was preparing to go foraging for food when their underground refuge was suddenly assaulted by a vicious gouging-stick of some kind. Within seconds the whole brood was exposed, as was the fiendish creature wielding the stick. They had thought, until hearing the stories of Cuspid and Jocko, that their predator was a Ghostie or Warlow exiled from Everdark, but knew now that it must have been the Tallwalker. Two of the youngsters were killed by blows from the iron stick and, as the ogrish two-leg squatted down to grasp them and stuff them bloody between his troll-teeth, the others managed to flee. And if it had not been for the sun going down at that moment, all would have been likewise devoured. After that, they had simply huddled together in a clump of brush – petrified and not distinguishing night from day – until the wayward bound of a jackrabbit jarred them conscious and put them in flight once again.

"Thank Gollah that three of your dear ones survived with you," Hubert said when Bucktooth had finished. He glanced at the hairless blobs tucked under their mother's belly.

"Enough of this foolishness now," Wylee said. "We've all been incredibly patient. But the sun is starting to rise behind us. We have chosen a leader. We have given him more than enough time to commune with Gollah through His sacred scripture. Either he has for us a plan for concerted action or the time has come for each breed to go its natural way."

Hubert's eyes widened. "Tell us what to do, Gavin. Please."

Trisbert leaned close to Gavin and whispered, "You got to tell them something, Gav."

For the first time in his young life Gavin realized why woods-creatures needed the leadership and savvy of a RA; why those pretending to the position needed to be steeped in the history, wisdom and cumulative lore of animal experience; and why the elders of the High-Ring schooled and groomed more than one candidate so that they could choose only the one destined to succeed. His own education, alas, had barely begun. He had learned to decipher the code in which The Book of Coon-Craft was written, but had thus far read only judiciously selected tidbits. And Papa had let him sit beside him as he decoded the forbidden runes of the Tallwalker book. Now as he stared out at the animals huddled about him in an expectant circle, his head was suddenly agog with sayings, proverbs, beatitudes, commandments – pungent, ominous with meaning, but all jumbled together in a hopeless gobbledygook.

But soon a voice not quite his own rose up from somewhere deep within and formed words of its own choosing: "In The Book Gollah says, 'When the spirit fails, look death in the eye.'"

Struck by the eerie, prophetic tenor of Gavin's almost-voice, his followers were too awed to respond.

Hubert was the first to speak. "If it must be so, then it must be so," he said sombrely, and put a steadying arm around Renée.

"You had given us reason to hope," Quiver said. "And I'm ashamed to admire that I did so."

"Hold on here!" Wylee cried, almost tipping himself over in the effort to be heard. "Are you saying that Gollah expects us to lie down here in this, this hellhole, and let death take us where it will?"

"Well, I for one don't have strength enough left to tell another story," Jocko sighed.

"Nor I to listen to it," Adderly said.

Trisbert said, "Is that it, then, Gav?"

"We can't go down without a fight," Cuyler said.

But every creature present — whether raccoon, hare, beaver, snake, rabbit, fox or mouse — knew in its bones that the will to survive is surpassed only by the sense of resignation that sets in when survival is no longer an option and bequeaths, to the last moments of being, dignity and quiet acceptance. They would each find a suitable spot, and await the inevitable.

"But our spirit hasn't failed," Wylee said into the general gloom. "We don't need more spunk; we need food — flesh."

Gavin, whose eyes had closed and remained so following his delivery of Gollah's proclamation, suddenly said, "Looking death in the eye does not necessarily mean that we accept what he has to offer. Our spirit has not failed, as Wylee has reminded us, and until it does, we shall keep on walking towards Everdark — until we reach it or until we drop in our tracks!"

"We'll march out smartly as soon as the sun comes up!" Trisbert enthused before the tiny stir of hope in the animals could wane. The first streaks of light were already flickering behind them in the east.

But before Trisbert and Cuyler could begin organizing the motley crew, they were interrupted by a piercing cry.

Bucktooth was standing over the lifeless bodies of his newborn, who had, it seemed, looked death in the eye, and succumbed. It was Petite who had cried out for her lost babies.

Gavin was not in the least surprised when Wylee grinned triumphantly and spoke over the consoling murmurs of the other animals: "Well, now, it would appear that Gollah has provided us with both courage and sustenance."

Petite squeezed out a mouse-shriek and fainted.

"Now see here, you three-legged coyote," Hubert said, alarmed and appalled. "We've agreed to suspend Gollah's laws till we reach Earthwood. There will be no consumption of herbivore flesh while I – "

"In The Book Gollah says, 'A creature in need must be served by his fellows.'" Gavin tried to stop the dangerous flow of words but out they came, oracular and disturbing. What in the name of Earthwood was happening to him? His bones were humming like cicadas in Seedpod.

"Exactly!" Wylee said gleefully, and could not refrain from drooling. "I see you may be a wise young coon after all."

"Do something!" Hubert shrieked. "The monster will eat us all!" And to Wylee he said, "I carried you on my injured shoulder. If it weren't for me, you wouldn't have got this far."

"Well, if it's Gollah's will," Bucktooth said, trembling all over, "then we must accept it." Petite threw him a baleful look that suggested she was not to be swayed by Gollah's words out of the mouths of raccoons.

"But we made a pact, a solemn covenant," Hubert persisted, "didn't we, Quiver?"

"That is so," Quiver said. "But it seems to me this quarry is really one for the carnivores in our midst to settle."

"That's all right for you to say," Hubert snapped. "Who'd want to eat you!"

Meanwhile Trisbert had manoeuvred his bulk between the grieving mice and the rapacious fox: "We do nothing till our leader says so."

Again all eyes, except for those of the objects in question, swung around to Gavin.

"Your children are dead," he said to Bucktooth and Petite. "Murdered by the same Tallwalker stalking us. It would be a sin against Dame Nature to leave their little bodies here to rot in the sun. There are no buzzards even to pick the bones pure. I shall leave it up to each of the meat-eaters among us to decide for himself." He turned to Trisbert.

"No," Trisbert said. "What good would a bit of suckling mouse do to bring me closer to Everdark?"

Cuyler said, "I'm with my brother."

Adderly, who saw little in the dark and was not entirely certain what was actually happening, said, "A morsel of infantile mouse would likely make me feel hungrier, if such is possible."

There was no need to ask Wylee. He was already attempting to hobble over to the dead mice.

"Look, the sun is up!" the beaver twins shouted in unison.

"Wylee, stay where you are," Gavin said. "The rest of you will follow me to the edge of this brush-pile and, after Cuyler and I have made a brief survey of our position, we shall all walk together towards Everdark, the strong assisting the weak for as long as they can. We shall put our lives in the hands of Gollah Himself. We shall have no watch, no rearguard, no camouflaging manoeuvres. Every last ounce of our physical strength shall be employed in our walking."

"But you can't just leave me!" Wylee said, defiant and terrified. "We have an agreement!"

"Nor shall we. We'll leave you to enjoy your grisly feast, and when you've done, you can catch us up as best you can. If you do, you will then receive the same assistance as the others in need." With this decree, Gavin whirled and marched off through the tumbled underbrush. Behind him Trisbert and Cuyler marshalled the troupe.

Gavin could feel the first twinge of sunlight on the nape of his neck as he made his way towards the western border of their hiding-place. He paused for a moment to let Trisbert come up beside him.

"We've got them ready to go," Trisbert said. "Cuyler's carrying the mice." He was trying to catch his brother's eye, but Gavin was staring blankly ahead, as if dreading the last few steps that would compel him to see just how hopelessly distant Everdark lay.

Trisbert said quietly, "How long do you think we can last?"

"I've got a quarter-morning in me at best. The others less than that, I should think."

"I'll carry you, if I can."

"You carry Cuyler," Gavin said, and looked directly at his littermate.

Trisbert said, "I might not have another chance to tell you, Gav, but you've been a true elder-son. For a little while last annual I was jealous of you, seeing the special way Papa trusted you and all, an' me being born not an eyeblink after you. It didn't seem fair. It didn't seem right. But it does now. You would've been our RA-to-be,

I'm sure, and I would've been proud to stand beside you. As I am now."

Moved to tears, Gavin wished to point out that his leadership had brought them all to the brink of extinction, but managed only to mumble an inadequate, "Thank you, brother."

Trisbert brightened a bit and said, "Maybe there'll be a miracle."

Muted whisperings just behind them indicated that the troupe was eager to look death in the eye, whatever Gollah might have meant by that ambiguous commandment.

"I suddenly have the strangest feeling that we're here entirely on our own," Gavin said, not wanting to believe it.

"But you've got The Book – "

Gavin felt like tossing the leather-pouch and its impious contents into the bramble. After all, it weighed as much as Cuyler and had produced nothing miraculous. And for all he knew, the Tallwalker book inside might be anathema to Gollah, might have inflamed His righteous wrath whose sting they were suffering at this very moment. He made no move to jettison it, however. Perhaps I'm like Papa, he thought, who had kept it secret and profane against all reason.

"It's time to go, Gav."

Gavin could delay no longer. He crawled to the edge of the brush and peered out at the sunlit waste-ground that lay between them and the Forest, the strip of parched earth upon which, one by one, they would drop and perish. The terrain to the west, he could see, rose slowly in a series of undulations, unlike the unrelieved flatness they had endured the past two days and three nights. But the rising land was not steep enough to block out his view of the Forest of Everdark – with its living trees.

His sudden gasp was enough to bring an alarmed Trisbert to his side.

Trisbert, too, began to stare straight ahead. In a hushed breath, he said, "It's a miracle."

And it was, sort of. Travelling in the dark, as they had done again last night, they had had little notion of how far they had fared and no way of knowing how much closer their laboured march had brought them to their destination. Now in the sheer light of morning, they knew.

Above the horizon, as plain as the mask on a raccoon's face, lay the grim forest of their hopes, so near to them that they could make out the upper halves of pine, spruce and fir; the glistening silver trunks of beaver-birch; and the deciduous green of maple leaves prospering in a Meadowbloom breeze. A mouse could trot there in a morning.

"Gollah be praised!" someone from the excited troupe shouted.

"Gavin be praised!" Trisbert and Cuyler replied smartly.

Chapter 9

A Grisly Discovery

TRISBERT AND CUYLER LED THE WAY, while Gavin
·encouraged and shepherded his ragtaggle troupe from
either flank and occasionally from the rear. If there was a
visceral fear of what horrors might lie ahead in the
Forest of Everdark – whose flourishing treetops could be
seen drawing closer with each hunger-driven step they
took – the woods-creatures gave no outward sign.
Stoicism was as much a part of their nature as the
instinct to survive. That it could easily turn into
resignation and a passive acceptance of the inevitable was
Gavin's chief concern at the moment.

"A quarter-morning's walk! An after-breakfast stroll!"
he cried cheerily to Cuspid and the hobbling Paddle-Whee
at his side, and Paddle-Whee gave him a wincing smile for
his efforts.

"Fresh water and thick, juicy celery-root just ahead!" he
called out to Hubert and Renée whenever they stumbled
and looked as if they might decide not to get up.

It soon became apparent that Bucktooth and Petite,
who were not only short of leg but near starvation as
well, would have to be carried the entire way. Cuyler,
scouting in the lead, skipped and hopped too precipi-

tously (in his coonish enthusiasm) to provide a reliable ride. Quiver offered his sturdy back, but was politely turned down. Cuspid also volunteered and was accepted, but whenever he leapt suddenly sideways to steady one of Paddle-Whee's frequent lurches (walking three-footed was no easy feat, it seemed), the mice tumbled into the half-dried mud below and begged to be left there. Hubert was far too concerned for Renée, who was trying unsuccessfully to conceal the pain clenching her abdomen. Jocko, though weakened by hunger, still had too much bounce to his hop-walking to be of service. Trisbert, though robust enough to carry a pair of mice and much more, was dangerously exposed next to Cuyler – should the Tallwalker or other as-yet-unencountered enemies surprise or ambush. Gavin himself, despite his need to be on constant watch, would gladly have settled a mouse on each shoulder, but the swaying of the leather-pouch strapped there offered too perilous a perch for the famished rodents. And worthless and profane as the contents of the pouch might prove to be, they could not be discarded, because so much of the optimism that now propelled the animals beyond the limits of their endurance lay in their naïve belief in the magic of the tome they assumed Gavin to be carrying and in the wizardry he would use to interpret its mystical incantations.

"Well, I do not need you to spell it out," Adderly sighed. "We reptiles may be sluggish of movement, but our thoughts move faster than that dopey jackrabbit can run with a belly full of clover."

"Would you mind taking them, then?" Gavin said cautiously.

Bucktooth and Petite recoiled in horror, unable to emit any protest but for several pathetic squeaks. For a moment Gavin thought they might die of fright.

"We have – all of us – agreed to suspend the laws of Dame Nature until we reach Earthwood and the world is set right again," Gavin explained to the mice. "And so far, among us, you and the cottontails are the only mated pairs." He had no need to elaborate on the significance of this remark. Mice and rabbits aplenty would be required if and when they ever found the home-forest.

Adderly essayed a smile, but as it exposed his fangs somewhat and the elastic yawn of his jaws, the effect on the mice was not all it should have been. "Hop on near my tail," he said in what he took to be a casual manner, "if that makes you feel a little safer. And I'll slither along as smoothly as I can."

Before any further squeakings could delay the event, Gavin gently lifted Bucktooth and Petite onto the fox-snake's ample, sun-warmed back. Instinctively the mice dug their pointed claws into the leathery skin there, found the ride as smooth as promised, and soon settled down into their own fur and the tiny tremblings under it.

Quiver put a paw on Gavin's shoulder. A small tear squeezed itself out of his left eye. "Your efforts on our behalf have been truly magnifying," he said. "Someday your grandchildren will pursue your own chapter in The Book."

Before Gavin could deflect the compliment, however, a blood-curdling cry of pain and desperation brought the members of the little caravan to a sudden halt. As one, they turned to stare behind them at the source of the piteous sound. Wylee the fox lay spraddled on the ground where he had just fallen – too weak, it appeared, to move his maimed limb or any other mobile part. His pointed snout rose above his flaccid pink tongue and razor-edged teeth, but no further cry of woe or despair emerged.

"Let him be," Quiver suggested, and murmurs of assent echoed behind him.

Trisbert came back to stand beside Gavin. "Well, he did break the code," he said coldly.

"Cannibal!" Bucktooth hissed from the snake's back.

Gavin walked slowly back towards Wylee.

"It's my leg," he whispered up at Gavin. "The splint came off. I can't take a step."

"We're all in this together," Gavin said gravely. "But when you broke the rules, you chose to go your own way. May Gollah be merciful." He turned back towards his comrades, who were eyeing him narrowly.

"I didn't eat the mice!" Wylee wailed, and when Gavin looked back, he added, "I swear!"

"That's not the point," Gavin said. "You could have come with us, but chose not to."

"May Gollah strike me dead on this spot if I am not telling you the truth. I buried the wretched creatures so the Tallwalker won't find them. Come and I'll show you!"

Several of the animals glanced skyward as if expecting Gollah's immediate answer from that quarter. But only the sun glared down from its early-morning eyrie, hot and indifferent.

"Who will volunteer to assist the fox, then?" Gavin said. "He cannot walk on his own."

"Let him slither," Hubert said on behalf of those among them whose flesh was fuel to so many of

Earthwood's mammals. "We're leaving a clear path for him to follow."

"And Everdark must lie just beyond the next rise," Jocko added with hopeful illogic.

Gavin turned to Trisbert, who shrugged grimly.

"He can lean on me, then," Gavin said.

"May Gollah bless you," Wylee sobbed as he clutched at the fur along Gavin's shoulder and, using one of the straps of the leather-pouch, hauled himself halfway to his feet.

Trisbert said sharply: "Gollah has nothing to do with it."

* * *

The sun definitely seemed more scorching this morning; the air was arid and enervating. The few puddles and anaemic ponds the animals encountered began to evaporate in the heat, some of them uttering little geysers of steam. The lifeless soil they trudged upon was hot to the touch, alternating between turgid gumbo and eddies of powdered dirt. The wreckage of tree and bush was everywhere, as it had been from the outset of their journey eight days ago, but now there was less of it, and the ground to the west of them began to undulate more regularly. As they plodded silently and diligently to the crest of each rise, the treetops along the next horizon-line began to take on recognizable shapes: spruce, fir, pine – unless of course all was mirage or hunger-born hallucination. Every once in a while Wylee whimpered, but no-one took any interest in his self-proclaimed suffering. (Gavin had reattached the splint, but it seemed only to occasion further complaint.)

As they were nearing what surely would prove to be the last hump of land between them and their goal, Trisbert stopped so abruptly that the creature immediately behind him bumped against his hind-quarter.

"Pardon my obtrusion," Quiver said, but, exhausted, sat where he had tottered after the brief collision.

Trisbert took no notice of the quill-marks on his flank. He and Cuyler were bent over examining something on the ground between them.

"It's a footprint," Cuyler informed the others.

Setting Wylee down carefully, Gavin trundled past the others, who were not uninterested but far too weary to become alarmed. "Tallwalker?" he asked.

"It's not one of their hoofprints," Trisbert said. "It's huge, though, with five toes . . ."

"Could be a monster," Cuyler said with mounting excitement, "from Everdark."

The footprint was solitary, most likely because the drying earth around it had been roughened and scattered by some thing in a hurry or in flight.

"I don't know of any one-footed ogres," Gavin said. "There have to other tracks."

While the animals stood stupefied in their own tracks and Wylee moaned softly to himself, the raccoons fanned out over the rumpled ground until Cuyler's cry brought all three of them together a few yards to the north of their column.

"Two-footed," Trisbert said, sniffing the spoor.

"Our Tallwalker without his boots," Gavin said.

"And these blotches here are blood," Trisbert said.

"His own," Gavin said.

Hubert had managed to drag himself over to the scene. "Is this the end, then?" he said tonelessly.

Gavin considered the question. Fatigue and the gnawing hunger inside him made it hard for him to think: his thoughts were shimmering like the heat-wave in front of him. "These tracks are fresh, all right. But, see, they go off to the north towards that collection of broken trees. Tallwalker's feet are cut and bleeding. He is staggering from foot to foot, as you can tell if you follow the side-to-side splayed pattern of the prints. And they're deep in the ground, as if bearing some intolerable weight."

"He won't be back, then?" Hubert said.

"I doubt it," Gavin said.

"Shouldn't we make sure the tracks go past the trees over there?" Cuyler said. "He could be hiding in there right now, for all we know."

"And his firestick can reach us easily, even if he can't run out here after us," Trisbert cautioned.

"All right, then," Gavin decided. "The three of us will go as far as those trees – "

"But Everdark is just over this rise," Hubert said, surprised that he could still muster some feeling about the matter. "We could make a dash for it. Some of us are bound to make it."

"That is a notion well worth our confabulation," Quiver called out from his sitting position.

"I say we make a run for it," Wylee shouted from the rear of the column. Then, realizing his error, added hastily, "as long as somebody agrees to carry me!"

"So be it," Gavin said agreeably. "We will check out the Tallwalker while the rest of you keep on moving westward. Be not so foolish as to run. If you do, none of you will make it. If all is clear over there to the north, my brothers and I will follow you. If not, we will do what we can to distract the humanoid. Quiver, I'll leave you in charge."

Wylee effected his most tragic whimper, but no-one volunteered a paw or a shoulder.

Then Paddle-Whee said, "I'll help him. Between us we've got six good legs."

*

The brothers set off to the north along the ghoulish trail laid down by the Tallwalker. The story of his struggle was told in the frenzied, plodding pattern of his footsteps: bare, bleeding flesh against barren ground. Although much younger and inexperienced, Cuyler was a keener tracker than Gavin and quicker of foot and eye than the shambling Trisbert. But even he in his excitement proceeded cautiously: the lurching yaw of the Tallwalker was becoming more pronounced with every step he had taken, and the bloodstains were now alarmingly fresh.

"He can't have made it too far into that mess of trees," Gavin whispered.

They peered at the bramble and enmeshed branches piled high as any ring-tree in Earthwood, into which the footprints were undeniably luring them.

"These roundish holes at every other step have likely been made by his firestick," Cuyler said. "He's using it like a crutch."

"But if he dragged himself into the brush," Trisbert said slowly, "he could be lyin' in wait for us – with his thunderstick pointed up, not down."

"Then I'm sure we would have been shot at by now," Gavin said.

"Maybe so," Trisbert said, "but there's no sense in all three of us stickin' our chests out. You two keep behind me, and I'll start movin' towards the brush. If I get hit, you must promise to leave an' make a run for the others."

Cuyler started to object but was silenced by a look from Gavin, who crouched low behind Trisbert's valiant bulk and waved at Cuyler to do the same. Then slowly but steadily, his head held high and defiant, Trisbert led the way to the point among the brush-piles where the alien footprints disappeared. The only sound was the rasp of Trisbert's breathing. Seconds later all three of them were standing among the detritus of dead trees and staring – awe-struck – at the sandy clearing just ahead of them.

It was a Tallwalker's habitat, no doubt. Immediately in front of them stood a shelter made out of the hairless skin that humanoids used to clothe themselves, but wind or water or both had ravaged it: gaping rips in the walls and roof, tattered pennants a-droop from the stiff framework of what had to be its entranceway, and shredded remnants drifting about its perimeter as if some persistent animal had torn at it nightly. In the searing sun of mid-morning, the Tallwalker's dwelling-place looked forlorn and long abandoned.

Just beyond it, the raccoons could see a cairn of blackened stones that had once, days or seasons ago, brightened an evening with the cosiness of a fire. Several metal containers and utensils lay a-tilt and rusting in the dust nearby. (RA-Mosah had told a hushed assembly of elder-scholars about his many sightings of the Tallwalkers who, generations ago, had come by the score to the fringes of Earthwood and the shores of the Lake of Waters Unending to hunt and take fish, and had built temporary encampments in the lee of trees: humanoid beings who charred their flesh-food with flame, boiled water in iron pots and swallowed it steaming, who possessed little fur of their own to protect them against frost and sun, and tottered about clownishly upon their hind feet.) Here and there the brothers could see that deep gouges had been made in the earth as if by some burrowing animal who had temporarily forgotten how to dig. And everywhere they looked, they saw tin containers not bigger than a fox's snout torn open, and empty.

"He's been diggin' for roots," Trisbert said. He did not need to add that such activity had been as futile as it had been exhausting.

Suddenly Cuyler said, "I see the footprints again — there, just past the skin-shelter."

"Careful," Trisbert said, steadying Cuyler with one paw.

"I don't think there's any need for that," Gavin said, and he stepped boldly towards the tent-thing, glanced through the open entrance-hole, and disappeared around the far wall. Trisbert and Cuyler stayed where they were. A moment later they heard Gavin's voice, low and solemn: "I've found him."

The Tallwalker lay face-down in a patch of half-dried mud, as if he had stumbled, collapsed, and had no strength to rise again or no will to try. His hairless hands were stretched out above his head and clenched in a last gesture of anger or unhope. The firestick lay nearby where it had simply been dropped. With his head spinning with incoherent snippets of stories and images, Gavin looked long and hard at this figure of legend and animal nightmare, the demon-spawn of Zeebub. His cloth-coverings were nothing but rags and tatters where thorns had ripped and burrs stuck. The grub-greasy skin showed through everywhere, and the flesh underneath it was so sparse that the arm-bones and leg-bones stuttered out. No skin remained on the soles of the feet that stared up at Gavin like a pair of gory eye-sockets. Like any woods-creature, Gavin recognized starvation when he saw it.

But it was the strange mange-sores on the back and thighs, the pocked and puckered skin, and the rotting tufts of hair on top of the head that drew Gavin closer — despite the stink of putrefaction. The Tallwalker's flesh appeared in places to have turned liquid and boiled, the blood bubbles darkening into scab or re-erupting in blackish pustules. The pain must have been unendurable. Death, sometime before dawn, had surely been welcomed.

"Don't touch it," Trisbert warned, edging away with Cuyler at his side.

Gavin didn't answer. He was staring at the objects he had just noticed protruding from the muck close to the corpse: pages from a book of some kind splattered with words or signs. He reached down and carefully brushed away the dried mud from what must have been some volume or other — its jagged edge indicating that it had been wrenched off in rage or despair. The Gibberlish-like markings leapt out at Gavin, but they were untranslatable. Perhaps the Tallwalker had kept the book in the knapsack that dangled by a single strap from one shoulder. Other pages, loosed from their mooring, lay mud-smeared nearby.

"Gollah be praised! The Tallwalker has been given his just contribution!"

Don Gutteridge

Gavin and his brothers whirled around in time to see
Quiver enter the clearing with the rest of the refugees at
his heels. Bucktooth and Petite were dozing contentedly
on Adderly's back. Embarrassed by his sister's
selflessness, Cuspid had Paddle-Whee leaning on one
shoulder and Wylee on the other.

"What are you doin' here?" Trisbert demanded. "You
were supposed to be on your way to Everdark."

"They refused to budge without Gavin's comman-
dership," Quiver said sheepishly.

"All creatures together, if I recall our covenant
correctly," Hubert added pointedly.

"Well, there's no hurry now," Jocko said, glancing at
the corpse, "though we hares are a hurrying kind of
quadruped."

"I think we should get out of here as soon as
possible: that stink may be poisonable," Cuspid said,
letting go of Wylee, who teetered, caught himself up, and
limped forward a few paces. The slits of his fox-eyes
narrowed upon the sprawled remains of the Tallwalker.

"Why don't we eat him?" Wylee said. "After all, it's
just carrion."

The herbivores drew back in disgust.

Gavin spoke: "Cuspid may be right. Furthermore, we
don't know for certain that this Tallwalker was alone. RA-
Mosah told us time and again that they ran in packs, like
wolves." Gavin forgave himself this small, motivating lie.

"What about his softsack?" Wylee said, limping closer.
"There could be food in there. Perhaps a dried turnip or
root of some kind." And he grinned at the rabbits.

"Well, it may be worth risking a peek inside it," Hubert said. "On the off-chance. Madame is feeling quite queasy and – "

"Gavin's given his opinion," Trisbert said bluntly.

"I'll open it myself," Wylee offered, "even though there's no likelihood of it containing any flesh-food."

"Why, how monogamous of you, fox," Quiver said. "You are truly one of us after all."

Wylee grinned till his tongue hurt, then looked at Gavin, who nodded assent. In his eagerness to show off his newfound sense of collaboration, Wylee stumbled once to his knees, grimaced theatrically, then limped gingerly to the malodorous carrion. Hooking a set of fox-claws under the strap of the knapsack, Wylee pulled it slowly off the shoulder and then down along one arm until it was freed. The animals gasped as most of the arm-flesh was stripped away by the strap in its descent. The Tallwalker's arm-bones gleamed in the sterile sunlight. Wylee fumbled with the hasps for a moment before Gavin, who had been observing the fox's every twitch and twinkle, stepped over and opened the knapsack with his deft coon-fingers.

It was empty.

One of the rabbits swooned. Paddle-Whee stood over Hubert and fanned him until his eyes blinked open and Renée's smile rekindled his breathing.

"We oughta take the sack-thing with us anyways, eh, Gav?" Trisbert said. In Earthwood, natural containers and carryalls were as scarce as cocoanuts, and those few dippers and bowls long ago salvaged from interloping Tallwalkers were preserved and prized in the raccoon's domain. "You never know what we may need to carry."

Gavin picked up the knapsack. It had a creature-smell to it, but it was not the odour given off by the Tallwalker's decomposing body. "We'll take it with us."

"I'm most pleased to have been of service," Wylee grinned, and grinned again when Cuspid and Paddle-Whee reached his side and hoisted him upright.

"Let's get going, then," Gavin said. "Cuyler, lead the troupe back to our original trail. Bertie and I will finish searching this site and join you shortly. Nothing can stop us from reaching Everdark now."

With Quiver's assistance, the animals were arranged in their proper order and led off by Cuyler.

"There's nothing more to find here," Trisbert said as soon as they were alone.

"I know," Gavin said. "I just needed a few quiet moments to think."

And have a discreet peek at The Book of Coon-Craft, Trisbert smiled knowingly to himself. He turned to leave Gavin to it, and was at the edge of the clearing when his brother called out to him: "You might as well take the sack-thing with you."

Trisbert came back, took the Tallwalker's knapsack and slipped it over both shoulders. "You put something in it?" he asked.

"Just some pieces of parchment I found here. If it gets too heavy, we can toss them away."

Trisbert, who did not think to question or wonder at his elder-brother's decisions, smiled and said, "It won't be too heavy for me."

As soon as Trisbert was gone, Gavin went over to the Tallwalker. While every animal instinct and the voices of his tutors warned him of the folly of what he was about to do, some urgency more compelling than his own safety, some half-whispered and not-quite-wordless temptation drew him forward. Pinching his nostrils shut against the putrid reek of death, Gavin got both forepaws under one shoulder and heaved the cadaverous lump up and over. Ribbons of the humanoid's flesh came away in his claws, but he did not notice. He was staring down into the wide-open, demon eyes of the Tallwalker, Zeebub's henchman, the epitome of all that was forbidden and un-animal, the scourge of Earthwood and any other realms where Gollah might presume and preside.

Gavin did not see what he had braced himself to see in the dead eyes that stared back up at him – their final thought not yet utterly extinguished. Bewilderingly, he looked away: at the forlorn tent, the abandoned fire-pit, the vacant vessels, the ragged ring of protective branches, the gashed and tuberless earth, the utter loneliness of the ravaged land everywhere around. And he knew that, whatever else he might be, this particular humanoid was no demon.

Chapter 10

Treachery

THERE WAS A COLLECTIVE SIGH OF RELIEF among the animals when they spotted Gavin coming out of the Tallwalker's brambled abode and walking meditatively over the waste-ground towards them. He's been consulting the sacred Book, was the general but unspoken opinion, and a comforting one it was. Gollah had spared them for a reason, and only Gavin had the means and heart to discover it. See how the gravity of such a responsibility even now weighed heavily upon him, making the fine raccoon-brow droop and the naturally nimble raccoon-step grow laboured and ordinary!

"I was just about to send Cuyler looking for you," Trisbert said in a voice too weary to conceal the worry in it.

"I felt a bit dizzy," Gavin explained, casting an eye on the bedraggled disciples he was about to lead to food, drink and temporary salvation. "But I'm all right now." Gavin drew Trisbert a little to one side. "Do you think everybody has enough energy left to get over the next hill or two to Everdark?" he asked in a grave whisper.

"If there aren't any more than that – yes," Trisbert said. "The rabbits are not faring well. They don't have the fat we do. The beavers started out exhausted, but that Paddle-Whee is amazingly strong: if only she had all of her feet . . ."

"What about Adderly? He says so little, it's hard to tell."

"Well, snakes can go a long ways without eating, but I think it's the sun that's slowing him down. I'm afraid he might boil to death."

"It's somewhat premature to be composing my epitaph," said Adderly, who had seesawed nearby. "And if you must do so, I'd prefer something more commemorative than 'he boiled to death'."

Gavin laughed briefly just in case Adderly was attempting to be funny. He wasn't. Gavin turned back to Trisbert. "Bertie, you help Hubert and Renée. I'll look after Wylee. Put Cuspid and Paddle-Whee between us in the column where we can watch them. Jocko, Adderly and his passengers will go ahead of them. Then Quiver, and Cuyler in the lead."

"We don't know what we'll find, Gav, even on the edge of Everdark." It was as close to an objection that Trisbert could come.

"Yes, I agree. But Cuyler will be all right. Believe me when I say that we are no longer in danger from any Tallwalker. Everdark, whatever its challenges, is our only hope. If Gollah wishes it to be the place where we relinquish our lives and give our spirits up to join those of our ancestors, then we shall all meet that grim fate whether we are at the front of the column or the rear."

"I won't go down without a fight," Trisbert said.

"Gollah would be astonished if you did."

Trisbert smiled and clapped his brother on the back, jostling Papa's leather-pouch and its "sacred" contents. "If this gets too heavy," he said, indicating the Tallwalker's knapsack on his own back, "should I throw it away?"

Gavin appeared to give the question some thought. "Not unless your life depends upon it. If we find food, we may well need something to carry and store it in. And the parchment pages could be used to write on, should I ever be granted that luxury. I'm trying to look ahead – as far as I dare."

"You can depend on me."

"I don't have to look ahead to know that, Bertie."

* * *

Cuyler was happy to take the lead. Despite his diminutive size, he seemed to have an inexhaustible reserve of energy, as if he could run forever on the optimism of youthful naiveté itself. But as the morning inched towards high-sun, the heat grew brutal. The sun's searing glare seemed determined to seek out every foot-scrape, belly-bruise or muscle-ache it could find, and expose them in sadistic delight to the sufferer.

Their progress was agonizingly slow. They were a quarter-morning traversing a single rise that was no more than a wavelet in the now gently rolling, flood-sculpted terrain. Adderly oscillated in a drugged torpor, as if he were merely dreaming of locomotion. Thrice the mice dozed off, toppled to the ground, and had to be adroitly scooped up by Trisbert before Adderly's tail lolled over and crushed them. Quiver's quills, increasingly coated with dust and mud, clanked and dragged like chain-mail.

Cuspid pretended to be steadying his three-pawed sister, but more and more of his weakening weight fell against Paddle-Whee's massive torso, which would have been pleased to accommodate it if only the absent forefoot had been willing to bear its share of the burden.

Hubert and Renée rested their emaciated rabbit-length on one or the other of Trisbert's shoulders and settled unrabbitlike into the big raccoon's ponderous, swaying rhythm. Just ahead, Jocko kept wandering to the north or south for several paces, as if asserting his species' need for independent action, but appeared to remember in the nick of time where he was and what he was about – and wobbled back into line.

At every fourth or fifth step Gavin had to temporarily abandon the disabled fox in order to reach ahead and prevent Paddle-Whee and her burden from pitching sideways, then reach back and catch Wylee before he struck the ground. No-one looked up or peered ahead: that would take too much energy, and the sudden leap of hope or the inevitable sag of disappointment were emotions too enervating to be risked. But Wylee, more or less being carried by Gavin, was in the mood for conversation.

"It is said among the elders of the Great Fox-Den that RA-Mosah himself liberated that leather-pouch you're wearing from the body of a Tallwalker asleep upon the sands at the edge of the Lake of Waters Unending."

Wylee decided to take Gavin's silence, or inability to speak, as assent. "You yourself come from noble stock, then. I am not surprised that, young and callow though you be, you survived the deluge, and have brought us this close to prolonging our day of doom."

Taking this as a compliment, Gavin managed a polite nod.

"And it was rumoured among the more credulous woods-creatures that you might have become RA after your papa. I must say that I now find such an assumption most credible."

Gavin let go of Wylee while he grasped and righted Paddle-Whee, but caught him neatly before he canted over and ungraciously met the ground.

"Thank you," Wylee said. "You raccoons would be amazed to learn that we foxes share some of your Gollah-given traits. I have been told by my great-grandfather that many, many annuals ago, according to legend, there was a clan of reynards who were granted their own alphabet by the mighty Gollah because their prudent ways and rich wisdom had become too vast to be contained in the head or in the communal memory. But, alas, their forepaws could not manipulate the quill-scratcher, and so – this is what our legends tell us – a family of upstart raccoons was engaged to act as scribes, and then – O perfidious day! – the masked rascals – "

Wylee's climactic comment was squelched by a sudden cough or burp, one that caused the fox's eyes to water as he sought strenuously to suppress it. When he could speak again, it was not to finish his tale of ringtail perfidy but to cry out instead: "I smell trees and water!"

Gavin signalled him to be quiet, but Wylee could not contain his excitement. "There are trees, living trees, and sweet, tumbling water, I swear! Just ahead! Over the next rise!"

A tremor of anticipation rippled through the members of the column. Cuyler stopped, and the caravan drew to a ragged halt behind him. He too sniffed the air to the west, its tantalizing scents drifting suddenly towards them on a freshening breeze.

"I think Wylee's right," Cuyler said. "Everdark must be over the next little hill."

Quiver dropped to his fore-knees as if he were about to kiss the dust before him. "Oh, Gavin, you have delivered us from certain death! You have led us safely to the portals of salivation!"

Too exhausted to echo these formal halleluiahs, the others murmured as best they could the two-syllabled name of their hero and friend.

Gavin was too overwhelmed to respond. Instead he collapsed softly into his own fur and let his muzzle rest gratefully in the dust. His eyes in their bold mask glazed over and closed.

Trisbert and Cuyler were quickly at his side. Cuyler pulled off the encumbering pouch while Trisbert nudged his brother over onto his side and began to lick the fur around his face as tenderly as he would wash his food in an icy stream.

"Is he dead?" Wylee said, who, with his crutch gone, was now seated unceremoniously in a mud-patch.

Gavin replied by opening one eye. "Not quite," he rasped.

"By Gollah, but you gave us a scare," Trisbert said.

"One sip of that creek-water I can now smell and I'll be fine."

"You been carryin' too big a load," Trisbert said with an acid glance at the fox.

"We all have," Gavin said, raising his head weakly.

Trisbert looked at the others, who had dragged themselves into a circle around their stricken leader. "We'll rest for a bit, until Gavin's well enough to walk."

No-one demurred.

"Indeed," Quiver added, more to fill the deep and awful silence that now descended upon the apostles of Gavin the elder-son, "our saviour requires time to rejuvenile." And, he might have appended, recover sufficiently to help them face the fresh perils of Everdark.

And so they sat, on haunch or belly, and tried to think only upon food and water and the not-unpleasant notion that in the very least they would not starve to death. Several fell sound asleep, and dreamt of fruit or flesh.

"Do you want me to go up to the top of the rise and have a peep at Everdark?" Cuyler said to Trisbert and secondarily to Gavin who still had not recovered enough to stand on all four feet.

"Save your energy, Cuy," Trisbert said. "We'll soon have need of it."

Then Gavin spoke, and the sound of his voice brought everyone except the mice awake and alert; "Friends, we're going to walk up that hill and down into Everdark together – not in a column like mechanical ants, but side by side like brothers and sisters." And with that, he sat back on his haunches and stretched out his forepaws in comradely invitation.

"Everybody up!" Trisbert shouted. "This is it! We're on our way to Everdark. And may Gollah be with us!"

Fatigued, famished, benumbed, the hardy animals – woods-creatures all – staggered into a lateral rank and prepared to face whatever lay over the next hill. Gavin opened his mouth to utter the cry that would launch them – hand in hand, as it were – irreversibly forward. It never reached the air.

The cry that did reach the air came not from Gavin but from Renée: a metallic shriek, followed by a sighing moan that seemed as if it would never end.

"Madame is about to bring forth!" Hubert gasped, and as he reached out to his beloved mate with a consoling paw, he fainted dead away.

* * *

Trisbert used the last ounce of his ebbing strength to help Renée over to the only shelter anywhere near them – a tangle of barberry bush and shattered elm-branch not much higher than the tips of Jocko's ears. She seemed to be in more pain than was normal in such circumstances. Giving birth was a necessarily painful business, and one universally accepted by female woods-creatures as their appointed lot. For cottontails, it was destined to be a frequent appointment with discomfort, followed soon after by the joyous sight of suckling, dependent, and sometimes grateful offspring. An occasional whimper was the usual sign of any inner turmoil.

But Renée had not whimpered. Huddled back in their circle again, the other animals could hear her shuddering gasps, and were glad that Hubert had not yet wakened from his faint – despite the ministrations of Paddle-Whee and Quiver (who was considering whether or not he should try some form of obtrusion to revive his companion). Gavin wobbled over to Trisbert, who had placed his bulk between the brush and the anxious onlookers to give Renée as much privacy as the situation permitted.

"It shouldn't be long," Gavin said hopefully. It rarely was with cottontails.

"She may be too weak to survive this," Trisbert said, and winced as Renée let out a shrivelled shriek that raised the hair on the nape of his neck. Then no sound at all. Then a series of soft, hiccoughing moans. Finally a voice not recognizable uttered hoarsely, "It's over."

Gavin stepped around Trisbert and the brush. Renée was lying on her side with her body curled in the foetal position, the visible eye milky and blinking as if begging for sufficient light to see the young she had just propulsed into the world, such as it was. And young there were, a full complement of them by the look of it, Gavin thought, as he peered down into the U-shape made by the curl of their mother's body.

"Where's Hubert?" she sighed.

"Right here, cherie," Hubert said, coming upon the scene and kneeling beside Renée's slumped head. "How are you?"

"I'm fine," she said with a wan smile. "This is not the first time, remember. And how are you? You have not re-injured your . . ."

Hubert did not get to answer Renée's question, for he had glanced down at the squirming, hairless blobs that would have quite dramatically become furred and hopping youngsters within days – had they not suddenly stopped squirming and had their blobbed shapes remotely resembled newborn cottontails. Hubert did not faint, but he did rock back on his heels and cast a beseeching look at Gavin.

Gavin leaned down and spoke quietly into Renée's ear: "They are stillborn, dear lady. All of them. Bertie and I will carry you back to the others, and when you are well enough, we will walk with you to Everdark."

Renée closed her eyes, took a huge, trembling breath, and said, "It is probably for the best." Then she rose slightly and said to Hubert, "Je suis désoleée, mon mari."

Hubert nodded sympathetically, then he and Trisbert helped Renée to her feet. When she twisted about to take a look at her dead babies, Hubert laid a paw across her face and said, "Don't, my darling. It's better if you don't."

Whether it occurred to her that she or her darling Hubert might profit by eating the dead offspring – as frightened or confused rabbits have been driven to do – or whether she merely wished to say goodbye to them in their brief existence on Gollah's ground was of little consequence. Hubert and Gavin knew that she must not see them. Nor must any of the others be told what they themselves had been compelled to witness, and remember. The wee creatures had been born alive, but so deformed and lurid that they could have been mistaken for dwarf Warlow or infant Karkajim untethered from the nightmare regions of Serpentine Ridge. That they had perished – writhing and frothing – within moments was a blessing and a relief.

What on earth is happening to us? Gavin thought as he scrabbled in the dirt until he had dug out a trough deep enough to cover forever the genetic monstrosities of Renée's womb. And where would it all end?

* * *

Still dazed by what he had just seen, Gavin turned to go back to the others, who had formed a sort of comfort-ring around the grieving cottontails. Out of the corner of his eye he saw the flick of a bushy tail and then, a moment later, the blurred profile of Cuyler breaking away from the group and racing up the knoll that separated them from Everdark. As much as their fatigue would allow, the animals sent up a cry of consternation and umbrage.

"Stop him, Cuyler! Comprehend the thief!" Quiver was shouting as he waddled precariously on his hind-legs and rattled his quills.

"Traitor!"

"Liar!"

"Hippocritic!"

"Cannibal!"

It was Trisbert who broke the devastating news to Gavin: "It's Wylee. His leg was perfectly fine all day. He let you carry him to preserve his strength. Now he's run off."

"Good riddance to bad radish, I say," Quiver said.

Trisbert said to Gavin, but loud enough for all to hear: "Wylee's taken Papa's leather-pouch with him. It was here on the ground when you went over to help Renée."

Consternation turned quickly to despair.

"Gollah save us, then," Hubert wailed, forgetting for the moment even the catastrophe of his malformed progeny and his soulmate's fragility, "we've gone and lost The Book of Coon-Craft! We are doomed!"

"Cuyler will catch him," Quiver said, wishing he believed so.

"I hate to raise such a pusillanimous point of order," Adderly drawled, "but was there not an element of carelessness in the holiest of books being left vulnerable to the well-known treacheries and dissemblings of the reynard clan?"

"You must not blame Monsieur Gavin," Renée said in her tiny, sad and most loyal voice.

"The rapscallion'll be in Everdark by now," Jocko said with just a hint of envy. "The blackguard saved up all his energy and skedadelled quicker'n my Uncle Gingerheels."

"With The Book strapped to his back," Trisbert sighed, slumping to his knees and perhaps for the very fist time admitting to himself the extent of his exhaustion and how much of his stout determination had rested upon the faith he had placed in Gollah and in Gavin's eldership.

While this unhelpful sequence of monologues was progressing, Gavin had walked forward a few paces to cast a worried eye upon the crest of the knoll, above which the treetops of Everdark could be seen beckoning in a westerly breeze. Moments later the figure of his younger brother appeared on the rise, waved a despondent paw in Gavin's general direction, then dropped to its knees to catch its breath. But Cuyler's message was clear enough. The fox had scarpered into Everdark with the leather-pouch upon his traitorous back.

Seeing that Cuyler was now safe, Gavin swung back to his demoralized troupe and said briskly, "Please, friends, there is no need for alarm. Cuyler has returned – "

"But The Book?" Trisbert said forlornly.

Gavin actually laughed. "There's nothing to worry about on that score," he said soothingly. "I suspected all along that Wylee was going to be true to his kind. But there is a difference between cunning and wisdom, opportunism and foresight. I decided to assist Wylee so that I could keep a close eye on him. The first thing I noticed was the squiggle of blood on his grinding teeth and the reek of his breath when he burped – "

"He ate our babies!" Bucktooth and Petite cried in unison.

"I'm afraid he did. Then to further conserve his energy, he pretended that his hind-leg had not begun to mend – enough for him to trot on three legs – but I noticed that whenever I had to reach ahead to steady Paddle-Whee, Wylee toppled nicely, as you would expect a quadruped with a gimpy limb, but, alas, not quite on cue. There was always a split-second when his left-rear haunch remained quite stubbornly perpendicular."

Trisbert could contain himself no longer: "But The Book?"

"I'm coming to that, Bertie. Knowing as I did that Wylee was just waiting for the right moment to desert us, and noting the way he could not keep his canine's eyes off the leather-pouch or his conversation away from its contents and the past treacheries of raccoons, I determined to let him go, so long as he didn't abscond with anything other than his own wretched bones."

"But he's got the pouch," Trisbert insisted.

"True, but The Book of Coon-Craft and Animal Cunning is not in it," Gavin said (but of course only he knew that it had never been there in the first place). "It's tucked safely away in the Tallwalker's knapsack on your sturdy back!"

Cries of disbelief and gasps of wonder and admiration all around.

"No need to look," Gavin said quickly. "Back at the Tallwalker's camp, I took the opportunity to slip the sacred tome from my pack to Trisbert's, along with some scraps of paper I found near the humanoid's body."

"Then what is Wylee lugging?" Trisbert said, more astonished with each fresh revelation.

"Two middling stones I substituted for the weight of The Book and the other papers."

"No wonder you were so tired," Trisbert said.

"But why ever did you decide to carry, all this way, so much extra . . . uh, extra avoir-du-poundage?" Quiver exclaimed.

"Well," Gavin replied, "I considered that if he should succeed somehow in defecting with the pouch, I didn't want him thinking it was empty or having cause to check its contents before he was a long ways away from us – too far to come back and bother us again."

"How very clever," Paddle-Whee said sweetly, as if she had just discovered the cleverness of raccoons and of this one in particular.

Gavin beamed. He knew that he ought not to have stretched out the story of his ingenuity and insight-into-the-character-of-foxes, especially when dear steadfast Trisbert, and the others too, were heartsick at the apparent loss of The Book. On the other hand, he felt justified in savouring such a small but important moment, in treating himself to a personally administered pat on the back, as it were. There would be precious little time to celebrate any triumphs, modest or immodest, after they had feasted and drunk their fill in Everdark's forest and braced themselves for Gollah-knows-what.

Attention was suddenly diverted from Gavin's imminent beatification to the figure on the crest of the rise up ahead. Cuyler had regained his feet and had found enough reserve energy to begin waving his paw vigorously, in an obvious effort to signal the animals to come forward – at once.

"He's seen Everdark," Quiver said.

And so the refugees and their leader-elect rose once more to their feet (or belly) and, without a further word being exchanged, moved steadily and hungrily forward, and more or less side by side. Cuyler's voice was soon added to his frantic gestures but, in spite of its loud and penetrating urgency, seemed to lack the degree of enthusiasm that might have been expected within spitting distance of food and drink.

"My goodness Gollah," Jocko shouted as he hopped ahead of the others towards Cuyler's spirited cry, "what's wrong?"

"L-l-look," Cuyler gasped. "D-d-down there!" And he turned with Jocko as if to face, against his will, the sight before them.

Jocko froze, as rabbits do so naturally in the face of danger.

Gavin and Trisbert panted up beside him.

At the bottom of the rise they were standing upon, there lay not the fearful Forest of Everdark or Serpentine Ridge ominous above it, but a beautiful, placidly rolling, breeze-whipped expanse of blue water: at least half-a-day's swim across to the far shore, where indeed a darkling woods stared back at them. Its trees were so stupendous in height and girth that they had seemed to be a league closer than they actually were.

The beautiful blue waters, meanwhile, undulated serenely as far north and as far south as the keenest animal eye could see. Gavin spoke for everyone:

"We're on an island," he said.

Chapter 11

Dante

FOR A LONG WHILE NO WORD WAS SPOKEN – in anger or despair, accusation or consolation. There were no words in any language to convey the feelings of those creatures who gazed out upon the impossible width of water that separated them forever from the living forest of the mainland, and ultimately from Earthwood itself (whose inundated wastes lay mercifully hidden behind the granite-and-limestone rampart of Serpentine Ridge). Then, as if in response to a single, instinctive impulse, the speechless animals edged their way down to the rocky shoreline and, with incautious appetite, slaked their thirst and filled the hollow of their stomachs with cool, unpolluted water. Momentarily sated, they lay down on the sun-baked slabs of rock, and sank into a communal doze.

It was Cuyler who roused himself first, and spoke: "Well, Gav, the water is pure, and I saw a flash of silver a long ways out – it was a fish, I'm sure of it."

Gavin opened his eyes and said without turning his head, "You'd need to be an otter to catch it." The rocky shoreline and steep drop-off dashed any hopes a raccoon might have of paddling in shallows for clams or unwary chub. And now that he was closer to the channel, Gavin could see that the rolling swell of waves was intermittently threatened by narrow stretches of rapids – that roiled and spumed in spiteful fury. Even a beaver would risk drowning in such a torrent.

Cuyler appeared to be reading his brother's mind: "I saw the fox swimming towards the rapids out there," he said, "with Papa's leather-pouch on his back."

"Maybe the stones he stole sucked him under," Trisbert said lazily, coming awake and trying to lift his head.

"What're we gonna do?" Cuyler said.

Gavin found strength enough to turn towards Cuyler, but all he could say was, "I don't know."

Cuyler gave Gavin a long searching look, as if he were trying to recall something that had once been a part of his brother and to fix it in his memory. Then he laid his face in his paws and closed his eyes.

Sometime later, Trisbert said so softly he might have been speaking to himself, "Maybe you oughta see what The Book says . . ."

No-one, not even Trisbert, noticed Gavin get up, casually unstrap the Tallwalker's knapsack from his brother's back, then move off a ways and settle himself down behind a low boulder. He could not bear to look at the brave souls who had put their faith in him as much as in Gollah, and had followed him here to this bleak beach, where they would all lay down and accept, without complaint or recrimination, the capricious fate meted out to them. He knew also that Hubert and Renée would be curled together as one, with Quiver nestled as near as he dare to his newfound friends; that Adderly would have swooned into the sun's torpor, untempted to take a last supper of mice, who were also curled together in one of the warm loops of his generous body; that Cuspid and Paddle-Whee would be snoozing side by side with their leathery tails testing the element they had expected to spend their lives thriving in; that Jocko would be true to his breed by lying apart and independent to the end; that his brothers would be dreaming of Papa and Grandpapa Mosah and what might have been if only their elder-brother had learned his lessons more diligently.

Listlessly, Gavin undid the clasps on the knapsack. Inside, safe and sound, was Tales of Arthro and the few remnants of the dead Tallwalker's own book that Gavin had tossed in there – covered as they were with the signs and scratchings of Gibberlish. Could his failure here and now be connected in some way with Papa's own transgression? With the perverse pride Papa had taken in discovering Tales of Arthro and keeping it secret for many seasons, and coming gradually to decipher that exotic code? And finally, against the wishes of the omnipotent Gollah, availing himself of the seditious and profane stories therein? Moreover, Papa had compounded his sin by allowing his elder-son to share the secret, to sit at his shoulder and hear, perforce, Papa's mumbled phrasings as his finger traced the scroll and filigree of the alien dialect. And like Papa, Gavin had also been secretive, concealing from the others the loss of The Book in the floodwaters of Earthwood. What other choice did he have? Would even Trisbert the faithful have followed him this far if he had not assumed, in his trusting way, that Gavin was being guided by the word of Gollah? Still, it was fair to admit (and necessary also) that getting the animals here was not much to boast about.

So shaky were his fingers that Gavin dropped the knapsack before he could reach inside it, and several pages fell out in front of him. Gavin picked them up before the breeze caught them. In his forepaws he now held about a dozen parchment pages, linked together by two thin threads at one corner. They were covered with tightly packed Gibberlish script. Out of habit Gavin cast an interpretive eye along the neat rows, not unlike those in The Book itself (except of course that this was incorrigible gobbledygook). Had the humanoids perhaps learned something about writing and books and chapters from the ancient coon-elders? Or stolen from them the secrets of syntax and scribing as they had (it was said) snatched fire from the very hearthstones of North Holy?

Suddenly, as his eye roved idly along the exotic script, a strange sensation overcame him: a kind of dizziness, then a queasiness in the stomach, then a faint trembling through every muscle in his body, then a reverberating in his bones like the thrum of a voice-box. Hunger, he thought, about to demand its due. But if that were so, it was having an unexpected effect upon his ability to focus on the Tallwalker text, for the individual letters and the curious clusters they gave vent to became more sharply etched, not less. And the quiverings under his skin were not premonitions of death by starvation but a weird species of telegraphy, like the shorthand drumming of rabbits' feet against the resonant earth. And his head was spinning, not with vertigo but with the penumbra of words, the echo of phrasings, the chimera of plots desperate to be voiced.

Without conscious knowledge or effort, Gavin found himself reading whatever-story-it-was from a fragment of the dead humanoid's book: The Hollow Babble.

He read, and he read.

* * *

"Friends, do not trouble to open your eyes," Gavin said to the comatose animals upon his return, "but I beg of you to listen to what I have to say, and then make up your own minds whether or not it seems worthwhile to raise your heads and look once again at the world out there."

Several of Gavin's disciples disobeyed his charge immediately. Others gave a flick of the eyelids to indicate some small measure of attention, or respect.

"I have been studying one of the most ancient chapters of the good book," he began (asking Gollah's pardon for the necessary deception). "It tells about another momentous and world-ruinous flood visited upon earth's creatures, and how Gollah – heartbroken at the sorry and sinful state of His creation – unleashed His purging floodwaters everywhere at once, and how He in His infinite mercy commanded one faithful raccoon, named Noab, to gather about him his family and a single pair of each kind of animal, and place them two by two upon a huge raft that he and his sons would construct under the overlord's guidance – to be dubbed the "arkle." Upon this great raft they floated safely until the floodwaters subsided, and they re-entered their drowned kingdom and built it anew and, indeed, better and more honourable than it had ever been. Through this ancient tale in His most holy Book, I think that Gollah is speaking to us here and now. I think He is telling us how and why we are to save ourselves and return to Earthwood."

Cuyler, whose eyes had been the first to open, said plaintively, "What's an arkle?"

"A raft," Gavin said. "A set of logs bound together, like a beaver-dam tipped flat and floating on the surface of a pond."

The beavers, brother and sister, opened their eyes wide.

"I propose that we build such a raft, an arkle-of-old, big enough to carry us all across this channel to Everdark on the other side."

Only the mice failed to open their eyes at this startling and quixotic proposal.

"Even if we could build such a contraption, we have no strength left to do so," Trisbert said groggily, then added in an apologetic tone, "Not even me."

"First things first," Gavin said. "The sun is on its way down from its high perch, but it has already sucked dry our feeble energies. But if we use the cold water before us to refresh and revitalize, we may be able to get ourselves back to the Tallwalker's habitat."

Gavin braced himself for the sceptical outcry, but no-one bothered to put their misgivings into words. Gavin continued: "We can use the humanoid's skin-shelter and several of the larger tree-trunks there for shade against the sun. And with the ingenuity of each member of this noble tribe of survivors, we shall find materials and means to construct an arkle. And like Noab, we shall traverse the floodwaters."

With a glimmer of interest, Cuyler said, "Can we do it without food?"

"No, we can't," Gavin said, "but I remembered that the dead Tallwalker seemed to have feverishly dug a dozen deep holes in the ground around his shelter. I thought at first he had been delving for roots or tubers.

But his camp was in a clearing, with no sign of tree or shrub where he'd been foraging. Why would he not try digging nearer the uprooted cedars and birches all around the clearing?"

When no-one volunteered an answer, Gavin supplied it himself: "I believe he was looking for food all right, but not roots. Papa once told me that the Tallwalkers, when hunting or fishing long ago, would set up skin-shelters at the edge of woods or near the shore, and occasionally bury caches of food and missiles for their firesticks so that they could return another season and unearth them for use – like squirrels do with acorns. I think our Tallwalker has been on this dreadful island many times before, and thought he knew where he could find such a cache. And if it's one thing we animals do better than anyone else, it's dig."

* * *

Paddle-Whee and Cuspid led the parade into the vivifying waters of what Gavin, in the chapter of The Book of Coon-Craft he was composing in his head, called Heartbreak Channel (and the island it lapped, Deadwood). The raccoons and cottontails followed suit and then, more dubiously, Quiver. Shivering more with fright than chill, Jocko the hare allowed Gavin and Trisbert to immerse him, once, like a reluctant communicant. Adderly proved to be a more daunting challenge. Though normally an avid swimmer, he was now too lethargic to drop himself into the icy channel and not certain he could hoist himself out again onto the rock-ledge a coon's-length above the surface. So, while he stretched his sagging coils out along the rocky shelf, with Bucktooth and Petite cowering near, the beaver twins swam by and smacked their tails sharply enough to send a sheet of cleansing, cooling liquid over Adderly and the startled mice.

* * *

With the sun westering towards Serpentine Ridge (or the bank of white cloud that had been obscuring it off and on all day), Gavin and Trisbert returned to the Tallwalker's encampment ahead of the others (who were taking a final draught of channel-water in lieu of food). Their purpose was to bury the corpse and take stock of anything remotely useful to the project that now engaged the hopes and enthusiasm of the troupe: constructing an arkle. (Noab's advantage in having mated pairs ready-to-hand as well as direct instruction from his overlord was noted by many but not mentioned.) Trisbert was humming away, as he did only after a satisfying snack of brook-trout, and trundling too sprightly for Gavin to catch up (though this may have been more due to Gavin's mind still a-whirl with wild thought and unsettling sensation).

For instance, how had he been able to unscramble the Gibberlish script? Had those furtive evenings at Papa's side, under the weird glow of the moon, listening to a RA-to-be whisper the Tallwalker words into the bright breath of the ring-tree air really have been sufficient to have imbedded them – without his knowledge or consent – so deep that they could never be unremembered? Or was he, as elder-son and scion of a noble line of RAs whose chapters bejewelled The Book of Coon-Craft, blessed with a kind of second sight, like Minervah the owl? Not likely (even though many a credulous woods-creature attributed such wizardry to all raccoons), for the cumulative wisdom of the ages was meticulously taught to those raccoons most susceptible to the sayings and heroic stories recorded, chapter by glorious chapter, in Gollah's own dialect in Gollah's only book.

True, he was aware that many of the Gibberlish words in that fragment of The Hollow Babble had kept their meanings hidden from him and that he had guessed at the import of others, but the tenor of Noab's tale had struck him clear and vivid and almost whole, as if its ending had been poorly disguised in its beginning and, afterwards, seemed familiar. Of course, it might simply have been the obvious coincidence of Noab's deluge and the flood that Gollah had visited upon Earthwood. Strange, though, that the Tallwalker version should refer to their overlord not as Zeebub but as Jovah. Jovah's spite and vindictiveness, however, certainly marked him as a demon-deity; so much so that Gavin found himself both pitying and admiring Noab the Tallwalker.

"I don't want to touch him," Trisbert was saying. "Some horrid disease has been eatin' him from the inside out."

"Let's just dig a trench beside the body until he topples over into it," Gavin suggested.

And that's what they did, using their powerful hind claws to carve out a shallow grave and their nimble forefingers to scratch out the loose dirt just under the body until — with a sagging whoosh! — it shifted sideways and dropped in, a second before the raccoons leapt out of the way. They started to kick the loose dirt back onto the corpse when Gavin suddenly stopped and, squeezing his nostrils shut, leaned down into the grave. He came up with a piece of paper in his paws. It was a single scrap, ripped at the edges.

"What is it, Gav?"

"I don't know, but the fellow had it clutched in his hand as if it might be important, perhaps a matter of life and death. I'll put it in the knapsack and look at it later."

They finished burying the Tallwalker (Gavin made certain he did not encounter again those dead but eloquent and disturbing eyes) just as Cuyler led the other animals into the clearing.

"I'm so hungry I could eat a school of trout, bones and all," Trisbert sighed.

"I know, Bertie. You've carried more than your share of the load. But we're going to get ourselves off Deadwood Island – tomorrow. That's a promise."

But who would help him keep it?

* * *

Gavin wasted no time in outlining his scheme, only parts of which he made up as he went along (it seemed to him more like telling his companions an improvised but pertinent fable than detailing a plan for the construction of an arkle). "We'll have to start immediately, while there's still light. Everyone will contribute according to the skills and habits of his kind." (Surely that was the reason, Gavin mused, that Noab had taken the various breeds of animal with him: the world would not work if one of its interdependent parts was lost. Though how a Tallwalker, even a brave one like Noab, could be intricately connected with Gollah's favoured ones was very puzzling – disorienting even. Tallwalkers did not belong in Earthwood. They were the scourge of woods-creatures, the monstrous offspring of a jealous and rejected Zeebub. The Book said so, did it not?)

"A noble sediment," Quiver said, "but I fail to see how a pair of starved field mice will be of material persistence to our enterprise."

"I'm coming to that," Gavin said, hoping that he was. "Those of us who see in the dark will work all night. But first, Cuspid and Paddle-Whee will cut, from the broken trees around us, a dozen logs, so big and so long, after which the cottontails and hare will use their powerful hind-legs to roll them down to the water's edge."

Hubert gasped. "Surely you don't expect Madame, in her delicate state, to engage in such an activity. It will kill her."

"So will hunger," Renée said, and threw Gavin a pale smile.

"My gracious Gollah," Jocko said with a little chuckle, "but we hares – and thank you for that appellation – do find it difficult to cede our independence, even when our lives are on the line. But these are unnatural times, I'm bound to admit, and I must say in all candour that my vaulting legs are the most prodigious pistons in Earthwood."

"Thank you," Gavin said, much relieved.

Hubert, still irritated by the failure of anyone but himself to appreciate the delicacy of his mate's sensibility (including, alas, his mate), said, "And what will the royal raccoons do – besides thinking?"

"Bucktooth and Petite will take those vines over there – which Bertie, Cuyler and I will disentangle – and massage and masticate them with their tiny mouths until they are soft and pliable. For we must have something with which to bind the logs together into a seaworthy arkle."

"And we, with our lively forefingers, will do the binding!" Cuyler burbled.

"A wonderful plan, Gav," Trisbert said, swelling with brotherly pride.

Adderly cleared his throat like a moose regurgitating a wad of bulrush. "Ahem, and pardon me, but have you not forgotten to mention one or two of us?"

Gavin was taken aback for a moment only. "We'll need someone long and strong to wrap himself around the logs and squeeze them close together so that when we bind them, they'll be as watertight as a beaver's lodge."

"And I repose that you want a certain porcupine to keep well away and assist the project by not obtruding into anyone with more important work to do?"

"No, indeed, Quiver. Yours is to be the most important contribution of all. We will ask you to sacrifice a number of your quills with which to interlace the knots we must make, as best we can, in the ends of the vine-ropes."

Quiver glanced appraisingly at his tail, and said, "Well, I suppose I could afford to give up a few of the older ones. We must all make our retribution, eh?"

While the assembled animals were gazing with some wonder upon their leader-elect and reflecting upon the fortuitous parable from The Book that had been miraculously revealed to him, one of them slipped to the ground and lay there, very still.

"I told you! I told you!" screamed a distraught Hubert over the prone shape of his beloved.

"It's a great plan," Trisbert said to Gavin, "but I think it came to you one day too late. If we don't get food right away, we won't have the strength to build an arkle – or lift our heads."

Which was all Renée was able to do in spite of Hubert's heart-rending pleas.

"Then we must find food – now," Gavin said. "So let's start digging. It's our last chance."

And how many of those had they already had?

* * *

The raccoons were joined by Jocko with his prodigious hare-paws, and the four of them began gouging at the surface of the Tallwalker's camp-ground. The others watched, trying not to hope too hard.

"Ouch!"

"Sorry," Trisbert said to Cuyler who was closest to him.

"You didn't scratch me," Cuyler said.

"Ouch!"

Trisbert stopped digging. His jaw dropped onto his chest.

Out of the shallow trough he had just made in the ground in front of him popped the gray, furred forehead of some small, subterranean creature. Cuyler and Gavin came over to determine the source of Trisbert's astonishment. They too watched, open-mouthed, as the gray head soon produced a pair of slitted eyes, a set of whiskers, and a pair of rodent-like incisors.

And then a voice:

"Who's the dolt with the errant claw

Scratching my house with his coon's paw?"

"By the brindled beard of Gollah, it's a mole!" Trisbert said.

"And it's alive," Cuyler said.

"Of course I'm alive, are you blind?

Turn off the lights, if you don't mind!"

"And he's talking in rhyme," Gavin said, stepping aside to let the others come over and stare at the newcomer, who showed himself to be a mole as he climbed fully out of the burrow that Trisbert had disturbed.

"How else should I talk, I'm a mole

With a poet's sensitive soul,

Though I'm woods-creature all the same;

You've not asked, but Dante's the name."

"Good Gollah," Hubert sighed. "Another mouth we can't feed."

"And I sincerely doubt," Quiver added, "that a mole, half-blind and addicted to diversification, could offer any practical assistance in the business of constricting an arkle."

"I know not what an arkle be," Dante replied, squinting at the last of the sunlight skittering among those ringed around him, "but I know where there's food a-plen-tee!"

This rhyme, orthodox or not, stopped all comment.

Dante beamed, savoured the silence a little, then said:

"I've found what the human could not

With his light-brimmed eyes and a lot

Don Gutteridge

Of desperate digging with hands

Too starved for brain's commands.

But one who's at home in the dark

With a nose for grub and ground, hark!

And hear how I snubbed and snouted,

Tunnelled and molishly routed

A route to the Tallwalker's cache

Of tasties – woe and alas

'Twas sealed in a barrel of wood

And wire: so near! so dear! that food

I could smell but not eat, by the rood!"

Cuyler almost knocked the mole and his rhyme flying in his haste to gain the hole Trisbert had started and Dante had vacated.

"Well, don't bother with 'pardon me'

For a mole without pedigree!"

Moments later, one of Cuyler's claws scraped upon something wooden and hollow. "It's the Tallwalker's cache," he called up.

"Food," Gavin said. "At last."

Chapter 12

A Sadder Tale, In Rhyme

NO LEADERSHIP WAS NEEDED to orchestrate the series of actions required to unearth the Tallwalker's cache. Raccoon, rabbit and porcupine set to work with their powerful digging appendages to widen and deepen the vertical tunnel out of which Dante had popped with his life-giving news and Cuyler had probed with one forepaw far enough to touch the top of the barrel. When the excavation reached down as far as Trisbert's snout, Hubert and a recovered Renée burrowed in together and flailed away, as if exhaustion were their adrenalin or the Bogeyman-Ferret were an inch from their bobbing tails. Soon they vanished completely, and only the steady fling of scooped earth assured the famished onlookers that the mated pair had not been mercifully immolated.

The digging stopped.

"It's definitely something shiny and wooden," Hubert called up.

Said Dante:

"The Tallwalker's barrel for sure,

Whose victuals will help us endure."

"We'll have to dig around it," Renée said, "to see if there's a way into it."

"Tallwalker used an iron stick t'elbow / One of these open, once, seasons ago," Dante said helpfully, not noticing the deflating effect this rhyming comment had upon the animals, whose hopes and disappointments could take no more sudden swings.

"We'll just have to find an animal way in," Gavin said. "Come on, Cuyler, you and I will go down there and scratch out a space all around the barrel-thing."

Being wee and young and eager to be all the things his dreams had promised, Cuyler set to work with a will. His tiny forefingers clawed with a frenzied delicacy at the soil imprisoning the barrel's sides. When he reached the bottom of his half, he went over to assist Gavin, whose bulk was impeding his progress. Gavin smiled, then stood on top of the barrel while Cuyler finished the job.

The animals could now peer down at the polished wooden barrel fully revealed below them. It was as tall as a deer and as round as a she-bear. Think of the food it must hold! But, alas, there seemed no way in: not a hatch to be picked open or a hasp to be jimmied by a clever coon.

"Oh-me-oh-my, but this is a letdown of preposterous proportions," sighed Quiver.

Gavin crawled out of the hole, spat some dirt out of his mouth, looked at Paddle-Whee and said simply, "It's made out of wood."

Brother and sister swung into action. They dropped onto the top of the barrel, skidded into the narrow gap cleared along each side, and began chomping at the circumference where the lid met the vertical staves. The power and ferocity of Paddle-Whee's incisors at work were awesome (she was half again as big as her littermate, the runt of that pairing). Bucktooth and Petite had to seek refuge from the grinding sound in one of Adderly's coils (where they now felt most comfortable). It wasn't long before Paddle-Whee met Cuspid's teeth coming the opposite way, and the lid now sat unattached upon the chewed-up stave-tops. Gavin and Cuyler then slid down and lifted it free. The animals held their breath while Gavin, as was only proper, looked in to appraise the contents.

"Food," he said, and could say no more.

* * *

Oddly enough – certainly it caused Gavin to reflect upon it later – the Tallwalker's victuals were neither wholly alien nor humanoidly tainted. There were wizened turnips and carrots which the rabbits found tolerably tasty and which Quiver (who had no other choice) was able to pretend were roots. There were jars of dried fruit and nuts (conveniently shelled), whose lids came off in the persuasive fingers of Cuyler and his kin, and quickly filled the bellies of raccoon and beaver (such provender being gourmet to the former and fodder to the latter). And there were bags of seed that the mice found varied and delicious.

"I'm certainly not surprised that everyone but me – a lowly and legless, cold-blooded, non-mammalian gentleman – should be overlooked amid all this gorging and self-indulgence."

Gavin stopped gorging and dropped his jar of dried berries.

"Don't mind me, but I would not call this sort of behaviour 'sticking together' or 'all for one,'" Adderly continued. He stared avidly at the two mice plumping themselves with sesame seed. Fortunately they were too busy to notice.

"Wait just a moment," Gavin said, and he wriggled down into the barrel (most of its contents now lay scattered on the ground above), and came up with a jar in his paws. "Pickled fish of some sort," he said, flipping the lid off. "Smells terrific."

"Dead fish!" Adderly said, coming as close to exclamation as his breeding would allow. At least Gavin had the courtesy to look the other way when Adderly slid reluctantly over to the spilled fillets and started to consume them.

Something then began to tug at Gavin's tail. It was Dante.

"You only eat worms or grubs?" Gavin asked, knowing the answer to his question.

Dante nodded, resigned to his fate, it seemed.

"I saw a box down there with those hook-things that Tallwalkers used to snag fish long ago on the shores of the Lake," Gavin said aloud to himself. He went down into the barrel once again. With some difficulty he unsnapped the hasps on an iron box (on top of which several hooks lay where they'd been tossed, apparently) and opened it. Inside he saw what appeared to be wooden replicas of fish and frogs: that was all. The box itself was sitting upon a wooden crate of some kind, and when Gavin pushed it aside with his snout, a potent and familiar aroma caressed his nostrils. Worms. Dozens of them, writhing and thriving in a damp, mossy interior. Resisting any temptation to help himself, Gavin reached up, lifted Dante down, and placed him on the crate. Dante squeezed through a space between the slats, and was gone.

"You're welcome," Gavin said, but he was smiling. After all, they had food and water; they had a plan to execute; all was as well as it could be. He hitched the Tallwalker's knapsack onto his back again, rubbed his stomach contentedly, and lay down to savour the satisfactions of the moment.

* * *

No effort was made to begin the work on a reproduction of Noab's arkle that night. The opportunity for the animals to sleep deeply and undisturbed by hunger and fear was not to be missed. No discussion of the matter ensued, nor were orders of any kind issued. When the sun cooled and shattered upon the knife-edge of Serpentine Ridge far off to the west, one by one they found some makeshift lair or burrow, and settled themselves down in the blanketing darkness. No ghost arose from the shallow grave of the deceased Tallwalker to haunt or wreak vengeance or stir sympathy for the one who had perished unable to find the very sustenance that had preserved the lives of others.

At daybreak, Gavin roused the members of his troupe and marshalled them into the various facets of his "divinely inspired" plan. He was just about to issue the first sequence of instructions when Dante, who had asked Trisbert to lift him up and set him erect upon a

tree-stump, interrupted the proceedings with a
peremptory squeak:

"Good friends, woods-creatures all, O hail!

 I beg leave to narrate my tale

Of doings dangerous and dire,

Of moles and men and flood and mire."

Gavin glanced at Trisbert, who nodded. "Everyone
here has told his story, come what may," Gavin said. "We
can do no less than hear your tale as you choose to tell
it."

Dante smiled, cleared his throat, blinked his near-
blind eyes shut, like a robin swallowing a worm, and
spoke thus in rhyme:

"From the moment that time itself began,

Th' noble moles of Brightleaf (for so this span

Of ground was dubbed: worm-burrowed and grub-

Teeming) have prospered and throve in the nub

Of Gollah's eye; to Nature's rule we clung

And knew our humble place on the world's rung,

When once-upon-a-day in Granddaddy's time

The Tallwalker came with his grit and his grime,

Grass-pummelling boots and an earth-digger

Sharper than a shrew's front claws and bigger

Than a . . .beaver whose tail's like a . . . jigger.

Mole and human for th' same worms contended:

We to survive, he to tease on bended

Hook the brookies that burbled in our brook

(The one over there that the Great Wave took)."

"Gollah's flood, you mean," Hubert said, "the one
that brought us all to this sorry pass?"

"Hush, cheri, you'll disturb his rhyming."

Eyes sealed and yearning inward, Dante soldiered on
as if nothing had been said or could be said to disrupt
such ringing couplets.

"And thus we moles, who ordinarily cleave

To ourselves, learned the mysterious weave

And wicked warp of Zeebub's henchmen, so

In due course, did I (when Papa needs go

To his reward in North Holy). But lo!

To my surprise the Tallwalker in sun's

Seasons only made camp above our runs

And anterooms, fished alone on a log

By the stream or strolled the meadow with a dog

For company (a mongrel cur too lazy

To delve for moles), or sat serene in hazy

Dusks or dawns contemplating the mazy

Stars or feeding fawns with tenderest corn

That browsèd nearby in the misty morn,

Or scribbling Gibberlish in a book –

Till Witherstalk marauded and he betook

Him off to come 'gain in Greendaze season,

Leaving behind, for whatever reason,

That barrel of tasties we now feast on."

Dante paused to allow his rapt listeners to view said barrel and hence validate the truth and power of his awful tale.

"Tell us about his firestick," Jocko said hopefully.

Dante pretended not to hear (moles, after all, have only rudimentary ears):

"A thunderstick he brought, but, by the rune,

Only once did he blow it – at the moon!"

"And a dozen more 'onces' at Paddle-Whee and Cuspid and Jocko – and my best shoulder!" Hubert felt obliged to point out.

Dante's whiskers began to quiver, and his whole body trembled as if seized by a sudden and lethal chill. Gavin started forward to assist the storyteller, but was stopped by Dante opening his eyes and continuing his tale in a hushed and prophetic tone:

"Ah, woe to the world and alack-a-day,

The heavens above that sanctified the way

Of sun and season under Gollah's sway

Breachèd and buckled and loud be-thundered,

The rains flooded down, our homes be-sundered,

The very roots that kept the ground from heaving

Skyward, shrieked in a fury-of-leaving:

Mouse and mole, worm and chinchbug be-mudded,

We hove up to the querulous air, thudded

And drenched till every creature drowned

But me – by chance or Gollah's will – who'd found

Desperate refuge in Tallwalker's sack and

There remained till floodwaters slackened

And I, sorrowful to tell, wriggled free

And begged to be blinded rather than see

Granddaddy's world come thus to wrack and ruin,

And me the last of the line in moledom."

Renée could be heard gently weeping, while the others peered furtively around at the desolation, as if seeing it again through Dante's eyes.

"Not a worm survived, no grub left behind

Over or under, no body could I find

To grieve upon or gormandize except

To my horror the Tallwalker's – that leapt

Awake as if from nightmare: bedazed, shock'd,

His flesh a-droop and so gruesomely pock'd

He staggered and shrieked, and like a loot-

ing coyote went scratching around for root

Or rhizome, recalled his cache, and with boot-

To-spade gored the earth in mad disarray

(Just missing a mole, I hasten to say),

Then seized his thunderstick and tottered off

In fruitless search of prey, while I did doff

My grief in time to find that secret coff-

in (O easy for a mole of breeding!)

Alack, 'twas too oaken, I'd be needing

A pack rat's incisors to be feeding

Therein, when back came the human, wolf-eyed,

Demon-mouthed, his skin erupting and pied

With a pox Zeebub must have concocted;

He cursed the sun for shining, unlocked

The firestick, lay down, and died."

Though this was not news, it struck the listeners as if they were learning it for the first time. Finally, into the silence Quiver blustered, "And good riddling to bad rubbish!"

But the silence abided.

"I'd just decided my Papa to join

By crawling happily under some quoin

Of log or bole, when you folk irrupted

From nowhere and all my hopes abrupted.

Now I am destined to live and convey

In troubled rhymes the sad news of this day."

Gavin was about to stand forth and offer thanks to Dante for such a dolorous narration and repeat his gratitude for the disclosure of the food-cache, when the storyteller cleared his throat, clenched his eyes shut, and added this codiçil to his account:

"Although you may think me an amateur

Who prates in iambic pentameter,

I was born with a second inward-sight

And predestined our future to recite

In prophesying rhymes and dizzy riddle

For ill or good, even Gollah can't fiddle

The consequence of what I must foretell,

So hark all ye within hearing, while I spell!"

The assembled animals did indeed hearken to this unexpected revelation, but not before a minor debate broke out as to whether the future ought to be spelled out and, if so, whether it ought to be uttered by a lowly mole who had not tasted the air and greenery of Earthwood or anywhere important, and certainly could not have observed the future were he to have it plunked in front of his perpetual squint.

"Let him speak," Gavin said. "It will be up to us to decide how much credence to give to the mole's predictions."

Dante, who seemed not a whit perturbed by (or even interested in) the discussion, nonetheless took Gavin's cue and, adopting yet another voice (more akin to the rustling sibilance of leaves), carried on:

"Riddle-di-row, riddle-di-ree,

Hark while I pose this prophecy:

To navigate the path that's straight

Go round about and inside out,

In pieces shake to one whole make,

Gollah's law break for Gollah's sake,

Let darkest night be all your light,

Circles devise of the lowly wise,

In alien tongue thy hopes be sung,

Tho' guarded be 'gainst treachery

Of one alone amongst your own,

To kill a king's a blessed thing,

A kingdom won by brother's son!

Riddle-di-ree, riddle-di-run,

The future's spoke and I am done."

As it turned out, Dante was not quite done, for after the briefest pause and a lungful of fresh breath, the chant was taken up again. This time, however, the cantor lapsed into ordinary voice, and said with a wry twinkle:

"And in addition, I humbly aver,

Dante's not a him nor a he, but a her;

O ne'er judge what can be seen, more or less,

For that prophet may be this prophetess!"

With appetites appeased and thirsts quenched, the animals might have found Dante's surprise revelation amusing, and might have offered him – her – an appreciative chuckle or two. (Few of them had had occasion to observe the subterranean mole closely, and one mole-gender looked much like another to creatures who exercised their lives in the open air.) But their heads were still buzzing with her prophetic riddles and what they might portend.

For example, how could they go round about in order to go straight? Or use darkness as a guiding light? And though killing a king might be blessed and justified (if he were evil), as far as anyone here was aware, there were no kings, good or bad, in Gollah's world – only the wise and foolish, and the immutable order of species and clan. RA-Mosah was no monarch, merely a sage among sages. And what a curious and contradictory phrase was "the lowly wise"! Surely the lady rodent was playing another mole-ish joke on them?

Still and all, one of their own kind had proved treacherous already (and, one trusted, had been drowned for his perfidy), an act that Dante herself could not have witnessed or known about. And certainly Gollah's natural law had been violated at every turn since they had awakened so mysteriously here on Deadwood Island. But had the law been broken for His sake or their own? And what was that nonsense about an alien tongue? Gollah had bestowed upon the woods-creatures of Earthwood a common language; any other – Gibberlish or the ravings of Warlows on the Ridge – was babble (though one among the animals here knew differently).

While Gavin too was puzzled and intrigued by Dante's prophetic rhymes, he was equally fascinated by her earlier account of the Tallwalker and his island sanctuary. The images that refused to leave his mind – try as he might to erase them – were that of a fawn, trembling and innocent in a woodsy morning mystical with mist, licking corn from outstretched fingers more commonly found on the butt of a thunderstick; and a mongrel cur trotting companionably beside his master through a green, sunlit meadow. What terror or awful necessity, then, had driven the humanoid to rampage and flounder among the flooded ruins of Brightleaf?

"Thank you for telling us your story," Gavin said at last. "Like us, you have witnessed and suffered many calamities. Your knowledge of the Tallwalker and his paraphernalia should prove invaluable to us, as may your prophecies in the fullness of time."

"And I am pleased to add my thanks," said Quiver, "for your despiteful contradictions."

Dante acknowledged the compliments with a whiskery smile.

"And though you are not a native of Earthwood," Gavin said, "there is nothing here on Deadwood, your beloved Brightleaf, to sustain you or your kind. We woods-creatures, who found ourselves marooned here and then found each other, have banded together and assented to a covenant: which is to suspend the laws of Dame Nature – the imperative of predator and prey, the distinction and necessary separation of species – until we regain our lost homeland. And further, to do nothing as individuals that will not benefit all the others. I have been chosen leader until such time as the right and proper RA is discovered or until my leadership is found wanting. We would be most happy if you would accompany us."

Dante was quick to reply:

"This lowly mole accepts your offers kind,

To fate and Gollah's will I am resigned."

"That's settled then," their leader said. "Now, loyal friends, we've got an arkle to build!"

Chapter 13

Noab's Arkle

AND THUS BEGAN THE CONSTRUCTION OF AN ARKLE to ferry the lost survivors of Earthwood across the roistering waters of Heartbreak Channel to the shores of Everdark. Under Gavin's guidance (and, after all, he himself was being guided, was he not, by divine scripture and the shining example of Noab?), the tree-trunks nearby were selected for their heft, uniformity of size and potential buoyancy – after which Cuspid and Paddle-Whee set their teeth to work gnawing them into similar lengths. Quiver was able to assist them in stripping away the smaller branches and in determining how much "life," if any, resided in the log itself. In the meantime, Bucktooth and Petite trailed Trisbert and Cuyler into a brush-pile, where strings of grapevine were disentangled and presented to the mice for "softening." Time and again the desiccated vines would simply snap in spite of the best efforts of the mice to chew gently on them – often when they had almost reached the length suggested by Gavin. But the mice displayed amazing patience, and found Trisbert's antics amusing (a muffled oath followed by a vengeful jig upon the offending vine).

Don Gutteridge

As soon as the first couple of logs had been cut and trimmed, Gavin asked the rabbits to begin rolling them towards the channel. Using their strong hind-legs, the three of them soon had their first log rotating nicely across the clearing. However, when it reached the pathway that the animals had been taking in and out of the clearing, it stopped. And refused to move.

"The path is too narrow and too winding," Hubert said despondently to Gavin.

"Then we'll just have to move the brush and debris back far enough for the logs to be rolled through," Gavin said.

They surveyed the route of the path. The "brush" around it was composed of stubbornly entangled branches, partial trunks, and major limbs of full-sized trees – with sections of hawthorn and barberry interwoven like spiked belts. Some of the trunks were too heavy to be moved and too thick for even a beaver to gnaw through. And the various thorns and barbs could slash open a misplaced paw in a wink. There was no way through.

Hubert turned to a crestfallen Gavin: "What do you think Noab would have done?"

Gavin grimaced. "I'll call the troupe together," he said, "and ask for suggestions." (Noab, of course, would have consulted Jovah.)

When the others had left their tasks and gathered around, Gavin explained the problem and admitted that he had no ready solution.

Paddle-Whee spat out several birch-chips and said, "Many times we beaver have had to travel deep into a woods to find the trees most suitable for a dam, so far in

191

that we cannot nudge or drag the logs down to our pond. In such cases we use our digging-claws to make a trench from the cutting-place to the pond, so that the pond-water flows back up the trench to the cutting site. After that, we nose the logs into the trench, give them a little push, and they float the rest of the way down to the dam on their own."

"And we can do that here!" Cuspid said jubilantly.

Though the beaver clan was not thought to have been allotted more than a modicum of intelligence by Gollah at the beginning of things, the animals were happy to concede that that gift often came in small but surprising packets.

Gavin looked doubtful: "It's a very long way . . ."

"True," Paddle-Whee said, "but we've got a lot of diggers amongst us."

* * *

The distance from the clearing to the channel was not as far as they had supposed. The beavers, with their instinct for water, quickly traced a nearly-straight path to the water's edge, which, it turned out, was part of an inlet that shortened the distance between it and the Tallwalker's camp by almost half. Moreover, the proposed trench would meet Heartbreak Channel at a place where two rock-ledges overlapped to form a chute through which the water would run backwards and the logs downward — if they could but dislodge the single boulder blocking it. Again, beaver savvy came into play.

"We use stout branches to lever heavy things up and out of the way," Paddle-Whee explained, limping about the obtruding boulder and sizing it up. "When we get the trench dug this far, we'll flip this boulder over, and the channel-water will rush inland."

And so the trenching-burrowing crew swung into action: cottontails, hare, raccoons and beaver. The sun was barely past its high-point when the trench was completed. The thickening heat and the expense of energy left the diggers momentarily exhausted, but a fresh supply of food and cold water soon revived them. Also, by this time Bucktooth and Petite, assisted now by Dante, had produced a sufficient supply of pliant grapevine, and Quiver, working alone, had trimmed most of the logs required to complete the platform of the arkle. Adderly was pressed into service from time to time to deposit his length parallel to a log being trimmed in order to keep it from jiggling or rolling unduly. While he did so willingly, he was heard to mutter once or twice that there was little dignity and less reward in being a member of the humblest (that is, limbless) caste.

* * *

The troupe gathered along the shore of Heartbreak Channel to watch Cuspid and Paddle-Whee perform their magic trick upon the boulder – the only barrier that now lay between the empty trench and the vast waters of the channel. The boulder was intimidatingly large. Had Adderly been inclined to try, he could not have wrapped his length once around its circumference. To the three small rodents it might as well have been Serpentine Ridge. However, it was more bulky and rounded above than below, almost teetering on a triangular base. It was this aspect that the beaver twins had spotted earlier in the day, and which they now took advantage of. Cuspid wedged a stout cedar-branch under the base of the rock –

gripping the free end with his incisors and heaving all his body-weight down on it till it was jammed in tightly at a jaunty angle.

Paddle-Whee surveyed the shim with the practiced eye that had helped keep massive dams perfectly perpendicular. "Nice work, Cus," she said. "Now it's my turn." And she clambered up onto the branch, gripping it with her three feet and swaying back and forth alarmingly. Her left forelimb kept reaching out and waving at the air as if it still had a foot and claws to clasp and balance.

"Oh, madam, please stop," Quiver cried. "You'll give us all whirligo!"

"Oh, do catch her!" Hubert called out to Cuspid.

But Cuspid was otherwise employed. He had reached up and grasped the branch from below with all four paws, and began swinging on it like an opossum. The combined weight of Paddle-Whee above and Cuspid below had a surprising result — at least to the onlookers. The shim started to bend and sway downward but, as it did so, the boulder began to tilt in the opposite direction.

"Grab hold!" Paddle-Whee shouted with a grin. "We need more body-fat!"

Trisbert and Gavin leapt up beside Paddle-Whee and began rocking in rhythm with her. They were about to call on Quiver to do the same when the boulder — with a hollow, sucking sound — released its purchase on the ground and tumbled away, not stopping until it struck the water and sank. At the other end of the operation, the branch came popping loose, as did those hanging onto it. By the time Gavin and the others had picked themselves up and stopped laughing, channel water began surging into the trench through the gap they had just created. In awe, they watched it seethe and race away towards the Tallwalker's clearing.

"You've done it," Gavin said with a mixture of relief, satisfaction and pride.

"We do this every day, back home," Paddle-Whee said with a sad smile.

"Paddle-Whee does," Cuspid beamed.

"Right now we've got a few more logs to cut," Paddle-Whee said, but not before the grateful animals gave her a rousing cheer.

* * *

While the beavers and porcupine completed the task of preparing the last of the logs for the raft, the others were usefully occupied in different ways. The cottontails and hare used their hind-paws to roll the finished logs into Arkle Trench (as Gavin would later call it). As the water in the trench had grown still and currentless after its initial in-rush, the raccoons had to nudge them towards Heartbreak Channel. When a log reached the end of the trench, it found Adderly stretched across the gap that would otherwise have permitted it to float away into the broad, blue water, and beyond. Once again the rabbits' skills were required, but this time Hubert and Renée (Jocko refused to enter the water) went into the trench and, bracing themselves on one bank, used their hind-paws to bully and roll the log up the far bank and onto a flat ledge – where the arkle itself was to be constructed. When the last of the logs had thus been deposited, Gavin raised his paw for attention, and addressed his weary workers.

"The sun is three-quarters of the way across the sky," he said. "We will go back to the camp for a short while to eat, drink, rest, and reflect upon the wonderful work we have accomplished thus far today – each of us doing what he does best with the skills Gollah granted. Then we will come back here and proceed to build us an arkle. It may not be as grand as Noab's, which held a pair of every woods-creature in the world, but it will be stout enough to carry us across Heartbreak Channel. That is all we can hope for. For now. Before we return to the shore, though, I suggest that we collect all the instruments and paraphernalia of the dead Tallwalker and place them in the barrel, along with any food not yet eaten. We'll float the barrel down here and place it on the arkle."

"But we don't know what these weird contraptions are used for," Hubert protested mildly, ignoring Trisbert's glowering glance. "They'll take up a lot of space – "

"And they may have a hex on them," Quiver added, eyeing a twisted piece of iron with several ugly claws at one end of it. "Beware of all wishhards and necrodancers, I say."

Gavin looked down at Dante – who was neither wizard nor necromancer – and said, "You've lived beside the Tallwalker and his humanoid accoutrements. What do you say?"

Dante, who had her eyes closed but her ears open, replied thus:

"I saw no magic in his fork or spoon,

And the firestick spoke only to the moon."

"Then it's settled," Gavin said. "We take the Tallwalker's things with us." He did not add that the profane texts he carried in the knapsack were also things of the Tallwalker, and much more hazardous than a fork or spoon.

* * *

Gavin was certain that Noab would have admired the putting-together of the second arkle. After he had indicated the square shape he wanted for the raft's base, all able-bodied paws were enlisted to roll the logs in close parallel to one another on the rock-ledge (itself slightly tilted towards the channel and selected by Gavin for this reason). Then Adderly slid to one end of the side-by-side logs. He cupped his chin around one edge, then stretched his coils full out till his tail was able to cup the opposite edge. As the others watched in awe, the fox-snake deployed his mighty, pent-up, constrictive power: the muscles along his entire length clenched in spasmic waves.

He let out a wheezing groan. "That's it," he said. "As tight as I can get them."

While Adderly maintained his vice-like grip, Gavin and Cuyler hopped onto the logs and began wrapping the masticated vine-ropes around them, crosswise. Trisbert stood beside Quiver, who started to tremble and, finally, placed one paw over his eyes.

"Go ahead," he mewed, raising his tail like a skunk before a spray. "We must all distribute to the common clause."

On that cue, Trisbert plucked a dozen quills and handed them to his brothers. They in turn pushed them through the rope-ends and, manipulating them like tourniquets, wound the ropes tight, then attached them securely with a twist of the crochet-hook at the terminus of each quill. This sequence had to be repeated for the other half of the raft, much to Quiver's dismay.

"Some creatures have had to make a greater artifice than others," he was heard to remark during the second round of de-quilling. But he swelled with pride when he decided to open his eyes and view the wonder he had helped bring into being.

"Now," Gavin said to Paddle-Whee and Cuspid, "we've got to make it as watertight as the finest beaver-dam."

And the beaver twins, who seemed to thrive on work, eagerly plopped into the trench, scooped handfuls of muddy clay from the bottom, and began inserting it into the cracks between the logs.

"We'll need lots of sticks and weed-stalks," Paddle-Whee said, and moments later the raft was piled with flotsam from the drowned island, which the beavers mixed into the mud and then pressed the whole concoction into place like mortar. When it dried, the upper surface of the arkle would be as smooth as it was impenetrable.

Hubert suddenly noticed that there were four logs lying unused nearby, and was about to remark to Renée that the arithmetical ability of raccoons left something to be desired, when Gavin said, "We'll use these logs here to create raised sides, as some of us are rather tiny and might be washed overboard in the event of strong waves."

The tinier members of the troupe peered warily out at the channel-waters, now undulating peacefully in a light westerly breeze, praying no doubt that there would be no need for the proposed railings but happy to see them put into place nonetheless.

Finally, several bodies were required to roll the Tallwalker's barrel – with the food and his exotic accoutrements (all save the dreaded firestick) – onto the centre of the arkle's deck and, like the railings, it was secured with daubs of mud-mortar. This task was completed just as the fading light reddened around them like pools of diluted blood.

"It is done," Gavin said. "Now we shall rest. When the first light breaks, we sail for Everdark!"

* * *

While generations of elder-coons had known (and either marvelled or guffawed, according to their temperament) that some Tallwalkers floated on the Lake of Waters Unending in wooden contraptions that appeared to be propelled by the wind pushing against an oversized, leaf-thin skin called a "sail," no-one had ever been able to figure out how the feat was managed. Gavin had considered stripping the skin-roof from the Tallwalker's shelter and trying to rig it on a branch set upright on the arkle. But how would such a branch get itself attached firmly enough to bear the weight of the wind? So, that strategy was abandoned. Nevertheless, Gavin did realize that, short of the beavers paddling astern and attempting to nose the prodigiously heavy arkle forward through the resisting water, they would need some form of locomotion. Their craft, though sturdy, would not propel itself from one shore to the other. What Gavin was counting on was the action of wind and wave. He had observed closely the movement of a number of branches and sticks that were carried slowly but surely from the middle of the channel onto the shore of Deadwood. The problem here was that, so far, the daily breeze had blown persistently from west to east — the opposite of the offshore wind they themselves would need. His announcement, then, of a daybreak departure was based on nothing more than his prayer for a shift in the wind and Dante's whispered answer to his question in that regard:

"To the east the wild wind doth blow

Till sun bleeds red, then west 'twill go."

Well, the setting sun had just bled crimson, hadn't it?

* * *

Gavin opened his eyes to find himself squinting into the first rays of the morning sun. The breeze that fluffed the fur on his cheeks was directly in his face: from the east. He took this as an omen, as Noab had taken the dovey-bird: pure of wing and alabaster-white above the dark visage of the sea.

The business of getting the arkle off the rock-ledge on which it had been erected had already been worked out. Gavin had chosen a rock that angled slightly towards the water, a mere three paces away. So, when the animals arrived at the arkle in the sullen but warm sunshine of this auspicious morning, they beheld gently rolling waves under an easterly, offshore breeze, and gave silent thanks to Gollah and His young lieutenant. Then they waited patiently for Cuspid and Paddle-Whee to flop into the water, where they proceeded to whack their flat tails on the surface and splash foaming wavelets up and over the rock-ledge. Quite soon the ledge was as glistening and slippery as an otter's back. Brother and sister beaver were so enjoying themselves — laughing and daring each other to more strenuous efforts – that Gavin had to call out politely that their task was more than complete.

As Paddle-Whee climbed ashore (awkwardly with only one forepaw), Cuspid gave the water a final whap that sent a spray shooting into his sister's face and incidentally soaking a porcupine in the line of fire.

"Oh, pardon my obtrusion!" Cuspid chuckled, and nearly everyone joined in the laughter.

"First of all," Gavin said as soon as he had the chance, "those of us who shun swimming or have limited pushing-power, are to climb aboard the arkle before we shove it down into the water. Bucktooth, Petite and Dante: you will find a piece of Tallwalker cloth to cozy yourselves into. Adderly, you may coil wherever you feel most comfortable. Though I realize that you can swim, Hubert and Renée, you will feel safer in boarding now and settling down near one of the railing-logs or in the shade of the barrel – as will you, Jocko. The rest of us will launch the arkle, and then clamber aboard as best we can."

No-one moved yet, as Gavin had obviously not finished his address.

"Gollah has blessed us with a fair wind and cloudless day. We have nothing to fear from Heartbreak Channel. When we reach the shores of Everdark, I will reveal to you my plan for furthering our journey home." That is, Gavin thought ruefully, if I can think of one before then. In their generous naiveté, his believers assumed that the plan would be derived from The Book tucked securely in his backpack.

Those named by Gavin were helped aboard and bravely took up their places. Except for Jocko. When Trisbert and Cuyler attempted to boost him up over the railing-log, he planted his forepaws against the wood and couldn't be budged.

"We hares are not rabbits!" he cried piteously. "We do not swim. We repudiate ponds and creeks. We are the lords of the open field and broad meadow. We travel alone and ask nothing of our fellow creatures but respect for what we are. I cannot entrust my life and my honour to this . . . this pile of mud and wood. Please do not make me do this. Please leave me here to die alone with the dignity of my kind!"

But when Gavin replaced Cuyler, Jocko was soon flipped head over heels onto the deck of the raft, where he cowered beside the barrel, shivering and shamed. Gavin came aboard and sat down beside him.

"Everyone here, Jocko, has suffered a hundred indignities since we first woke up on this cursèd island," he said. "We do not understand why we, among thousands, were chosen to survive. We have broken one of Gollah's laws with every step we've taken and every word we've exchanged. But when we get back to Earthwood, and I swear that we shall or perish valiantly in the attempt, we will need every species and clan possible if those almighty laws are to be restored and the world reborn. We need you, Jocko. Earthwood will need the hare – with his independent spirit and alacrity of limb – to serve as example to us all of those irreplaceable qualities."

Jocko's shivering began to subside. Gavin could hear the restless buzz of those behind him on the shore.

"And remember, when we do reach Earthwood, Sprightleg may be there waiting for you."

Jocko didn't look up, but one ear stiffened, and stayed erect. Gavin turned and hopped back onto the rock-ledge.

Just as the pushing-crew was about to launch the arkle, Cuyler raised an eyebrow and said to Gavin beside him, "What happens if the wind changes direction when we're out there in the middle of the channel?"

Gavin replied in what he hoped was a jocular tone, "We go where the wind blows."

"But that could send us north or south," Cuyler said, "and out into the Lake of Waters Unending."

"The youngster's point obtains some vividity," Quiver said. "I've been told that drowning is not a pleasant way to expectorate."

Paddle-Whee said, "There is a way we might steer the arkle, you know."

"In spite of the wind and waves?" Gavin said. "How?"

Paddle-Whee gave her tail a flip. "How do you think we beaver steer ourselves under water? We just twist our tails this way or that, and off we go wherever we aim ourselves."

Gavin was impressed. He surveyed the arkle. "We would need a long, flat stick . . ."

"There's one lying beside the Tallwalker's shelter," Cuspid said. "I noticed it because I thought it looked a lot like my own tail, only bigger."

"I'll float it down the trench," Paddle-Whee said.

"But your tail is attached," Gavin pointed out. "And I can't think how to attach a stick to the rear railing-log so that it swings like a beaver-tail."

Cuspid's face fell, but Paddle-Whee said, "If we need to use it, Trisbert and I will hold it fast, and Cuspid can manoeuvre it." She scrutinized the rear railing-log for a long moment with her dam-builder's eye. "We'll need a notch in this log about here to keep the paddle from slipping." She nodded to Cuspid, who chuckled, and within seconds he had chewed out a serviceable vee.

Gavin's smile was as wide as his mask. The last of his concerns had been addressed. Nothing could now stop them from reaching Everdark.

So they waited while the beaver twins swam back to the camp and returned, likewise, with a long, flat stick that did indeed resemble a beaver-tail. Gavin had it placed carefully on the deck of the arkle, to be used only if necessary. It was time at last to push their craft into Heartbreak Channel and add a fresh chapter to their common adventure. However, they had succeeded in nudging the arkle only halfway down the slippery rock-ledge, grunting and puffing, when a keening wail rose up from somewhere aboard and stopped them in mid-push.

It was Dante. She had crawled, in her blundering fashion, to the top of the barrel, and stood there uttering an elongated ai-eee-ai-eee!

"What is it?" Gavin said. "What do you see?"

Dante replied in her singsong chant:

"Wind and wave bedevil the day,

Foam and fury shall have their say!

On crest and trough shall we be tossed

And one of us forever lost!"

Eager to reassure the others, whatever his own doubts might be, Gavin said, "But there isn't a cloud in sight except for that bank of white fluff a hundred leagues off on the western horizon. And with this brisk offshore breeze, I estimate we'll be in Everdark before the sun hits the high point of the sky."

Dante had nothing more to say. She closed her eyes, and seemed to be asleep.

"It's all silly riddles anyway," Trisbert said. "If we don't go now we may never get another chance."

One by one Gavin looked at the others. "We go," he said.

And Dante's sudden, wild, wee wail was smothered in the collective shout of Gavin's crew as the arkle irreversibly sallied into the welcoming blue of Heartbreak Channel.

Chapter 14

Foam and Fury

THE ARKLE SOON PROVED TO BE A SEAWORTHY VESSEL. It rode high and smooth upon the tender swell of the channel waters. The easterly wind nudged it wavelet by wavelet towards the far western shore, whose thick, deep woods and hovering escarpment beckoned in the bright morning. Aboard the craft, that rocked and lulled like an elm-bough in a Meadowbloom breeze, the animals dozed in the sun or sheltered in the shade of the Tallwalker's barrel. Whatever awaited them at the end of the voyage, they would put their trust in Gavin and the precedent of Noab.

Gavin himself did not doze, though he gave the appearance of doing so as he rested his chin upon his forepaws on the forward railing-log. Actually, he was scanning the opposing shoreline for the least flicker of movement. If Everdark were in fact greening and growing, the creatures that fed upon such abundance would be thriving also. Once in a while Gavin was startled by a fish breaking the surface nearby, and his stomach rumbled at the memory of live trout in Ambling Creek, and he thought of Papa's patience as he taught his sons how to locate and capture the wiliest and swiftest of fish, and remembered also strolling through misty dawns with bellies full and young legs happily tired (Papa still chuckling at one or another of their antics), and coming home, sleepy and proud, to the High Ring tree at the centre of their Realm – knowing in their hearts that this was the place they were born to and would inherit and keep faith with for the rest of their lives. But all the wisdom of all the ages had not forewarned them of the great flood, or saved them from calamity.

How then could he, Gavin – a partially educated tyro and untested elder-son – hope to accomplish what his betters could not? Oh, how he longed to peruse the Tallwalker texts in his backpack – Tales of Arthro and the fragment from The Hollow Babble – for, absurd as it might seem, it was possible that further insight and intimation for action were contained therein: more stirring stories perhaps, like Noab's, or the fabulous Arthro, whose glories Papa had hinted at during their last secret session. Absurd it must be, however, because RA-Mosah had assured his elder-pupils that all Tallwalkers were the demon-spawn of Zeebub at perpetual war with Gollah – humanoid, ogre-eyed apes whose periodic raids and forays into Earthwood were the subject of heroic deed and derring-do and righteous triumph for the woods-creatures designated by Gollah to keep his world sane and pure.

But Papa had not been so certain. Something had induced him to keep the dead Tallwalker's book that he and Uncle Sylva had come upon that fateful day. And if Noab were in truth a Tallwalker, why had he not been justifiably drowned with the other transgressors? How could Noab, whose chief interest in beasts as a humanoid was the target they presented to his firestick or the pleasure they gave him as he ran them down in his doomsmobile – how could such a one lead the animals two by two into his arkle and go with them to found a new world on the ruins of the old? Was Jovah not merely Zeebub in one of his many guises? (RA-Mosah had warned his elder-pupils that the spirit of Zeebub materialized in many shapes, not all of which were monstrous.) Was Jovah not really Zeebub, then, in one of his many seductive poses? Possibly, but Gavin could not blot out the image of the dead Tallwalker's eyes: the inextinguishable pain in them, the puzzlement, the sadness. And what was he to make of the fawn feeding from the monster's hand? Or the little cur kept only as a companion? Or the summery quietude of his encampment as it must have been before the flood devastated it? Or that paper seized in his death-grip, as if it had promised some answer and failed to deliver it?

Those eyes were not the eyes of an ogre.

What, then, should he make of this fabulous Arthro and his magic kingdom? Had Papa been seduced by false tales of the Tallwalkers, dreamt up to justify their wickedness and amuse their repugnant offspring at bedtime? Whatever the truth might be, Gavin knew that sooner or later, if his troupe should prevail, he must read far enough into these profane texts to have his many questions answered. At the moment, though, he could not – within plain sight of these simple believers – open the knapsack and risk revealing the deception he was practising upon them for their own sake. Yet even as individual trunks of Everdark's gigantic trees swam into focus, he knew he had no real plan to present.

Trisbert came up beside him.

"Well, Gav, you've done it. I can taste the brookies," he grinned, then added more soberly, "Papa would've been proud of you."

"He'll be proud of you, Bertie, when he hears the tale we have to tell."

"I was bred big and strong; you were born wise."

"But you were born brave," Gavin said. "And it's bravery we're likely to need when we creep into the dark forests ahead."

This brotherly game of trying to out-compliment one another might well have continued, had a voice behind them not interrupted: "We seem to be rocking more than is necessary, in my opinion. And Madame's stomach is extremely sensitive to such gyration as a consequence of her recent tragedy."

"The wind's changing direction," Cuspid remarked.

"It's coming from the north, I think," Paddle-Whee added.

"Then we'll be blown into open water and vanquish without a trace!"

The wind had not only shifted to the north, it had picked up its pace. The arkle was now bucking and pitching as the waves contended in several directions under it. Soon, however, the staunch wind from the north sent it skidding steadily southward. Every time the raft now slid down into the trough of a wave, a frenzied spume broke over the foredeck railing-log and washed across the main deck – toppling the mice and mole and frightening the others, who were certain the vessel would be swamped. Had Noab suffered such indignities at the hand of Jovah?

Gavin stared up at the sky. It was cloudless, from rim to rim. Where was the storm? The source of the howling wind and its rage against the unoffending waves of the channel? Suddenly the spray and spume rose, intensified, and lashed out to envelop them all, like a horizontal rain. Clouds or not, they were in the eye of a tempest.

"We'll have to use the paddle!" Gavin shouted as he tucked the wee ones behind the barrel and tossed a cloth over them.

"Right you are," Paddle-Whee called through the spray that was now so constant they could no longer see a tail's-length beyond the railing and so thick it might as well have been pouring rain. "Come on, Bertie, you and I will hold it steady in the vee-notch while Cuspid steers."

Trisbert and Paddle-Whee brought their combined weight and strength to bear upon the paddle, squeezing it into the indentation in the rear railing-log to form a fulcrum-point, which allowed Cuspid to work the tiller-end of the device. When this makeshift "rudder" dug snugly into the water, the fulcrum held fast – but the helmsman was flung upward into an unforeseen somersault.

"I can't hold it against the waves!" Cuspid cried.

Gavin arrived in time to bring Cuspid upright and, in tandem, they were able to dip the rudder back into the raging waves and hold it firm – at a sharp angle. The arkle lurched, groaned in protest, and altered its course.

"You have to bend it the opposite way to where you want to go," Paddle-Whee laughed. "You're sending us back to Deadwood!"

Obediently Gavin and Cuspid leaned the other way, and the arkle followed their lead.

Cuyler, who had come over to help steady the agitations of the rudder, hollered at Gavin, "How do you know where the Everdark shore is supposed to be? I can't see a thing."

"The wind switched to the north," Gavin shouted back. "I saw that clearly before the sky disappeared. If we hold this rudder against the wind, as Paddle-Whee suggests, we'll have to move westerly – south-westerly, most likely, but it'll get us to Everdark eventually. We weren't that far away when all this started."

"As long as the wind stays steady," Cuspid pointed out. "If it changes again, we'll have no way to get our bearings."

"And as long as we don't go under!" Jocko cried out from his cowering-place, just as a huge wave broke over the barrel and swamped the stern-section of the arkle. Fortunately, the corner-joints of the railing-logs had not been sealed, so the water did not accumulate in the well of the deck, where it might have drowned its occupants or sunk the craft summarily. As the arkle rode up to the crest of the next wave, the water streamed out of the rear corner-slots in two furious jets.

"Ai-eee-ai-eee-ai-eee!"

"What's wrong?" Hubert cried at Dante as he wrapped his soggy body around Renée's.

It was Jocko who replied: "The mice. They've been swept overboard!"

And which of them, he thought guiltily, will be the one "forever lost"?

* * *

"There they are!" Paddle-Whee shouted. "I'm going in after them!"

"But the paddle!" Cuspid protested. "If you let go, we'll spin like a dragonfly and be lost!"

"Someone else can take my place."

"Who? We need your weight on that notch."

"I can hold it by myself," Trisbert grunted.

Paddle-Whee took her eye off the bobbing, helpless mice for one moment to glance imploringly up at Gavin.

"I can't let go at this end either," Gavin sighed. "I'm afraid we've got to do what's best for the whole group." Besides, Gavin was not Paddle-Whee. His determination could not make up for his lighter weight.

"I believe I may be of service, even though I am seldom thought of in that regard."

It was Adderly. He had been near-anaesthetized by the morning sun, but the cool north wind and icy spray had roused him to consciousness, and conscience.

"But you've got no paws to grip with," Cuspid said, not unkindly.

"I've managed quite well thus far, as have my forebears, without the aid of extraneous appendages," Adderly said, and demonstrated his claim by crawling up onto the rear railing-log. Where, as the others watched in some amazement, he wrapped himself once around the rudder at the pressure point of the fulcrum (next to Trisbert's forepaws) and, letting his head and tail droop down to the deck, pressed their bulk tightly into the crease where deck and railing met. He then clenched his entire body. With Trisbert still manning his position, the rudder was as secure in its crotch as it had ever been.

Without waiting about for permission, Paddle-Whee now leapt into the whirling, foam-tormented waters.

"She'll drown," Quiver sighed. "The waves are too tem . . .temcrestuous!"

"There isn't a fish that can swim better than Paddle-Whee," Cuspid countered.

Though serviceable swimmers when they had to be, Bucktooth and Petite were out of their depth in such tempestuous seas. Whitecap after whitecap peaked and collapsed upon them, so that they vanished utterly for several awful moments before popping up farther away than ever from the arkle and gasping for what little breath remained in their exhausted lungs. They could not stay afloat much longer.

With a deliberate flip of her tail, Paddle-Whee dipped out of sight, and the onlookers held their own breath while they waited for her to surface somewhere in the vicinity of the floundering mice. It appeared to be Bucktooth who opened his mouth and hurled some wee mouse-words towards the fading arkle: was it goodbye or thanks? Then without warning the mice dissolved into spume and mist. They were out of eye contact with the arkle, as Paddle-Whee herself would be if or when she reached them. How would she know where to return?

Gavin heard the cries of dismay all around him but, swimming underwater, Paddle-Whee would not hear them and, if she did surface, they would be blown askew by the flail of the wind.

"She'll get back," Cuspid said, more to reassure himself than the others. "She'll hear the arkle slapping on the waves. It's very quiet under there, whatever's happening above."

"Oh my, oh me," Quiver keened, "she'll be inundulated!"

"Nothing good ever came from travelling on water," Jocko remarked glumly.

What worried Gavin, as much as the loss of Paddle-Whee and the mice, was the thought that they could not hold the rudder steady much longer, come what may. Adderly's constrictive powers would need relief very soon, and even if he could persuade Quiver and the rabbits to add some ballast to the fulcrum-point, the gusting wind, nearing hurricane velocity, would soon emerge the victor in this deadly tug-of-war. Gavin's forelimbs throbbed rebelliously. Soon the muscles would seize up in unbearable cramp.

"There she is!" Cuspid shouted.

Paddle-Whee broke the surface of the water only a few paces to the lee of the arkle. Bucktooth was clinging to her scruff-fur for dear life. Paddle-Whee appeared to be grinning but, surely not, since there was no sign of Petite, who had certainly been drowned. While those on the raft cheered her on, Paddle-Whee made it to the edge of the arkle, riding the waves that rocked it up and down. But she made no move to dig her single forepaw into the nearest log and climb aboard.

"I don't think she's got enough strength left to get up here," Gavin said.

"I'm going in after them," Cuspid said.

"Oh, please don't!" Quiver expostulated. "You'll all be lost in the refuge!"

But Cuspid was already braving the deluge. He surfaced alongside his sister, and uttered a brief word of encouragement or instruction (the din of the blast was now deafening). Then he clawed his way up the bucking side of the raft and stretched his body out full, like a ladder or stile. Her eyes slitted with fatigue, Paddle-Whee inched her way up the swaying incline of her brother's furry back, pausing every second step to gather her strength. Bucktooth's back teeth could be heard chattering above the maelstrom. But he hung on.

It was Quiver who reached down and helped them up onto the railing-log and then into the well of the deck. Paddle-Whee slumped onto her single forepaw. Bucktooth shinnied down her right shoulder. Cold and still terrified, he could find nothing to say – of relief or of sorrow at the loss of his mate.

"Well done, Paddle-Whee," Gavin said to comfort the intrepid beaver. "You did all you could."

Paddle-Whee parted her jaws to reply, but no words came. Petite skittered out in their stead.

* * *

The intensity of the tempest was increasing. The waves grew taller and angrier. Paddle-Whee relieved a grateful Adderly on the rudder, and Cuspid joined Gavin and Cuyler at the tiller. The force of Dante's prediction about "foam and fury" suddenly came home to Gavin, as did her earlier one: "In pieces break to one whole make." Were they all to be made one in death?

"We've sprung a leak!" Hubert cried. He was pointing frantically at a spout of water shooting up between two of the main logs, where the mud-mortar was slowly giving way. "We've got to swim for it!"

Adderly eased his stiff body over and inserted his belly-length between the two logs, thus serving as an elongated cork. The geyser fizzled and died. Seconds later, though, another one spurted up on the opposite side of the barrel.

"Put the mice and the mole on top of the barrel!" Gavin commanded. "A few leaks won't hurt us as long as the water can run out through the slits in the back railings. But we don't want any more bodies overboard."

"My muscles are cramping," Cuspid whispered in Gavin's ear. "I can't hold onto my end of the paddle much longer."

"Quiver, come over here and spell off Cuspid for a while!"

"Madame is getting waterlogged. We might as well be flopping about in the channel."

"Jackrabbits — I mean hares — don't swim!"

"You'll learn," Hubert snapped.

"The paddle's slipping out of the notch, I can't hold it!" Paddle-Whee called out to Trisbert, who put all of his weight down on it in a vain effort to prevent its slipping completely out of the vee.

Just then a vicious wave struck the arkle broadside. The rudder jumped free of the notch and the water. Gavin, Quiver and Cuyler at the helm were spun sideways into a heap.

"I've been obtruded!" Cuyler cried.

Without its rudder, the arkle was left to the mercy of the waves. First it was tossed upwards on a writhing crest, then dashed down into a steep trough. It skidded and careened. It shuddered.

With rapidly depleting energy (and not-a-little discouragement), Paddle-Whee and Trisbert managed to re-establish the rudder in its notch, and Gavin was joined by Cuspid, Quiver and Cuyler at the gyrating tiller. Slowly the arkle steadied, and ploughed once again south-westerly towards Everdark (that is, if the invisible wind had decided not to shift its course in the interim).

But the pounding endured by the momentarily rudderless craft had prompted several more leaks.

However, when Hubert opened his mouth to utter yet another warning, it was not about the arkle leaking:

"One of the vine-ropes has just snapped!"

"And another one!" shrieked Jocko, who jammed both forepaws into his eye-sockets, laid back his handsome ears, and let himself tremble all over.

Gavin could hear the vine-ropes snapping under the relentless strain of wind and wave. Without doubt the arkle was about to break up into a dozen pieces. He gazed helplessly out at the frenzied channel-water. Its raging had not abated one whit but, strangely, the wind on the side of his face was definitely slackening. The storm (if that's what it was buffeting them) was now blowing itself out, it seemed: but too late to be of comfort to the arkle and its passengers. Gavin knew they had no choice. High seas or no, they had to abandon their ship before it exploded in a fury and killed them outright.

"We're going overboard!" Gavin shouted and, ignoring the cries and gasps around him, continued: "Pull the Tallwalker's cooking devices out of the barrel! Quickly, Cuyler! Put the mice and Dante in that pot with the lid, and pitch them into the water. Jocko, take that round pan, squat low in it, and ride the waves into shore. The rest of us know how to swim. The winds are dying down. We should all be able to make it. We'll try to stick together out there, but until we get to Everdark, you may be on your own! Gollah be with you!"

Paddle-Whee and Cuspid flung the rudder away, dove into the water, and helped the others lower the cooking-pot (with lid) and the saucepan into the turbulent waves, steadying them until they were swept off into the mists ahead. Jocko's awesome squeals could be heard long after he had disappeared. Adderly, a strong swimmer, slid into the nearest trough and vanished. The raccoons, cottontails and porcupine left last, paw-paddling along the frothing surface on a course they took to be westerly.

Gavin swung his head around to have a final look at the vessel that had done its best to bring them to the far shore. As he did, the logs that comprised it burst apart on the crest of an immense wave, as if a troll's fist in a blind rage had struck them from below. The Tallwalker's barrel, its lid securely resealed, was tossed backwards in a long arc, seemed to hesitate for a moment, then hit the surface with a ringing slap. It held together, bobbed thrice, and floated jauntily out of sight.

Trisbert and Cuyler, their snouts poking just out of the water, were off to Gavin's right, and Quiver and the rabbits somewhere to his left. But it took all his concentration and ingenuity to keep his head above the whirl and froth of the waves and to persuade his four paws to propel him forward. The breeze, perceptibly lighter now, still blew aslant his right cheek, assuring him that he was aiming south-westerly. Once, he thought he heard Trisbert call out, but when he tried to answer him, his mouth filled with water. After a while, he could only hope that the others, especially the cottontails who were not long-distance swimmers, were doing as he was, and that they would arrive on the shore of Everdark not too far from one another. For the nonce, it was every swimmer for himself.

As he rose to the top of a swell, Gavin caught a glimpse of the trees shrouding the shoreline. The spume and spray had decreased rapidly with the dying wind (though the waves would undulate mountainously for some time yet), so that visibility was now quite fair. It was possible, Gavin mused, that the sun had been boiling down on them all along, obscured only by the fierce

surface-spray: a wind without rain, a tempest with a
target.

At the crest of the next wave, Gavin peered left and
right: no-one. Ahead he spied a yellow patch of sand
beach. He was almost there. He would make it. Would the
others?

When he rose again, the sandy beach was gone. So
were the trees. He shook the water out of his eyes. They
misted up immediately. What was happening now? He
stretched out, rolled on his side, and looked straight up:
no sun, no clouds, no sky. The breeze on his right cheek
waned and died. All around him the air was mysteriously
stilled. Somewhere above he heard the screech of a gull.
So there were birds along this shore, harbingers of
seasons, of life itself. If he could reach them.

Soon, however, he could not tell the trough of a wave
from its crest. He was swimming – who knew in what
direction? – through a dense fog in a serenely rolling,
gradually calming sea. With only the soft swells rocking
under him as a guide, he realized with a growing sense of
panic that he could well be paddling back out to the
middle of the channel or south into the everywhere of
the vast Lake. And it was suddenly so quiet that he could
detect the pitiful rasping of his own breath, and knew
how much his strength had diminished.

In a very short time he would have to jettison the
knapsack that was now becoming a deadly burden: the
very text that had promised salvation would itself have to
be sacrificed. Already he suspected that the pages inside
might be drenched and warped beyond repair, or use. He
was just about to undo one of the straps when a forepaw
struck sand. A following wave lifted him up and away, but
when it settled again, all four of his feet hit bottom. He
scrambled and clawed his way the final few paces up onto

the shore: the dry, hot sand of Everdark's beach. Should he thank Gollah or Jovah?

Still unable to see more than a leg's-length in front of him, Gavin crawled very carefully away from the mellow swish of the waves stroking the beach behind him: he didn't want to stumble blindly into the forest itself. Finally, he felt his body slump sideways into some long grass, and welcomed the sleep that seized him.

* * *

When he woke, the sun was low in the western sky. The fog had lifted. The air was warm and clear, the channel smooth as pond-ice. A sand beach stretched for leagues and leagues to the north and south of him, interrupted by tiny inlets and swollen with grassy dunes. Bees hummed. Grasshoppers buzzed. Overhead a white bird sailed serenely. A gull? Or Noab's dovey-bird?

Behind him he could feel the immense darkness of the legendary Forest. He did not look in that direction. Instead he stared anxiously north and south. He listened for the sound of voices. He climbed to the top of the nearest dune, and looked and listened again.

He was alone. In Everdark.

Book II

Everdark

Chapter 15

Brotherly Love

GAVIN AWOKE – THIRSTY, ACHING, AND STILL ALIVE.

This was not how he had imagined his arrival on Everdark beach. Even when the arkle had broken up, he had envisaged his companions being swept along side by side and inexorably towards the wave-beaten shore, where, dazed but thankful, they would be joyously reunited. Recalling now that his brothers had been swimming to the north of him, he stole cautiously up the shoreline in that direction. His eyes surveyed the beach and its grassy dunes, but seldom strayed to the shadowy edge of the forest. Every once in a while he would peer out at the unrippled channel, hoping against hope. But it appeared he had slept for half the day. Anyone who was going to make it ashore would be here by now.

He was scouring the channel anyway when, improbably, he spotted something metallic glinting in the low rays of the setting sun and struggling to make its way to shore. It was the saucepan they had pressed Jocko into. Without thinking, Gavin plunged into the water and swam out to meet it. With his heart racing, he reached up with a forepaw and gripped its thin edge. The pan tilted towards him.

"Jocko!" he called out.

But the Tallwalker-thing was empty. Poor Jocko, the one "forever lost," had met the death he had foreseen so many times in his worst nightmares. Gavin shuddered, then remembered where he was. He swam slowly back to shore. The saucepan followed, mournfully.

Gavin sat on the beach with his chin on his forepaws. He had been walking north for some time. Without checking, he knew the cooling sun lay close to the horizon along Serpentine Ridge. He shivered. For the first time since he had awakened on Deadwood Island ten days ago, he was deeply afraid. It was not the kind of sudden, instinctive terror – occasioned for instance by things like a Tallwalker's firestick booming behind you in the night – the kind that tremored through you and dissipated. No, this was cold, bone-dense, bloodless fear. Fully in its grip, Gavin was compelled to admit now that it had been the presence of Trisbert with his steadfast loyalty and raw courage that had given him liberty to be brave himself, and the presence of Cuyler and his youthful enthusiasm that had prompted his sworn guardian to be more paternal and more determined in his efforts to bring them all safely home. But now that he was alone, with no-one to watch over and no-one to watch over him, he was as frightened as a rabbit staring down a stoat's throat.

He might have sat there on the beach and let the night swallow him whole, had his stomach not reminded him that he was hungry. And hunger reminded him that he was still alive and that, afraid or not, his lot as a woods-creature was to survive until Gollah – or whoever had supplanted Him – decided he should die. Wearily he got up and trudged towards the forest, keeping his gaze on the ground. He heard the creek before he saw it: off to his right, just over the next dune.

It was a modest little stream, bubbling out of the woods and feeding into the channel. Insects darted across its surface. It was live water flowing out of a living forest. Farther up, there would be fish – trout and chub – and frogs and salamanders: raccoon delicacies. Already he could see how dark it was in there, and surmised how much darker it would be when the sun had fully set. But raccoons were night-prowlers. His plan was to paddle along upstream a short way until he found enough food to satisfy his hunger, then retrace his steps back here to the beach, where he would climb a tree – within sight of the channel – and rest until dawn. When the sun rose, he would take out the Tallwalker's texts and see what he could see. He realized too late that he should have taken them out of the knapsack and let them dry out in the sunlight, but he hadn't. Some leader! Some RA-in-the-making!

The stream was shallow with occasional deep pools, so he was able to walk most of the time, ambling along, as raccoons are wont, with snout down, ears pricked, eyes alert for the slightest movement below the surface of the water. In short order he caught a fingerling trout napping, a complacent chub, and a couple of lounging clams. There was food enough here for a colony of ringtails. He crawled onto the bank of the stream and sat back to open the clams with his teeth and fore-claws. As he did so, he could not help but notice the forest around him.

The trees were enormous, their trunks three times the circumference of the grandest pine or oak in Earthwood. They soared limbless above him for a long while before the first branches leapt laterally out of them, branches that were so interwoven with those from neighbouring trees as to form an impenetrable canopy over the forest floor. Scant sunlight would ever reach it. A permanent gloom would prevail, day or night. He didn't recognize the tree-bark or the strange nuts that littered the mossy, fungus-draped ground about him. The soil itself was very damp. Perhaps the great flood had swept through here and subsided without doing irreparable damage. These titanic trees would not easily be uprooted, and the living things along the forest floor obviously throve in the humid gloom.

Gavin washed the clams and ate them. He began to feel much better. His mind started buzzing with plots and plans again. But first he must get back to the beach and find a secure tree for the night. Best, though, to let the food digest a bit. He would hate to have to run for his life with this weight on his back and this lump in his belly. He closed his eyes. My, but he was tired – again.

* * *

Something splashed against his bare snout. Gavin opened his eyes, expecting to see the wake of a speeding trout. But a trout didn't growl. Instinctively, even before the rush of adrenalin struck, he flipped over to his left, and kept on somersaulting. He heard the scrunch of claws on a mossy rock, smelled the foul breath and rotted fur of some lunging predator. As he came upright, he caught a shadowy glimpse of slavering jaws and a bushy, twitching tail. A wolf. Who, having missed his prey, had tumbled into the creek, splashing and flailing in thwarted rage. The creature was scrambling to its feet, amber eyes ablaze, between Gavin and the way out.

Gavin knew that his best hope for escape lay in his climbing the nearest tree, but that was too far away to risk. So he plunged into the deeper part of the creek and began swimming upstream. It was very dark, and the wolf, not able to see Gavin's protruding muzzle, would have neither image nor scent to follow. When Gavin had put sufficient distance between them, he would wait for an overhanging limb to present itself, then swing up into the thick branches above it, and thence trapeze from tree to tree until the wolf would have no spoor to track and no hint of where his quarry might have alighted. This was one of many such stratagems, recorded in The Book of Coon-Craft and Animal Cunning, that had preserved the raccoon's place at the top of Gollah's hierarchy: brains over brawn.

Having heard the splash, however, the wolf decided to join his victim in the stream, and came floundering vexatiously in Gavin's direction, skidding and knocking its bones against jutting rock and root. Every few seconds it let out a wounded howl, as if it were being throttled. Though frightened, Gavin found that his fear in these circumstances drove him deeper into his instinct for survival: his mind was wonderfully concentrated. He swam steadily and noiselessly, and guessed from the thrashings and yowls behind him that the wolf had little idea how close it actually was. Every few paces, the creature would foolishly scrabble up to one bank and then the other, checking for an exit scent, then plummet back into the ever-deepening waters of the creek.

As he rounded a sharp bend, Gavin saw, just ahead, a thick branch hanging halfway over the stream. Perfect. The wolf hadn't rounded the bend yet and thus would not see Gavin swing up into a convenient tree and vanish without a trace. But Gavin realized too late that the reason the branch was so vivid before him was that a break in the canopy above had permitted a bright slice of moonlight to illuminate both branch and creek. He managed to swing up onto the limb without mishap, but as he was tight-roping along it towards the trunk, the wolf rounded the bend and spotted its prey, flood-lit and vulnerable. It emitted a trumpeting yip, and charged.

Gavin froze. All he had to do was dive back into the water and its camouflaging shadows, but he could not move a muscle. Nor could he take his eyes off the approaching beast. It had a wolf's face all right: pointed muzzle, glistening fangs, lolling tongue, slitted yellow-eyes, gray fur stiffening with hunger-lust. But it was charging him on its hind limbs like a bear on shrivelled feet, and uttering a guttural, groaning howl like no animal Gavin had ever heard. This was no wolf.

Whatever it was would have seized him whole, had its undersized feet not stepped in a hole and caused it to make an ungainly tumble into the water. At the same time, Gavin made a desperate leap from the branch into the creek. In doing so, his left hind-paw got wedged between two smaller branches and, as he fell, it twisted horribly before tearing loose. Gavin shrieked with pain. When he hit the water, he found himself paralyzed. His whole body was shrieking. Fortunately he had landed in a shallow spot, and was able to roll himself onto the far bank. The pain began to ebb a little. He would have to run for it, on three legs like poor Paddle-Whee, for he doubted whether he could swim or climb a tree-trunk quickly enough to escape. He heard the beast lurch to its feet and howl out another unearthly vowel of rage. Perhaps it hadn't seen him.

Soundlessly, Gavin limped into the pitch-blackness of the forest interior, away from the stream towards he knew not what. After a few tentative attempts, he soon adjusted to a three-footed canter. But it was so dark in here that even he, with his night-vision, could see nothing. He bumped into trees and tripped over lichens-slick boulders. And very soon he was lost.

He sat down to rest, and think. He could detect no crashing footsteps behind him. Well, he had apparently put the beast off the scent. For the time being. Now he could possibly climb a tree, awkwardly but safely, and spend the night shivering in its upper branches. After a bit, he was able to make out a stout trunk nearby with several bulbous lumps along its lower length that would act as a sort of ladder and help him climb with only one hind-paw for traction and leverage. Still in pain, he eased over towards it. And came face to face with the beast.

Somehow, trundling over the mossy ground, it had managed to track Gavin in silence. Now it stood before him, its bear-like paws swaying just beyond its flared nostrils, its eyes fierce and merciless, its teeth slobbered and agleam in the dark, as if they had some inner light-source of their own devising. Just as it was about to clamp him in both paws, its jaws widening to tear at his flesh, Gavin noticed a loose lump jiggling obscenely at the back of its neck.

The jaws never closed. Instead they opened even farther to allow a piercing bellow to explode out of them into the ebony air. Gavin tottered backwards with the force of it, and fell. When he looked up, he saw that the beast had been attacked from the rear by some other twisted denizen of this mad forest. The creature had sunk its teeth deeply into the hump, and was hanging on. Far from being a senseless bag of flesh, the hump must have been ripe with nerves, for the beast howled in agony and swatted haplessly at the attached assailant with its front paws. Then, unable to reach it (for the other beast was as small and agile as it was fierce), the wolf-beast began to lurch about blindly in an attempt to crush the other against a low limb or tree-trunk or boulder. Several times it managed to do so but, despite the battering blows it took, the wee-fiend tightened further its death-grip, and the victim howled out its anguish so obstreperously that Gavin felt the forest tremble in sympathy. Finally the wolf-beast and its tormentor went crashing away through the bush, and the piteous cries faded and died.

Gavin could not move. He knew he should climb the nearest tree while he had the chance. But somewhere inside him a voice was whispering to him that the Forest of Everdark was not an abode where ordinary woods-creatures would long survive. Death was going to come, and it would be a terrible going. Why not let it happen now rather than later? If any of his companions had indeed made it to the beach and been tempted, like him, into these woods in quest of food, they too would have been relentlessly tracked down and devoured. Who was he to try and hold out?

Gavin heard a light tread coming his way from the direction in which the two monstrosities had disappeared: the wee-beast, having driven off the competition, was coming back for its prize. Gavin crouched down and closed his eyes. His last thoughts would be of Papa, proud beside RA-Mosah at the top of the High-Ring tree with The Book of Coon-Craft in his hand, his eloquent voice hurling its wise words into the brute face of the storm that had swept them away. All of them.

"You can open your eyes now, Gav."

* * *

"This is not a dream, then?" Gavin said. "It is really you, Bertie. Oh, dear, dear Bertie."

"It's me, Gav," Trisbert said in a faint but familiar voice.

Gavin brushed his forepaws over Trisbert's face and ears. "You made it to the beach. I knew you would."

"Couldn't find anybody . . . looked everywhere . . . waited all day . . . went into the woods . . . found this little stream . . ." Trisbert's voice was growing hoarse and more faint, as if he were trying to shout under water.

"And Cuyler?"

"Don't know . . . thought everybody was gone . . . heard . . . heard this roaring . . ."

"You've been hurt!" Gavin cried, and cursed himself for being so stupid and selfish: it had been Trisbert who had latched onto the wolf-beast's hump, and was battered from tree to tree – unwilling to let go until his brother was no longer in danger, absorbing all those body-blows until the creature had staggered far enough away.

Trisbert moaned, and slumped to the ground. Gavin lifted up his head and leaned down: Trisbert was still breathing – in intermittent, shallow drafts. Gavin ran a forepaw gingerly down Trisbert's side. Though he could not see it, he felt the blood, oozing from a slash just below the shoulder. The beast had taken one swipe at his fleeing tormentor, and made the most of it.

Well, there was now good reason to live: Trisbert needed him, and together, somehow, they would have to find Cuyler, dead or alive. Alert once more – mind and instinct, training and native cunning now resurgent – Gavin crawled partway up the nearest tree, pricked both ears, and listened. Soon the sound of water prattling over stones arrived, just audible but clearly in the direction away from the path of the beast's retreat. Setting the creek's position firmly in his mind, Gavin crawled back down and oriented himself. Then he raised the bulky dead-weight of his brother onto his shoulders (his head resting on the knapsack), and started to walk – on all fours. Every time his left hind-paw touched the ground, Gavin grimaced with the pain, gritted his teeth, and pushed on. The chatter of the creek became more prominent as he struggled with his burden and the excruciating pain – giving him hope that he could hold out long enough to reach the buoyancy of water.

The hoot of an owl and the griding of its wings brought him up short. I'm much too big for you to tackle, he thought, unless the owls here were also gargantuan. The wing-whirr faded, and Gavin staggered ahead, pace by painful pace. Just as he was about to collapse from exhaustion he caught the scent of water, and stumbled forward the final few steps to the creek's edge. He laid Trisbert gently down and anxiously checked his breathing: weak but still there. Next he bent over and tenderly licked the wound with his cleansing tongue. He didn't want the scab forming before he had disinfected the gash. From his probings he estimated that it was long but not deep. It would heal, if Bertie were able to recover from the pummelling his body had taken: it must be one big bruise.

When his own strength returned, Gavin again draped Trisbert over his back, but this time he slipped into the water and the two of them floated with the current downstream towards the mouth of the creek and the safety of the beach. On several occasions Gavin had to scramble precariously over stony sections. And as it neared the channel, the stream grew too shallow for him to float at all. Ahead he could now discern moonlight where the beach would be, and he imagined it glittering on the blue-black water as sweet and beguiling as it had shone on Ambling Creek in Earthwood before the world had upended itself.

Suddenly Gavin found he could not get up. His belly lay pressed against the rocky bottom of the stream. Trisbert's weight was crushing him. His foot throbbed like a ruptured boil. Only a dozen paces more and they would be home-free on the beach! But the icy water rippled past his unmoving form, chilling them both. If he collapsed here and passed out, they would perish of the cold and wet before sunrise.

Just then Trisbert groaned, and his breath started coming in frightful gasps. Gavin heaved himself upright. He felt no pain, no fatigue, no elation as he lunged and lurched forward – and fell snout-first into the welcoming sand of the channel shore (forever after referred to as Desperation Beach).

Sometime later – the moon had advanced a considerable way up the arc of the star-filled sky – Gavin rolled Trisbert onto the warmth of the sand, packed it around him, then curled his own length around Trisbert (as far as it would go): willing his own robust heartbeat into his brother's intrepid and loving body. Together they lay in sibling embrace, as they once had in their mother's nest, until morning.

* * *

Trisbert's wound was scabbing up nicely. His breathing, while weak, was becoming more and more regular; but he did not open his eyes. Oh, how often Gavin had been witness to woods-creatures like this, who, mortally wounded or ill, simply closed their eyes against the world and waited for their breathing to cease. Gavin would have wept if weeping had been of any use.

While seagulls whorled overhead and bass leaped out in the channel, Gavin again stared hopefully north and south along the beach. No sign of anyone, friend or forest-foe. He was not certain what to do: how long would it be before one beast or another sensed their presence here on the open shore? Trisbert would not die alone and friendless, however: of that he was certain. Right now, though, Gavin needed food. So he decided to slip a few paces up the creek to garner a minnow or two or perhaps scratch in the embankment for earthworms. And he would do so without letting Trisbert out of his sight. He tested out his injured foot: sore, but not cripplingly so. Good.

He was sidling into a shadowy section of the stream when he realized with a start that this was not the same creek he had followed into the forest last night. He and Trisbert must have made their escape on a second creek, perhaps the very one that Trisbert himself had used to begin his own quest for food and kin. Another thought struck Gavin almost simultaneously: he was now on a different patch of the beach than he had been on yesterday! Maybe he ought to go back and reconnoitre the area more thoroughly. Whisking a couple of tasty minnows into his mouth and chewing on them ruminatively, Gavin trotted back to Trisbert. His breathing was still regular and a little less shallow.

Satisfied that his brother was all right for the moment, Gavin walked southward towards a large dune set back a fair distance from the shoreline. The reason for this quickly became apparent: it was part of a good-sized inlet whose sandy stretch had been hidden from his view when he had made his earlier, perfunctory survey. He started to climb up the near slope of the dune, and had not quite reached its summit when he thought he heard voices – hushed but excited. And dangerously close.

He paused. Had some wolf-beasts and their kin on the far side of the dune heard him climbing? Were they lying in wait to ambush him? If he tried to scramble back down, especially with his stiffening hind-paw, he would make even more noise and attract instant attention. What if they then spotted Trisbert, defenceless a mere dozen paces away? He concluded it was best to creep around the slope of the dune facing the forest, where he would make a deliberate scrabbling noise and then flee into the bush to draw the beasts away from the beach and Trisbert. It was the least he could do.

One tentative step at a time, he inched sideways until he was almost halfway around the dune. With his head down he didn't see the other creature (also inching), who had just poked its own snout into view.

"Oh! Pardon my obtrusion!" said the other creature.

Chapter 16

Gavin the Great

GAVIN HARDLY KNEW WHOM TO HUG FIRST. Cuyler, of course. And Quiver (carefully). The rest of the troop was arrayed along the slope of the dune, having been alerted by Quiver's cry and whoop of delight. Gavin was speechless.

"We thought you'd been drowned," Quiver said, "swallowed up in the spiny deep."

"Oh, Gav, it's wonderful to see you," Cuyler said, clapping his brother on the shoulder in the familiar manner. Then he stared past him and asked, "Where's Tris?"

Gavin finally found his voice, and said loud enough for the others to hear, "Trisbert's over by the creek. He'll need a little assistance to get over here." Very quietly he said to Cuyler, "He's been hurt – badly."

A great cheer went up from the troupe below them.

"Cuspid and I will fetch Trisbert," Paddle-Whee said, "while you come on down and have a gander at what we've found."

* * *

What the others had found was a spacious ruins of some kind, a rectangle of broken and jagged stone – in most places as tall as a rearing bear – which would offer protection from the wind and the sun (in its shady corners). There was even a gap in one wall that would serve as a convenient entrance-way. Trisbert was carried gently inside and propped comfortably in a shaded spot carpeted with marsh grass. Much concern was expressed about his health but, for the time being, Gavin thought it prudent to tell his friends only that he and Trisbert had encountered some trouble the previous night and that he was confident that his brother would be fine after some desperately needed rest. But Cuyler was not the only one to stare anxiously at the slash on Trisbert's shoulder, now scabbed and wizened – like a grimace.

"I want to hear your stories first," Gavin said.

"There's really not much to tell," Cuyler said. "When we jumped into the channel, it was so misty and wild that we soon began to lose sight of one another. You and Trisbert just vanished on me. But Quiver and Hubert and Renée – " (here, those named smiled at Gavin as if they were being introduced to him for the first time) " – were close together, and somehow we managed to keep close for most of the way in. A little ahead of us we could hear Jocko keening in his Tallwalker saucepan and Dante chanting in a weird voice."

Here, Dante felt compelled to interrupt the narrative:

"To be weird or strange I've often been thought,

But not for chanting in a hollow pot!"

"But then the wind dropped and the fog arrived," Cuyler continued. "We stuck together by listening for each other's painful breathing, but we had no idea whether we were still moving in the right direction."

Hubert picked up the story at this point, with a nod from Cuyler. "Quiver and Cuyler, I must emphasize on behalf of Madame et moi-même, swam deliberately slowly so that we rabbits, as less accomplished swimmers, should not lag behind and be lost. However, though compact of body, we are capacious of ear. Renée and I (Madame was first to do so) could suddenly hear a tinny, rattling sound ahead of us. 'It's the lid on the mice's kettle,' Renée remarked immediately. ''Tis so,' I responded. And surmising (correctly) that the Tallwalker's kettle would ride the last of the rolling swells onto the shore, we determined to follow it. And Cuyler and Quiver followed us."

"As soon as the wind died and it got quiet in the fog," Quiver said, "we called out for you and Trisbert. We set up a verifiable consternation of yells and shouts."

"But what made the lid continue to rattle after the wind died?" Gavin asked.

"Dante doing her death-chant," Hubert said, "and Bucktooth and Petite trying to join in."

"And then when we landed on the beach," said Cuyler, carrying the tale forward, "we found the kettle and its occupants safe and sound – "

"Safe and sounding!" Hubert interjected with an affectionate glance at Dante.

"And lolling in the sand nearby were Adderly and the twins."

"Well, swimming underwater in a tempest is somewhat of an advantage," Cuspid grinned.

"We had planned to help the others find their way," Paddle-Whee said, "but we could barely see because of all the sand roiling down there and, whenever we surfaced, the waves and general din made it impossible for us to see if we could guide any of the others in. Then the fog came."

"I swam the whole way underwater," Adderly said. "It's the optimal way to navigate, you know, though we reptiles are seldom given credit for it."

"But where's Jocko?" Cuyler said with a guilty start. "We thought he was behind you."

The animals, who had been in a jocular, upbeat mood ever since the arrival of Gavin and the safe bestowal of Trisbert, went suddenly silent. No-one spoke for a long, solemn moment. When Gavin finally informed them of the empty saucepan floating in the channel and the inescapable conclusion to be drawn, the silence deepened. The troupe had suffered its first loss. Dante had been right: their collective triumph had come at a high price.

"How tragical," Quiver managed to say, "that Jocko should drown and the likes of Wylee survive the channel-waters unscythed."

"Wylee?" Gavin said, taken aback.

"We spotted your leather-pouch on the beach over near the mouth of the creek," Hubert said. "It was empty. But when I reached down and tried to salvage it, a wave came suddenly and washed it back into the channel."

"Wylee must have thrown the two stones overboard," Cuspid grinned, savouring the thought.

"We saw his tracks leading into the forest," Paddle-Whee said.

"So Wylee will know that we still have The Book of Coon-Craft," Cuspid reasoned.

"Well, if he has plans to return for it – provided he hasn't already been eaten – he'll need a lot more than a foxy deception to get it again," Hubert said.

"I doubt very much if we'll see his face again," Gavin said.

Thus reassured, the others now urged Gavin to tell his story. He did so by giving them a judiciously edited version of the horrific events of the night past. Even so, Hubert felt obliged to cover Renée's ears at certain points, for which courtesy he received a jab in the ribs.

"How in the name of Gollah will we ever make our way to Serpentine Ridge past wolf-beasts like that?" Cuspid mused when Gavin had finished.

"Where the Warlows and Karkajim are praying that we do," Hubert sighed.

"Our whole situation is impostrous!" Quiver added, and Gavin found himself hard-pressed to find a more apt epithet to describe their plight.

* * *

Having made sure that Trisbert's breathing was still regular, Gavin asked to be taken on a tour of the ruins. It turned out that the main contingent of the troupe had come ashore very near the mouth of a creek, and when several of them set off to look for strays, they discovered on the other side of the first dune they crossed a perfect shelter in which to catch their breath and which they might utilize as a base for any excursions farther afield.

Gavin now brought his full attention to bear upon the details of their discovery. The stones that comprised the four walls, though chipped and roughened along the top now, were too neatly sculpted to be natural. And the presence of a number of shards scattered both inside and outside the perimeter indicated that the walls had once been much higher. Also, the littered bits of spongy wood and iron sprouts suggested that the shelter had once had a wooden roof. Unquestionably they were in the remains of a Tallwalker building (what Papa called their house-habitat), one that – long ago – had served as a permanent abode. It was not the great flood that had ravaged these long-rotted boards and crumbling stones, Gavin thought: they were very, very old. Sometime in the distant past Tallwalkers had lived in or beside the Forest of Everdark. But why?

The surface of the habitat's interior was now a pleasantly matted floor of marsh grasses and mossy nooks. Bits and pieces of iron scattered about may have been tools or instruments of some kind (perhaps Dante would be able to explain the function of some of them). Just before they went out to survey the exterior, Paddle-Whee pointed to an object placed on end in a shadowy alcove facing the forest: a rusted, ancient firestick.

"We wanted to show you this before we told you what happened to us before sundown yesterday," she said. "You tell him, Cuspid."

"Well, after we all had a nap, we decided that we should look for food first, then organize a search for you and the others. Adderly found frogs galore in the creek. Paddle-Whee, Quiver and I gorged ourselves on some tender-looking willow-shoots along its banks, and the mice, rabbits and mole found unexpected delicacies just beyond this wall – "

"We'll show him that in a minute," Hubert said. "Kindly return to the main point."

But Cuspid was not about to relinquish the limelight hastily. "Well, we did then try to organize a search, but – I am chagrined to say – we were not all that clever when it came to arranging the kind of matters that are best arranged when one has an experienced arranger to – "

"We needed you," Renée said sweetly to Gavin.

"That's about it,' Cuspid said. "But we were still in the midst of discussing – "

"Arguing," Hubert said.

"Inquisitioning," suggested Quiver.

" – when we heard a terrible roaring sound from somewhere in the forest, as if two wild beasts were locked in a death-struggle. We were petrified, as you can imagine. What would we do if one of them heard us or smelled us in here? We had been foolishly noisy in our . . . discussion. Most of us could hit the water again, but that would mean abandoning Bucktooth, Petite and Dante."

"We told them to go ahead," Bucktooth piped up. "No monster would be interested in eating tidbits like us."

"Besides which," Petite added, "we had lots of places to hide."

"It was Paddle-Whee who thought of the firestick," said Cuspid proudly. "Once we decided to stick together – after all, how long could we swim out there in the open water with a carnivore stalking us from the beach? – we had to find some way of defending ourselves. Quiver suggested rolling stones off the wall onto the beast's head when it came in after us. Hubert proposed that Adderly drape himself along the west wall and drop onto it from above and, while it was tangled up in his coils, we would scratch its eyes out."

"If it actually possessed oracular orbs," Quiver said.

"You are wandering from the point again," Hubert said.

"Yes, you're philandering all over the place!"

Gavin began to understand why few decisions had been arrived at yesterday.

"Paddle-Whee guessed that these Everdark Warlows might be afraid of a firestick. Would the Tallwalkers who owned it long ago not have loosed its venom upon them? So, with Adderly's help we manoeuvred the firestick up onto that ledge there (after considerable discussion as to which end should be pointed outward), aimed it at the forest, and waited."

Hubert could bear it no longer: "To cut to the quick of the tale, we very soon saw a gigantic shadow stretch itself out of the woods, and behind it came lumbering a creature of dreadful mien and contorted form."

"What did it look like?" Gavin asked.

Monstrous! Terrifying! Horrible! Ghastly! and other unhelpful descriptions poured into Gavin's ears. Someone suggested it was a three-toed Karkajim driven by the flood down into Everdark from its phantom eyrie on Serpentine Ridge. (But the creature that had stared Gavin in the eye and battered brave Trisbert within an inch of his life was no refugee from a nightmare.)

"It was a sort of cougar," Paddle-Whee said hesitantly, while the others either nodded assent or shook their heads in disagreement. "A wildcat of some kind, with cat's eyes and sharp cat's teeth. But it had a bushy tail and it yapped and howled like a coyote."

"And its front legs were shorter than the hind ones, so it kind of waddled instead of loping like a cougar or coyote."

"But when it saw the firestick waving at it from the ledge, it stopped dead in its tracks," Paddle-Whee said. "You could see it sniffing at the breeze, knowing something animal and edible was near, and its drool was slopping over its chin – but there was cold fear in its eyes."

"That's when Paddle-Whee smacked that chunk of wood there against the Tallwalker's kettle," Cuspid said, "and to our amazement and delight the beast-thing waddled away into the forest as fast as its misaligned legs would carry it."

"And we've neither seen nor heard of any others since," Hubert said.

Gavin congratulated them for their courage and their ingenuity.

When they stepped outside, Gavin was surprised to see that from the southern wall of the dwelling a low stone-barrier, square in shape, stretched out for some distance in that direction. More surprising still, the ground within its perimeter was not a sandy beach swaying with thin grasses, but a rich loam, part of which was covered with dense green grass and clover, and a larger part of which was hummocked with straight rows of wild legumes and tubers – some familiar, others strange. The rabbits had already made some inroads in the two rows of leaf lettuce. Although choked with competing weeds, the wild carrot, beans and other exotics had survived, it appeared to Gavin, from season to season on their own merit. That they had once been arranged and tended by the hand of a Tallwalker was also evident.

("The sacred Book tells us, RA-Mosah had told his pupils solemnly, "that the Tallwalkers, at Zeebub's behest, corrupt Gollah's natural bounty by stealing its seed and planting it in sterile ranks surrounded by stone ramparts to keep the animals from enjoying what has been given freely to all His creatures." "They call them gardens," Papa had added.) Here and there in this "garden," random flowers raised their vermilion or yellow petals to be caressed by the sea-breeze or flattered by drowsy bees.

"Food! Here and over at the creek, for as long as we need it," Hubert said with deep satisfaction.

As if to illustrate the point, the mice and Dante disappeared into the grass and, moments later, into the earth under it. Bucktooth poked his head up and out of a burrow he had just made and said, "If you need us, just have one of the rabbits drum three times above us with its big hind feet."

"And we've got the Tallwalker's barrel, too," Cuspid said. "It's over there beside the wall facing the shore. We can roll it inside, if you like."

They had everything, Gavin thought – but Jocko, and Trisbert restored to life.

* * *

After everyone had had a good feed, Gavin gathered the troupe together inside the house-habitat. He unstrapped the knapsack and laid it on the ground – unopened. In a private moment sometime soon he would have to take the papers out and see how much damage had been done. At this moment, though, he was expected to resume his leadership, dubious as that had been. Even now he was not sure whether the parable of Noab and the arkle had been a gift from the gods or a fiendish trick to undo them all.

"Friends, we have been blessed by Gollah," he began, tapping the knapsack with one hypocritical paw. "We have crossed Heartbreak Channel. We have found each other. We mourn the loss of Jocko. We pray for the swift recovery of our dear Trisbert. And we have been led — divinely, I aver — to this wonderful sheltering-place. I propose that we establish ourselves here for the time being. We will bring food inside these protective walls in case we are besieged. We'll make nests of our own kind in here. When Trisbert has regained his full strength — for we shall require his courageous spirit and stout body — I will organize us into reconnoitring parties. For we must find a way to penetrate the Forest of Everdark, safely and surely. At the moment we have no guide except the looming presence of the Ridge, whose own terrors we must also negotiate if we are to return to Earthwood . . ."

Even as he listened to the drone of his own voice mouthing platitudes and soothing homilies to his world-weary troupe, another part of Gavin's mind was generating other, more profound thoughts. He was thinking, oh how sadly, of those loved ones he would likely see no more: Papa and RA-Mosah and the dozens of soft-masked raccoon-faces — friends and kin and elders — that had been part of his world and his growing up into it; and lost, too, would be the stories Papa told at twilight or dawn that brought back to life those faces already departed: dearest Mama and poor Aunt Rootha and Uncle Sylva whose lives had been cut short by the casual cruelties of the Tallwalkers.

He was thinking also that Jocko would never get to see his intended, Sprightleg, who even now might be waiting somewhere far away and alien to be found and rescued.

Nor would Jocko ever again be able to assert the independence that marked his breed, unless there was need for it among the spectres of North Holy. Nor would he, Gavin, ever again know the joy and challenge of the elder-school: the wise and patient teachings there, the shy glances that passed between him and Tee-Jenn, elder-daughter of Grayfur and Sleekcoat. (Though it was true that Cuspid and Paddle-Whee had observed her clinging with her parents to a tree upon the floodwaters, was it not? Dare he allow himself to hope that she might still be . . . ?)

He was thinking, moreover, that, should the troupe somehow make it back to Earthwood, where would any of them find mates to start the world up again? (Noab had been luckier: with Jovah's connivance he had brought the animals along on the journey.) And, dwarfing all other sorrows, was the loss of The Book of Coon-Craft and Animal Cunning and the RAs who could deliver its wisdom to the dominion of the animals.

He was puzzling, too, over Dante's prophetic riddles: the fact that they had indeed broken in pieces only to be made one again, that in the maelstrom of the channel waves they had been turned round about and inside out only to end up on the same creek on the same beach, and that in the darkest dark his valiant brother had been able to see and save him (though their chances of stumbling upon a king in this vestibule of Zeebub were nil, nor was there any brother's son or nephew to kill him blessedly, as Dante had also prophesied).

He was wondering as well where Gollah was hiding – and why, so far, it had been the corrupted things of the demon Tallwalkers that time and again had saved them all from certain death: the life-restoring cache of food at the encampment on Deadwood, the discarded fragment of The Hollow Babble that just happened to contain the story of a flood and miraculous arkle (told in a Gibberlish mysteriously familiar), the paddle-rudder that had kept their vessel from spinning off the southern edge of creation, the cooking kettle that had ferried the mice and mole safely to shore and rattled its lid to guide the others in, and now this house-habitat and garden and monster-frightening firestick!

And, above all, he was thinking that, if Trisbert did not recover, he could not bear to carry on.

". . . and we shall succeed in this new endeavour in the same way and for the same reason that we have succeeded to this point in our arduous journey: by drawing upon our individual skills and strengths for the common good in a just and united cause. Gollah be with us!"

Gavin's oration touched the animals deeply. For a moment no-one moved. The entire assemblage rose as one.

"Three cheers for Gavin!" Cuspid shouted.

But Cuyler (and Trisbert, who had just awakened, wondered for a bit where he was, then toddled over to join his brother) shouted even louder:

"Three cheers for Gavin the Great!"

Chapter 17

King Arthro and the Invincible Sword

GAVIN THE GREAT SOUGHT OUT A SHADED BOWER under the shadow of the east wall of the house-habitat, next to the barrel they had salvaged from the dead Tallwalker's camp and had now dragged inside. (Only the firestick had been left behind, where the humanoid had dropped it in his despair.) The sun was nearing its high point, was warm against the stones of the ruins, but it was not, Gavin noticed with some satisfaction, the searing, unseasonal sun that had bewildered them on their journey across Deadwood Island. Whatever calamity had befallen Dante's beloved Brightleaf and transformed it into a wasteland – jarring loose the sequence of the seasons ordained by Gollah since the Beginning of Things – it had not laid as catastrophic a hand upon the Forest of Everdark. Not thirty paces from where he sat huddled and meditating, there was a living woods – with streams abounding in trout and chub – where the everyday drama of life and death was being played out, a drama that was the lot of all who belonged to the order of Dame Nature. That the animal creatures who apparently inhabited its grim corridors were monstrous in the eyes of those from Earthwood was neither here nor there. Except, of course, that somehow Gavin the Great was expected to find a safe passage through such dangers, after which only the perils of Serpentine Ridge and its phantom menace would stand between him and home.

Gavin brushed these shivery thoughts from his mind. Now that he was certain that Trisbert was on the road to recovery and before the cougar-beast decided to renew its assault from the forest-edge, Gavin knew that he must take this opportunity to come up with some sort of plan – first to insure the immediate safety of the troupe that had chosen to elevate him to its leadership and, secondly, to devise a set of actions that would in the least give this motley collection of woods-creatures the semblance of doing something that might get them back to Earthwood. In short, he had to provide hope where all seemed most hopeless. But of course each one of his followers fervently believed in magic, in the divine superiority of the clan coon, in the imperishable wisdom accumulated and faithfully recorded in The Book. If he were to tell them the truth – that The Book had been lost in the flood – they would abandon all hope, whatever clever plan their leader might produce. What, then, to do?

Use your brain, Gavin said sternly to himself (though he heard Dante emit a responsive squeak nearby), because that is what Gollah gave to every raccoon from the most humble to the most holy. Start with the positive. Well, they had survived the crossing of Heartbreak Channel with the loss of only Jocko – not counting Wylee, who seemed to have reached Everdark on his own (though how long he might last in that carnivores' country was anybody's guess). They had access to food suited to each species within the troupe. They had shelter of sorts in this broken-down habitat on the beach. They had turned aside the first attack upon it by using the threat of the Tallwalker firestick they had found nearby. They could eat, drink, rest, keep watch, and grow strong enough to brave whatever perils lay between them and Earthwood.

Which reminded Gavin of the negatives in their situation. It was clear that without his firm hand on the controls of the troupe, its members would squabble and dither and be tempted to forsake the covenant they had sworn to uphold until their return should be accomplished. So, although he did not feel in any way that he deserved to be hailed as Gavin the Great, he realized that it was necessary to continue the fiction that he was invincible and was being guided by the magical words upon the pages tucked in his knapsack. More practically, he would have to find a way to systematically explore the regions of Everdark in order to discover a passage through the granite outcrops of Serpentine Ridge – if such a throughway existed. But how? Even the valiant Trisbert had come close to perishing in the jaws of one the forest's innumerable monsters.

Unable to think his way further, Gavin opened the backpack and let its contents spill out in front of him. If their own sacred Book had been lost, then perhaps – despite all he had been taught and had observed in his brief time on Earthwood – he would have to turn again to the demon lore of Zeebub's henchmen: the dreaded Tallwalkers.

First he picked up the battered fragment of The Hollow Babble. He skimmed over the story of Noab and the Arkle, hoping for some further parable he could adapt or use. But the fragment stopped just as Noab and his mated pairs touched down upon dry land. Gavin could see where dozens of pages had been ripped out. Had the dying Tallwalker torn them out in some sort of rage? Had the book's prophecies proved to be false? Had its sayings and commandments been lies? Gavin noticed, however, that the ruptured pages had been in the middle of what must have been a volume much thicker than The Book of Coon-Craft. Luckily a few dozen parchment-sheets remained attached near the end. Gavin held his breath, and flipped them open.

They were blank. Not a single scribble of Gibberlish. One by one he flipped back through them. Nothing. But a raccoon's five toes are the nimblest of all Gollah's creatures, and Gavin's soon sensed that one of the pages seemed thicker and heavier than the others. Using one of his claws with a dexterity his father would have admired, Gavin picked at the thick page until it slowly divided itself in two. And there on the inside surfaces he spotted what had to be Tallwalker writing.

On one page he saw what he took to be letters in the Gibberlish tongue. He stared hard at them, as he had done with those that had risen up and brought the story of Noab to life. But no words grew together out of these squiggles. He moved partway into a shaft of sunlight nearby and held the document up to the blazing light. Still, the squiggles refused to speak. He sighed back against the barrel. And, without much optimism, turned his attention to the facing page. More squiggles, of course, but around and amongst them sat a series of thin lines − curves, circles, a square or two, a cross, and a great many curlicues that might have been poorly formed letter "n's." Again, he stared hard at the strange markings, blocking out all competing thoughts in his head as RA-Mosah and Papa had taught him whenever he attempted to interpret the runes and lexical enchantments of The Book of Coon-Craft. Suddenly, his mind emptied, and the blood-thump of his heart faded away. Soon a gauzy, mesmerizing mist began to swim across the path of his vision — between it and the scratchings on the page. Then, without warning, it started to lift itself, and shred, and vanish as silently as it had arisen. And in a single, blinding flash, he knew what he was looking at!

It was a diagram, what RA-Mosah had called a map, something the Tallwalkers were fond of making to guide them from tree to tree because they were too stupid to do so on their own. But a map of what? Gavin continued to stare, in desperate hope. The n-like squiggles began to sway, and he was forced to blink to try and hold them still. It didn't work. Annoyed at his failure to maintain his trance, he squeezed his eyes shut, then slowly opened them again. The n-squiggles steadied. And began once again their irritating swing and sway.

Waves. They were swaying like waves because that's what they were — quill-scratched wavelets to suggest to the inept Tallwalkers where the waters were. And, here, they were surrounding something that wasn't water: but land.

Now he knew precisely what he was seeing, what the dead Tallwalker had drawn on one of the blank pages at the back of his Hollow Babble. And the scribbling on the page opposite was, he was sure now, the fellow's final, pathetic effort to record his own thoughts as hunger gnawed at him and his flesh began to melt away from his bones. But he had been unable to quill the letters clearly enough for Gavin to interpret them, however hard he stared. The map, however, was as clear as a cardinal's call to the first hint of dawn-light. It showed him the Lake of Waters Unending curled around the length of land that harboured Earthwood and Everdark, with the wriggling granite-and-limestone terror of Serpentine Ridge forever dividing them. And the circle to the east in its midst was surely Deadwood Island. If so, then the cross-mark opposite it on this shore was the Tallwalker abode they were squatting in. There was much more on the map, but for the moment it remained indecipherable.

Suddenly, Gavin's heart thudded against his chest, and the trance was broken.

* * *

"Gav?"

It was Cuyler, edging around the barrel.

"It's all right," Gavin said. "You're not interrupting me."

"Tris is sound asleep. He's gonna be fine."

"I never doubted it," Gavin lied.

"Quiver and I have propped the firestick up on the wall in case the monster comes at us again. Everybody else is snoozing."

"I won't be much longer," Gavin said, aware that Cuyler's "snoozing" remark was meant to warn him that the others were anxious to hear from their anointed ruler. But wisdom, whatever its source, could not be hurried.

"I'll tell them," Cuyler said. But he did not leave.

"Well, Cuy, what is it?"

Cuyler bit his lip, but seeing the look in his brother's eye, he said hesitatingly, "Some of the troupe think we should just stay here."

"I was afraid of that. And in a way it makes sense, doesn't it?"

"Oh, no!" the youngest coon cried, lifting himself up to his full height. "We've got to get back to Earthwood. Papa and RA-Mosah will be expecting us!"

"Don't worry. I believe that too, little brother. But remember that we woods-creatures know when to die, and how to do so. What we must do, above all other things, is convince our fellows that now is not the time and here is not the place, as cozy and secure and food-bountiful as it might seem."

"And you can do that, can't you, Gav?"

Gavin smiled, and taking that as a "yes," Cuyler vanished, leaving the great one to his greatness.

* * *

What Gavin was hoping was that somewhere on the Tallwalker's map would be information that might lead them to a passage through Everdark and over Serpentine ridge. But he realized that the markings would only start to mean something to him when he himself, with the help of the troupe, acquired more details of the terrain that surrounded them. For example, the squirming lines running through Everdark could be creeks or rocky ridges. And several of the larger blobs could represent mounds or hills or even valleys or caves. If they could just manage a foray or two into Everdark to confirm Gavin's guesses, then perhaps the entire landscape of Forest and Ridge would be revealed to them – and a safe passage to Earthwood.

Thus had Gavin the Great begun to reason, and to formulate a possible plan of action. But there was still the more pressing business of motivating the members of the troupe, with all their differences and conflicting needs. With a sigh, he turned to the book he had not yet thumbed, the one that Papa had salvaged from the Tallwalker's wrecked doomsmobile many annuals before: Tales of Arthro. Papa must have had a reason to have kept such a forbidden document, to have secretly brought it out into the moonlight, to have suffered alone (and afraid perhaps) the agonies of cracking its Gibberlish code, and finally to have risked his own future and that of his elder-son by letting the lad sit on his knee and help him turn its sacrilegious pages one by one until the black magic of the Tallwalkers' scribble-tongue had unwillingly and unbeknownst entered the boy's head.

Again and again, RA-Mosah had assured the elder-sons and elder-daughters in their schooling that the Tallwalkers were universally evil, the devil-enemies of Gollah, and that the woods-creatures and their clan-coon leaders had been put in the world to keep pure the laws of Dame Nature he had provided for their benefit. They in turn were to abstain from all contact with these contaminating demons. In particular, RA-Mosah had warned them that the Tallwalkers had, in olden times before the ascendancy of the woods-creatures, concocted fantastic stories of their own derring-do and their role in the creation of the world and its working-out. But they were all lies, perverse deceptions designed to please the baby-Tallwalkers and baffle Gollah's chosen ones, should they ever grow careless and unwary. If so, then why had Papa not only kept these subversive tales, but tried to pass their perversions on to his son?

Gavin shuddered as he turned to the first page of Tales of Arthro. It was a shudder of fear, but also of anticipation. He thought he heard the sweet shiver of Papa's voice rippling through the evening branches of the

High-Ring tree. His father was dead: that much he knew. But Papa had left him this, hadn't he?

With growing confidence, he began reading.

* * *

At the insistence of the others, Gavin stood on one of the four-legged platforms to address the assembled troupe. He waited patiently while the mice and mole were placed on a similar chair beside him so that they could see and hear as well as the larger animals. Gavin could detect in their faces the depth of their hope and their simple faith in his RA-like powers. And behind this, he knew all too well, lay the distinct possibility that if he were to disappoint them during the next few minutes in which he had their rapt attention, they would revert instantly to their ancient animal ways – and one by one be doomed. Trisbert was awake, but had not taken up his usual position beside his leader, nor did he have to summon up strength enough to call for silence, for nobody dared speak. The wavelets from Heartbreak Channel slapped happily on the beach a few paces away, and a bright little breeze ruffled the fur around Gavin's mask.

Gavin cleared his throat and began: "I have spent the past little while poring over the ancient texts rescued by Gollah's grace from the devastation of the great flood. By the most incredible stroke of luck, I came across a chapter which I had not, in my school days, been privy to as yet, and to which RA-Mosah made no reference. It appears to be the oldest and, I presume, the wisest of the elder-stories."

Several of the listeners nodded enthusiastically at this smoothly delivered lie.

"I have studied it carefully, and have come to the conclusion that it contains within its fabulous tales and adventuresome saga, the means of our salvation – chapter and verse." (As he said these words, he suddenly recalled another of Dante's rhyming prophecies: In alien tongue thy hopes be sung.).

Such was the clamour of approval that followed upon this proclamation that no-one noticed the proclaimer blushing furiously.

"We knew you wouldn't let us down, didn't we, chérie?" Hubert cried to his mate and, through her ready smile, to the others.

"Tell us what we must do," said Paddle-Whee in her customary straightforward manner, "and we'll get it done."

"That I shall do," Gavin replied, "in due course. But first I have much to explain and interpret so that you will understand the meaning of any course of action decided upon."

"You've got a story to tell, I hope!" Cuspid said to the satisfaction of those nearby, including at least two of the rodents on their plateau.

"In a way, I have. It's the story told in an ancient chapter of The Book I've been deciphering during your naptime." And thus, while his audience sat back on their haunches, as Woods-Creatures will whenever a tale is about to be spun for their pleasure and enlightenment, Gavin recounted the marvellous and death-defying feats of King Arthro and his Knaves of the Round Tablet. They heard about the princeling who was raised in secret by the wizard, Merlah, with his cousin, Sir Kain, and how they travelled through ever-dark woods to the place where stood a magic swordstick imbedded in a rock, harder than the granite of Serpentine Ridge. And the one who could pull the swordstick free from its stone-prison would be hailed supreme ruler of his kind. Placed there by Gollah, and named Hex-Calibre, it had defied all attempts thus far. But young Arthro removed it with the single flick of a wrist, aided of course by the wizard's magic. And in spite of his young years, he had been made ruler of his world.

When Gavin paused to catch his breath and his evolving thoughts, no-one dared interrupt. And soon they were once more enthralled by what came next (it had dawned on more than one listener that the youngish prodigy in the story bore more than a little resemblance to their own nominee for rulership). Arthro, it appeared, ruled over a divided and troubled land. Raiders from the outside, called Sacksons, ravaged their borders with all the ferocity of Tallwalkers stalking deer. His own followers, alas, were given to arguing amongst themselves, preferring to hunt and feed their own kind rather than help their neighbours. Then one day Arthro got a brilliant idea. He called together the leaders of each tribe and territory in Anguishland, and seated them around him in a way that was both cunning and winning.

"From this point henceforth," Gavin said, imitating as best he could what he assumed to be the voice of the mighty Arthro, "you shall be called my Knaves, and the circle around which I have seated you shall be known as the Round Tablet. Our land will be governed only by the laws and decisions which we make together around this sacred circle. I will lead you into battle, and provide advice as needed when you are sent abroad to carry out your duties across the far hills and dales of our blessed country. If we act as one and if we remain true to the principles of the Round Tablet, we shall never be defeated or go wanting. No enemy can withstand the power of Hex-Calibre. But our success and our prosperity depend upon absolute loyalty and purity of purpose. And these shall be tested again and again by those who envy us and wish us to be brought low."

These remarks were greeted with jaw-dropping awe. Where would they, in their own need, find such Knaves? Such an invincible swordstick?

Gavin sensed their misgivings, and plunged relentlessly ahead. He turned to a prop he had retrieved from the dead Tallwalker's barrel. "Gollah has placed before us a swordstick as potent as Hex-Calibre. I found it lying beside me as I read." He held up before them an elongated leather container of some sort, out of the end of which protruded a thick, twig-like appendage, fashioned of animal bone. Gavin felt the general shudder of his fellows at the sight of such a ghastly and profane use of a body-part by the ruthless raiders from the south.

"Awful as this perversion might be," Gavin said, swallowing hard, "it is still a sign to us from Gollah. Behold!" With a magisterial flourish, he reached down, grasped the bone protuberance in his right forepaw, made several grimacing attempts to pull it free from its casing, and then at the third effort pretended to stagger back and almost topple off his platform. In his grip there gleamed, steady and dazzling in the sunlight, a silver-bladed swordstick!

"Hex-Calibre," breathed Hubert, and was undecided whether he should shield his lady's eye or his own.

"Yes!" Gavin cried, looking as awe-struck as he could manage.

The animals drew back, frightened but unable to look away. Finally, Quiver said, "But you are already our pointed leader, O Great One."

"True, but I have not yet the sterling Knaves I require to give the invincible sword of Gollah its strength and purpose," Gavin said solemnly.

The puzzled assembly glanced here and there around them, expecting, it seemed, further divine interventions. Before they could say or do anything more, however, Gavin leapt boldly off his platform, kicked it over into a corner, strode to the centre of the large space they occupied, and placed the point of Hex-Calibre into the dirt that had blown in and over the floor of the alien habitat. Striding as if his motion were being guided by powers beyond him, Gavin drew a continuous line in the dirt until he met it again where he had begun. He had described a perfect circle, as fine and remarkable as the one formed by the circumference of RA-Mosah's High-Ring tree in Earthwood.

Gavin leaned upon the swordstick, and spoke thus: "This is our Round Tablet, as the elder-story foretold." (And Dante had uncannily echoed in her "Circles devise of the lowly wise.") "I shall consent to be your leader in battle and your spiritual guide. Around this Tablet, I shall gather my Knaves and their Squirelings. We will swear a solemn oath to Gollah – who has now sanctioned all that we shall choose to do or be required to do – regarding our agreed-upon principles, and then proceed to work out a plan of action for the triumphant return to Earthwood!"

Everyone now peered at the Round Tablet, and tried to imagine a dozen or more bravehearts seated at its circumference. Hubert almost stepped on the sacred line, and fell back upon his unsuspecting lady with a dreadful gasp.

"But where are the Knaves and Squirelings?" Cuspid said at last.

"I'm looking at them," Gavin said.

Chapter 18

Sir Gavum and the Cougar-Beast

THE SOLEMN CEREMONY OF NAMES TOOK PLACE down near the water. One by one, those appointed to be Knaves of the Round Tablet stepped up and knelt before their leader (except for Adderly, who had no knees to kneel with and wouldn't have accepted such had they been offered). In turn, Sir Gavum – as he was soon to be called – dipped Hex-Calibre in the wave-washed sand at his feet, raised it up into the sunlight, paused, and then laid it gently upon the knave before him, depositing a decorous daub of muddy sand on the honoree.

To Cuyler he said, in a voice reminiscent of RA-Mosah's (though an octave higher), "In the name of Arthro, I daub thee Sir Kayla, Holy Questor, who shall sit at the leader's left hand."

Cuyler wriggled with such delight at this pronouncement that the royal daub flew up into the breeze like a puff of dandelion dust.

To Quiver, whose excited quills soon disposed of Hex-Calibre's muddy deposit, Gavin said, "In the name of Arthro, I daub thee Sir Quivelot, Guardian of the Home Gate."

To Hubert, who protested (mildly) that he should receive no honour not offered to his lady as well, Gavin said, "In the name of Arthro, I daub thee Sir Percibert, Protector of the Squirelings." Gavin nodded to the mice, Hubert blushed, and when the Squirelings cheered, he blushed again.

To Cuspid, Gavin said, "In the name of Arthro, I daub thee Sir Cuspidon, Watcher of the Skies and the Waters under them." Cuspid smacked his tail upon an incoming wave to signal his pleasure and intimidate any sea-beasts in the channel who might be thinking about interrupting the ceremony.

To Adderly, Gavin said, "In the name of Arthro, I daub thee Sir Gaddelad, Warder of the Walls." No-one was quite certain just what this very important post was, but they applauded anyway.

To Paddle-Whee and Renée, Gavin made a deep bow, placed Hex-Calibre on the sand before their feet, took each in turn by one forepaw, and said, "To you, Lady Morga-Whee and to you Lady Relaine, we commend the Custodianship of the Royal Treasure."

Hubert thumped the beach so vigorously at this remark that Bucktooth toppled into Petite and Dante dove into a nearby crevice in the sand.

Neither the newly dubbed ladies nor their knaves had any doubt as to the nature of the treasure that was to be hoarded and protected at all costs. (Only their leader knew that the "sacred text" they might be required to lay down their lives for was in fact a profane remnant of the Tallwalkers' ruined world.)

"What about Trisbert?" Cuyler said into the hubbub that had been raised at the awesomeness of the naming ritual.

"I have saved the greatest honour for the last," Gavin said. "Please assist your brother."

Cuyler and Paddle-Whee went over to the crumbling wall of the house-habitat where Trisbert had been dozing in the sun and half-observing the ceremony. Without complaint, he allowed himself to be lifted up and helped across the beach until he was able to slump before the figure with a swordstick in his coon's grip.

"In the name of Arthro and with the blessing of Gollah, I daub thee Sir Tristum, Holy Questor and Warden of the Sword, who shall sit at my right hand."

Trisbert blinked, smiled until the pain of his wound stopped him, and then clung to his assistants as they guided him back to his resting place.

"But we have no Arthro," Hubert said quietly, not wanting to break the spell that had been cast here on this miraculous beach, but feeling that someone ought to be practical about matters of such importance.

Gavin had his answer ready. "There was only one Arthro," he said solemnly, "and, of course, you have just taken on the names and duties of those storied ancestors of ours who arrived in Earthwood at the Beginning to help carry out Gollah's divine plan. You cannot be those mighty heroes of old, but you can, by assuming their duties, gather unto yourselves, by gradual degrees, the wisdom they employed to make the world work. Like you, I can only, and most humbly, take on the role of one of Arthro's knaves. I shall be Sir Gavum, and sit at the Round Tablet where the great Arthro would have seated himself. But I will not be your king: only your elected leader and only that as long as I may prove worthy of your confidence."

There was some muttering and protest at this declaration – they had heard it before – but not enough to dampen the general enthusiasm that had been aroused and abetted by Gavin's elaborate deception. If he wished to insist on pretending that he wasn't Gollah's chosen one and future RA, so be it. That mattered little when each member of the troupe – bereft of that animal identity that defined their behaviour and gave meaning to their lives, bewildered by the collapse of Dame Nature's laws, and having been tossed willy-nilly into a random collection of flood-battered survivors – now possessed, however temporarily, a fresh identity, an assigned role, and a renewed purpose. What else could they hope for?

"We have one more honour to bestow," Gavin said, surprising the Knaves, Ladies and Squirelings but in no way diminishing their satisfaction with the proceedings. "In the olden days, as I've said, Arthro was aided and advised by a wizard-prophet named Merlah, and I call your attention to the fact that Gollah has seen fit to provide us with a soothsayer of our own."

After only the briefest pause, the troupe turned an eye towards the crevice where Dante had last been observed. As if on cue, though none had been given, the mole popped her head up into the light and squinted painfully at the spectators, who were staring at her in expectation.

"From time to time, dear Dante," Gavin smiled, "we shall call upon you for prophecy, and the wisdom within it. You shall be our Merlah."

Dante coughed, and appeared mortified by the honour just bestowed. She opened her lips to speak, and her whiskers stiffened and quivered alarmingly. When words at last reached the air, they were shrivelled and shaking — audible only to those nearest her.

"You may blame the channel-waters, of course,

But Gollah, I aver, has struck me hoarse:

My song's unsung, my tongue unstrung, ah me,

Nor gloom nor day-bright prove my prophecy."

Dante's lips kept moving, but no sound of any kind emerged. Well, Gavin thought, so much for wizardry and second sight. He would have to make his own magic. Still, it was not possible, was it, that the wizardry of old was merely the "magic" of seducing others into accepting what their common sense and ordinary daylight-eyes would not otherwise believe? That sorcery was only a kind of trickery or sleight-of-hand? It was a disturbing notion, but Gavin knew that he must not let the momentum of the naming-ceremony sag because of Dante's laryngitis or his own doubts.

So he leaned upon the haft of Hex-Calibre, and its strength, and said with all the authority he could muster, "I call together the first assembly of the Knaves of the Round Tablet in the seat of power: Castelot."

"Castelot?" Cuyler said, looking about with the others.

"The ancient fortress of Arthro's kingdom," Gavin said, pointing at the rubble of the house-habitat behind them. The troupe turned to behold the seat of their power and centre of their new-found kingdom, and for a moment as the sun caught its powdering bricks and odd-angled wood in the fierce halo of its noonday shining, they were certain it glowed golden with promise.

"Are we going to formidable a plan of action?" Quiver said excitedly.

"I trust so," Hubert said, "as Madame and I are eager to play the part of knave and lady, as only befits a couple with our breeding and savoir faire."

"And where are these walls I'm supposed to warder?" Adderly grumped. "Whatever that means."

"All will be explained at the Round Tablet," Gavin assured them. "So let us repair thence immediately."

"I – I don't think that'll be palpable," Quiver suddenly quivered.

"What do you mean by such an imperti – " Hubert began, but stopped his protest when he spotted the fear in Quiver's eyes and then followed their gaze to the edge of the forest to the north and west of Castelot.

"It's the cougar-beast!" Cuyler cried.

And it was. It was standing a pace or so beyond the tree-line, blinking into the sunlight and oscillating its shaggy head, snout upward, as if testing the odours wafted its way on the fitful breeze. Its fearful tongue lolled out of its jaws like a drugged snake, and its drool glistened and polished its jagged, mismatched teeth. Suddenly it uttered a high-pitched yowl – like a coyote's ravening on a spoor, yet as stuttering and guttural as a cougar's growl. If this were a woods-creature, it was of a kind never before seen or imagined.

Slowly, as if dazed and uncertain of itself in the abrupt sunlight of the barren beach, it began shuffling towards the Knaves of the Round Tablet and their supporters. There was no time for talk, or a plan of action – however inspired.

* * *

"Into Castelot!" Gavin cried, "before it decides to attack!" His heart was trying to leap up into his throat and become a word: help! But there was no help to be had. Trisbert, the only one of the troupe likely strong or brave enough to face such a monstrous opponent lay sound asleep outside the east wall of Castelot.

"I'll carry the Squirelings!" Paddle-Whee shouted, and scooped the mice and mole onto her flat tail.

"Oh dear, oh dear, oh dear," Hubert chanted and had to be helped upright by Renée as they tottered towards the opening in the wall a few paces away.

"We can't hide, Sir Gavum," Cuspid said, still beside his leader, who had not moved or taken his eyes off the cougar-beast, which had stopped once again – somewhat puzzled it seemed by the sudden movement and jumble of voices. But it was no more than five giant strides from the closest wall, and its slobber dripped scarlet with the blood of a recent kill, staining the white sand of the beach.

"And I fear the walls of Castelot are not high or stout enough to install the monster!" Quiver cried, tugging at Cuspid to follow him to the dubious safety of the house-habitat.

Cuyler, anxious for his dozing brother and assuming his leader would be close upon his heel, had dashed over to Trisbert and, as soon as Paddle-Whee, her passengers, Cuspid, Quiver and the rabbits had made it through the opening, began tickling Trisbert along that part of his belly exposed to the sun.

"Come on, Tris, wake up! We're under attack!"

Trisbert moaned, began to giggle and then chuckle and then laugh loud enough to wake himself up. But his eyes were glazed and his befuddlement deep. "I need to sleep, Cuy," he sighed, and his lids came down.

"Roll him onto my back," Adderly said as he glided up to the scene.

"He'll fall off!" Cuyler said. "Where's Gavin?"

"Sir Gavum the Great is, I'm sorry to say, occupied at the moment in contemplating his swordstick."

When Cuyler turned back towards the channel, he saw that Adderly was right. Gavin had not budged. Both forepaws were gripping Hex-Calibre, and the swordstick was gripping the sand as if it were granite-stone.

"Wave the firestick at him!" Cuspid could be heard shouting within the fortress.

"Gavin! Gavin!"

"We can't stand upon ceremony," Adderly suggested. "Roll the fat coon over."

Cuyler wanted to dash back and fetch Gavin, but he sensed that Trisbert was the more immediate priority. Besides, Gavin was Gavin, and if he had made the decision to stand out there – to distract the beast while his people retreated to the only refuge available – then that was his royal prerogative. So, with great difficulty, Cuyler pushed the dead-weight of his older brother over onto Adderly, who squirmed and shuffled his generous length until Trisbert lay raccoon-belly to fox-snake's back with four legs acting as braces. Then, deploying only the front half of his body in its customary side-to-side sliding motion – so as not to topple his rider – Adderly eased his way into the shady interior of Castelot.

"Oh, no! You've gone and dropped it!" It was Hubert's hectoring complaint.

"Quick, get it back up on the ledge!"

"Not that way!"

"Oh, Gollah! The beast has smelled us! It's coming to eat us!"

"No, no, the other way! It'll never act as a detergent stuck up there like that!"

"Then do it yourself!"

"I don't suppose the monster'll enjoy crunching down on these quill-points, will he?"

These desperate and panicky remarks floated out to where Gavin stood rooted to the swordstick and the sand that held them both. Without his steady guidance, the others — brave or not — were unable to co-ordinate their efforts. The ruse of the firestick was not about to work a second time. What was the alternative? Gavin's plan had been to attach a sense of the miraculous to the Tallwalker's hunting-knife and then put it into the powerful right hand of Trisbert. Together, he knew, they could face any enemy, any challenge. He himself had been selected for possible RA-ship not because of his size but because of his brain. Size itself was never enough, though Papa had assured him that long ago his Uncle Sylva had possessed both bulk and brilliance (and only his untimely death had stopped him becoming a veritable Arthro!) But surely he and Trisbert combined would make the perfect leadership team. Alas, Bertie lay wounded and disabled in the fortress. The swordstick was in his own hands.

Well, he had already shown a kind of courage, hadn't he? Out there on the storm-tossed Channel? In carrying Trisbert on his back through the darkness of the beast-mad Forest? But he had not — yet, at least — faced and

---

passed the ultimate test of physical courage. He had not stood eye to eye with a predator and tasted its bloodied breath upon his nostrils, and dared it to do its worst. As Arthro must have done a thousand times.

The cougar-beast let out a horrific howl-groan. Its eyes had adjusted at last to the brightness about it. It had spotted Gavin, solitary before it. As the others had described it earlier, the beast's head was shaggy and lion-like, while its rear parts and bushy tail were those of a coyote. The legs, fore and aft, were mismatched and misaligned, so that as it moved past the house-habitat towards Gavin, it wobbled and skidded. Gollah had had no hand in creating this mutant monstrosity.

Still, Gavin found he could not move. The roar of the beast had brought the terrified members of the troupe up to the north and east walls of Castelot. In mute horror they watched as the distance between predator and prey lessened second by second.

I'm going to die right here on this spot, Gavin thought. Surely, though, Gollah would bear his spirit away to North Holy, where he would be reunited with those of Papa, Mama, Aunt Rootha, Uncle Sylva, and dear, dear Tee-Jenn. He had been as true to his kind as he knew how. And surely Gollah would know why he had been compelled to call upon the corrupt and contaminating texts of The Hollow Babble and Tales of Arthro, and would forgive him. After all, cunning was His creed and that of His chosen clan.

"He's going to use Hex-Calibre!" Hubert suddenly cried from his post in front of Renée.

"He's setting a trap!" Cuspid shouted.

"He's going to prosecute the beast with it!"

"Atta boy, brother!"

"Think of Tee-Jenn!" Paddle-Whee encouraged.

What had been cries of panic, near-despair and recrimination just a few moments before had miraculously turned into a chorus of encouragement and confidence in the invincibility of Sir Gavum and his magic swordstick. Gavin's purpose in drawing upon his hazy reading of Tales of Arthro – of giving his crew fresh hope and pride and valour – had begun to work. Not one of them had any other expectation than that their leader would vanquish the cougar-beast and save them all! Gavin fervently wished that he could believe in the illusions he had so meticulously concocted for the others. But he couldn't. Hex-Calibre was a hunting-knife, nothing more. And, alas, the one now holding it had reached deep down for a tidbit of physical courage, and had found it not. Gavin stood where he was and shook with fear.

The cougar-beast paused to take note of the continuing cheers and plaudits from the nearby walls, but its eyes – yellow and oozing with pus and cross-hatched with broken blood-vessels – had fastened upon the victim, and stayed there. With a short shuffle, it stopped no more than three paces from Gavin. Its stink was overpowering, its breath acrid and foul.

"It's going to spring!" Paddle-Whee screamed.

"He's waited too long!"

"Ei-eee! Ei-eee! Ei-eee!" The wizard had found enough voice to wail out a bone-chilling lament.

The cougar-beast sprang – lop-sided and decidedly un-cat-like, but straight enough to effect a teeth-crushing seizure of the paralysed raccoon. But just as those slavering jaws were nearing their target, the victim – in a reflex action that was born of pure animal-panic – reared back to postpone the inevitable, and in doing so inadvertently yanked the swordstick up and back (as it was still frozen to his forepaws), and then fell onto his tail with both eyes squeezed shut and his jaws clenched against the anticipated pain.

The cougar-beast's death-dealing leap ended right where the collapsed victim crouched and awaited his fate. A multi-sided shriek of disbelief soared out of Castelot. The airborne weight of the blood-crazed creature plunged down upon Sir Gavum with the force of a felled oak, even as its scissoring jaws slightly overshot their mark and thudded into the sand – which exploded on every side like a sheet of flame.

Silence then. Everywhere. The once-cheering chorus on the wall now stood without speech or breath at the suddenness of the calamity just witnessed. Their champion, crushed beneath the sprawling monster, was either dead or else knocked senseless and about to be devoured before their horrified gaze. The predator itself, stunned by the abrupt landing, lay still – as if assessing, in its tiny and muddled brain, what had actually happened and what might be needed next in order to ensure a satisfying supper.

The silence continued. No-one could look away. Trisbert chuckled in his sleep and began to snore. At last, the cougar-beast began to lift itself, one misaligned leg at a time, until it stood trembling on all fours above its kill. The force of the impact had driven Gavin into the soft sand so deeply that only his forepaws were now visible. They were not moving. The cougar-beast opened its mouth, smeared with drool and grit, spread its jaws wide, and emitted a sort of whining wail that started out loud and intimidating but slowly began to fade and run down. Then, with a gargantuan gasp it tipped over, stiff-legged, onto its right side and thudded onto the beach, where it lay amazingly still. A drizzle of blood seeped onto the sand. In the rib-cage, within which its mutant heart once beat – sunk to the hilt and still quivering from the force of its entry – sat Hex-Calibre, Sir Gavum's invincible swordstick.

It was Cuyler who slipped off the wall and tiptoed out to confirm what each member of the troupe – Knave, Lady or Squireling – knew to be so: their champion had sacrificed himself to save his comrades. Cuyler began brushing the sand away from his brother's near-buried corpse – very gently, as one sweeps grit out of a fresh wound. Gradually, the familiar mask came into view. Thankfully, the eyes were closed.

As Cuyler allowed the first tear to make its way down his left cheek and was about to turn and deliver the devastating news to his comrades, one of the eyes opened.

"Is this North Holy?" Gavin said.

Chapter 19

A Satisfactory Council

SIR GAVUM CALLED THE FIRST MEETING of the Knaves of the Round Tablet to order. The sun was now approaching the jagged edge of Serpentine Ridge looming above the tree-line of Everdark, and Gavin felt that he must take full advantage of what had happened a few paces away on the beach when the sun had still been high in its daily flight. At the shocking sight of the cougar-beast skewered by Hex-Calibre and the miraculous revival of their fallen champion, those watchers on the wall had burst out in spontaneous cheers, and several dropped to their knees in thankful prayer to the mighty Gollah. The moment it was determined that Gavin had merely had the breath knocked out of him (that he might have fainted from fear was inconceivable), the beavers hoisted him upon their shoulders and bore him aloft through the praise and applause of his disciples, and sat him down in the very centre of the fabulous Tablet.

Sir Kayla had been so excited and so proud and so instantly brave that he'd sprinted back to the slaughtered beast, hopped up on its blood-smeared belly, grasped the bone-haft of Hex-Calibre in his forepaws, and pulled the swordstick free of that foul flesh with such a sudden swoosh that both he and the sacred weapon toppled happily upon the sand. And while the others, including Trisbert who had been propped up on a casement to observe the proceedings, ringed their hero with awe-filled, worshipping eyes, Cuyler dashed into Castelot and placed Hex-Calibre, still dripping monster-blood, at his brother's feet.

Still dazed and not quite certain how he had come to play the hero, Gavin had had the good sense to blink, smile and nod until he was able, from the comments and recapitulations of his well-wishers, to piece together the incredible sequence of chance events that had ended in the cougar-beast's defeat. That he had been no hero, he knew only too well. But the others, even Cuyler and Trisbert, believed otherwise. Moreover, the Tallwalker swordstick had somehow (on its own, perhaps?) managed to find its way precisely into the beast's heart. If not, the creature would have been merely wounded, and his own fate quickly sealed. Was it possible that he, elder-son of the clan coon, had been able to endow the ordinary hunting-knife of their ancient enemy with magic powers? If so, then why had he not been able to make himself brave? Surely that was simpler than conjuring magic out of a metal blade?

But Gavin had realized, basking in the praise of his grateful troupe, that such thoughts were a luxury. If fate or luck or sorcery had made him a hero in their eyes, then – embarrassed as he was and still very much afraid – he still had to make use of the opportunity if they were to survive and get back to Earthwood. Even now, other cougar-bests or worse could be gathering at the forest's edge, preparing for an assault on Castelot. So, he had hauled his bruised body (the cougar-beast had given it a stiff pounding into the sand) up to its feet, looked as princely as he could under the circumstances, and ordered his followers to the walls to keep a constant watch. Then he and Paddle-Whee had hoisted the rusted firestick up into a crevice between two bricks and pointed it in the right direction, while Cuyler stood ready to rap on the tin kettle to simulate the weapon's "thunder." But only Gavin had seemed to take these precautions seriously. The others had been quick to obey his every suggestion, but he could tell that they really felt there would be no further attack, at least not right away. They muttered and buzzed amongst themselves incessantly, and cast adoring glances at their leader and the enchanted instrument he had placed conspicuously at his side. In their view, though no-one said so aloud, their champion had jousted in single combat with one of the ogrish denizens of Everdark, and had triumphed. Crows, gulls and other scavengers were already at work upon its polluted flesh, their noises and commotion surely noticed by its companion-beasts twenty paces away in the woods. These would have witnessed the fury of Hex-Calibre and the valour of the one who had unleashed its power – and would not dare leave the safety of their own habitat.

The day had worn on. The scavenger-birds went winging away in search of fresh carrion. No cougar-beast or any mutant cousin came charging at Castelot. No sudden movement was seen among the branches next to the beach. No yellowed eye, harrowed by hunger, squinted at them out of the gloom. Trisbert fell asleep. The beavers dozed. The mice and mole slipped underground to cool off and rest. Cuyler was daydreaming about swordsticks and applause. Quiver wondered whether his sacrificed quills would grow back any day soon. Hubert and Renée snuggled, then snoozed. And so, before the rush of enthusiasm and bolstered confidence of the day died away entirely, Gavin had tapped Hex-Calibre upon the kettle, startled everyone awake, and announced that it was time for the Knaves, Ladies and Squirelings to congregate at the Round Tablet.

Refreshed by their various nappings and not a whit less bumptious than before, they hopped to their commander's command. And as soon as the Tablet had been redrawn (large sections of its circumference having been accidentally erased during the triumphal march back into Castelot) and everyone had been seated where they thought their kind and dignity ought to be, Gavin was able to call for silence and start the discussion.

"Knaves, Ladies and Squirelings," he began, "we have all seen for ourselves how powerful and prophetic has been the story of Arthro as set down in The Book. It seems clear that Gollah placed Hex-Calibre where I, or any one of us, could discover and claim it – "

"But it was you who did so!" Cuspid cried.

"And it was you who found the ancient texts and read them a-rightly!" Hubert protested.

"And it was you who distracted the swordstick from its casing!" Quiver put in.

"Thank you, thank you," Gavin said. "But you must remember the whole of the story and its meaning. The swordstick is no more important than the Knaves who benefit from its enchantment or this Round Tablet that provides us with a forum in which wisdom can flow from our shared thoughts and our faithfulness to the covenant we have sworn to uphold."

"Well, I'm certainly glad it wasn't me that Gollah chose to hold Hex-Calibre up before that slavering beast," Hubert said. "I'm sure I would have fainted dead away, wouldn't I, chérie?"

"But not if you had been defending me," Renée said loyally.

"And, oh," Cuyler gushed, "not even Tris would've been strong enough to hold Hex-Calibre up long enough to find its way straight into the beast's heart!"

Trisbert, too weak to speak, nodded his agreement.

For the good of the group Gavin accepted these accolades, but he too had wondered how, paralysed by fear and losing consciousness, he had managed to grip the swordstick until it had done its worst. The only answer he could come up with was that he had let go of the weapon and that its handle had become imbedded in the sand beside him in such a way that the collapsing and misguided weight of the cougar-beast had fallen on its blade-tip. So, lodged securely in the ground, Hex-Calibre had assisted the unlucky creature to stab itself.

"Again, my thanks, fellow Knaves, but we really must move on to the pressing business of our first council meeting," Gavin said with a pleading look that gradually quelled the river of praise and congratulation. When at last they could hear the wavelets lap and the leaves rustle once again, Gavin spoke to the sacred circle: "We need to do two things right away: make Castelot into a defensible fortress to ensure our safety and then – when we have had a few days to rest, eat, and recover from the strain of the past three or four days – to lay plans for those quests which might bring us closer to our beloved Earthwood."

"Why don't you just tell us what to do?" Cuspid suggested helpfully.

"Yes," Quiver added, "we'll obey your every construction to the letter!"

"But you must understand, all of you," Gavin replied, "that the Tablet is round for a reason. Although I am your elected leader, anyone seated here is free to offer advice or request that any stratagems put forward by me may be altered or overruled by the assembly. And that includes the Ladies and Squirelings."

Since only Cuyler and Trisbert had any experience of this kind of joint decision-making, a regular feature of the councils of the Ring-Tree and a habit ingrained in all raccoons from the Beginning of Things, it took the others a few moments to have the meaning of Gavin's remarks sink in.

"Well, then, if that is settled," Gavin continued, "may we move to the first item of business? Who among my Knaves and followers has an idea for how we may make Castelot attack-proof?"

Gavin waited, and when it became clear that he himself was not about to offer the first suggestion, several Knaves and one of the Ladies began muttering to themselves. Finally, Cuspid put up a forepaw.

"You don't need to seek permission to speak," Gavin said kindly. "As long as no-one else is doing so, you may merely begin yourself."

In a small voice, Cuspid said, "Paddle-Whee and I are very adept at building things to hold back other things."

"Like dams," Paddle-Whee said.

"And we think we can quickly take the square stones lying all about here and tuck them back into the holes and gaps in the walls," Cuspid said more forcefully. "We'll use mud and shore-grasses for mortar."

"We'll make the walls as high as the cougar-beast's chin," Paddle-Whee added, "so it can't jump in on us."

"A capital idea, eh?" Gavin said, and waited for the chorus of approval. "Who else would like to contribute?"

"If a cougar-beast does come up to the new beaver-wall," Quiver said, "I'll walk along the top and osculate my quill-tail in its face!"

"Splendid, mon ami," Hubert said. Then, with a nod in the direction of his mate, he carried on: "Madame and I have observed in one of the many corners of Castelot a pile of discarded and rusty iron-sticks once used by the Tallwalkers who lived here and befouled its air. When Madame accidentally stepped on some of these dreadful utensils, they rattled and shivered to a degree that came near to startling our dear Lady Relaine."

"So what's your requisition?" Quiver interrupted, but was silenced by a stern glance from Gavin.

"My proposition is simply this," Hubert said in a tone which hinted that what was to come would be anything but simple, "Madame and I will place these rattle-items in one of the kettles, put its lid on and, when the cougar-beasts come, we'll hop aboard and thump the kettle with the combined rabbit-power of our hind feet. The resultant shrieks and clattering will lead the attackers to think that Castelot is full of Ghosties and Warlows."

Renée beamed at the brilliance of her soulmate.

"Excellent," Gavin said.

And before anyone else could get in and steal his contribution, Cuyler piped up: "I'll man the firestick and bang the kettle beside it – especially at night, when I can also act as lookout."

"And since we'll be free after we build up the walls," Cuspid said, "my sister and I will take turns as lookout during the day. And we can use our tails to whack the snouts of any cougar-beasts foolish enough to poke them above our rampart."

"Or bite out their eyes with our incisors!" Paddle-Whee said.

Gavin thanked those who had spoken so far, then looked at Adderly.

"Well, then," Adderly said in his slow, sidling way, "if you all insist, I'll make myself into a coil of rope under the outside wall, and when a cougar-beast steps inside my loop, I'll squeeze him until he topples."

"Splendid, Sir Gaddelad," Gavin said. "That's the spirit!"

"But what may happen after that is anybody's guess," the fox-snake appended gloomily.

"But you see, my fellows," Gavin enthused, "how much we have been able to imagine when each of us, so different in our ways, is called upon to contribute to the common cause?"

Hubert cleared his throat.

"Ah," Gavin chuckled, "you're wondering what I will add to our defence?"

"But you will dash out instantly and drive Hex-Calibre through the monster's breast!" Cuspid said.

"It's one thing to be brave," Gavin replied solemnly to the murmurs of assent from the others, "but to be foolishly so is an unforgivable folly. What I shall do at the first sign of an attack, with Sir Tristum's assistance when he has recovered, is stand upon the west wall of Castelot brandishing Hex-Calibre in hopes that the sight of it, of the stout ramparts we'll have built, and the protruding firestick — along with the rattle-shrieking of our Ghosties – will be sufficient to instigate an immediate retreat."

While not as romantic and thrilling as hand-to-hand combat, Gavin's strategy was certainly more practical and likely to succeed.

"Anything further in the matter of our defence?" Gavin said.

"What was that?" Quiver said, looking anxiously behind him.

"It's the mouse trying to talk," Hubert said.

And so it was. Gavin reached over and sat Bucktooth on his left forepaw. "Go ahead, young Squireling," he said.

"Petite an' me'll go down into the black soil under the garden and nose up some proper mud for the sticky stuff the beavers'll need to hold the rock-pieces together on the wall."

"Great idea!" Paddle-Whee said somewhat more enthusiastically than was required. "The sandy stuff around Castelot isn't right for the job, and nobody wants to venture into the forest to find the damp loam we usually use."

"Well, then," Gavin summed up the proceedings to date, "we have had contributions from every member of the troupe – "

"But one," Hubert pointed out. "And that particular one has lost its voice and hence cannot even predict when the sun will go down over Serpentine Ridge."

This valid but somewhat harsh judgement brought everyone's attention around to Squireling Dante, their designated but disabled Merlah.

"I think she's trying to rhyme," Petite squeaked, and pressed her ear next to Dante's quivering lips.

"What is she saying?" Gavin said. "Can you tell?"

"Yes!" Petite replied and, closing her eyes in imitation of Dante in a trance, she uttered the mole's words on her behalf:

"I watched Tallwalker in the dark

Strike rock on rock to make a spark,

'Twas shiny and tiny and quick

Like the glint-glow of a firestick."

For a long moment Dante's second-hand pronouncement silenced the troupe.

Finally Hubert said, "Is that all?"

"I find the rhymes comestible," Quiver said, "but even a fine rhyme ought to make a little sense."

"What do you make of it, Sir Gavum?" Paddle-Whee said to one she assumed was adept at interpreting things, even puzzling rhymes.

Gavin smiled. "I make it to be another excellent contribution to our defence of Castelot."

"You do?" Cuyler said, amazed yet again at his brother's seemingly endless array of talents.

"You may have frightened off the cougar-beasts yesterday by pointing the firestick over the wall at them and banging a pot," Gavin explained, "but the Tallwalker weapon makes a fiery puff along with every bang. I believe that Dante, our Merlah, is suggesting that if we could make such a spark, beside the firestick, whilst striking the pot, our deception would be complete.

Moreover, if we are attacked at night, only such a spark will convince the beasts that the firestick is real."

"But where will we find such magic rocks?" Cuspid said with a sigh.

"I will search through the Tallwalker's things in the barrel we brought with us, and experiment until I find the proper combination – as soon as we have dealt with the final item on our agenda."

"I was dearly hoping that we had reached that point already," Adderly grumbled.

"I recall you saying something about we Knaves becoming guests," Hubert said, pointedly ignoring the reptile's rude complaint.

"Quests," Gavin said, and the expression on his face brought the entire assembly save one to rapt attention once more. "According to the story of Arthro, after he created the Round Tablet, on the instructions of Gollah – "

Murmurs of "of course" and "we knew it" followed this critical claim by their leader, who was in turn astonished at how easily the lies were leaping from his lips.

" – he sent his bravest Knaves into the wicked world outside of Castelot on a series of quests, which are – as far as I can tell, for I have read only a fragment of the text – journeys of adventure and derring-do."

"How exciting!" said Sir Cuspidon.

"How romantic!" said the Lady Relaine.

"When can we start?" said Sir Kayla.

"And would these questions be dangerous and life-threatening?" said Sir Quivelot.

"I trust they serve some useful purpose," said Sir Percibert.

"Oh, indeed," Gavin said. "There were dragons to be slain and damsels to be rescued."

"Well, then," Cuyler said, "you have already had a quest, haven't you?"

"But there is still a forest full of cougar-beasts and other mutants, isn't there?" Cuspid said with youthful enthusiasm.

"That is what I am suggesting, yes," Gavin said. "And after we have made our fortress impregnable, it behooves us not to wait for the monsters to come to us as they please. We will have to venture into their territory and find a way through it."

"Which means we'll have to be prepared to fight," Paddle-Whee said.

"Moreover," Gavin said, "the greatest quest of all seems to have been the search for the Golden Quail."

The silence prompted by this remark was not occasioned so much by awe or reverence as it was by sheer puzzlement. Quails they knew about and could picture in their minds – all feathery and trotting – but none so far had appeared in Earthwood in a plumage of shimmering gold.

"I'm not quite sure, yet, what the old texts mean by this, but it's something more wonderful and enchanted than Hex-Calibre. At any rate, I believe our instructions are clear enough. I have found among the dead Tallwalker's papers something called a 'map' – a curious set of squiggles that show us where we are, and may point us to a way through Everdark and even indicate a passage through the formidable rock of the Ridge. But the only way I can be sure of what the squiggles represent is for my Knaves to go questing and then return to describe what they have seen – of creeks and mounds and valleys and crags and caves and swamps, and so forth. If I can then match these features on the map, I am confident that I shall be able to plot a safe route home for the entire troupe." Even this exaggerated and dubious promise rolled easily off Gavin's tongue, and (sadly perhaps) was accepted as gospel by his credulous followers.

"Tomorrow, then, we complete our fortifications, and the next day we venture into the unknown with Gollah and Hex-Calibre at our side!" Gavin shouted, and slammed one forepaw into the other.

Sir Gavum was cheered to the echo.

The first council of the Round Tablet was concluded with a silent prayer for the successful passage of Jocko's animal spirit over the wild waters that separated the world from the serene and restful valleys of North Holy – Gollah's own dwelling-place. Just as the assembled Tableters were about to open their eyes, they were shaken awake by a piercing cry:

"Ai-eee, ai-eee, ai-eee

A dragon's cave I see!

Brimstone and fire and death,

A damsel's dying breath!"

Merlah had recovered her voice, and its penchant for dire prophecy.

Chapter 20

Questward Ho!

GAVIN'S PLAN TO HAVE THE WOODS-CREATURES in his care organize themselves along the lines suggested in Tales of Arthro was carried out to the full over the next three days. Before dark descended shortly after the first great council of the Round Tablet had concluded, they had had time to prepare for any night-attack only to the extent of propping up the firestick and posting a keen-eyed raccoon or two to keep close watch on the looming forest. But true to his promise, Gavin rummaged through the Tallwalker's barrel until he found a pouch containing two sharp-edged rocks which, when struck smartly together (as Dante had predicted) produced a flash of flame startling enough to frighten the mice and give Hubert indigestion. This effect, timed to coincide with Cuspid's tail-rap upon one of the metal pots, was rehearsed so often during the evening hours (the timing of Cuyler's "spark" and Cuspid's "bang" never seeming to be quite perfect enough) that Adderly went so far as to suggest that he might prefer the distraction of a cougar-beast or two to such an infernal, dream-disrupting racket. No assault was launched against them that night.

So it was they were able on the following day to accomplish the other tasks put forward during the council. Bucktooth and Petite burrowed under the garden below the vegetable roots (while the rabbits grazed on the wild lettuce above them) and mined more gooey clay-mortar than the beavers could use, as they industriously set about patching and raising the level of the four walls of Castelot. Cuspid was particularly proud of the neat ledge and gap they left as a cradle for the firestick and its sparking apparatus, though Paddle-Whee was far too busy filling in a nearby window to pause with her brother while he invited the others to admire their joint handiwork. As each new segment of the wall was completed, Quiver practised prancing along the top and thrashing his "spears." Beyond the wall Adderly made a cunning loop or two, before falling asleep. Renée and Hubert − the latter no longer limping, except once or twice when he felt his mate's adoring gaze upon him − gathered the eccentric bits of metal found in the barrel or plucked from the dust of the abandoned house-habitat, and put them into the biggest kettle, whose lid they sealed with some of Bucktooth's mortar. After which they began to take turns thumping its hollow sides, causing it to sway and give out a shrieking clatter that stopped every other member of the troupe in mid-task, and nearly deafened the drummers themselves. No further rehearsal was deemed necessary.

Meanwhile, Gavin walked around Castelot offering words of encouragement and approval, and using the newly dubbed names of the Knaves, Ladies and Squirelings. "What a fine stout wall, Sir Cuspidon!" "Here, Lady Morga-Whee, allow me to steady that stone while you seal it in place with your powerful forepaw!" "What a joyful noise you've conjured up, Sir Percibert, and so ably assisted by the Lady Relaine!" "Oh, Sir

Quivelot, do stop rattling those spears, you're terrifying the gulls above the Channel!" "Stand by your weapon, good Sir Kayla!" "Oh, such noble burrowing, Squirelings Bucktooth and Petite: burrow on!" "Behold Sir Gaddelad in the dune-grass, feigning sleep to deceive the lumbering beasts!" "Do not strive to speak, oh mystical Merlah! We'll have need of your prophecies by and by."

The members of the Round Tablet made an effort to use the names assigned to them whenever speaking to a fellow worker, but found in thinking of that same fellow out of his or her sight that the old name clung stubbornly. Moreover, conceiving of themselves or others as Knave, Lady, or even Squireling was well nigh impossible when Gollah Himself had decreed each breed of animal to be unique and forever true to its own kind. Otherwise, the laws of Dame Nature could not operate, and their common enemy – Zeebub and his Tallwalker minions – would be loosed to work their evil upon Earthwood and whatever lay beyond it. However, their faith in the lessons recorded for their use in The Book was almost as great as the instincts passed down to them through countless generations. And was not Gavin a true interpreter of those texts? And so they tried as best they could, trusting that the courage required to make their new selves real would somehow catch up on its own.

When not working on Gavin's defence scheme or standing sentry in their turn, the troupe busied itself with the business of eating. The abundance of appropriate food within hopping, crawling or trotting distance was both an unlooked-for boon and a potential hazard. The instinct half of the animals' nature cried out for a permanent settling-in, especially if Castelot should prove defensible in the face of an all-out attack: sleeping dreamfully and feeding extravagantly were deeply satisfying animal activities. The thinking-observing half of their being, however, prompted them at regular intervals (or whenever Sir Gavum dolloped them with praise) to consider the circumstances of their plight and their desire – part need and part wish – to return to Earthwood and re-create their kind.

By the second day, following another uneventful night, everyone was free to assist the beavers in completing the wall. If Lady Morga-Whee had had the use of both forepaws, she and Sir Cuspidon would have finished the job by then, but as it was they were happy to have the stronger members dig up any castaway stones or bricks, drag them to the wall, and help hold them in place when required. Before the sun set below the Ridge that evening, the rampart reached all the way around Castelot and stood twice as tall as Sir Percibert on his tip toes. Sir Gavum declared the fortifications complete, and set out the guard for the coming night. Then, as he had done every hour of every day since his arrival here, he took Sir Tristum a pair of fresh-caught trout or a fistful of clams, examined the wound (healing nicely), and whispered encouraging phrases in his brother's ear.

"I'll be ready to start questing in another day," Trisbert insisted as Gavin settled in beside him. Above them on the west rampart, Cuyler was scanning the ground between him and Everdark, and listening. Trisbert wasn't quite sure what was involved in rescuing damsels or bearding dragons in a cave, but he was eager to try.

"I'm planning to set up the quests tomorrow," Gavin said, "but we won't start out until the morning after that. We all need to be well fed, strong and alert, if we are to succeed."

"I'll be with you, won't I?" Trisbert said.

"You will, brother, for it is only you who will be strong enough to carry Hex-Calibre for any distance and to wield it in combat, should that be necessary."

Trisbert glanced at the swordstick that lay between them, glinting in the moonlight. "But I saw you – "

"A lucky stroke, I assure you," Gavin said. "It took all my strength to lift it above my shoulders. It is you who must bear it into battle."

"But it is you who gives it its magic," Trisbert said solemnly.

Which was only too true, Gavin sighed to himself.

"If I ate twenty trout a day, I'd soon be big enough to help carry Hex-Calibre," Cuyler said from his nearby perch on the wall.

"Or become the swiftest and most resolute scout in the company of Knaves," Gavin said, grinning up at him.

"Or too fat to waddle," Trisbert said with as much chuckle as he could muster.

His brothers chuckled with him. Then for a while they were quiet – each one content in the others' presence. From the depths of Everdark came the unnerving sound of an animal scream, the kind that precedes a deadly pounce. It was quickly followed by a screech of pain or terror. Then: a series of thrashing and gnashing noises. Two of the monstrous mutants of that foul place were locked in bone-crushing, mortal combat. The silence that ensued was more chilling to the inhabitants of Castelot than any bestial cry could be.

"Can you see anything?" Gavin asked Cuyler.

"Only a pair of yellow eyes where the moonlight's hitting the edge of the woods," Cuyler said. "Staring out at us. But they've been doing that off and on since sundown."

"Perhaps I'd better relieve Cuspid and Quiver at the firestick," Gavin said.

"I'll go," Cuyler said, and sprinted nimbly along the wall towards his fellow Knaves.

After a while, Trisbert said, "Say, Gav, I been thinkin'."

"You have?" Gavin tried not to look too astonished.

"Well, I haven't had much else to do, have I?"

"Go on."

"Well, after I heard your speech at the council, I begun to wonder about our names."

"You mean the ones I took from The Book?"

"Well, it was them that got me thinkin'."

"I see."

"Haven't you ever wondered about the queer names Papa gave us when we were born?"

Gavin smiled, somewhat relieved, for the question really didn't surprise him. "I know that our names are not ones used by any other raccoons in the clan. But I suppose Papa, being a candidate for RA-ship, felt his own sons would someday be as special as he or Uncle Sylva were, and thus deserved unique names."

"I did, too, but the thought just popped into my head last night that Gavin, Cuyler and Trisbert are awfully much like Gavum, Kayla and Tristum."

Gavin said nothing. He realized that his ability to decipher Gibberlish words in the Tallwalker book that Papa had stolen was not perfect: much of the time he was merely guessing at the sense. Even so, the royal names he had bestowed upon his followers were very like the ones he had found in Tales of Arthro. He had merely twisted them a bit so as not to have them sound totally unfamiliar to the sceptical or anxious members of the troupe. But under Trisbert's unexpected prodding, the originals now leapt into his mind – clear and yet puzzling: Kay, Tristram, Lancelot, Percival, Galahad, Morgana, Elaine, Accolon and, of course, Gawain. Without doubt, Papa had named his sons after the Knaves of the Round Tablet, in defiance of all tradition and even common sense. But why? It must have been something in that forbidden Tallwalker text that was too valuable not to be passed on – whatever the cost. Gavin suddenly felt that he was destined in the next few days to find out exactly what that might have been.

"So what do you think, Gav?"

"I think Papa found the names in the beginning chapter of The Book of Coon-Craft and thought they deserved to be used again. That's all."
Gavin was hoping that this lame explanation would suffice, but he need not have worried: Trisbert was asleep, and snoring loud enough to frighten a cougar-beast.

* * *

The day before the quests were to be launched was the most pleasant one the troupe had spent since they had wakened on Deadwood Island and found themselves estranged from Earthwood. They fed and dozed and dawdled in bright sunshine, and made a pretence of guarding Castelot against a predator they were pretty certain would not risk suffering the same fate as their cousin beast whose bones were now bleaching on the sandy shore. Which was not to say that such beasts would not hesitate to tear the worthies of the Round Tablet to pieces should they so much as put a toe into Everdark. Knowing this, and having heard the terrible gnashings and death-struggles in the night-forest next to Castelot, Gavin suggested that the questors travel by day, even though several of the Knaves would have been more comfortable questing in the dark.

At the second council of the Round Tablet late in the day, Gavin outlined the purpose and nature of the quests. The first group would consist of Gavin, Trisbert (now well enough to participate) and Cuspid. They would go along the beach towards North Holy, noting all landmarks and, where possible, following streams inland and memorizing their path. The second group would consist of Cuyler, Paddle-Whee and Quiver, and they would go along the beach in the opposite direction towards the Tallwalker territory, exploring and "mapping" (as Gavin termed it). Each group of questors was to complete its work and return to Castelot by nightfall. The reason for their travelling on the open sand-beach was threefold. First, they could move more quickly there than they could within Everdark itself while still being able to spot hills, crags or possible valleys in the landscape of the Ridge above the tree-line. Secondly, as all streams flowed down from the Ridge into Heartbreak Channel, they could begin mapping their course from the mouth, working comfortably inland as far as they dared. Finally, the nameless carnivores of Everdark seemed reluctant to leave their shadowed lairs and risk the blinding daylight of the wide beach and gently rolling dunes. And while the questors were questing, Castelot itself would be guarded by Hubert and Renée, assisted by Adderly and cheered on by the mice and mole. However, should the propped firestick and rattling kettle prove ineffective in warding off an attack, the rabbits and rodents were to scamper into their burrows and stay there, while Adderly was to hide in the dune-grass and keep watch.

When Gavin dutifully called for further suggestions, he was met with respectful silence. Everyone was aware of the importance of these missions to their eventual return to Earthwood. No-one wished to disturb the absolute perfection of Sir Gavum's scheme with a careless or eccentric comment. So Gavin turned to Dante and said, "Merlah, do you have anything to prophesy for this worthy council?"

The council waited. From her pedestal, Dante spoke in a painful whisper:

"Noble one, full of wit and clan-coon pluck,

I can only wish you the best of luck."
We'll need more than that, Gavin thought.

* * *

At the crack of dawn Gavin said goodbye to Cuyler and the others. Then he and his group set off up the beach towards North Holy. A brisk breeze had arrived with the sun and was wafting blue wavelets upon the sand at their feet. The blood-red sun, low above Deadwood Island to their right, cast an eerie, shivering light along the water's edge and over the dunes between them and the woods. Cuspid could hardly contain his excitement, but heeded Gavin's warning to keep silent as they travelled – with one eye always upon the thick blotch of Everdark on their left. While Cuspid and Trisbert were given the role of lookout, Gavin took it upon himself to note and memorize the terrain they were exploring. He had considered bringing along his knapsack with the

Tallwalker's texts and his map in order to mark down on the empty pages those things that needed to be recorded – using a stick and mud-ink if necessary. But he had dismissed the notion as being too cumbersome. Also, woods-creatures had reliable and prodigious memories, for their very lives depended on knowing where they were at all times and where potential dangers lay. And so he had left the pack and its vital texts tucked under some stones in an obscure corner of Castelot.

The more important decision, whether or not to bring along the invincible Hex-Calibre, had been made for him. He had hardly begun to suggest that it might prove to be too heavy to take on a daylong journey when the others had interrupted, with something close to dismay in their eyes, and begged him to bear the great swordstick with him at all times and at any cost. Without it, they assured him, all would be lost. Moreover, if it were left at Castelot, was there not the chance that it could fall into the enemy's hands? And then what hope would any of them have?

And so, as the sun now rose fully into the morning sky, it was Trisbert who lugged Hex-Calibre beside him while Gavin was free to observe and record. The first thing that Gavin did was look for any sign of the pouch that Wylee had stolen, but the waves had washed it back into the channel, as Cuspid had reported, along with the traitor's pawprints. Nor was there any sign of Jocko's sleek jackrabbit body, waterlogged or picked clean by crows. Not that he was expecting to find it, because any creature drowned in Heartbreak Channel would have soon been swept north in the currents and out to the far reaches of the endless Lake.

As they moved on up the beach, what Gavin observed was not encouraging. The barren rock of Serpentine

Ridge was forever visible above the tree-line of Everdark, presenting an impassable barrier between the forest here and whatever remained of Earthwood on the other side. Even if there were no Ghosties or Warlows inhabiting those razor-sharp crags and treacherous crevasses (Gavin's own view was that these were more the product of woods-creatures' nightmares than Zeebub's sorcery), there was no way that the members of the troupe could scale those heights – exposed at they would be to birds of prey and deadly gusts of wind and inevitable exhaustion. What they needed to find was a pass through the crags, a deep valley along whose shady bottomland they could travel in complete safety. But league after league the Ridge offered no break in its relentless, menacing silhouette. The only way past it was over it. Behind him, Gavin could hear Trisbert puffing and wheezing.

"I could carry the swordstick," Cuspid said after a while.

"I'm all right," Trisbert panted. "It's no bother."

Gavin stopped. "I think you'd better let him try, Sir Tristum. If we're attacked, we'll need you to deploy all your mighty strength against the enemy."

Trisbert smiled at the compliment. "As you wish, Sir Gav," he said, and handed Hex-Calibre to Cuspid, who promptly dropped it.

"Just drag it along, Sir Cuspidon," Gavin said helpfully. "A little sand won't rub off its magic."

Unburdened by the swordstick and refreshed by a mid-day snack at the mouth of a generous stream, Trisbert's energy soon returned, and the questors continued walking northwards. Gavin's plan was to scout the Ridge itself from the beach until they could go no farther and, then, on the return journey, explore the most promising creeks inland. Very soon they discovered that the beach began to narrow, so that they found themselves having to travel ever closer to the forest's edge. Trisbert took up the swordstick again.

"This is as far as we can go," Gavin said as they drew to a halt. A dozen paces distant, the beach faded away completely. A sheer cliff rose out of the waves as high as an eagle could fly, where Serpentine Ridge met the Lake of Waters Unending and then continued on as far as the eye could see. Beyond that, in the mists through which only the souls of the dead could navigate, lay the abode of Gollah and his fellow deities: North Holy. They had come as far north as any woods-creature had ever ventured, or ought to. There was no way around the Ridge and, it seemed, no way over it.

"I guess we'll have to have a look at one of those creeks we passed back there," Cuspid said. "There could be an underground stream through the Ridge somewhere."

Gavin nodded, but his eye had caught something odd on the Ridge immediately above them. "What's that up there?" he said.

Cuspid and Trisbert looked up. Like Gavin, they soon spotted a dip in the hogback of the Ridge, not enough to suggest a deep valley or ravine running through it, but worthy of mapping nonetheless.

"You think there might be a passageway through the Ridge up there?" Cuspid said, trying to appear more enthusiastic than he felt.

"Maybe," Gavin replied, "but it's that vee-shaped dip in the rock that intrigues me. Look carefully at the bottom of the vee."

"It's only a little bump of sorts," Cuspid said, squinting at the object in question. "An outcrop or ledge, I'd say."

"That may be, Sir Cuspidon, but rocky outcrops don't glitter in the sun."

Just as Gavin pointed out this phenomenon, the lumpy outcrop emitted a near-blinding flash as the sun struck it full on. "The only things we've seen glitter like that are made of metal," Gavin said.

"You mean like Tallwalkers' iron?"

"Yes, the stuff they put on the outside of their doomsmobiles and twist to make the sticks they use to eat with."

"And the blade of Hex-Calibre," Trisbert said, holding it up against the sky-high sun until it gave off a series of glints and fiery winks.

"But what could it mean?" Cuspid said, peering back up at the Ridge.

"I don't know," Gavin said, "but my guess is that it could be the roof or some other part of a Tallwalker house-habitat."

"But what would it be doing stuck up there — next to the Ghosties?" Cuspid said as he edged closer to Trisbert and the swordstick.

"Who knows, eh? But remember that the house-habitat on the shore back there at Castelot is in a strange place as well. It's possible that at some time — many annuals ago, perhaps — Tallwalkers hunted in Everdark as they once did in Earthwood until all the deer were slaughtered. And they may have built some house-habitats here and there to protect themselves from the cougar-beasts or other predators."

"Then, if we could find a way up there, we could build another Castelot, couldn't we?"

"Was that bump marked on your map?" Trisbert said.

"By Gollah, I believe it was!" cried Gavin. "I'll need to check it out as soon as we get back. The more marks we can pinpoint on that map, the more we'll know about where we are and where we need to go."

"But right now," Trisbert said, "we gotta turn around and look for a nice, fat trout stream."

"Right you are, Sir Tristum – on both counts," their leader replied cheerfully. But he was thinking this: there was a lot in Gollah's world he knew nothing about – of its mysterious past or its future, if it had one.

Chapter 21

Minervah

ON THE TREK NORTHWARD Gavin had made a mental note of three good-sized streams flowing into the Channel, wide and swift-moving enough to be worth investigation. When they came to the first of these on their return journey, they paused to eat and drink (Cuspid finding the tender shoots nearby particularly to his liking). Then Gavin ordered them into single-file, with Trisbert trailing him and Cuspid. Arranged thus, they waded into the middle of the shallow rapids and began treading upstream. Trisbert held Hex-Calibre high above his head and waddled heroically on his hind legs. Gavin scouted the terrain directly ahead, and Cuspid kept a sharp beaver-eye on the shoreline where branches overhung the water and provided shadowy pockets for would-be bushwhackers. As long as the creek remained broad, as it did near its mouth, the questors were able to advance in full sunlight, but as they progressed north-westerly towards its source, the forest gradually closed over them, and the creek became narrower, more winding, and much, much darker. They began to move slowly and cautiously, though Gavin was still able to calm his fears sufficiently to memorize each bend and oddity of the stream's course. Very soon, they felt themselves walking steeply upwards, while the water thrashed about their legs and bubbled over their snouts.

"We haven't come very far," Gavin mused to himself, "not even a quarter morning's walk, and already the creek is starting to climb sharply."

"What does that mean?" Cuspid whispered.

Gavin turned and replied as softly as he could, "The Forest of Everdark is not very wide, at least not here. It seems to hug the space between the Ridge and the Channel."

"So we could all cross it a lot more quickly than we did Deadwood?"

Gavin nodded, buoyed by this happy prospect.

Behind him Trisbert stirred and coughed. Gavin followed his brother's gaze to a spot in the gloom of the left bank: a branch was swaying where no breeze could blow. Moments later, a pair of large, slitted eyes revealed themselves in the blackness, as yellow and bloody as smashed robin's eggs.

"A cougar-beast!" Cuspid said, and prepared to dive underwater.

But before he could move and before Sir Gavum could issue a command (that is, find his voice in order to do so), Trisbert raised Hex-Calibre in both forepaws, bellowed some wordless battle-cry, and charged across the stream towards the beast. The swordstick could not glitter because there was no light to assist it, but something in its menacing whip – as Trisbert slashed at the air – was enough to frighten the yellow-eyed creature. It uttered a high-pitched howl and rattled off through the undergrowth behind it.

"Well done, Sir Tristum," Gavin said, still whispering, though Trisbert's cry would have wakened half of Everdark.

Cuspid's jaw dropped and stayed there. "Another miracle," was all he could say – his eyes glued to Hex-Calibre.

Even Trisbert, ever brave and self-sacrificing Trisbert, seemed in awe of the swordstick's effect.

"I want to go on just a little bit farther," Gavin said, "to see if this creek begins way up on the Ridge or tumbles out of its side lower down."

Feeling less vulnerable in view of Hex-Calibre's performance, Trisbert and Cuspid dutifully followed Gavin around a sharp bend, where the streambed became rocky and seething with rapids. Around the next bend, steeply upwards, an unexpected sight froze them in their tracks.

"Where's the woods?" Cuspid said, looking about, bewildered.

"Gone," Gavin said. "We've reached the Ridge."

While not exactly a cliff, the rockface that loomed up before them – shorn of vegetation – was too steep for anything but a mountain goat to scale. And slightly to their right, they suddenly saw where the creek originated. Out of a gaping hole in the rock, ten paces above them, a frothing stream of water poured and then dropped straight down upon a scattering of boulders, polished smooth by the pummelling cataract.

"I don't think even a beaver could swim through that channel up there," Cuspid sighed.

"Even if you could scratch your way up there," Trisbert said.

For a long while they stood silently watching the waterfall and wondering whether its backwards course rushed all the way to the Earthwood side of Serpentine Ridge. But Gavin was now looking elsewhere. His gaze was fixed upon what appeared to be an ancient goat-path that began at the foot of the falls and meandered northwards along the slope of the Ridge about twenty paces or so above the treetops. He followed its outline until it seemed to veer upwards, about a morning's walk from where Gavin stood, and then suddenly stop. Above this point, only a darkish blob was visible. A house-habitat perhaps? A cave in the hillside? He couldn't tell.

"What is it, Sir Gavum?" Cuspid said.

"Only a goat-path," Gavin replied, but a very interesting one. Had it not appeared as a squiggle on the Tallwalker's map?

"We'd better move along," Trisbert said. "We got a couple more of these creeks to have a look at."

"Right. We must be back at Castelot before dark." And before any night-attacks by enraged cougar-beasts.

* * *

The sun was sinking towards the edge of the Ridge when Gavin's questors found themselves following the last of the creeks deep into the forest. While they did not see or hear anything untoward, Cuspid did notice several gigantic footprints in the mud near the banks of the stream.

"I don't think there's much to see in here except darkness and trees," Trisbert suggested, "and a fat trout over there waiting for his supper."

"The current's still moving slowly," Cuspid pointed out. "And there're more bends in this creek than water."

"True," Gavin agreed. "I don't think we can afford to follow it to its source on the Ridge. At least not today." He was just about to give the order to retreat when a low, sad, long, hootish sigh sailed down upon their ears from somewhere in the gloom above.

Trisbert raised Hex-Calibre in readiness. "What was that, Gav?"

"It came from over there. Somewhere up in that giant oak, I'd say."

"An eagle?" Cuspid said, darting behind Trisbert and squinting upwards.

"Not in here," Gavin said. "But then we haven't seen a normal creature in Everdark since we arrived. Even the crows picking at the cougar-beast were as big as turkeys."

They decided to stand still and listen. The creek barely gurgled, and in the windless, dank air any wayward sound would be quickly noted and distinguished. Moments later, the solemn sigh was repeated, except that just as it was about to die away, it was concluded with a short, and pathetic, hoot.

"It's an owl," Cuspid said.

"Yes, I believe it is," Gavin said, but instead of leading his Knaves off to safety, he paddled ahead until he stood directly below the big oak, whose branches swept imperially over the insignificant little stream. He peered up, scanning the limbs and leafy bowers, aided by occasional slivers of sunlight leaking through from above.

The hooting sigh came again, directed not at the intruders but out at the world that had caused it.

"Stay where you are and stand watch," Gavin said. "I'm going up to have a look."

With the protests of his fellow questors ringing in his ears, Gavin scrambled up the trunk and began ascending the thick-limbed, ancient tree. He was almost at the top, with only three or four short branches to negotiate, when he spotted the creature. It was indeed an owl, though no owl had ever voluntarily perched itself thus – with one wing wedged securely in the crotch of two limbs and a single claw wrapped around one of them. The other was clenching and unclenching in mid-air.

"Is that you, Gavin?"

The voice was thin and hollow with hopelessness. "Yes, Minervah, it's me. How in Gollah's name have you gotten yourself here?"

* * *

Gavin had recognized the owl as Minervah – the bird of wisdom-past who had been a fixture of life in Earthwood even before RA-Mosah's time, but only because of her eyes. Like any great-horned owl's, hers were as round as clams, but they were also sightless, their lids wide open to dark or light, as if she were trying to swallow the world whole with them. (She had been blinded some time ago when, feeling it to be her duty, she had flown south to observe the Great Burning in the Tallwalker territory.) And these blighted eyes were now all that was recognizable. For the glory of her plumage and fearsome wingspan were no more. In their stead, on body or wing, there fluttered a few wispy pin-feathers interspersed with the broken and jagged stumps of their longer and more resplendent cousins. In an instant Gavin grasped what must have happened. Minervah had somehow got her left wing wedged in this crevice and, unable to pull it free, had flapped and jerked about until most of her feathers had snapped off or given up. Slow starvation had done the rest.

"Do not fret about me, dearest Gavin," she said as Gavin started towards the branch that had been pinioning her. "I am very near my death. I can hear the siren song of North Holy beckoning me. But perhaps I can be of some last service to you and your companions before I take my leave."

"Do you know how you came to be here?" Gavin asked as soon as he realized that there was nothing he could do to save the owl or delay her soul's departure. "And how is it that almost a dozen of us from Earthwood survived the flood?"

Minervah blinked in the prodigious blinking manner of owls everywhere. Gavin knew, of course, that Minervah had been born with the gift of second sight, except that in her case she was able to see backwards in time and visualize events from the past that neither she and nor any other living creature in Earthwood had lived through or heard about — things not recorded in the multitudinous chapters of The Book.

"I cannot forget those terrible events," she began, and Gavin shuddered as he noted the trembling of her featherless, famished flesh as she uttered each painful phrase. "I see them still in the blazing eye behind these dead ones. It is not the rain-driven flood that sweeps the creatures of Earthwood up and over the Ridge, though thousands drown before that happens. It is a mammoth wave roaring in from the Lake of Waters Unending, a wall of water as high as the Ridge itself. I see hundreds dashing in desperation up the craggy slopes, many of them are almost at the top when the big wave arrives and carries them over the steepest peaks and then down across the drowned treetops of Everdark and then out and out to the endless ends of Gollah's lake, so their souls have but a short way to reach the shores of North Holy."

"But not everyone?" Gavin prompted.

"Many of the cleverest and most nimble of Earthwood's creatures seize upon uprooted trunks and severed tree-limbs, and those swift enough or with luck to spare are floated – tumbling and roiling – through gaps in the hogback just as the water-wall rolls up behind them. And these few, and only these, get tangled in the tallest trees before the deluge plunges over them, carrying their unfortunate brothers and sisters and mothers and fathers to a watery grave in the vast beyond."

"Tangled in a tall treetop, as you were?"

"I am winging my way above the Ridge and Gollah's rain is drenching my wing-feathers, I can barely fly, I am blundering downwards, I strike this oak at full throttle, I flap about in wild confusion, blind and helpless and begging Gollah to – "

"It's all right," Gavin said quietly. "You've told me what I need to know." Then, half-aloud to himself he said, "There must have been giant trees on Deadwood Island before the flood, and a mere handful of resourceful and lucky woods-creatures were snagged by their upper branches as the water-wall surged out into the Lake. Those trees in turn succumbed to the flood, while the rock-rooted ones here in Everdark have somehow survived."

"I have clung to this branch an age or more," Minervah continued, her voice now merely a hoarse croak. "My only comfort has been the sound of woods-creatures crawling out of their logs and astonishing the saturated air with their cries of delight and thanksgiving at being impossibly alive. I can see their faces now — raccoons, foxes, skunks, adders, beaver — as they stagger into the grim damp of Everdark: dazed, mourning, happy-sad, eager to survive as Gollah taught them, yet resigned to their fate."

"But I was referring to the dozen who survived with me on Deadwood!" Gavin cried, as his heart leapt. "Are there dozens more somewhere here in Everdark? RA-Mosah and Papa and Tee-Jenn?"

Minervah opened her beak as if to continue, but without warning her eyelids began to close. "Take my last tail-feather, please," she said with fading breath. "Someone must write the past and the future." The shuttered lids now extinguished all light, outer and inner. They would not open again.

Sadly, Gavin crawled up to the dead owl and sat beside her on the branch. He said a silent prayer for her soul's safe passage. The body, what there was left of it, would be carrion for some grateful scavenger. From his new position, however, Gavin could now see that a solitary but splendid tail-feather did indeed remain on Minervah. He reached across and plucked it. Its quill would make a fine writing instrument.

* * *

Sir Gavum gave his worried Knaves a brief account of what had happened up in the oak tree.

"So there could be others about here like us?" Trisbert said when Gavin had finished.

"But we haven't seen a soul from Earthwood anywhere, have we?" Cuspid said, though he dearly wished he could say otherwise. "Not a footprint on the beach all day or one here that wasn't that of a monster-beast."

No-one said so, but all three were thinking the same despairing thought: the chances of bewildered and starving woods-creatures – dropped into strange and hostile territory – of avoiding the slobbering jaws of a cougar-beast or other carnivore were slim and none. On Deadwood, Gavin's troupe had had only the dying Tallwalker to contend with, had found a temporary food source, and had been granted several days to get their bearings and develop a strategy for survival. Here in the tropical gloom of Everdark there would have been no reprieve, and no mercy. Still, while they had found no evidence of survivors here, they had not as yet stumbled upon the bones of any carcase.

"Let's go home, Gav," Trisbert said.
"I'll take that as an order," Gavin said, and did his best to smile.

* * *

While Sir Kayla had been put in charge of the second group of questors, it was Sir Gavum who had laid out their marching orders. They were to travel southwards along the beach as close to the water's edge as possible until the sun reached its high point – observing the nooks and crannies of the hogback above them and memorizing any promising oddities in that forbidding rampart. They were then to start back towards Castelot, pausing to explore any creeks that looked as if they might lead up to a valley between the craggy humps of the Ridge. Gavin had agonized over sending Cuyler out questing at all, ever mindful of Papa's command that he take care of his young, impetuous and unworldly brother. He had considered the option of taking one day to explore northward and another to explore southward, but had rejected it. He did not want to spend a fifth day at Castelot because he was afraid that the members of the troupe would become complacent and comfortable with their circumstance, particularly since no cougar-beast had even threatened to attack and the food supply was succulent and plentiful. Secondly, he felt that the longer they remained in the fortress, the less effective would be their deceptions – the mimicking of the firestick and the ghost-rattlings of Hubert's kettle – in fooling any would-be predators. After all, he and Trisbert had seen a different but equally ferocious mutant that first evening in Everdark. Sooner or later, one breed or another of these misfits would sniff them out, and launch a deadly assault.

And so, he had reluctantly decided to team Cuyler up with Paddle-Whee and Quiver. While Paddle-Whee had only three feet, she was quite fearless and could wield her tail with the force of a bear's paw. And Quiver was capable of thrashing his quills about without a pardon and with more than an unpleasant intrusion. Whether they or any of his own team could in reality withstand the full charge of a cougar-beast in the near-dark of the forest was questionable, but it was a risk they each had to take. And while Gavin had at first hoped that he could bring Cuyler with him and Trisbert, he knew in his heart that a raccoon-questor was needed in each group for his keen vision, resourcefulness around water and trees, and retentive memory.

Sir Kayla was happily unaware of Sir Gavum's doubts, however, and tripped away at the head of his squad without a backwards glance. Like Gavin's group, they soon found little to raise their hopes as they scanned the bleak and formidable escarpment of the Ridge. But their disappointment was not reflected in their leader's words and deeds.

"Lady Morga-Whee, please take a note: above the mouth of the third creek and a forepaw to the south lies a vee-shaped gap that might possibly be sheltering a hidden valley."

Paddle-Whee, of course, had no notebook in which to record this critical remark – or any of the dozen others thus pronounced – and no pen to write with even if she had learned to do so. But each time she faithfully replied to her squadron leader: "Duly noted, Sir Kayla."

"Sir Quivelot, is that dark blotch just below the highest crag up there not the mouth of a cave?"

"I believe so, Sir Knave," Quiver said, squinting at the Ridge with his less-than-coon-like vision, "but I cannot truthfully say with resolute certaintude."

Cuyler took this response as a firm "yes," and ordered that it be duly recorded.

At high-sun they stopped at the mouth of a creek, and ate and drank greedily, with the beaver and porcupine edging upstream far enough to obtain the tenderest roots and shoots near the forest's edge. Sir Quivelot suggested a nap might be in order, but was turned down by his leader, who was still bouncing as if their quest had been a dazzling success.

"Time to nose our way up these streams," he declared, "and frighten the cougar-beasts."

However, when they began treading along the next big creek into the overarching gloom of Everdark, even Sir Kayla moved with extreme caution and not a little agitation of the heart's beat. From time to time they could feel malevolent eyes pressed upon them from the shadows along each bank, and twice they got a whiff of something so foul they wondered that it could be alive. Finally they arrived at a place where the trees ended and the steep slope of the Ridge began. The stream could be seen hopping and skipping down the hillside from some hidden source – a spring, no doubt – about halfway up. No valley or friendly ravine presented itself.

This reconnoitring manoeuvre was repeated three more times with similar disappointing results. Eventually, Sir Kayla stopped uttering critical remarks and made no further reference to their being duly noted. They were about a third of the way back from what was to be their last inland foray – the sun was dropping rapidly – when the trouble began.

Chapter 22

Squeezels

FORTUNATELY THE ATTACK CAME with a few seconds advance warning. A chorus of shrieks, loud with rage and bloodlust, shot through the air above the questors, who were knee-deep in the stream. The violence of its din stunned the trio of woods-creatures. They froze at first, then swung their heads around in slow befuddlement towards its source. Fear had not yet penetrated shock nor set the adrenalin a-gallop. The shrieks continued, but now out of the murky shadow above the left bank there materialized the half-dozen beings uttering them. Knowing they should turn and run for their lives, Cuyler, Paddle-Whee and Quiver instead stood stock-still in deadly fascination at what was roaring down upon them: a howling pack of predators so like one another they could have been clones. Narrow-jawed, dog-toothed, rodent-eared and weasel-eyed they were – with a loping, elongated stride. But the weasel-bodies ended in a flaming tail, and everywhere they were covered with a shag of fox-fur. More to the point, they were twice the size of Wylee!

"Head for deeper water!" Paddle-Whee cried at last, hoping that these malformed giants were not fond of swimming.

"It's too late," Quiver yelled, "we're being overwelcomed!"

"Stand and fight!" Cuyler commanded, and bared both teeth and claws.

One of the fiends was strides ahead of its companions, who came to a sudden halt as soon as their feet struck water, as if they had decided not merely to avoid further contact with the repulsive element but also to enjoy the spectacle of their champion chewing up the easy prey on his own. The latter made an acrobatic lunge at Cuyler, and its wide, slathering, loose-tongued jaws would have chomped the young raccoon in two if they had not been rudely forestalled by a paralysing smack from some sort of paddle – a hidden weapon perhaps that the fiend had not noticed in time.

"Way to go, Lady Morga-Whee!" Cuyler cried, trembling and laughing at the same time. "You saved my life!"

"You've knocked him subconscious with one mighty swat of your tail!" Quiver added. "Now I think we oughta get out of here!"

But the fiend was not unconscious. While its comrades remained where they were (with something close to a chuckle sputtering from their weasel-mouths), it staggered back to its feet, and just as Paddle-Whee turned to dive safely away, it bit her on the tail with a horrific snap of its jaws. Paddle-Whee cried out, more in fear than pain, and struggled without success to break free. A quintet of grunts and wheezes from the sidelines seemed to be suggesting that the beaver be dispatched quickly and mercilessly for her tail's impudence. And as if these monsters could indeed communicate in some primitive babble-tongue, their leader let go of Paddle-Whee and — with a swift, arching movement characteristic of weasels on the prowl — leapt at the beaver's throat.

But this time it wasn't a paddle that thwarted the attack: it was something infinitely worse. What should have been a cry of triumph and carnivore-satisfaction turned amazingly into a stutter of piercing screeches, followed by a series of writhing, floundering twists and somersaults. The cheerleaders near the bank set up an immediate yipping bellow of outrage. Their Goliath was thrashing about in agony with a dozen porcupine quills imbedded in the tender flesh of its nostrils, lips and drooling gums.

"Now let's go!" Quiver said, and plunged into the water beside Paddle-Whee.

"You'd better hop on my back," Paddle-Whee said. "You weren't designed for swift passage in a shallow creek!"

Already winded and soggy, Quiver did as he was told.

"And I don't want to hear any more 'pardon my obtrusions' from you," the beaver added. "Those prickles of yours saved me from certain death."

Behind them they could hear the mutant creatures splashing about their fallen champion — surprised, outraged and confused.

"Where's Cuyler?" Paddle-Whee said as they rounded a bend and put more distance between themselves and the shrieking behind them.

"I saw him heading for the nearest tree as soon as the thing started to get up after you paddle-whipped it."

"Yes, that's what raccoons do, isn't it?"

"And I believe those beasts don't like water any more than trees — at least that's my consumption."

For the next little while, neither spoke again, pouring all their energy into the business of escape, even though there was no further sign of their being pursued. The skies were starting to darken, and they had to get back to Castelot soon. A few paces from the creek-mouth, Paddle-Whee stopped, and Quiver hopped off gingerly.

"What do you think those beasts were?" Paddle-Whee said.

"Squeezels," Quiver said.

"How do you know?"

"I've seen them in my nightmares," Quiver said.

"Then Squeezels they must be," Paddle-Whee smiled at her improbable friend and ally.

They paddled slowly out to where the beach cradled the mouth of the creek. Peering north, they could see the last, horizontal rays of the dying sun strike the bright walls of Castelot, a mere two hundred paces away.

"We're going to make it," Paddle-Whee said, proud and relieved.

"How's your tail?"

"It stings, but it still works. I can swim with a missing forepaw, but not without my trusty rudder." She gave her tail a jaunty flip to reassure Quiver that it was still in fine working order.

"We oughta wait for Cuyler, eh? He'll follow the creek along the treetops until he's sure he's safe — I've seen raccoons do it all the time in Earthwood — and come out right here."

"Yes. And if we're waiting, he'll know he won't have to go back in search of us."

So they hunkered down, listening to the frogs start up their early-evening fugues and to the lapping of waves upon the shore, and keeping a sharp eye out for Squeezels. None came. Nor did Cuyler. They waited until it was almost too dark to see a half a pace ahead – the moon had not yet risen in the east – and then with a resigned sigh they trudged wearily and anxiously towards Castelot.

* * *

As his squad approached Castelot from the north, Gavin declared himself satisfied with the quest, assuring his weary companions that they had helped him to acquire detailed information about the size and course of streams and the relation of their position to specific peaks and noticeable crags on the Ridge. These he would be able to compare with the wavy lines and squiggles on the Tallwalker's map to see if they matched. Best of all, the curious structure at the far north of the Ridge and that dark blob above the waterfall might prove to be of vital importance. And, of course, there would be the report of the questors led by Cuyler to add to what they themselves had discovered. The sun had not yet sunk below the escarpment when Gavin, Cuspid and Trisbert – the latter holding Hex-Calibre bravely aloft – rapped on the swinging gate that the Tallwalkers used for an entranceway.

"Anybody home?" Sir Gavum called out, while Sir Tristum scanned the nearby woods for any sign of trouble. "We're back from our quest!"

Cuspid gave the gate a push, and it creaked inward.

"That's odd," Gavin said. "Hubert or Adderly must have rolled the blocking-stone away."

"They must be expecting us, then," Trisbert said, letting the swordstick drop to his side.

"Sir Percibert! Lady Relaine! Sir Gaddelad!" Gavin shouted as they walked cautiously into the house-habitat, puzzled and not a little anxious.

"They're not here," Cuspid said. "And the others aren't back from their quest either."

"Check the garden, Sir Cuspidon, to see if the Squirelings are about."

When Cuspid had gone back out, Gavin peered about in the fast-fading light. "Someone's been here, Bertie," he breathed. "And made a mess."

The Tallwalker's barrel had been toppled and its motley contents scattered about. The rusty firestick was missing from its slot in the wall and was nowhere to be seen. Hubert's kettle was knocked on its side, and much dented.

"The cougar-beasts?" Trisbert said.

"We'd still smell them if they'd been here," Gavin said.

"I'd better check outside for tracks," Trisbert said.

"I should have been more careful about that when we arrived," Gavin sighed.

After Trisbert went outside, Gavin cast his gaze about Castelot. He examined every corner with increasing concern. Where were those he had left in charge of the place? There was no sign of blood anywhere or ripped fur, though an odour of animal presence was still strong. It was none he recognized.

Trisbert and Cuspid came back in together, and both began speaking at once.

"The footprints are huge and – "

"I think I heard the mice – "

" . . . there's six or seven – "

" . . . under the garden but they won't – "

" . . . with a weasely smell to 'em – "

" . . . come up."

" . . . and they're very fresh."

"All right, all right," Gavin said. Thank you, both."

"What does it mean?" Cuspid said.

"It means that half a dozen strange creatures, ones we haven't yet encountered, came in here a short while ago, bent on wrecking our defences and – "

"Carrying off our friends!" Cuspid cried, his sudden despair tempered only by the knowledge that Paddle-Whee might be safe somewhere on her quest.

"It appears so," Gavin said truthfully. "But why is there no blood, no sign of a struggle? Predators pursue their prey to feast on them, not abduct them."

"Maybe the cottontails went burrowing," Trisbert said, remembering that such a plan had been suggested in the event of an all-out attack.

"Of course!" Gavin said. "How stupid of me to forget that!"

"And the mice must be doing the same," Cuspid said with rising hope.

"Let's have a look, then." Gavin went into the darkest corner of one of the square spaces, pulled up a flat stone like the others next to it on the floor of the habitat, and said cheerfully to a hole in the ground, "It's all right, fellow Tableters. They've all gone and we're back – in charge."

There was a long and anxious pause. Then a muffled voice floating weakly from the depths of the burrow below: "Is that you, Sir Gavum?"

"It is, my Lady. Please come up and join us."

"Is Sir Percibert down there with you?" Cuspid said.

"He is, but he's suffering from a bad case of laryngitis."

With that apology for her mate's uncharacteristic silence, Renée eased her head up into the dim light, blinking and then smiling broadly at the sight of Gavin and his questors. Once fully out of the burrow, she reached back and hauled Hubert up by a forepaw. He was trembling from his ear-tips to his cottonball tail, and still speechless.

"And he's gone and caught a cold from the damp down there," Renée said sympathetically.

"Can you tell us what happened here," Gavin said, "and where the others are?"

Quite calmly, and with Hubert tucked under one foreleg and still shivering, Renée explained what had induced her mate's sudden laryngitis and fever-shakes. "It happened just a little while ago. They came quickly and quietly out of the woods. We banged on the pot to make the firestick 'boom' and rattled the kettle. But they had no fear in them."

"Who's them?" Cuspid said.

"Not the cougar-beasts. Oh, no. These were gigantic weasels with fox tails and fur, and they moved as swift as the wind and leapt over our walls as if they were not even there. Hubert and I dashed for our burrow, squeezed into it, and drew the stone over the entrance."

"But surely these raiders would have seen or smelled you?" Gavin said.

"And weasels like nothing better than a rabbit supper," Cuspid said, and regretted doing so, for Hubert's teeth began to chatter alarmingly.

"We could hear them above us, rummaging about and tipping things over and kicking the kettles and pots. But they never tried to lift our entrance-stone."

"So they weren't after food," Gavin said, then added, "Where was Sir Gaddelad when all this happened?"

"He was making his loop-trap in the dune-grass, as promised. I saw one of the creatures trip over him, but Adderly wasn't quick enough to ensnare it, and I heard the poor Knave yelp as if he had been bitten. Then we were running for our hiding-hole."

"And the Squirelings?"

"I heard them squeaking in the garden, so I'm sure they too went underground."

"Thank you, my Lady, for a thorough and courageous report," Sir Gavum said in a brave and business-like voice, though he was anything but calm inside. These fearsome raiders had come here looking for something, as if they had known what they might find when they arrived and had already known in advance that there was no real danger to them from the defences in Castelot. But how was this possible? Had the troupe been watched and spied upon since their arrival? Such a possibility made

Gavin shudder, but in spite of his own fears, his immediate concern was the fate of Adderly.

"I'll go out and have a look for our wounded comrade," Gavin said.

"I'd better come too," Trisbert offered.

"No, please rest. All of you. I'll go."

The dune-grass between the fortress and the woods was entirely in shadow when Gavin began treading through it looking for Adderly, alive or dead. So it was that he stepped on him before he could stop himself.

"Ouch! I thought you raccoons had night-vision, but I see now that your prowess has been exaggerated."

"Adderly! Thank Gollah. We thought you'd been killed by the raiders."

"Merely bitten on the tail and left to suffer the indignity," Adderly said, yawning and making an effort to raise his head. "But I'll survive, though I'm not sure why I should bother."

"You'd better come inside, nevertheless," Gavin said, smiling to himself. "Your friends are terribly worried about you."

"This knavehood business isn't all it was cracked up to be," Sir Gaddelad opined.

As they were making their way back towards Castelot, they heard a wild halloo from the beach to the south of them.
"It's the other questors!" Gavin cried, forgetting to be calm and leader-like. Everyone, it seemed, had survived one more day on the bleak shores of Everdark.

* * *

"But where can he be?" Cuspid said, glad to see his sister safely returned but, like the others, distressed at the absence of Cuyler.

"Don't worry," Gavin — worried sick — said to his followers. "Sir Kayla's a raccoon. He's as at home in a tree as in creek-water. And when the moon comes up, it'll be clear as daylight for him. He'll be back here by dawn, you'll see."

"And the Squeezels can't climb," Quiver pointed out. He had been the one to describe their frightening encounter, Paddle-Whee's heroism, his own fierce counter-attack in the face of danger, and the unexplained disappearance of Cuyler. "And they've got hydrothermia, fear of water."

"I'll stay up on the wall an' watch out for him," Trisbert said.

"All right," Gavin agreed. "The firestick's been stolen, but we can still rattle the kettle and do whatever we can in the event that the cougar-beasts take advantage of our weakness and charge in force."

"If they do," Quiver said, "just wake me up and I'll give them what I gave to that Squeezel in the creek."

"So, do you think the Squeezels were after the Tallwalker weapon?" Cuspid asked Gavin. "It was the only thing they took."

"Ei-eee, ei-eee, by hook and crook

The Squeezels went off with The Book!"

It was Dante, rhyming from her perch on the wall next to the garden. Bucktooth and Petite were beside her.

"Not The Book of Coon-Craft and Animal Cunning?"

"Yes," Bucktooth squeaked. "We watched them from the lettuce-patch. They found Sir Gavum's pouch-thing and carried it off into the forest — with the firestick."

No news, not even the disappearance of Cuyler, could have struck more dismay into the troupe than this. Cries of woe and despair poured out of them, and Gavin could see that his Herculean efforts to mould this eccentric collection of woods-creatures into a functioning unit and give them a sense of purpose and confidence beyond their individual natures was in danger of collapsing — here and now and irreversibly. Only he knew, of course, that what the Squeezels had stolen was not The Book but bits and pieces of Tallwalker text they would not care a fig for. Was it time at last to tell them the truth: that all their success thus far had been due to Tallwalker tales, Tallwalker utensils, Tallwalker habitats? He looked about him at the slumped and defeated posture of his comrades — their initial outpouring of shock and disbelief having given way to quiet resignation — and decided that he could not do so. Even if he were to lie to them by holding out hope that Gollah's sacred texts were likely to be safe and sound somewhere in Earthwood, he realized that they might well lack the stamina and willpower to get there. And he now believed that with the aid of the Tallwalker's map, they could soon find a way through or over Serpentine Ridge.

He cleared his throat, and spoke: "Knaves, Ladies and Squirelings — my good friends — please do not lose hope. We have come this far and I promise you that within two days we will set foot upon our homeland. The sacred texts that conveyed to us Gollah's will and divine advice have guided us here in safety. And they shall continue to guide us to a passage through Serpentine."

"But how?" Trisbert said. As stalwart as any three of them, he had nonetheless tossed away Hex-Calibre and crawled into the shadows. "They're gone forever."

"Perhaps. I was – am – an elder-son. I have a prodigious memory." He tapped his head meaningfully. "I have memorized those parts that we shall need to ensure our safe return."

The effect of this deception was instantaneous. Within seconds the Round Tablet had re-formed around its most noble Knave – waiting once again for the word.

"You are with me, then?"

Cheers of assent greeted this unnecessary question. Trisbert had once more taken hold of Hex-Calibre.

"Your wish is our commandment!"

"Hurrah for Gavin the Great!"

Sir Percibert sneezed.

"Is that a 'yes'?" Cuspid said to him with the twinkle back in his eye.

"What I shall do," Gavin said when he had everyone's attention, "is sit in the moonlight and study the Tallwalker's map – "

"But it's gone!" Paddle-Whee said suddenly.

"Not so," Gavin said. He went over to the gate, reached down and lifted up a floor-stone. A sheet of paper floated up into the moonlight with his forepaw. "I took the precaution of hiding it separately from the texts. This is all I need – thanks to you brave questors and what we have learned – to work out a plan of action. And I shall do so by sun-up."

"Will we be leaving Castelot?" Cuspid asked, hoping and worrying in the same breath.

"I'm afraid so. It is no longer safe here. This fine abode has served us well, but now is the time for all of us to make a dash for the border. It's now or never."

No-one responded to this remark, but in their silence Gavin was sure he detected more resolute determination than animal doubt.

"What about Cuyler?" Trisbert said softly.

"He'll be here before morning," Gavin said. "And it'll be one for all and all for one!"

The hurrahs that followed on this ringing reaffirmation were heartfelt and prolonged. Now, if only Cuyler were alive and making his coon-like way through the moonlit treetops . . .

Chapter 23

The Bear-Beast

GAVIN HAD NOT SHARED ALL HIS THOUGHTS about the raid of the Squeezels. It seemed clear to him that what they had carried off was merely a backpack. From Renée's account, it didn't appear that they had opened it, but rather had gone searching for it knowing beforehand what was inside. But who could know that such a pouch might contain anything of value? Only one candidate suggested himself: Wylee the fox. He had already attempted once to steal what he assumed was The Book, and discovered too late that he had swum Heartbreak Channel lugging a pair of stones. But Wylee had reached Everdark. Paddle-Whee had seen his tracks on the beach, heading into the forest. The fox certainly wanted The Book badly, thinking no doubt that it contained the wisdom he would need to survive, or perhaps to rule over any of those woods-creatures who might have outlasted the flood. And although Wylee himself had not come here to get The Book, it was impossible to believe that anyone other than he had informed the Squeezels of its whereabouts and the importance of its contents. Moreover, those mammoth mutants were part fox, were they not? Had Wylee somehow worked his wily stratagems upon those ignorant beasts? Was he holed up somewhere nearby in command of these ruthless henchmen? If so, then it was vital that the troupe make their dash for Earthwood at first light, even if it meant leaving Cuyler to his own devices. Please, forgive me, Papa.

Gavin found himself a quiet, moon-mellowed spot and sat down with the map and the details of the terrain he had kept in his head. To his delight, he soon concluded that the wriggling lines were indeed representing the course of the streams he had observed to the north of Castelot. Furthermore, the waterfall was indicated at the end of one of the creeks by several short, wavy lines. And there beside it, and meandering its way along the slope of the Ridge, was a double-line — which had to be the goat-path he himself had taken special note of. The paw holding the paper was trembling as he followed the "path" up to where it stopped at a shaded oval. Next to the oval he could make out a Gibberlish word. Perhaps it was the moonlight or even an unexpected gift from Gollah, but its meaning leapt instantly into his mind: cave. The goat-path led to a cave. And came out again, for the double-line continued from the other side of the cave and kept going northward up the Ridge, ending — and here Gavin could hear his heart begin to hammer wildly — at a square-figure which could only represent the structure whose metal roof had glinted in the sun earlier today. And this structure was very near the top of the Ridge! If they could get that far and find shelter — it could only be a house-habitat — surely they could summon courage and strength enough to make a final climb to freedom, and home. In any event, it was their only chance, and one that Gavin was determined to take.
Near the barrel, among its scattered contents, Gavin found one of the leather straps that Tallwalkers tied around their waists. He wrapped it around his chest,

fiddled with the buckle till he got it latched, and tucked the map inside it, along with Minervah's tail-feather. Then, exhausted, he fell asleep.

* * *

Although everyone, including the Squirelings, noticed that Sir Kayla had failed to return during the night, no-one had the courage or the desire to remark on his absence or speculate what might have happened or not happened to him. Sir Gavum gave no outward sign as he quietly went about preparing to abandon the fortification that had begun to seem just a little like home. At his urging the others ate and drank their fill, as when and where the next meal might occur was anyone's guess. Gavin deliberately avoided looking towards the woods to the south, but his ears were pricked in that direction. Nor could he look dear, dear Trisbert in the eye for fear that his brother's anguish would set his own spiralling out of control. And he would need all his wit and more valour than he had as yet been able to muster if they were to get as far as the waterfall and the cave beyond.

The sun was fully up when the troupe at last organized itself in single-file, with Sir Gaddelad guarding the rear and Sir Tristum at the front brandishing the invincible swordstick. Gavin was set to join him as soon as he was satisfied that the column was ready to march.

"Where are the Squirelings?" he said suddenly. "I thought they were going to ride on Lady Morga-Whee?"

"They are," Paddle-Whee said, "but they've gone back to fetch Merlah, who seems to have forgotten the time."

"Well, I trust that they will hurry," Sir Percibert said, "as the morning dampness is settling into my bones and threatening another bout of fever."

"The sun and the walk will do wonders, chéri," his lady sympathized.

"I certainly assumed that the well-being of the knave-class superseded that of the Squirelings," Hubert complained, "or what use is a Round Tablet?"

"I suppose," Quiver said, "one should not jump to confusions about such matters."

Just then Bucktooth and Petite tripped out from under the gate.

"What's wrong?" Gavin asked.

"She won't come," Bucktooth said.

"She's decided that since Earthwood is not her home and the garden here would make a suitable abode for a mole, she intends to stay on," Petite explained. "She wishes us well, and offers her thanks to you all, and especially to our leader. She even forgives Wylee the fox and his treachery."

"Well, that's just dandy," Hubert said. "It's all very well for her to think only of herself, but what are we Knaves to do without our wizard, our sorcerer, our prophet?"

At this less than polite remark, the delinquent Squireling herself appeared on top of the gate.

"We respect your decision," Gavin said to her, "and wish you good health and long life."

Dante smiled her gratitude.

"You wouldn't happen," Quiver said hopefully, "to have in your rhyme-pouch just one more predilection for us, would you?"

Dante squeezed her eyes completely shut. The troupe waited nervously, for the next day and night were likely to determine their fate one way or another, and it would be helpful – even if her predictions were not always right – to know which way it was to be. Gavin of course was concerned that her reply might have more to do with Cuyler than the troupe.

At last she spoke:

"Ai-eee! A darkling tunnel I do see

From Tallwalker house to a far countree!

And Gavin the Great, with no plots pending,

Shall tell his tale with a happy ending!

By moon and sun, my rhymes are done."

And so, with these hopeful words ringing in their ears, Castelot's troupe set off upon their final quest.

* * *

As they trekked northwards along the beach in bright sunshine towards the stream that would lead them to the waterfall, no-one spied upon them from the woods on their left, while on their right the waves from Heartbreak Channel washed whisperingly at their feet. At the mouth of Good Luck Creek (as Gavin would always remember it) they paused just long enough to re-arrange themselves for travelling upstream in shallow water. The mice continued to ride on Paddle-Whee's back, buried in her thick fur. Quiver held onto Cuspid's tail and allowed himself to be towed whenever his body, unused to maritime locomotion, sagged and his paws ached from paddling. The cottontails, who could swim but preferred not to, piggy-backed on Trisbert and Gavin, while Adderly slipped along on his own with only his head swaying above the surface. Hex-Calibre was clamped firmly in Trisbert's teeth, who was compelled to stop every few moments to rest his jaw and catch up on his breathing. But with the loss of the sacred texts, Gavin knew that his comrades had transferred their hopes to the death-dealing swordstick, and so he had been obliged to carry it along, cumbersome though it be.

Knowing the terrain now (he didn't need to refer to the map on his belt), Gavin led the way with as much confidence as their perilous situation permitted. As long as the sun continued to shine through the trees onto the middle of the creek where the troupe was travelling, there was little danger of the cougar-beasts or other gloom-loving mutants attacking them – at least that was Gavin's optimistic conclusion. But very soon the shadows of Everdark's enormous canopy of branches began to stretch all the way across Good Luck Creek.

Trisbert suddenly stopped and let Hex-Calibre drop into the water. "I meed to ged my jawdones worging again," he mumbled to Gavin.

"But you don't have to stand on your hind feet to do so," Hubert complained from his dry perch aboard Gavin. "You're getting Madame's paws needlessly wet!"

"I'm perfectly fine, chéri. Sir Tristum has been most gallant."

"I can smell beasts in the woods over there," Cuspid said.

"And I can hear their slobbery breathing," Hubert added.

"The waterfall, and the safety of the barren Ridge, is only about twenty paces beyond the next bend," Gavin said. "The water here is deep enough to have everybody swimming or riding. We'll catch our breath for a bit, and then make a run for it. It's our only hope. If we're attacked, I want everyone to keep going, whatever happens. Don't look back or glance sideways. Some of us are bound to make it through. And remember, you are Knaves, Ladies and Squirelings."

This commentary silenced the troupe, even Hubert, whose fur was near ruin from the inconsiderate splashing of others.

Everyone held their breath until at last Trisbert picked up Hex-Calibre, and Gavin, beside him, gave the signal to advance. Beavers, raccoons and fox-snake dove with determination into their element, carrying their comrades with them. They paddled with the fury of desperation. The thickets and shrubs overhanging the banks suddenly shook and rattled with the excitement of equally desperate pursuers. Only when Gavin rounded the bend and could look up to see the shaft of sunlight that indicated where Everdark ended and the Ridge began, did he come to a halt and turn back to see how many had survived along with him.

"We're all here," Adderly said from the rear of the column. "We've run the gauntlet."

The others, excited and breathless, looked to Gavin.

"Listen, friends, and you'll hear the waterfall where the creek comes down from the Ridge, just to the north of where the sunlight's shining up ahead."

"I think we'd better go there now," Cuspid said. "I can hear teeth grinding close by, and they aren't my own."

"Right you are, Sir Cuspidon," Gavin said, and making sure that Trisbert was ready to bear the weight of Hex-Calibre once more, he plunged into the icy rapids. However, when he brought his head up to begin his steady stroking and make sure that Hubert was still safely aboard, he froze. His paws hung lifeless in the current. Trisbert bumped into him, almost unseating Hubert, who was too surprised to deliver any rebuke.

"What is it?" Trisbert spluttered.

"L-L-Look," Gavin whispered, though he'd intended to shout.

The others, who had now stopped as well, stared up at what had brought their leader to a paralysed halt. There, ten paces ahead and half in the shadow of Everdark and half in the free-shining light beyond it, stood the monster of all monsters — blocking their escape and dashing their hopes utterly.

Sometime long ago its ancestors had begun life as bears, for the creature was as big and bulky as a grizzly, with a bruin's vicious and terrifying jaws — all razor-sharp teeth and lolling tongue — and a bear's beady, pig-like eyes. And its general shape was lumpy and bearish. Then somehow, through successive mutations, it had lost its lustrous fur, for this beast was as hairless as a newt and the pulpy flesh under its glistening skin was tortured by warts as fat and venomous as toads. As it reared up on its hind legs and shook its forearms in concert with its tree-trembling growl, only one of them had claws. The other ended in a stump.

Gavin felt his bowels turn to liquid with fear. Even if he had had the strength to wield Hex-Calibre, it would work no miracles on this gargantuan spawn of Zeebub. And brave Trisbert, who would test its magic anyway, would be crushed like a clamshell.

"Use the swordstick, please," Renée whispered in Trisbert's ear. "Dump me off. I'd sooner drown than be eaten."

Behind her the others were speechless, though prayers to Gollah were being lipped – begging quick passage to North Holy. Gavin had now recovered enough to stare back up at the monster. He remembered Dante's prophetic rhyme about a dragon and a cave. This "dragon" wasn't breathing fire like the ones described in Tales of Arthro, but it would do in every other respect. Gavin's gaze was suddenly returned by the beast, whose introductory bellow had settled down to a menacing growl. Its piggish eyes were staring directly at Gavin, who must have appeared to it no larger than a mouse to a lynx. They gleamed with the ruthless ferocity of all unchallenged predators, but behind them somewhere deep and abiding Gavin was certain he detected a kind of sadness. For the merest eyeblink, it reminded him of the look on the dead Tallwalker's face as he lay among the ruins of his retreat and the scattered pages of the books that had failed him.

Then the bear-beast raised one huge foot and took a first harrowing step towards the troupe. What could they do? They could retreat back into the gauntlet of dangerous dark they had just successfully run, where cougar-beasts waited to pounce. Even so, the "dragon" would be over them in three simple strides. That left only the banks and the forest itself. And a similar fate. Gavin realized, though, that there was no need for a command of any kind. The Round Tableters were now woods-creatures once again, and would submit individually to their fate.

Just as the bear-beast was about to take another step, one which would have brought it right up to Gavin and Trisbert, there came from somewhere high up and nearby in the treetops a wild chittering noise. The mutant's floppy ears shot up, and it slowly swung its thick head up towards the source of the distraction. The noise grew louder and closer – a chirruping, taunting refrain that seemed to catch and hold the bear-beast's attention, against its will almost, for dinner was laid out within easy reach at its feet. Gavin and his troupe watched with increasing fascination and suspended terror as the slobbering carnivore swivelled its entire bulk around to confront the maddening and foolhardy interruption. The upper branches of a deformed elm were seen to shake acrobatically while continuing to camouflage the impudent intruder.

With a roar that rocked the troupe backwards into the water and shuddered its way down Good Luck Creek, the bear-beast stomped towards the south bank of the stream in the direction of the offending elm-tree. The chittering increased in volume, as cheeky as a chipmunk's taunt. With a snort of rage, the bear-beast lunged into the forest, wrapped both forearms around the trunk of the elm and began to shake it. But it was too late. The offender had taken its taunt to a neighbouring tree. The enraged bear-beast lurched after it, but in doing so it lost its bearings, swayed and seesawed this way and that, and finally stumbled and crashed to the forest-floor with the thunderous whump of a felled redwood.

"Quick!" Gavin yelled. "Let's go! To the waterfall!"

* * *

Incredibly, every member of the troupe made it out of Everdark onto the goat-path that began just above the cataract – where it was sunny and safe. For a long while no-one spoke, such was their relief, their wonder, and their gratitude to Gollah for sending them a saviour in their hour of need. Their delivery had not, it seemed, been due to the power of the Round Tablet or to Hex-

Calibre or to their own animal instincts. It had been a miracle of another kind entirely.

Gavin of course was as relieved and grateful as the rest. But they were still only partway home. On the path above, a cave with unknown dangers stood between them and the Tallwalker house-habitat farther above (where, if Dante was right, some sort of passageway might lead them back to Earthwood). The troupe would still need the courage of their Arthro names if these fresh hazards were to be faced and overcome. But he could see plainly that his comrades had accepted the intervention as the work of Gollah, and were most likely to be happy to put their faith and hopes back in His hands.

It was Trisbert who spoke first. "What sort of creature do you think it was who helped us out back there, Gav?"

"I couldn't see, Bertie, and the noises were pure nonsense to me."

Hubert and Renée lay upon a warm boulder, letting the sun dry their matted fur. Paddle-Whee and Cuspid, never fully at ease too far from water, huddled in the boulder's shade and listened to the music of the falls just below.

"It's almost like it wanted to save us."

True, though it's hard to believe anything in Everdark would be friendly," Gavin said. But was it possible that Minervah had seen only part of what had happened after the flood? That scattered throughout Everdark was a handful of survivors, like themselves? Could some of them have made it up to the cave, or to the house-habitat with the metal roof?

"If only Sir Kayla had managed to reach us," Paddle-Whee sighed.

"But he has!" someone cried as he bounded up the path and parked himself proudly in front of the troupe. It was Sir Kayla himself, beaming.

* * *

Cuyler was cheered and hurrahed, and then cheered again for good measure. How clever he had been to trail them up Good Luck Creek and then, when the coast was clear, slip past the befuddled bear-beast and the waterfall to join his fellow Tableters.

"You had us very worried for a while," Gavin said, but his eyes were dancing with pride and brotherly affection.

"And how did you ever find us?" Quiver said. "You must be a regular cart-logger!"

"Raccoons don't need maps or cartographers to find their way in a forest," Gavin laughed.

"Sir Gavum's right," Cuyler said, delighted to be the centre of attention and not sure he wished to relinquish the pleasure. "I just climbed the highest tree I could find and had a sunny look over Everdark. You were just disappearing into the shadows of that nasty creek back there when I spotted you."

"But we must have the whole story," Paddle-Whee said. "We were not sure where you'd got to after the Squeezels attacked."

Once informed just who the Squeezels were, Cuyler was most happy to recount the details of his own improvised quest. He had indeed taken to the nearest tree, but had remained in a lower branch, prepared to counter-attack if his comrades should be unable to escape the onslaught. As it turned out, his valour had not needed testing, for Paddle-Whee and Quiver had got safely away – after transforming the champion Squeezel's mouth into a prickly pear. Its howls of outrage brought its henchmen into the fray, though it was clear that none of them could stand to be in the water for more than a moment. So, Cuyler informed his rapt audience, he decided to make certain that his fellow questors were able to get safely all the way to the beach – by taunting the half-dozen Squeezels and drawing them away in the opposite direction. He leaped from branch to limb just above their outstretched paws, sticking to the trees overhanging the creek so that the maddened Squeezels, stumbling and cursing below, were often toppled into the water, where their curses increased tenfold. At last, tiring of the game, Cuyler went aloft and easily lost his pursuers. By then it was pitch black. He had moved so far inland that he could not be sure which creek was which. Moreover, he was exhausted, and so decided to find a cosy limb-crotch and rest. Once or twice he thought he saw a three-legged owl skimming overhead, but he soon fell so soundly asleep that only the heat of the mid-morning sun woke him up.

"Did you happen to notice whether or not the Squeezels were carrying anything?" Gavin asked when Cuyler paused for breath.

Cuyler looked puzzled, then brightened and said, "Why, yes, I did, Sir Gavum. One of them was dragging along a pouch, very like the Tallwalker's knapsack."

At this point it became necessary to tell Cuyler of the Squeezels' raid on Castelot in the questors' absence and the missing backpack – with its "sacred" contents.

"But what would Squeezels want with The Book?" Cuyler said, more puzzled than upset.

"Wylee," Quiver said, "and his deviant machineries."

"You didn't happen to see the rascally fox in all your surveying?" Cuspid said.

"Only cougar-beasts," Cuyler said with a tremor in his voice that brought the attention of the troupe back where it belonged, "and hawks with webbed toes – and that ghastly bear-thing in the creek."

"Then you must have seen the strange creature who so cleverly detracted the bear-beast with his gobbledy-gobble," Quiver said, as the others – including Gavin (who had suspected the truth from the start) – leaned forward to learn the name or species of their saviour.

"Please, do tell us who it was," Renée said sweetly.

Cuyler had the good sense to blush before saying quietly, "I was the clever distracter."

"Well, you were always good at doin' that!" Trisbert said with a burst of brotherly laughter. And all the Knaves, Ladies and Squirelings joined in.

"Three more cheers for Sir Kayla!" they shouted.
Not only was Cuyler back, Gavin thought with deep satisfaction, but the Round Tablet as well.

* * *

Gavin insisted that everyone take a long drink at the waterfall before they set off up the goat-path on the next leg of their journey to Earthwood. There would be no food, for the path appeared to follow the line of a ledge jutting from the cliff-face itself. The terrain above and below was barren limestone, devoid of shrubbery and grass. Forming the single-file they were now accustomed to, they began to pick their way carefully along the rocky course: anyone tumbling off would drop to an instant death on the jagged scree below or else lie maimed at the edge of Everdark until one of its carnivores slipped out and devoured him. Difficult as the climb was, the mood among the Tableters was hopeful, almost buoyant. The membership was intact, and their quests thus far had been spectacularly successful. They had lost the sacred texts — for now — but their leader had memorized the necessary bits. And they still had Hex-Calibre.

The sun was beginning to slide down from its high point when Gavin held up a paw, and the column drew to a halt. Tallwalker's map was true: thirty paces ahead and slightly above, the path vanished into the dark mouth of a cave. Farther on up, the path appeared to emerge from the other end of the cavern, and continued northward towards the sun-washed roof of a house-habitat — still some leagues away but now tantalizingly visible. Gavin scanned the bald terrain around the cave's mouth: there was no way for the troupe to reach the upper path without going through the cave.

"Sir Tristum and I will go ahead and see what's in the cave," Gavin announced. "The others will proceed cautiously until I give the all-clear."

Clamping Hex-Calibre between his teeth, Trisbert trailed Gavin towards the cave. With the sun now in the western sky, the large opening before them was still dark, and the hollow behind it darker still. Surely if there were survivors from Earthwood in there, they would come out to welcome him. Hadn't Dante mentioned something about a damsel? Tee-Jenn, perhaps? His heart skipped several beats. "I guess we'll just have to go right up and have a look," he said at last.

"I'll be right beside you," Trisbert said.

Gavin suddenly remembered the exact details of Dante's prophetic rhyme. He was just about to mention this to Trisbert when the black oval of the cave's entrance exploded with a burst of smoke that hissed and writhed, and then poured over their heads and down towards the troupe ten paces behind them. This was followed immediately by a hollow howling, that was part moan and part rage.

"Another beast," Trisbert coughed, as he took Hex-Calibre into his powerful forepaws.

"Merlah's dragon," Gavin sighed before he too began to cough.

Chapter 24

Dragonslayer

GAVIN AND TRISBERT BACK-PEDALLED down to the others with as much dignity as they could muster in the face of the belching smoke and fading howl. The troupe, having nowhere to hide or cower safely except the bare and narrow path, simply cringed and slowly grew petrified.

"It's D-Dante's dragon," Hubert mewled as his mysterious fever struck again.

"What'll we do?" Cuspid said through the paws he had placed in front of his face.

"Perhaps Sir Kayla might subtract him," Quiver suggested through a screen of quills.

"He must be bigger than a m-moose," Paddle-Whee said in a tiny voice unsuited to the high status of a royal lady.

"Oh, please stop shaking," Bucktooth cried from his handhold on the Lady's back. "We'll perish of the trembles!"

"It's only to be expected." Adderly said, suppressing a sneeze.

"We've got Hex-Calibre, haven't we?" Cuyler said behind the bulwark of Trisbert's rump.

"Yes," Trisbert said, "we have."

All eyes, where possible, turned to the one who must, according to the most holy of texts, wield the invincible weapon.

Gavin was leaning against a boulder in a vain attempt to stop his legs from trembling. He was afraid and angry and demoralized all at once. The fear was easy to explain: the cave blocking their only escape route was inhabited by a creature more terrible and vindictive than any of the pathetic mutants they had encountered thus far. The tales he had read in Arthro's book had spelled it out: this was the beast sent by the forces of darkness to plague the world. It could only be vanquished in single combat with the chosen champion of its enemy. At least that's what the Tallwalker stories seemed to suggest. But as telling as the wisdom in them might be, they were just fantastic tales, were they not? Suddenly he found himself angry, he felt like shouting to his followers that Hex-Calibre was not an enchanted swordstick but a cheap utensil discarded by some careless Tallwalker ages ago! And their chosen champion was a charlatan, a trickster who had used the Athro tales to give them a courage and purpose they were ready to abandon at the first sign of adversity or failure! And of course he was crushingly disappointed in himself: he was no more a warrior prince than they were Knaves of the Round Tablet! Here, at last, each member of the troupe would have to face the inescapable reality of his or her own nature.

"I'll carry Hex-Calibre up there as far as I can go," Trisbert was saying, "and hand it to you when you're ready to strike the fiend."

Gavin startled himself by replying, "Yes. Thank you. I'll need to save all my strength for the killing thrust." For the horror of my ignominious death, he thought. But at least he would die with his beloved and impossibly brave littermate at his side. Their souls would fly together to North Holy.

Sir Quivelot was about to call for a round of cheers in support of their champion when the dragon let loose with another barrage of smoke and roaring.

Before Gavin could change his mind, Trisbert set off with Hex-Calibre in his jaws. "Don't come near the cave until I give you the signal to move," Gavin said to the troupe, grateful that his coughing disguised the tremor in his voice.

The brothers made their way through the oily smoke, brushing it from their eyes in an effort see what kind of monster could breathe such fury. Gradually the air cleared before them, and they braced for another blast, one that might easily scorch or suffocate them – so close were they now to the entrance. Slowly out of the smoky haze there took shape an incredible form: half as high as a Ring-Tree in Earthwood, draped with loose, flapping, pock-marked skin, the massive bulk of its chest completely filling the cave-mouth. Its neck and fire-spewing jaws had to be somewhere near the cavernous roof of its dragon-lair.

I cannot even reach its knees, if it has any, Gavin thought, just as Trisbert placed Hex-Calibre in his forepaws and whispered, "Gollah be with you." Quaking all over, as if in the final throes of hydrophobia, Gavin tried to raise the Tallwalker's hunting-knife above his head in a manner that might resemble a threat to the dragon – but failed. His forelimbs were paralysed with pure, animal terror. He simply stood and waited for the fiery demise that was his due.

The fatal blast of fire-breath did not arrive. Instead there was a tiny spurt of smoke that seemed to come not from the jaws in the blackness above but rather from somewhere behind the beast. Was there a second one? A whole caveful of them? Summoning up the last of his fast-waning strength, Gavin forced himself to take one more step towards certain death. This move, while in no way menacing, provoked from the cave-creature a vocal response. But it was neither ear-shattering nor awesome. It was muffled and frightened and unceasing.
Something nearby was sobbing its heart out.

* * *

Gavin stepped around the drooping hide. Four or five paces behind it, squatted on its haunches beside a smoky wood-fire, sat the strangest-looking creature Gavin had yet seen in this country of mutants and misfits. Its head and shoulders were that of a very large warthog, except that it had no tusks and its eyes were as round and glassy as an owl's. Its slim, sleek-haired body could have been that of an otter – with delicate, coon-nimble forepaws – though no self-respecting otter would have boasted a set of hind-legs that were utterly hairless and considerably bowed, as if they had long ago given up supporting the weight of that comical, bulbous head. The creature's face was contorted by sobs and other tearful shakings that shuddered down through the mismatched parts below. Beside it, near the fire where it had been tossed, lay a pouch-like leather contraption.

Without looking up or interrupting its sobbing, the would-be dragon said suddenly, "Just kill me quickly and get it over, will you?"

"Who are you?" Gavin asked, as all his earlier terrors began fading discreetly away.

"I knew I couldn't fool you fellows forever," the creature continued, as if the intruder had not spoken. "But, then, no-one lives forever, does he?"

"I have not come to eat you," Gavin said in his most kindly voice. "Please, stop your crying."

The sobbing let up a little or perhaps was merely running out of steam. "It's not being eaten that's so sad, it's the failure of my monster to keep you and your cougar-beast cousins out of my home. You see — being ugly and out-of-joint and all alone — it was the only thing I had to be proud about, and now that too is to be taken from me before I am ruthlessly devoured." The sadness of this last thought brought on a single, blubbery sob.

Gavin set Hex-Calibre down and walked over to the creature until he was standing no more than a hand-span from its pig's snout. "I am Gavin of Earthwood," he said. "I am the leader-elect of a group of woods-creatures who are making their way home. We will not harm you, good sir. We wish only to take passage through your cave to the path beyond it."

The big head swung slowly upwards. The owl-eyes took in the features of the stranger. "You are not a cougar-beast." The voice, disentangled from the sobbing, was surprisingly deep and sonorous.

"I am a raccoon. And you are — ?"

"I call myself Barbar. I find it easy to pronounce." Then, when Gavin appeared to be expecting more, he added, "I've been told I am a male."

Gavin took the liberty of settling down next to the fire, which was quickly dying down. "But did your parents not give you a name when you were born?"

Barbar gave Gavin a sceptical look, as if he thought his question might be mocking him, then said, "My mother took one peek at me and trundled off into the forest."

Gavin now recalled the deformed and grotesque shapes of Renée's babies back there on Deadwood Island. "Are all the beings born in Everdark – are they all . . . ah . . . unusual?"

"Thank you for that thoughtful remark. In fact, that's the kindest thing anyone's ever said to me or any other mangled soul in this blighted country." Barbar looked as if he might weep again. "But if you have been here long, you must surely have noticed that our inhabitants are universally malformed. We are mutants, each generation more twisted and repulsive than the previous one."

"Are you alive in there, Gav?"

It was Trisbert calling from the entrance. Gavin could see his silhouette backlit by the afternoon sun.

"Everything's fine, Sir Tristum. The dragon has been taken care of."

"Oh, wonderful news!"

"Please, go back down to the others and tell them to wait until I call them up here. I'll only be a few moments."

The brave Trisbert, who had no doubt been waiting to follow his brother into death's jaws, turned and ambled dutifully off to carry out his commander's request.

"There, Barbar. Now we can talk."

"We can?"

"Yes. I need to know as much about Everdark and what's happened here as you can tell me – if I am to devise a successful plan of escape for my knaves-in-arms."

* * *

While it was obvious that Barbar had not had a friendly chat – or any sort of chat for that matter – in a very long time, it was equally clear that he knew how to tell a story and had done so quite often in the past. He began quite properly at the beginning. He remembered being born and abandoned on the very same day. That night he had been chased by a ravenous beast and nearly eaten, and later had been seized by an owl's talons and lifted treeward until the half-blind bird blundered into a limb and let him drop. Fortunately he found that he was a herbivore and that there were roots and bulbs and tubers galore in the spongy soil of the forest. Then by chance he came upon a gang of young misfits – no two of them the same – who took him in and let him accompany them on their nightly maraudings. They killed and ate and bullied at will. They fought with each other for pleasure or release from the pain of their ugliness and isolation. Some of them mated, producing offspring even more hideous than themselves.

"Do you have any idea why Gollah would have visited such a plague upon Everdark?" Gavin asked at this point, "or have allowed Zeebub to do so?"

"I do," Barbar said, and he spoke then of the Great Burning. The gang had adopted — for reasons more related to mockery and abuse than to kindness or mercy — a very old badger-beast, who taught them to tell stories to amuse themselves and to make them up when the truth wouldn't do. One evening he explained to them how the once-proud animal paradise of Everdark had become a menagerie of mutants. An annual or two after the birth of his grandfather, the Tallwalkers, carrying out Zeebub's evil plan, went too far in their attempts to sow turmoil and destruction, and the result was the Great Burning. So thick was the ash from the conflagration that the sun ran off and hid for seven moons. Everdark itself was spared, the old badger said, because its long, peninsular finger jutted up into the Lake as close to North Holy as any land was allowed to be. But the ordinary forest to the south, where his grandparents and a hundred other thriving species had dwelt since time began, had been suffocated by the falling ash. And those few who survived had fled north, as their instincts dictated — into the sanctuary of Everdark.

"But if Everdark was spared from the fallout of the Burning, how did it get corrupted?" Gavin asked, fascinated now by this story and where it fit into the other stories and fragments of story he had been accumulating since the flood.

"Ah, that is the saddest part," Barbar said, as a fat tear rolled down his snout and hung, sadly, from his left nostril.

The babies that were born to the animals who had fled to Everdark were either stillborn or grotesque mutants. Moreover, the mutants that survived turned out to be much larger and stronger than their parents, and began to mate randomly with one another. Mostly carnivores, they sought to devour the ordinary species in an orgy of killing and feasting. Within two annuals, not a single creature ordained by Gollah – of either those who had been resident in Everdark or those who had fled there – remained. The forest had become a grim battleground for contending monsters.

"That is by far the saddest tale I have ever been told," Gavin said.

"But it will end soon," Barbar said. "No offspring of any sort has been born now for the past ten moons. Those of us here now are the last of our misbegotten kind."

"But you still haven't explained how you came to be in this place?" Gavin said and, glancing at the weird apparatus on the ground beside Barbar, added, "or why you set up this make-believe dragon and its smoking breath."
"Oh, that's because it only happened after the arrival of the weasel-beasts and their king, Lord Gnash," Barbar said.

* * *

"Can we come up now?" Cuyler called from the cave-mouth. "Are you sure you're all right, Gav?"

"Yes, I'm fine."

"Is the dragon really dead?"

"It's gone, Cuy. But I'm making sure the cave is safe for our passage. I'll give you a shout when I'm finished."

Barbar kindly waited until Cuyler had gone before continuing his tale. "The weasel-beasts – "

"We've begun calling them Squeezels," Gavin said.

"Very well, then. We're not fussy about names any more. These Squeezels as you call them arrived from the southern forest and took up residence on the ridge to the north of us."

"In the abandoned Tallwalker house-habitat?"

"The same. And these mutants were twice as quick and twice as wily as anyone else in Everdark. They hunted mainly at night, slipping into the woods in squads of five or six and wreaking havoc, even among the largest, most ferocious monsters."

"Like the giant bear-beast?"

"Even it. Soon my own group broke up in panic and disarray. I knew my chances of survival were non-existent if I didn't find some sort of refuge. I searched about until one day I found this cave. Only I wasn't the first one here."

What Barbar had discovered cowering in the dark here was a dwarfish Squeezel, who had been abandoned by the pack and driven out to fend for herself. Unable to do so, she had crawled into the cave to die peacefully, rather than be eaten. Against the odds, the two had become friends and partners in the survival game. Sleekit, for that was the Squeezel's name, informed Barbar that her kind were leery of water and terrified of fire. Barbar then came up with the idea of producing a fire-breathing monster to guard the cave and frighten off all attackers, Squeezel or otherwise. He had often prowled through the derelict house-habitat on the beach opposite the island. He recalled the old badger telling him how the Tallwalkers created sparks and built cooking-fires. He sneaked back there one night and returned with three essential items: jagged stones for making sparks, a flame-puffing device, and a large moose-skin he had pulled down from one of the walls.

Using his dextrous, coon-like forepaws, he built a framework of interlocking branches, and the partners draped the hide over it to resemble the chest of a mammoth beast. Gathering damp wood from the edge of the forest every day, they used the stones to ignite a fire – more smoke than flame – and while Sleekit worked the bellows to drive the oily froth out of the cave's mouth, Barbar set up a deep-throated roar whose echo and re-echo in the cavernous interior produced a sound boisterous enough to make a bear-beast quake in its own sweat. After about a dozen failed attempts by various carnivores to storm the dragon-lair, the attacks were reduced to the occasional foray by some creature driven to extremes by starvation. Such was the general fear of the place and its monster that Barbar and Sleekit found they could sidle down to the forest-edge and feed to their heart's content (though Sleekit had been slow to adapt to a vegetable diet).

"But where is Sleekit today?" Gavin asked, peering about in the increasing gloom.

Tears filled Barbar's enormous eyes. "Sleekit passed away in her sleep two moons ago. I've been alone ever since."

"I am sorry to hear that," Gavin said, thinking of Dante's prediction concerning a cave, a dragon and a dying damsel. "So you've had to operate the dragon-device all on your own?"

"I have, though lately I have begun not to care very much whether the fire lives or dies. But you and your friends are the first ones to challenge the smoke-monster since dear Sleekit passed away."

"I apologize for giving you such a fright." Though the fright had been mutual, Gavin mused.

Barbar's face brightened. "A few days ago, though, I had high hopes that I had found a new partner."

"Another shunned Squeezel?"

"No, no. It was a very small fox-beast."

Gavin's heart lurched. "His name wasn't Wylee by any chance?"

"You knew him, then?" Barbar said, surprised.

"He was one of us, but deserted at the first opportunity."

"That explains why he seemed so well-proportioned, beautiful even. Like you."

"Did he come here to attack you?" Gavin asked, quite aware that Wylee's handsome swagger camouflaged a streak of cunning selfishness.

"Oh, no. That morning I heard a low moaning down on the path by the falls. I ignored it as long as I could, but it was so pitiful and so unrelenting that I slipped outside in the bright sunshine and looked down there. The wee creature was near death, I was sure. I don't know why, but I decided to help. I dragged him up here to the safety of my cave. After a while he woke up and asked for food. Under cover of dark I fetched him some from the creek, and he nibbled at it. By the next morning he was strong enough to tell me that he had been attacked by enemies on the island and had been forced by his tormentors to swim the channel with two stones strapped to his back. This cruelty so exhausted him that he could only crawl towards the Ridge, where he expected to find a way out – he didn't say where to."

"A fine tissue of self-serving fibs," Gavin sighed.

"Alas, the poor chap took to shivering before the next morning, and died soon after. I was devastated."

And you were lucky, too, Gavin thought. He also concluded that Wylee could not have been the one to have organized the raid on Castelot or even the one to have told the Squeezels what was there that was worth stealing.

"His bones are over there," Barbar was saying. "I put his carcase out for the crows to pick clean, and when they were done I brought the remains in here. I find them strangely comforting."

"He's probably getting up to mischief in North Holy," Gavin said kindly.

Barbar made an effort to smile. "And he was one of yours, you say?"

"He was. He and my ten companions were swept away from Earthwood by the great flood, and met only by chance on the island we called Deadwood."

"Ah, yes. The flood." Barbar gave a shudder that set his mismatched parts in exaggerated motion.

Gavin took a deep breath and said, "We've been told by an owl who survived in Everdark that many of my fellow-creatures from Earthwood found themselves alive and marooned in your forest when the mighty wall of water passed on."

Barbar let his shudder subside into a long sigh.

"You've seen or heard of them?" Gavin asked, hoping against hope.

"In a way," Barbar said, staring at the fire. "I was down by the falls when I heard the roar of water and looked up to see a wave as big as a thunderhead come washing over the ridge a league or so away. We had had no rain here, so my first thought was that Gollah had sent a deluge to destroy us – mercifully and outright. My second thought was to scramble back into my cave like a coward and wait out my fate in the cosy darkness of my own nest."

"But the waters didn't reach you?"

"I guess not." He looked up sheepishly for a moment. "I was so scared I just put my paws over my eyes and pretended to sleep. Days went by, I think – I've no way of knowing for sure. But I knew the waters had passed over or through the forest because I could hear the wails and cries of a hundred beasts – in torment."

"Oh, please, Barbar, do not upset yourself with such memories. I need to know only if you heard or saw – "

"The big wave swept many beasts out into the lake, I'm sure, but others clung to the trees and those who didn't drown survived. I heard their bodies dropping onto the forest floor. Then I heard the Squeezels – "

"The flood didn't harm them?"

"Their lair, like my cave, was too high and too close to North Holy. They must have watched the horrors with glee, then came slinking down to feast on the maimed and dying. It was dreadful. I lay in the darkness here and could not help but listen to the crunching of bones and the pitiful cries of the forsaken – and prayed for my own death."

"No-one found your cave or sought refuge up here?" Gavin said with a sinking heart.

"No-one – from Everdark or . . . or Earthwood." Barbar looked up, shame flooding his face. "But I did hear a lot of tiny shrieks and strange, alien death-cries . . ."

Then Minervah had been right: animals from Earthwood had made it alive to Everdark, only to be devoured by Squeezels or worse. Any hopes of seeing Papa or Tee-Jenn again this side of North Holy had been dashed by Barbar's sad account.

"There was nothing I could do," Barbar was saying.

"There was nothing any of us could do," Gavin said. Then, remembering why he was here and where his duty lay, Gavin pushed these sorrows aside and gathered his wits about him. It was time to redirect the dialogue towards more practical ends. "My troupe and I have reason to believe that if we can get to the house-habitat north of here, we will find a passageway through the Ridge to Earthwood. Is there an exit at the other end of your cave that would allow us to resume our climb?"

Barbar frowned, then smiled and said, "Yes, there is. I've got it blocked with a stone only I know how to remove, but it would give me great pleasure to open the way for you and your brave friends."

"That's most kind of you, considering the fright we gave you. Perhaps you'd like to join us on our quest. You'd be most welcome."

Barbar smiled again, and brushed away a tear. "Thank you, young Gavin. Your offer is more than I deserve, but my leaving here would serve no purpose. My fate was sealed with my birth. But you have given me the courage to play out my part to the end. When your friends have passed through, I shall stir the fire again and practise my best dragon's bellow." Barbar's smile vanished as he added, "But you must reconsider any plan to approach the palace of Lord Gnash."

"We are quite aware that we may have to outwit any current occupants of the place," Gavin said, both puzzled and alarmed. And we have an invincible swordstick, he was about to boast before he realized the foolishness of such a claim.

"But Lord Gnash is not a Squeezel," Barbar protested.

"Another kind of mutant, then?"

"No, sir. He is much, much worse than any misbegotten beast of Everdark. And ten times as dangerous."

Gavin blinked, speechless.

"He's a mad Tallwalker who wants to be king of the world!"

Chapter 25

Lord Gnash

WHEN GAVIN HAD RECOVERED FROM HIS INITIAL SHOCK
at this dreadful news, he stumbled back to the entrance
and hollered down to the troupe that he would be ready
to bring them forward shortly. As he turned to go back
in, he heard the beginnings of a hurrah – and wished he
hadn't.

Back inside, Gavin said to his host, "Tell me all about
this Lord Gnash."

So Barbar, reluctantly – for he was saddened by the
worry that kept worsening in his guest's face – began to
tell Gavin about the renegade Tallwalker. His main source
for the known facts was Sleekit, his exiled Squeezel-
friend. Although no-one knew exactly when, Lord Gnash
had appeared at his "palace" (as it was thereafter called)
sometime soon after the invasion of the Squeezels.
Within days, he had used his Tallwalker skills and
ruthlessness to take over the lives of those Squeezels
already living there. One moon later and he was in
command of every Squeezel in Everdark – that's when
Sleekit had been "recruited" – using them as his
bodyguards and foragers, designated killers, and all-round
henchmen. With their speed and his treacherous

stratagems, he was quickly the master of Everdark. The Squeezels brought him the choicest morsels from their frequent kills. The two largest, fiercest and most acrobatic Squeezels stood constant guard outside his throne-room at the rear of the palace.

"But you said he wanted to be king of more than Everdark," Gavin said, wishing he didn't have to ask.

"That is so, according to Sleekit. Lord Gnash has his sights set on Earthwood and, after that, whatever is left of the Tallwalker territory to the south, where he is said to have been born and raised."

"But Earthwood has been flooded away," Gavin said, again wishing it were not so.

"Nice and empty, then, isn't it? For Lord Gnash to populate with Squeezels – or worse."

Gavin shuddered. The news was getting worse with each sentence.

"Sleekit was sure that Lord Gnash had some secret plan in store for Earthwood, but before she could learn any details, she was cast out by her own kind."

"Did she actually see this Lord Gnash?"

"Once, and only then from the middle of a crowd – there are many, many Squeezels and they are possibly still reproducing themselves, Sleekit said. He seems to be short for a Tallwalker, but has one of those hairy faces they adopt to try and resemble Gollah's chosen ones, and there's a metal ring stuck stupidly on his head. His coverings are all of the Tallwalker type, garishly coloured and drooping. He astonished his followers by speaking every known creature-tongue, as well as Gibberlish."

Gavin sighed. "Whatever he is and whatever he is plotting, we have no choice but to try and get past him –

by hook or by crook – and find that tunnel. We have come too far to quit now."

"I don't expect it'll help much," Barbar said as he gave the fire a friendly poke, "but Sleekit told me all about the palace and the strange terrain around it."
For the first time in a while Gavin began to hope.

* * *

With some good grace Gavin endured the cheers and hurrahs of his troupe ("Hurray for Sir Gavum the Dragonslayer!" being the most popular) as he led them back up the slope to the entrance of the cave. In the murky gloom there was just enough light for the Tableters to see, off to their left, the remains of the dragon Gavin the Great had slain. And what a mammoth beast it must have been! Only its enormous back and flank were visible, but protruding from the former was Hex-Calibre itself, buried to the hilt in the fiend's heart! Gavin made no move to retrieve the invincible swordstick. (And only Gavin noticed the great beast flinch as Barbar, hidden underneath its hide, shuffled uncomfortably.) A few paces farther on, the cave turned slightly and, once around this bend, everyone was relieved to see an oval of light at the far end. (Barbar – bless him – had removed the keystone before putting out his fire and tucking Wylee's bones in next to him under the fake dragon.)

Moments later the entire troupe stood upon the goat-path once again, and stared in wonder and relief at the house-habitat where all their hopes were about to be realized.

"Aren't you going back for Hex-Calibre?" Cuyler said to Gavin, who looked as if he were about to set out on the final leg of their quest without the fabled weapon.

"Oh, we must have the swordstick," Quiver said, agitating his quills. "It's residential to all our success!"

"If it's stuck in the dreadful beast, Sir Tristum will gladly help you pull it out," Hubert suggested with a pleading glance at Trisbert.

"Do not be alarmed, my friends," Gavin said. "I intend to leave Hex-Calibre where it belongs — in a dragon's heart."

This remark caused a great deal of trembling and consternation among the members of the Round Tablet, but Gavin cut them short. "Please listen to me carefully." He waited for everyone (except Petite who had fallen asleep in Paddle-Whee's fur) to calm down and pay attention before continuing. "Hex-Calibre and the wisdom we've gleaned from Tales of Arthro have brought us through thick and thin to this point in our journey home. We have fought off cougar-beasts and bear-beasts, and now a dragon. The names and parts we have taken on from the story of the Round Tablet have given us a strength beyond strength, a courage beyond courage. I am proud of you all. But what we must do next, before dawn tomorrow, will depend solely upon the skills and instincts we were born with. The plan I have conceived will require only that we act collectively and rely upon the ancient lore of coon-craft and animal cunning."

A puzzled silence greeted Gavin's speech.

"You want us to go back to our real names?" Cuspid said at last.

"But I was just getting used to mine," Hubert said, "and Madame of course will always be a Lady."

"We can discuss this further when we reach our destination," Gavin said, and with that he turned and began striding up the narrow cliff-path with a swagger and confidence he really didn't feel inside. Barbar had given him enough detail about the defences of Lord Gnash's palace and its daily routines to suggest to Gavin a plan of attack. But it was full of risk and would require the courage, cool-headedness and unwavering commitment on the part of every member of the troupe – whatever name they chose to fight under.
"Follow your leader!" Trisbert snapped, and was quickly obeyed. After all, the fellow they were following was a dragonslayer, was he not?

* * *

The sun was almost touching the edge of the Ridge, above them and to their left, when Gavin called a halt. And there, suddenly, they saw what he did: a valley nestled between two rocky crags with steep cliffs on either side that dropped straight down to the Lake of Waters Unending. At the northern end of the valley the house-habitat – Lord Gnash's "palace" – was built into the rock-face, its metal roof intact and ablaze with the slanting rays of the sun. Around it on three sides was a grassy depression – what was called a moat in Tales of Arthro, though this one had no water in it. And racing down from springs in the Ridge above and curling close to the moat was a violent, frothing stream that continued on past the palace and eventually tumbled down the hillside to Everdark. Between this curve and the moat lay a field of patchy stubble that once, before the Great Burning, must have been one of those grain-crops the

Tallwalkers were said to grow (being too lazy and inept to forage on their own). It was brown and very dry.

"Is the tunnel down there?" Cuyler asked with growing excitement.

"If Dante is right, yes," Gavin said, "but I'm afraid we cannot go looking for it, at least not yet."

"What are you saying?" Quiver cried. "I trust you didn't get us all the way up here under false pretensions?"

"See for yourself," Gavin said gently, and he pointed to a spot in the moat just below the west-front corner of the palace. There the grass seemed to be swaying despite the absence of the slightest breeze.

"Squeezels," sighed Cuspid, "taking a nap by the look of it."

"Oh, dear," Hubert sighed, "I don't know how many more disappointments my brave lady can stand."

"But if this path is the only way in or out of that valley," Cuspid said, "we are in danger of stumbling over Squeezels any moment!"

"Don't fret about that," Gavin said quickly. "I've checked the path at every dip and bend. No-one has used it for a very long time."

"Then the Squeezels must have another way down into Everdark," Cuyler said. "And that means – "

"The Ridge up here is riddled with dried-up, underground streambeds," Gavin said.

"All this talk of tunnels is making me dizzy," Adderly grumbled from his rearguard position, but Gavin's remark had its intended effect: a wave of excitement rippled through the troupe. If they could outwit bear-beasts and subdue dragons, surely they could outmanoeuvre a dozen or so Squeezels!

"But just to be certain that we are not seen up here, I want you all to take refuge in this cave." And Gavin pulled back a scrawny thorn-bush to expose the entrance to yet another cavern. How he knew it was there no-one could guess, but he did — and that was all that mattered.

"Bertie, would you please lead the group inside, and move them along until you come to an opening in the cliff-face that will provide some light and give you a clear view of the valley and the house-habitat."

Had Gavin been given second sight? Would the wonders of his coon-cunning never cease?

But just as Trisbert was set to carry out his brother's request, Gavin called Paddle-Whee aside and began whispering in her ear. Bucktooth and Petite were seen to scramble up to her neck and appeared to be listening as well. Then, without further ado, Paddle-Whee and her passengers headed down the steep slope towards the stream and the outskirts of the house-habitat. In stunned silence they watched Paddle-Whee swim casually — despite her missing paw — through the rapids there to the other side.

"I'll wait here for Paddle-Whee while you take the others inside," Gavin said to Trisbert.
Puzzled but fully confident of their great leader's judgement, the troupe filed into yet another cave.

* * *

The cave was comfortable enough. The opening Gavin referred to was a long, wide slit that let in fresh air and moonlight. In a hollow behind them, the animals found a pool of pure water formed by a constant drip from somewhere above it. Gavin had asked them to rest and relax, though it was hard to do either in the circumstances. Paddle-Whee had returned not long after they had settled down – to Cuspid's great relief – but the mice were not with her.

"Drowned or deserted, I expect," Adderly opined with no touch of malice or blame.

Gavin said nothing. Instead, he spent the entire time gazing down upon the moonlit expanse of the valley and the house-habitat, as if committing to memory every bump, dip, bend and hollow. Oh, how they wished their leader would end the suspense and reveal to them the master plan that would see them through! But, then, those with second sight required silence and solitude, didn't they? Still, the tension in the troupe – even Trisbert and Cuyler were pacing nervously – had almost reached the breaking point when Gavin turned away from his vigil at the opening and called Paddle-Whee over to him. Again, instructions were whispered, and Paddle-Whee trotted away into the dark.

"Please, don't be concerned," Gavin said calmly. "She's just gone to fetch our spies." With that he turned back to his gazing, more to still his thumping heart than to learn anything further about Lord Gnash's fortified palace. Everything depended now upon the smallest and most vulnerable members of the troupe. Gavin had meant it when he'd said that their success would require the particular talents of everyone.

"Here she comes!" Cuspid cried, and Gavin turned gratefully around to see the brave beaver loping down towards him. The squeaking from her shoulders told him all he needed to know. Thank Gollah, and Barbar.

Gavin took the mice aside and listened intently as they told him everything they had seen. For, while Barbar had provided chapter and verse about the palace grounds, he had been able to give only the sketchiest account of what lay inside the building itself. Bucktooth and Petite, true to their rodent propensities, had had no trouble finding a way inside, and once there they moved with the speed and caution of their kind. Gavin nodded his head and smiled. It was very much as he had thought – and hoped.

At last he was ready to address the troupe and put an end to the awful suspense. "Friends, Bucktooth and Petite have given me the specific details I required in order that we may execute the master plan. Now please listen carefully, for this is what we're going to do . . ."

* * *

Into the false dawn, with its hazy light and ghostly shadow, Gavin's troupe made their way down into the valley. They could see, in the little hollow of the moat below, two dozen or more Squeezels sleeping soundly after a night of successful and gluttonous killing – certain in the knowledge that they would be undisturbed in their secure kingdom. Still, the sight of so many ruthless creatures – who could, if prematurely awakened, gobble up the brash invaders in an eyeblink – was frightening enough. Everything, they knew, depended on the element of surprise.

Soon they reached the fast-moving mountain-stream that circled the valley before catapulting down to Everdark. The beavers of course could swim across despite the swiftness of the current, as could the raccoons. But Quiver could not do so. Even holding onto a beaver tail might prove disastrous, and Quiver was vital to the plan. The cottontails shuddered at the mere sight of water. However, as soon as they reached the near bank, Adderly swam across the narrowest portion he could find, bit into a clump of sod on the far bank, waggled his tail-end back until it could be curled around the stout branch of a nearby willow, straightened it out, and offered himself as a makeshift bridge.

When everyone had reached the other side, Gavin cautioned them once again to be silent, then motioned them to hunker down in the thick grass of the bank. Less than thirty paces away the Squeezels lay slumbering in the comfort of the dry moat. Gavin led Paddle-Whee and Cuspid down to the spot where the stream began its lazy curve around the edge of the valley itself. Here there appeared a log-structure of some kind, made no doubt by the Tallwalkers who once lived here, and now so mossy and overgrown with grass and brambles that it could not be seen by anyone who was not looking for it. As they had been instructed, the beavers set to work doing what their kind did best: chewing wood. Wood-chips and bark went flying in every direction as they chawed happily on the rotting barrier.

When they had worked their way through that part of it that appeared to hold the whole apparatus in place, Gavin raised a forepaw to signal the others to be ready. Moments later, the barrier snapped open, squealing on its rusted hinges, and a goodly portion of the stream was suddenly redirected – into the hollow of the moat. The screech of the hinges brought the Squeezels to their feet, groggy but animal-alert. What greeted them, however, was not a stray and foolish mutant-beast from Everdark, but a wall of rushing, foaming, invidious water! With a howling chorus of yips and squeals they whirled and sprinted towards safety. No-one made it. The roaring

stream caught them all and swept them along in the
element they most detested. As the low bank of the moat
happened to be the one on the outside of its semi-circle,
the shuddering, panicked gang of henchmen scrambled
off in that direction until, shivering and quaking with
rage, they collapsed onto dry ground. Meanwhile, the
waters continued on until the entire moat was filled to
the brim. One or two of the Squeezels staggered upright
and gazed forlornly across to the palace – which they
could no longer reach or defend.

Gavin's troupe had no time to witness the success of
this initial manoeuvre because they had had to dash
across the dry moat at its highest point near the corner
of the palace before the water backed up and cut off
their assault. Once they had all reached the broad, flat
lawn in front of the building, they turned immediately to
the next task. As Barbar had informed Gavin, the
imposing wooden door of Lord Gnash's private quarters
was guarded only by two Squeezels – but they were the
brawniest, swiftest and most ruthless of the bunch,
dedicated to defending their master to the death.
Somehow they had to be eliminated before his majesty
could be approached and dealt with.

"This is it," Gavin said. "Good luck to you all."

With that Hubert and Renée sprinted out into the
open. The Squeezel-guards had come away from their
station a few paces – they had sworn never to desert their
post – to find the source of the disaster unfolding in
front of them. All they could see in the ghostly light was
their comrades gesticulating wildly and helplessly from
the other side of the watery moat. One of them pointed
upwards to the cliff-face, and from this angle several
other cave-openings were visible. As Gavin had feared,
and anticipated, there no doubt existed a subterranean

entrance somewhere that would carry the Squeezels under the moat.

But there was no time to worry about how far or how long it might be before the dazed henchmen recovered and found it. The cottontails had now been spotted, and at first the Squeezel-guards merely grunted and made threatening gestures at them. At which Renée bobbed right in front of them and wiggled the white puff of her tail. This was too much for the Squeezels. They lunged at the presumptuous rabbit, and missed, for Renée had executed the abrupt, sideways swerve that had frustrated predators since the beginning of the world. Moreover, being three times the size of ordinary weasels was a decided disadvantage for the guards, for their own quick gambits were too outsized for the prey they were pursuing. In attempting to swerve with Renée they jumped clear over her and skidded onto their chins: only to look up angrily and see Hubert's rump just a whisker away. So off they went after the second zigzagging cottontail, pouncing upon the very spot it had occupied an eyeblink before their mistimed efforts. Whenever Renée passed across their vision, one of them would break off in fruitless pursuit of her, occasionally colliding with his fellow Squeezel, at which calamity each would scramble about and screech something uncomplimentary at the other's ineptness.

This erratic tag-game on the palace lawn had scarcely begun when Gavin slipped along the edge of the moat and entered the dry stubble-field. From their place lodged in the fur beneath his chest-strap, Gavin drew out two spark-making stones given to him by Barbar. On the third try he was successful: a spark fluttered into the stubble and set it alight. Gavin dashed back towards the lawn in front of the palace. Behind him the withered stalks and grasses of the crop-field were a wall of flame and rising smoke. A great wail went up from the Squeezels on the far side of the moat. From their vantage-point, Gavin was certain that, seeing the flames crackle skyward, they would assume the palace itself was on fire. Until they might learn otherwise, he hoped they would be too frightened and discouraged to attempt a return – by any means.

As he skipped along the bank of the stream, he saw now that the others had joined in the business of eliminating the Squeezel-guards. And herein lay the most perilous part of Gavin's carefully sequenced scheme. Hubert and Renée would soon begin to tire, and so the arrival on the scene of Quiver, Trisbert and Cuyler was critical. So obsessed were the enraged Squeezels with punishing the rabbits that they ignored the blazing stubble-field and paid no attention as the raccoons sped up behind and sunk their teeth into a hind-leg – right where a tendon ought to be. And whenever one of them, yipping with pain or annoyance, stopped in order to take a swipe at the ankle-clinging creature, Hubert or Renée would dash right under its nose and dare it to resume the pursuit. While agile and ruthless, the Squeezels had little brain and no imagination. They practically tore themselves in half as they lunged at a rabbit and in mid-lunge tried to twist and swat at the raccoon biting even deeper into a leg. Very close at hand, Quiver squatted and waited his turn.

Gavin could not wait, however. He could only hope that the outcome of this battle would be as planned, for now was his best chance to gain access to the inner chamber – and the tunnel it was shielding. He ran up to the huge door and leaned against it with all his might. It didn't budge. Bucktooth had assured him that it was not barred or latched – the Squeezel-guards were all the protection the crazed Tallwalker and would-be king apparently required. But it was the sheer weight of the thing that was now thwarting him.

"Perhaps we can help," Paddle-Whee said behind him.

And soon she, Cuspid, and even Adderly were leaning and puffing against the barrier – accompanied by yelps and shrieks of frustration from the mêlée on the lawn. Just when Gavin was about to try some other strategy, the door sighed open far enough for him to squeeze in. His assistants turned back to their primary tasks, leaving Gavin alone to deal with Lord Gnash.

The layout of the royal chamber was exactly as the mice had described it. Along the side walls a row of tiny flame-sticks illuminated the room with a flickering, shadowy glow. Bulky, boulder-like things, upon which Tallwalkers slept or sat, loomed here and there, but the thick dust that blanketed them suggested that neither Lord Gnash nor his guards had rested on them. It had been Petite who had discovered a smaller, adjoining room at the back, in which the dwarfish lord was observed fast asleep and snoring like a hog in a wallow. Tripping carefully around the sleeping-platform, she had nosed her way under the boards guarding the wall and – lo and behold and halleluiah! – there was the entrance to what she was certain was a tunnel. Where it might lead she did not know.

Gavin's plan was to sneak into the sleeping-chamber before the sun could slant in to wake up his majesty – and sink his teeth into the Tallwalker's jugular vein, holding on till the life bled out of him. The very thought of such a cold-blooded act set his lips a-tremble and his breath jittering. But it had to be done. And it was only right and proper that he should be the one to do it.

Don Gutteridge

But a sudden movement off to his left brought him up short. Someone else was in the room. Perhaps his spies had not seen all that needed to be seen. Gavin ducked behind a chair and held his breath. The door had made no noise in opening, so it was possible that his entry had gone unnoticed. Slowly he raised up until he could peer above the edge of the chair. The movement had been made by some creature, for even now it was sidling – no, staggering – towards the high, broad writing-platform that the mice had described, littered with papers, books and quill pens. It could be no other than Lord Gnash himself, wakened by the wails and cries outside and drawn to a wide window in the west wall of the palace, where he would have just seen the blazing field, the flooded moat, the stranded Squeezels and the struggling guards. More fascinated than afraid, Gavin watched the staggering figure reach the platform and slump into a chair behind it. A great sigh escaped his lips. He reached across to a tin cup, dropped something into it, then drew the vessel two-handed up to his lips. And drank.

Gavin stared at Lord Gnash, just as the rising sun slashed through an east window and illuminated his every feature. Barbar's description had been uncannily accurate, as had Bucktooth's in adding more current detail. Lord Gnash was indeed a squat Tallwalker, no taller than a bear-cub but twice as fat. His bevelled paunch pushed against the edge of the desk and strained at the cloth covering trying to contain its girth – testimony to a gluttonous and greedy life. Most of him was hidden behind ludicrously (and needlessly) coloured humanoid-garments, but the backs of his hands were hairy, and his face sprouted whiskers everywhere except around his eyes, which lurked unseen behind dark glasses (noted often on Tallwalkers in bright sunlight). Upon his head he wore a metal ring, or crown (as Tales of Arthro called such a decoration).

Gavin stood up. He was counting now on Lord Gnash's corpulence, slothful existence and general sluggishness to make his elimination possible. Certainly there was no firestick or any other weapon on the desk. But Gavin could not be sure that those hairy hands had not sufficient strength or will left to seize his assailant by the throat and throttle him. However, he was left with no choice. It had come down to single combat after all – champion versus champion.

Gavin moved unsteadily towards the desk, furious that his fear should be so blatant and visible. As he himself edged into the shaft of sunlight, Lord Gnash raised his head with a jerk. The spectacles tipped off his nose and clattered onto the desk. He stared at Gavin with a single, malevolent eye: the left one was a blank blob.

"So, Gavin," he said, "you've come at last."

Gavin rocked back on his heels, stunned. "Hello, Uncle Sylva," he stammered.

Chapter 26

A Riddle Resolved

IN THE YARD OUTSIDE THE PALACE, the battle between the Squeezel-guards and the woods-creatures was nearing its climax. Hubert's gimpy shoulder was beginning to tell on him, and he started to slow down alarmingly. Only the drag-weight of Trisbert on the Squeezel's hind-leg saved the cottontail from being seized and bitten to death. Renée also was visibly tired. Her breath was coming in short, agonizing pants. Cuyler, only half as heavy as his brother, was clamped onto the other Squeezel, but was being bounced about and bruised like a mouse in a cat's paw. Quiver hovered nearby but could not make his move until one or both of the Squeezels went down. Adderly decided on his own to enter the fray, and proceeded to slither and slide over the lawn in a series of improvised figures that served to distract the Squeezels visually and once in a while to make them stumble blindly over him.

Hubert had done what he could. His hammering heart was fit to burst. With a terrible wheeze he slumped into the grass, rolled over, and presented his throat to the Squeezel on his trail. Paddle-Whee risked her own life by running straight out towards the Squeezel and squeaking frantically in a vain effort to divert its attention. But

Hubert's taunting had infuriated his pursuer, and it was Hubert's blood he wished to taste. Paddle-Whee reached the fallen rabbit first, however, and flopped down in front of him. The Squeezel coughed with rage, then batted her away with a vicious swipe of his razor-sharp forepaw. Paddle-Whee yelped and collapsed in a heap — which brought Cuspid roaring out towards her. The Squeezel, certain now of the kill he lusted after, calmly waited until Cuspid arrived and aimed another lethal swat at the foolhardy beaver. Only Cuspid's agility and a sideways leap saved him from a bloody death. The Squeezel then leaned over to seize Hubert's jugular, and would have done so had not Cuyler at that precise moment managed to sever a vital ligament in its lower hind-leg.

With a horrified shriek, the creature went down writhing and struggling to kick off its tormentor. With his task completed, Cuyler let go and scampered away. Cuspid now saw his chance, moved in, and rolled the exhausted Hubert out of reach. Meanwhile, Renée was about to do what her mate had done, but was luckier in that Trisbert's teeth had already done their work on the leg of the other Squeezel, who promptly dropped to the ground, howling in pain and disbelief. Unfortunately for Trisbert, however, before he could leap to safety, the other, unsevered hind-leg swung across, and its claws raked him along his soft underbelly. He gasped, and lay still in the grass.

Quiver now made his move, as instructed. He trundled out to Hubert's Squeezel and lashed it once, face-on, blinding it instantly and depositing half a dozen darts in its lips and nostrils. Its piteous cries were soon joined by its partner's, who had just suffered a similar blow.

"Come on!" Cuyler cried. "We've got to get inside before the other Squeezels find their way back here."

Hubert and Renée had recovered enough to regain their feet, and Paddle-Whee, bleeding from the shoulder, was otherwise unscathed and undeterred. Cuspid was unmarked. Cuyler was badly bruised and Quiver was missing a quarter of his quills. Adderly had been stepped on, but only his dignity had been injured. Trisbert, however, was unconscious, and had to be dragged across the ground to the partly open door to the palace, where Bucktooth and Petite were waiting for them.

"We can't drag him all the way to Earthwood," Cuspid said with a huge sigh.

"You fellows go ahead," Paddle-Whee said, wincing with pain. "Cuspid and I will weave a bed we can lay him on and pull — out of willow branches. Tell Gavin it won't take very long."

"Well, then," Quiver said. "I guess we'd better go in and see what sort of bromocide our leader has committed upon Lord Gnash."

* * *

"But Papa told us that your dead body was carried off by the Tallwalkers after their doomsmobile ran you down," Gavin said to the grotesque figure behind the book-strewn writing-desk. Surely this one-eyed, fur-masked ringtail was some gruesome parody of his lost uncle.

"But I was not dead, you see, although I'm certain your Papa wished it to be so. He was ever jealous that it was I who was destined to be the next RA."

"You were taken off to the country of the Tallwalkers?"

"It's a long story. I haven't got the time to bore you with it." Lord Gnash let the lid of his good eye droop, as if sleep were about to ambush him.

"I have come here to lead my troupe back to Earthwood through the tunnel whose entrance is in that bedchamber," Gavin said with a trembling voice, while his mind raced and buzzed with questions he too had no time to deal with.

"I know. And I will not stop you, though before I staggered awake a minute ago and looked out that window, I would have had you and your ragtag disciples killed and tossed to my soldiers for breakfast."

"You've seen the moat-flood and the stubble-fire?"

"You are as clever as your Papa thought he was," Uncle Sylva said with a sort of grim smile on his face. "You have devastated the grounds of my palace and disabled the royal guard."

"But your mutant soldiers will come back here after we've gone."

"There you are not so clever. The loyalty of those distorted creatures rests solely on my ability to provide them with food and shelter. They feed on the mad beasts of Everdark, but it is I who supply them with the delicacies they crave. When they see my guard destroyed and their resting-ground polluted with water, they will not hesitate to tear me limb from limb and eat me alive."

"Then you must come with us."

A look of surprise took hold of Uncle Sylva's face, followed by a smile less grim than the first. "So you are like my brother, clever but hopelessly sentimental. But, of course, I cannot accompany you or anyone else – not if the lethal berry-juice I've just swallowed does what it was created to do."

"You've poisoned yourself?"

"I have only a little time left. I am getting weary already, and the feeling has gone out of my legs."

"I'm sorry to have to leave you like this," Gavin said sincerely, "but I must call my troupe inside and lead them to the tunnel."

"Don't you want to know how I came to be like this?" Uncle Sylva said, staring at the ridiculous drapery he was wearing and reaching up to touch his crown. In a bowl nearby Gavin saw for the first time a brown smoking-tube, the sort of thing, he had been told, that Tallwalkers stuck between their lips and drank smoke from. On the digits of his uncle's left forepaw there glittered several bits of hard-rock or glass.

"You tried to become a Tallwalker," Gavin said with disbelief.

"Not really. It was the Tallwalkers who tried to turn me into one of them – and, as you can see, they almost succeeded."

"But how?"

Uncle Sylva grimaced as a spasm of pain struck somewhere below his bloated belly. "I was not badly injured when the doomsmobile hit me that day. When I woke up, bruised and dazed, I found I was riding along with two Tallwalkers, who took me to their home deep in their territory. They nursed me back to full strength, feeding and petting me so well that I began to feel that they were – despite all we have been taught – becoming my friends. Soon they were dressing me in cut-down versions of their own cloth-coverings, and gradually tempted me to sample and eventually begin to crave the food they themselves ate – all the time suggesting to me, in word and gesture, that raccoons were the brightest of all animals and that with their tutelage I could be remade in their image. Yes, by then I had already begun to understand their Gibberlish, and later on I was even able to write its alien words on paper with a nimbleness of forepaw they marvelled at. They tried to get me to speak their lingo, but that was the only Tallwalker skill I did not fully succeed at. But I could write down what I wanted and what I felt – and I did."

"You wanted to be returned to Earthwood."

Uncle Sylva sighed. "No. I wanted to be mistaken for one of them. They had taught me so well that I forgot about my own kind and their place in Gollah's universe. So many annuals had gone by that I was certain RA-Mosah had passed on and that my less talented brother had succeeded him."

"So you became one of them?"

Uncle Sylva moaned softly, either in pain or at the memory of that dark time. "Not as I supposed. My benefactors brought their friends into our home and I was flattered into performing for them – dancing on my hind-legs and scribbling words on a slate as they were tossed at me by the sceptics. You see, it turned out that I was merely the object of a wager between the two who had rescued me and their companions. I was to them, in the end, no better than a jackdaw doing a mating dance on command before a flock of jeering tanagers. I was shamed and furious."

"But how did you get here, so far from where you were?"

"Aah . . ." Uncle Sylva's good eye glistened. "I decided to play their game, but all the while I listened and read their books and scripts, and learned more about them than they knew of themselves. And two days before the Great Burning – which I had anticipated – I escaped and headed north. You see, every Greendaze I had accompanied my keepers to this summer home here above Everdark. So, while they maimed and annihilated one another, I reached this refuge safely. And not long after that, the deformed and pathetic creatures from the forest below came fleeing here – and with them the gullible weasel-beasts."

"Squeezels, we call them."

Uncle Sylva clutched his stomach and grimaced, but was determined to get his story out before the poison finished him. "Like the other beasts here, they were solitary and murderous – killing each other as often as their intended prey. I took them in and, using my superior intelligence and things I had learned from the wicked ways of the Tallwalkers, I moulded them into a fighting unit. They agreed to do my bidding in return for the protection and effectiveness of my organization. I taught them to hunt in packs, to forage food for me, to dig and weed the Tallwalker garden out there to provide me with delicacies I'd come to depend upon."

"Why didn't you just slip across to Earthwood, and come home?"

"You don't understand. I had already begun to plot how I would use my soldiers to invade and take over Earthwood – not as RA but as its lord and master – though I had little hope that life there would be much different from the monstrosities of Everdark."

"But the flood came."

"Yes – drowning most of whoever and whatever remained there, and then sweeping the remainder over the Ridge and across Everdark on a giant tidal wave." He peered at Gavin for several moments before adding, "And depositing a lucky few in our very midst."

Gavin started, trying without success to hope where hope was foolhardy.

Uncle Sylva's expression darkened even as a malicious grin took hold – one that sent a shudder through Gavin. "My troops got them all, before those lumbering half-wits out there could dig themselves out of the mud and wonder what had washed over them."

And devoured them, Gavin thought with a pang, but he could not bring himself to say so.

"They are still with me," Uncle Sylva said. It was a vicious whisper, smug and a-brim with spite and self-congratulation. His eye widened and fixed itself upon his nephew.

"They're alive?" Gavin said cautiously, not ready to accept such news at face value.

"More than a hundred of them – even now." The smirk on his face was interrupted by a cough, and then a gasping for breath.

"Papa and RA-Mosah?"

The smirk deepened as the breathing resumed. "I wish they had survived. It would have given me exquisite pleasure to have them throttled in front of me and their carcases thrown to the cougar-beasts. Alas, they didn't. But dozens of others did. And they soon became part of my grand scheme – to make myself Lord of Everdark and then Earthwood and then whatever's left of the Tallwalker world. I donned this crown and these regal robes, salvaged from a play-actor's trunk in the other room, and made my plans. I bribed my soldiers by giving them any of the Earthwood animals I had no need of – as rewards for good behaviour and exceptional service."

"Had no need of?"

"Don't you see? I thought it would be obvious to an elder-son and offspring of Uthra. I needed only mated pairs of each species to take back to Earthwood to repopulate it – should it ever revive. And I would be their king." Here Uncle Sylva coughed again, and his good eye seemed to go milky. "But, alas, while I had learned from the Tallwalkers to be cruel and ruthless and unflinching in my ambitions, I had at the same time forgotten much that I once knew about animal craft and cunning."

"You needed The Book," Gavin said, the truth suddenly dawning.

Uncle Sylva tried to smile. "Very good, young elder-son. So you see when I was informed that you and your eccentric friends had survived and were encamped on the beach and that you had in your possession the only thing I now needed to rule the world, I was ecstatic."

"But why not simply have your troops attack and destroy us without mercy?"

Uncle Sylva groaned, but managed to say in an almost regretful tone, "Oh, but I wanted to test the mettle of my brother's brood . . . to enjoy, if you like, a last bit of coon-play."

"So you merely sent your henchmen to steal it?"

"I did. But when I opened the pouch that was placed before me, it contained nothing but a useless Tallwalker book of childish adventure stories and a fragment of their Holy Bible. I threw them there with the other trash, and had my informant beaten to death – slowly. My scheme had been cruelly thwarted. The Book has vanished with RA-Mosah."

"But who could have known what I was supposed to be carrying in that backpack?"

"He's over there behind that curtain. You may see for yourself." Uncle Sylva gave a shuddering gasp, and his head dropped onto the desk next to Tales of Arthro. The crown spilled sideways and rattled onto the floor.

"Where are the prisoners from Earthwood?" Gavin cried, suddenly fearful that his uncle would die without giving him the most important piece of information of all.

The good eye opened halfway – glazed, its light fast fading. "Only one coon survived, and she was to be my queen. Now it's all gone. Everything."

Gavin reached around and pulled Uncle Sylva's head up by the scruff. "Where are they? You must tell me."

Something close to a chuckle curdled and died away in the old raccoon's throat. "In a dungeon off the tunnel. But it's . . . barred . . . need the key . . . or they'll all die . . . like me."

The open eye remained open, but it saw nothing more in this life.

The "key" must be some Tallwalker device to open the bars on the prison. But Gavin didn't know for sure what it might look like. Such an implement was mentioned somewhere in Tales of Arthro, but he couldn't remember where.

Right now, though, he could hear the piteous groans of the blinded and crippled Squeezel-guards outside and the murmur of familiar voices near the door. They needed to hurry. Quickly Gavin picked the knapsack up from the floor beside the desk, tossed in The Babble fragment, Tales of Arthro and several other Tallwalker books nearby, then strapped it onto his back. In doing so, he happened to glance at the dead monarch and noticed that his right forepaw was clenched, as if gripping some object too precious to release – even in death. He went over and pried the paw open. It held an oddly shaped metal implement: a key.

Elated but still thinking with a clear head, he next moved across the room and pulled back a cloth-hanging. He needed to know who the informant had been. What he saw curled up on the floor was not a surprise, but what did startle him was an eye opening and staring mournfully up at him.

"Oh, Gavin . . . That coon-creature told me that my darling Sprightleg was down there. He promised I could be with her again and we would be free to roam the meadows of Earthwood once more," Jocko said, each word renewing the pain that wracked his battered body. "We hares have always been loners and free spirits . . ."

"Don't try to say anything more," Gavin said quietly.

"My goodness Gollah, but I am sorry," Jocko sighed, and closed his eye against his grief, his regret, and the cruelties of the world.

Gavin said a brief prayer for his comrade's spirit-flight to North Holy, then turned back to gaze in sorrow and wonder at the stiffening body of the elder-coon who might have become the greatest RA in the history of Earthwood, an uncle to revere and model his own life upon. At that very moment, the last of Dante's riddles popped back into his head:

Be guarded against treachery

Of one alone amongst your own,

To kill a king's a blessed thing,

His kingdom won by brother's son.

So it had been Jocko and not the slippery fox who had been the traitor amongst them (though his tale of the knapsack and The Book had probably saved the troupe from instant annihilation at the hands of Lord Gnash's troops). And even though Gavin himself had not stuck a swordstick into his father's brother or prepared the poison berry-juice, he had, all the same, killed him.

This sad thought was interrupted by the cautious opening of the big front door.

"Sorry we took so long, Gav," Cuyler said, coming in, "but Tris got hurt and we had to wait while the beavers made a bed to carry him home in."

"And that's where we're going," Gavin replied.

Chapter 27

The Golden Quail

GAVIN LET BUCKTOOTH AND PETITE LEAD THE TROUPE
past him and the body of Lord Gnash to the rear chamber
where the mice reported seeing the tunnel. As the troupe
passed by, one by one, Gavin felt his heart swelling with
pride and half a dozen other nameless emotions. Without
the courageous reconnoitring of these mice, he could not
have begun to formulate a plan of attack. Next came
Quiver, his proud porcupine's tail utterly denuded of
quills: one sideways snap of a Squeezel-guard's jaw could
have ended his life. Then came Cuspid, the wee beaver
with a titan's teeth and plenty of grit, now bruised and
exhausted from his efforts on behalf of his companions.
Next: Hubert and Renée, their ears flopped over, their fur
knotted and stained – still winded from the zigzagging
sprints whose speed and nimbleness would live forever in
the annals of rabbitdom. Behind them Adderly slithered
awkwardly, trying not to show the world where he had
been stomped upon in the heat of battle. A step behind
him Paddle-Whee limped and took no notice of the gash
in her side, her valour and selflessness every bit as big as
her massive physique. Finally, his baby brother: with a
sapling-strap across his chest, by which he was hauling
the sled that the beavers had woven – now occupied by

the unconscious form of a badly mauled Trisbert. Cuyler was no longer a pup.

"The bleeding's stopped," Cuyler said in a matter-of-fact voice. "It won't start again if we can keep him from being jostled too much."

Gavin smiled his thanks and stepped in behind the sled.

As they passed the slumped corpse of Lord Gnash, the troupe resisted the temptation to ask Gavin just how he had accomplished yet another miraculous triumph in face-to-face combat with the forces of darkness. But they had no doubt that he had done it again, and this time without the aid of an invincible swordstick. Oh, what a leader Gollah had chosen for them!

Once inside the bedchamber, the mice pattered over to a far wall and pointed at a wooden panel. Gavin went over to it, and pushed and joggled until it suddenly slid sideways. In the opening beyond it lay the secret tunnel. Although elated, the troupe was too exhausted to cheer.

"I'll lead the way," Gavin said. "Cuyler, please follow me with Trisbert. We still don't know for sure where this tunnel actually goes. It may well be booby-trapped. Lord Gnash is not to be trusted and we have only Dante's prediction to go on."

This remark sobered the troupe somewhat, but their faith in Gavin was now complete and irreversible. They happily followed him into the darkness.

The first thing that Gavin noticed was that, as he had surmised, the passageway was the dry bed of a defunct underground stream, and as such its floor was as smooth as a rain-slick boulder. Trisbert would have a jog-free ride. Next, as his keen night-vision cleared, he detected a source of light that was washing back towards them and providing enough illumination for them to move along at a steady pace. The panel at the entrance had been slid back into place and was not likely to be discovered by any returning Squeezels, who were more apt to start feuding and feeding on each other with the failure of their king and his blinded sentries. Nevertheless, there was urgency in his stride, especially as he soon realized that the glow ahead was too near to be the tunnel's exit into Earthwood. Thus he found himself ten paces beyond the troupe and standing – with a wildly thumping heart – next to an imposing iron grate set in a rectangular gap in the wall. Slowly, afraid to hope and fearing to look, he eased his head between two of the iron bars and let his mind absorb the scene below. What he saw stunned him, and then sent him reeling back against the opposite wall.

Catching his breath in agonizing gasps, he returned to the grate and forced himself to look again. What he saw was a very large, steep-sided cavern with a hole in its roof that was letting a single shaft of sunlight sail down into the depths thirty or forty paces below. From the grate, a crude set of steps had been hacked out of the rock, providing a way up and down to the horrors on the cavern-floor – that is, if one could first negotiate the iron bars. Even in the scattered and dissipated light down there, Gavin could see that the rock bottom of this hideous dungeon was carpeted with living beings: the captured woods-creatures Uncle Sylva had boasted about.

While he couldn't make out individual forms and traits, he was certain that they were varied in shape and size. Soft moans, whimpers, keenings and sighs rose up to him like a cacophonous chorus of the damned. A savage anger surged through him.

"I am Gavin the Great!" he shouted. "I have come to lead you all back to Earthwood!"

This frantic proclamation drew the troupe quickly up beside him, and they too peered down into the dungeon, awe-struck and horrified.

"They're woods-creatures," Gavin explained, "our fellow survivors from Earthwood."

"We must get them out," Paddle-Whee said. "Let's see if we can push this metal dam aside."

"We may not have to," Gavin said as his anger slowly gave way to the need for clear-headed action. "I think this key-device will open the barrier for us."

Oh, would the marvels of the clan coon and its leader never cease?

Gavin shoved the key into the only slot he could see that might accommodate it and activate its magic. He fidgeted and wriggled it, and just as Paddle-Whee was about to launch her ungashed shoulder against its might, there was a metallic click, and the great iron thing swung open on its own.

"I'll go down," Gavin said. And he started down the stone stairway. "It's all right," he called out in a firm but not-threatening voice to those below. "I'm Gavin, and I've come to take you away from here."

He got no response, except for a slight increase in the volume and variety of moans and a muted shuffling of bodies inured, it seemed, to fear. Then, as he neared the bottom step, one figure detached itself from the crouched and cowed mass of woods-creatures, and stood upright. It waited while Gavin stepped fully into the shaft of light from above.

"Is it really you, Gav?"

The blood rushed so fiercely to Gavin's head that he almost fainted on the spot. "It is," he whispered. "And are you really . . . Tee-Jenn?"

She smiled wanly. "I've grown a mite, but I'm still me," she said.

A mite? Little Jenn, the elder-daughter who had tormented and dazzled his dreams in the season before the flood, was now bigger than he was, almost as tall as Trisbert and nearly as robust — despite the terrors and rigours she must have suffered down here. But those eyes, radiant with intelligence, kindness and empathy, were exactly the same — only deepened perhaps by the experience of Uncle Sylva's dungeon.

"Who else is here?" Gavin asked diffidently, for he was strangely overcome by a wave of shyness.

"There were almost two hundred of us at first, several of every kind of woods-creature. But twice a moon or more, the giant weasels would come down, choose one of us they said was 'unnecessary' to their lord's scheme, throttle the poor soul before our eyes, and carry off the body." Tee-Jenn shuddered as she recounted these horrors, but there was more anger than sorrow in her eyes.

"Are you the only . . . ?"

Jenn smiled as best she could. "No, I'm not. My cousin Marla survived the flood with me. Soon after we were captured and placed here, she gave birth to twin pups, females. The day after they were weaned, the guards came for her. I've managed to keep the twins hidden ever since, as they most surely would have been deemed 'unnecessary' to the lord's scheme."

"Are you the . . . leader, then?"

"I am an elder-daughter," she said brusquely. "I did my duty according to my station."

Trisbert and Cuyler would be overjoyed to learn of the twins' survival. "We have little time to spare," Gavin said, finding his leader's voice once again. "I've opened the barrier up there. I believe the tunnel goes all the way through to Earthwood, whatever's left of it. Can you persuade these poor, suffering souls to get on their feet and follow me?"

"Yes, I can."

"Some of my companions above may be able to help. I myself must go ahead and make sure of the way, but I'd like you and all the others to follow after as soon as possible."

"But you haven't told me how you and your friends managed to survive and find your way here, and avoid being slaughtered by the weasel-fiends."

"Well, Jenn, that's a very long story."

"We'll have more than enough time for it to be told when you and I get home," she said, and smiled beautifully with her beautiful eyes.

Gavin smiled, too. He liked that "you and I" – very much.

* * *

As soon as it became clear that Jenn would be able to rouse the captives out of their torpor and despair, and get them up to the tunnel, Gavin set off down the passageway with Cuyler – and Trisbert in tow. No word was spoken between him and Cuyler as they moved through the increasing darkness of the tunnel. Very soon the light from the cavern behind them gave out altogether. After which they had to grope their way along, bumping into walls when the tunnel bent suddenly and drew a muffled groan from Trisbert on the sled. Gavin now regretted bringing his stricken brother along, but he had thought that the bright sunshine of home might bring him out of his coma and begin to revive him – body and soul.

"Hold onto my ringtail," Gavin said to Cuyler after a particularly severe bump. "I'll do all the banging about, and when it's safe, you can follow right behind me with Trisbert."

While slowing their progress, this arrangement minimized the jostling for Trisbert, who – Gollah be thanked – actually began to snore in his old, ear-battering way. At last they crept around a bend and were greeted by a pale glimmer of light. Some sort of exit must lie not too far ahead. As the light gradually increased, they were able to move faster without jarring Trisbert.

"That's it!" Cuyler cried. "As big and round and bright as the sun!"

Yes, there it was, the sun-lit exit. And if Dante were right, they had just made their way through Serpentine Ridge from Everdark to Earthwood. And not a Ghostie or Warlow had whispered or siren-sang or wailed to them!

Gavin was first to step out. He was standing on the Ridge, and laid out below him were the remains of his homeland. Cuyler came up beside him, and together they stood and stared.

The flood had uprooted every living tree in the territory, and the ground could not be seen for the twisting, rotting trunks and limbs, and leafless branches – that covered it utterly.

"The Realm of Ringtail is gone," Cuyler said numbly. "I'm afraid there's nothing alive here except us."

Gavin set down his backpack and began walking down the slope until he came to the edge of what once had been their forest. He bent over, his nostrils twitching. Something green was growing somewhere: its pungent aroma was unmistakable. He lifted a nearby branch. A patch of lustrous grass sprang upwards, reaching for the sudden light. At the base of a fractured tree-trunk, several brave little shoots gasped for air. Gavin stood up and took a deep breath. Then from some distance came a distinctive and lilting sound: birdsong. A few paces farther on, he spotted a miniature creek rippling under a screen of branches. As he stared – his blood surging and his heart hammering – a fish leapt skyward and splashed joyfully back into its element.
Earthwood was alive. Like its own estranged creatures, it had found the will to survive, and prevail.

* * *

Gavin walked back up to his brothers. To his great relief he saw that Trisbert had wakened, and was sitting up – letting the sun lap at the gash on his belly, while sniffing at the fresh breeze and the welcome news it carried. Gavin went over and held the tuft of grass he had plucked under Trisbert's nose.

Trisbert sucked in its fragrance. "We've found the Golden Quail," he said.
"So we have, Bertie. So we have."

* * *

Don Gutteridge

Cuyler was delighted to be given the happy task of returning to the others still in the tunnel to inform them of what Gavin had found, and to lead them home.

Meanwhile, Gavin sat beside his brother, snoring robustly on the sled, and let his thoughts roam where they might. The forest of Earthwood – with its marshes, streams and grassy shoreline – would slowly renew itself. The hundred or so pairs of woods-creatures would find enough food to keep them alive, and as their offspring arrived to repopulate the territory, the land and its waters would grow with them until someday Earthwood would begin to resemble the original created by Gollah. But would the ringtails rule as once they did? The Book of Coon-Craft and Animal Cunning was lost forever. And while it had served to govern the behaviour and welfare of all woods-creatures for time out of mind, it had not contained in its successive chapters all the wisdom there was to be known in the world. Nor had its account of how the world worked told the whole story.

Gavin and his fellow survivors on Deadwood had stayed alive and prospered in their efforts to return home not because they were guided by The Book alone (only fragments of which Gavin had been privy to), but because of the parables and examples – the wisdom, if you will – of the Tallwalker texts: The Hollow Babble remnant and Tales of Arthro. His own father had so believed in those Gibberlish tales (and in all likelihood had possessed many more of them) that he had named his sons after several of their heroes. And was it coincidence that his own name – Uthra –resembled that of Athro's father? Was it not possible – even – that the idea for the High Ring of the clan coon had come from some long-ago reading of the Arthro stories? It was all very confusing, and yet at the same time exhilarating!

Nor, as they had been taught from birth, were all Tallwalkers evil and self-destructive — the henchmen of Zeebub, prince of darkness. Arthro's knaves had been Tallwalkers, as Gavin well knew. Noab was a Tallwalker who, like those courageous souls behind him in the tunnel, had risked all to save both his and animal kind, and were about to replenish a flooded earth. And of course there was Dante's tale of the last Tallwalker, who doted on his dog and fed the fawns beside his woodsy camp, whose flesh had disintegrated after the Great Burning, who had taken up his gun to hunt only when starving, as any living thing had the right to do. What is more, Gavin had looked into his eyes as he died, and seen not wickedness there but suffering, sorrow, and regret.

So, after all that had befallen them and all they had endured, what would now happen here when the survivors arrived? Would each kind — despite the fact that only by abandoning the separate instincts of their species and acting collectively had they prevailed — would they revert to their long-established behaviour? Would they suffer the raccoons to rule over them and once more supervise the affairs of Earthwood? Gavin did not know, and Dante was not here to foretell the future. All he knew for certain was that his world was about to begin from the beginning — again. And what they had already learned from the Tallwalkers and from the secret braveries they had discovered in themselves would surely make it a world quite different, and hopefully more wonderful, than the one it was destined to replace.

Gavin glanced at the books he had taken from Uncle Sylva's desk. The Gibberlish titles leapt vividly into his head: The Arabian Lights, Gullivah Travelling, Mobile Dick, The Tempester. He would read them all, for their wisdom and their sacrilege alike. Knowledge, he now realized, could not be stopped once it was loosed to the free air. With quiet deliberation he took out the quill-feather Minervah had graciously given him and the container of berry-juice ink he had scooped up at the last moment before leaving the palace. At the end of the Tallwalker's Babble fragment there were dozens of blank pages, he recalled. He flipped through it in search of them. It was then that he noticed that on the page before the blank section, the Tallwalker had written his own words – in letters Gavin had not been able to decipher. He stared at them again, and this time, to his amazement, their meanings jumped out at him:

Tuesday, the first

I have decided I should keep a journal of these final days, in the faint hope that someone somewhere has survived the holocaust we brought upon ourselves. My flesh has begun to melt away, and the pain is staggering. But I shall try to die gracefully, in this island refuge I have loved and protected since I was brought here as a boy. Is it too much to hope that on some far-flung island not polluted by mankind there might be a colony of animate creatures whom the firestorm did not consume? If so, I'd like to die thinking that they might retake the earth and make it something better than human.

I can write no more

Gavin heard excited voices in the tunnel behind him. He turned the journal-page over to the blank one following it, dipped Minervah's tail-feather in Uncle Sylva's ink, and began to write:

The Book of Cunning

Chapter One

A Flood...

Afterword by Brian T. W. Way

Gavin's Search
for the Golden Quail

The spring rains have come to Earthwood but, with them, disaster. For these rains do not stop. They continue to fall and fall, becoming a flood, a catastrophic deluge. It may be an after-effect of the Great Burning in the neighboring nation-state but, whatever the cause, a great wave of water now rises and rises and begins to sweep away all of the civilization that the wise young racoons of Earthwood have ever known. Earth melts into swamp, trees topple into ruin and a dense fog rolls across the land, all but decimating this land of the Ring-tails. The only escape, to rush to the high ground of Serpentine Ridge and broach the border of Everdark, but that is no escape at all, for in that direction lies certain death at the hands of fierce predators and whatever other evil might exist beyond. Gavin, the oldest of three brother-racoons, all separated from their father and the other elders of the clan, knows that his survival and that of his brothers, Trisbert and Cuyler, is his responsibility. He has to become their leader. He has to rely on his abilities and on the wisdom he can recall and enact from lessons given to him from *The Book of Coon-Craft* and his training as next RA-to-be. But the situation is so dire, so uncertain, and the fog so thick...

So begins Don Gutteridge's fantasy-fiction, *The Perilous Journey of Gavin the Great: a fable*. And a fable it is, a story set in an animal world where wise and resilient racoons reside at the centre—the word *fable*, itself, derived from the Latin *fibula*, meaning "a story," in turn, from *fari* meaning "to speak." The flood has swept a family of racoons toward the strange and foreign land of Everdark and the young racoon named Gavin must assume the role of leader and somehow guide his brothers and a host of others on the desperate quest to return to their home. Gavin's Troupe becomes quite the assemblage, three racoons, a trio of rabbits (or hares), two beavers, a porcupine, some mice, a mole, a fox-snake and a wily fox, in effect, a true Tolkienesque 'Fellowship,' in this case a 'Fellowship of the Ring(tail)s'.

There are many forms of narrative, many ways to tell a story—epic, allegory, folktale, religious myth, satire, sermon, confession, documentary, novel, romance, and more. And the fable. The fable as a form of story-telling dates far back into the history of human narratology; probably the best-known are those attributed to a slave of ancient Greece named Aesop (*Aisōpos*—circa mid-6th century BCE). Aesop probably never wrote down his stories (in fact, Aesop may simply have been an invented name attached to the genre) and there is certainly no evidence that any were published in his time—his was an oral tradition (the true *fari* from which the word derives)—and, although the selections and inclusions in publications ever since have been extensive and sometimes wildly unverifiable, Aesop established a genus with a lasting tradition. There have been many excellent fabulists since including the likes of the Roman, Phaedrus (also a slave), Jean de la Fontaine (who revived Aesop's fables in verse form), Tomás de Iriarte, José Núñez de Cáceres, Rafael Pombo, Beatrix Potter, and those great nineteenth century fable-*auteurs*, academics and anthologists, Jacob and Wilhelm Grimm. And the fable-form has been extended into several notable novels—*Animal Farm* (Orwell), *The Jungle Book* (Kipling), *The Wind in the Willows* (Grahame), *Le Petit Prince* (Saint-Exupéry), *Watership Down* (Adams*), Life of Pi* (Martel), *The Boy, the Mole, the Fox, and the Horse* (Mackesy). In addition, writers such as James Thurber, Edward Gorey and Jon Scieszka have all written satiric parodies of the fable.

In its original form, the fable was a short fictional tale (often very short) in which, anthropomorphically, actual or mythic animals (and sometimes plants or forces of nature) recounted a story with a moral or a cautionary lesson, often finishing with a clever maxim. From Aesop, for example: "The Tortoise and the Hare"—*Never giver up*; "The Lion, the Ass, and the Fox"—*Learn from the failure of others*; "The Lion and the Mouse"—*No act of kindness is ever wasted*; "The North Wind and the Sun"—*Kindness is better than force*; "The Milkmaid and her Pail"—*Never count your chickens before they hatch*, and so on. According to one Classics' scholar and translator, S. A. Handford, 207 fables can be attributed definitively to Aesop although that number has often been debated and amended by other scholars and publishers.

In spite of its incredulous nature, though, the essence of the literary fable lies in its prescient revelation of some aspect of the human condition (good or bad). And in that, it must behave like all fiction. In his *Biographia Literaria*, in commenting on the philosophical sensibility that led to their compilation of the landmark *Lyrical Ballads* (Wordsworth and Coleridge 1798), Samuel Coleridge makes his famed, and most succinct and significant, insight into the nature of literary art:

> It was agreed, that my endeavours should be directed to persons and characters supernatural, or at least romantic, yet so as to transfer from our inward nature a human interest and a semblance of truth sufficient to procure for these shadows of imagination that willing suspension of disbelief for the moment, which constitutes poetic faith. Mr. Wordsworth on the other hand was to propose to himself as his object, to give the charm of novelty to things of every day, and to excite a feeling analogous to the supernatural, by awakening the mind's attention from the lethargy of custom, and directing it to the loveliness and the wonders of the world before us.
>
> (S. T. Coleridge *Biographia Literaria* ch. 14 1817)

No matter the situation, no matter the genre, literary fiction needs to generate a "willing suspension of disbelief for the moment, which constitutes poetic faith." Here lies the "human interest and a semblance of truth" that tap the human imagination and unveil the human condition; here lies the interlocutory compenetration that welds both reader and text in a genuine bond; here lies a sense of verisimilitude, the veritas of being that brings meaning to fiction. Whatever the tale, if it is about liars or con-artists or telemarketers or racoons (maybe especially if they are liars or con-artists or telemarketers or racoons), storytellers want their characters and their tale to offer some wisp of believability to the sensibilities of the reader. It can take place in a galaxy far away, or on a raft in the middle of the Mississippi, or along St. Urbain street in

Montreal, but it needs plausibility. And in the writing of fabulous fiction, that challenge may be greater than in the writing of most other forms of fiction. The principal characters in fables are usually animals. And as the central purpose of a fable is invariably didactic, to deliver a moral or a message to help the human reader avoid or understand some folly or pitfall, the correction of which will lead to a better life, when a rabbit or a pig or a racoon stands up to tell a tale, there are many who would put the book down, who would disallow any suspension of disbelief. So, over the years, writers of fables have developed many techniques to enhance and make believable their tales, to make their readers keep reading, their audience keep listening—to manufacture and enable a genuine belief—to know that we humans can learn even from the folly of pigs or rabbits.

Initially, most fables were short; only a paragraph or so and that helped. And they were often whimsical and humorous—almost a kind of joke with a punchline—a message that delivered some logic or common sense, and it was delivered quickly. The persistent tortoise outraces the frivolous hare, so, *never give up*—then on to the next tale. As fables began to be lengthened into novels, though, techniques needed to be applied to keep the reader's attention and develop complexity in the fiction, to assure a suspension of disbelief. First, of course, an interesting story, clever, fast-paced, engaging. And often with illustrations, diagrams, maps. Additionally, very often the form of fables, which were almost always symbolic or representational (and instructive), turned to allegory and/or political satire. In *Gulliver's Travels*, for example, a country run by horses (the Houyhnhnms—the sound a horse might make) who are logical to the exclusion of all other things (including feelings like love and sorrow), mesmerizes Gulliver (gullible as his name implies) so much so that he essentially loses his sanity, ending the novel back in England and living in the barn with the family's livestock. George Orwell's political satire, *Animal Farm*, allegorically recreates the Russian Revolution on a farm where each animal represents a significant figure or force (the owner of the farm, Mr. Jones, is Czar Nicholas, Napoleon is Stalin, Snowball, Trotsky, and so on). Beatrix Potter creates her *Peter Rabbit* series (twenty-three books in all, each the shape and size a child might hold) with such beautiful and scientifically precise illustrations that the natural realism charms as much as the stories or the lessons to be learned—the rabbits may wear clothes but they still seem like real rabbits and we would not want them any other way. All cloaked in enticing watercolours, to boot.

In some of the extended beast fables, while animals may think and behave and speak like humans, they clearly maintain an animal inclination or spirit. In Kipling's *The Jungle Book*, the laws of the jungle apply. The tiger, Shere Khan, conniving and devious and arrogant as any human antagonist might be, still exists as a deadly killing machine. He also fears fire as an animal does and, outsmarted and trapped in a canyon by the boy-human Mowgli's cleverness, he is trampled to death in a buffalo stampede. And Mowgli, although he lives in the jungle and communicates with the beasts there, remains innately human and consistently superior in reasoning and ability (not unlike the way the British in India probably viewed themselves). (The same is true of his literary cousin Tarzan who, although he readily talks with a menagerie of jungle creatures in all his adventures, always exhibits a human superiority in this "nature, red as tooth and claw" world. So, too, with Dr. Dolittle.) In Kipling, the consistent infusion of this hint of Darwinian reality into the fable provides a contrast that enhances and intensifies the action and somehow makes the drama more compelling, makes the fable more than less believable. And this is a technique that Gutteridge applies in *The Perilous Journey of Gavin the Great*. Although the beasts, both natural and mutation, all think and act and speak as humans, the narrative reminds the reader that they speak a common tongue known as 'animal'—these creatures are still wild beasts. They are compelled to follow a commandment issued by their *uber-god* Gollah: "Gollah had decreed that there should be but one written code for all woods-creatures, that it should be kept and passed down..." (38). Before they can trust one another to join forces as Gavin's Troupe—the fox is always tempted by natural instincts to kill and eat the mice and rabbits, the porcupine always tempted to use his quills in defense—all must agree to alter their animal instincts. As Gavin essentially reminds them on several occasions: "We have—all of us—agreed to suspend the laws of Dame Nature until we reach Earthwood and the world is set right again" (95). Only then, we presume, will they once again return to animal instincts, to hunt, feast on and fear one another.

In other beast fables, such as *The Wind in the Willows, Charlotte's Web*, or *Silverwing*, even the allegorical *Narnia Chronicles*, human mannerisms, dialogue and concerns dominate the action so much so that a tale inhabited by talking beasts does not seem unusual. As readers, disbelief is suspended and we accept (or maybe forget) that a spider named Charlotte is writing her web-messages, that a Lion named Aslan is sacrificed and resurrected for the sins of His world. And in our contemporary age, as beast fables became electronic (Bugs Bunny, Daffy Duck, Yogi Bear, Bullwinkle, and a host of "Looney" others), aside from the desire for a carrot or two, an absolute morphing of beast into the human situation usually drives the tale and tends to eliminate any disbelief. 'Hunting Season' always seems open and the Acme Corporation has an endless supply of implausible gadgetry. "What's up, Doc!" indeed. And so, in a literary context, the fable seems to inhabit a wide spectrum, on one side, the cartoon-tale filled with animals behaving, inhabiting—literally, animating—the human condition to, on the other side, the realistic story in which the tales of animals are represented sympathetically in a natural manner—while humans talk, animals do not, satisfied and impelled to do animal things.

One variation of such an extended beast fable is represented in novels like Jack London's *The Call of the Wild* where, in a realistic setting, Buck, the other dogs and the wolves, never speak but, through the narrative, the reader is placed in an empathetic relationship that enables one to think and feel what the dog thinks and feels. Books like Bodsworth's *Last of the Curlew*, Sewell's *Black Beauty*, Kjeldgaard's *Big Red*, and Gipson's *Old Yeller* function in similar ways. (Another variation by London, *White Fang*, flips this around; here the story is presented through the perspective—the thoughts and feelings and observations— of the wolf/dog. Although the animal never actually speaks, we feel as if he is telling his tale.)

And so, *The Perilous Journey of Gavin the Great* neatly fits into the traditional format of the fable. As well, fundamental to its fabulist narrative structure is the iconic journey: the novel tells the tale of a band of racoons and other animals displaced by disaster who set out on a quest to find their homeland. The journey home is a fairly common motif in children's literature (in literary works, in general) and central in many fabulist novels as well, including familiar works such as *The Wonderful World of Oz* (Baum), *Alice's Adventures in Wonderland* (Carroll), *Peter Pan* (Barrie), *The Lion, the Witch and the Wardrobe* (Lewis), and *The*

Don Gutteridge

Little Prince (Saint-Exupéry). Helpful in any recent consideration of the journey paradigm are the copious studies of anthropological researchers and critics—the likes of Frye, Campbell, Jewkes, Zimmer, Jung, Gaster, Eliade, Frazer, Weston, and others—who have studied a diverse breadth of cultures and civilisations and noted patterns and symbols common among them; these shared features, what Jung calls the collective unconscious or Yeats refers to as *Spiritus Mundi*, have been well-documented at least since the turn of the twentieth century and the ideas broadly disseminated. According to the research, in general, almost all cultures have such conceptualizations as a creation story, most have a flood myth, most have a variety of gods or goddesses, and/or demonic versions of the same operating in various domains for various purposes, most have some elements of magic or the extraordinary, most have stories of heroes, most have some kind of after-life and, within all, exist sets of archetypes that unify and illuminate events (recurring motifs such as good, evil, innocence, experience, a perfect existence lost, the rebel, the kindly helper, the trickster or jester, the unpleasant step-parent, the journey or quest, and so on). In Gutteridge's fiction, in particular, at the centre of *The Perilous Journey of Gavin the Great* is Gavin, himself, as protagonist, as the once and future leader and hero-to-be. Accordingly, from the anthropological research, the emergence of the hero in a culture invariably occurs in a set of stages and, while different sources provide different variations, some with greatly detailed steps (Joseph Campbell's "Monomyth" from *The Hero with a Thousand Faces* cites seventeen; Chris Vogler in *The Writer's Journey* lists twelve), essentially the journey of the hero can be deduced to five broad stages: the birth of the hero, the education (arming and preparation), the perilous journey, the great battle, and the return of the king.

I might note, briefly, from 'Ranger Rick' of the National Wildlife Federation to 'Bobby Coon' in Thornton Burgess's canon to 'Doc Racoon' in the *Catfish Bend* books to 'Chester' in *A Kissing Hand* to the Beatles' "Rocky Racoon" to the exuberant 'Rocket Racoon (89P13)' of the *Guardians of the Galaxy* and many more, racoons appear frequently in literature aimed at children and adolescents (adults, too). One suspects the devilishly attractive appearance of these bandit-branded creatures and, in actuality, their familiar adaptation to human habitats in relatively non-threatening ways makes them appealing to many writers and a large audience.

The Perilous Journey of Gavin the Great

The Perilous Journey of Gavin the Great begins *in medias res* with Gavin and his brothers already uprooted from their homeland and cast into Everdark: "Devastation was everywhere, and everywhere it was complete" (41). Beginning a tale in the middle is not too unusual a narrative strategy—Milton's *Paradise Lost* is probably the grandest example in English; the *Odyssey* and *Divine Comedy* are classic examples—one could even argue that *Hamlet* begins this way, conspiracy and adultery and murder in the court already over when Shakespeare begins, cutting quickly to the core of the plot and his primary dramatical interests—"Who's there" cries the anxious guard from the parapet of Elsinore and the play begins. Many popular detective-crime stories, the *who-dun-it* variety, also begin in this way. It is a method of instantly catching the reader's attention, of absorbing the reader in the fiction. In *The Perilous Journey of Gavin the Great*, details about what has happened are filled in gradually through exposition, much of it in Gavin's final conversation with Lord Gnash. In effect, Gavin and his Troupe do not actually know much about what has occurred, or why, and so some gaps (such as why the Great Fire happened or the exact fate of the father) are never quite recounted—call it fictive verisimilitude, if you will.

What the racoons do know—to survive, they must begin their journey home immediately and, though tentatively reluctant as so many heroes are (the likes of Moses, Odysseus, Achilles, Sherlock Holmes, Frodo, Luke Skywalker, Simba, Tyrion Lannister, Neo, and such), Gavin takes on the leadership role—he knows and accepts the fact that it is his responsibility as the eldest brother and as one who is in training to be the next RA of the clan. So, while the "origin story" has almost become a central genre-in-itself in the world of Superhero comics and blockbuster films, not too much is made of it Gavin's tale. He has been raised as the eldest son in a family of racoons and knows what lies ahead for him. With his father now lost in the flood though, and his mother killed in a doomsmobile accident (67), Gavin is suddenly an orphan, again aligning with the lineage typical of the archetypal hero (Moses, Oedipus, Beowulf, Pip Pirrip, Peter Pan, Heidi, Anne Shirley, Huck Finn, Clark Kent, Luke Skywalker, Harry Potter—as actor Tatiana Maslany quips as *She-Hulk: Attorney at Law*: "I'm not a Superhero. That's for billionaires, narcissists—and adult-orphans, for some reason!"). Orphans, by their very situation, of course, are outcasts, isolated and vulnerable and such is certainly the case with Gavin; on numerous occasions, as he tries to gather himself and sort out what he must do, he simply sinks into a meditative distance. And from those moments he often finds in memory or cleverness or imagination the solution that is needed, quite often finding an arcane piece of advice from one of the holy book-scraps he carries or by making up what he needs: "In short, he had to provide hope where all seemed most hopeless" (249).

The symbolic significance, etymologically, at least, of Gavin's birth-name is noteworthy. From English origins, *Gavin* means, "the white hawk of May," a potent image of spring and rebirth, courage and singularity. And its Medieval spelling would be Gawain, one of the most prominent knights of the Round Table and nephew of the titular King Arthur. Sir Gawain is important for several reasons, but most notably, first, his involvement with the Green Knight and the beheading game, a myth of Spring and the cycle of the seasons, and two, his involvement with the Lady Ragnel, surely one of the most poignant of all Medieval romance-stories. Central to all of the accounts, Gawain is exposed as one of the most human of the knights, in sincerity and in weakness. Central in the Green Knight's tale, surreptitiously he succumbs to kissing the Lady of the Castle (the Green Knight's wife), then lies about it, and so is nicked, but not decapitated at the beheading ceremony (and ridiculed about his failure later at Arthur's court). And with Lady Ragnel, he is tricked into agreeing to marry the horrific hag and expresses his disgust, although honourably he continues with the betrothal. And so, in the final Grail quest of Camelot's court, Gawain will fail in his bid to secure the Holy Grail—simply, being too human and flawed, he is not pure enough. But in some way, we can relate and we admire Gawain all the more for this. Some versions of the tale have both Gawain and Percival arriving at the Grail Castle; Gawain fails while Percival claims the holy prize. In essence, Gawain represents the human virtue and frailty that are central themes of the Arthurian romances—after all, it is human deceit and betrayal that bring down Camelot.

In *Anatomy of Criticism* (1957), situated in the history of criticism interstitially between the elite New Critical theorists of Modernism (Ransom, Richards, Wimsatt, Forster) and the more recent Postmodern approaches (Derrida, deMan, Foucault, Baudrillard, Steinem), Northrop Frye attempts to codify all forms of literature as part of a unified mythic whole cohesively interconnected with various modes, symbols and archetypes. In considering the fiction of romance (the type of literature that Gavin's tale is), Frye writes:

> The complete form of the romance is clearly the successful quest, and such a completed form has three main stages: the stage of the perilous journey and the preliminary minor adventures; the crucial struggle, usually some kind of battle in which either the hero or his foe, or both, must die; and the exaltation of the hero. We may call these three stages respectively, using Greek terms, the agon or conflict, the pathos or death-struggle, and the anagnorisis or discovery, the recognition of the hero, who has clearly proved himself to be a hero even if he does not survive the conflict (187).

Perilous journey then can be envisaged conceptually—structurally and thematically—as a decisive technique in delineating the development of the prose fiction as a whole. It is the agon before the ecstasy, both method and means, technique and idea, and can be seen as the foundation on which the fiction operates. Through the perilous journey, the quest at the core of the story, physically and psychologically, is laid out and, from that, the personalities of the characters, their motivations, their strengths and weaknesses, the details and outcomes of the story and its themes and its morals.

So the details of Gavin's origin and of his education are revealed retrospectively as he undertakes his quest. Part of Gavin's education and training is, in mythic tradition, the acquisition of combat skills and weaponry—Gavin, for instance, acquires the hunting knife (Hex-Calibre) and it will serve him in the same fashion that other famed weapons serve other great heroes—as Caliburn/Excaliber, Goswhit and Pridwen do Arthur; Mjõlnir and Megingjörõ, Thor; the River Styx, Achilles; Nægling, Beowulf; the Genii's lamp, Aladdin; Asi, Mahabharata; Tablets of Stone, Moses; the Aston Martin DB5, James Bond; Sting and Mithril, Bilbo; the Elder Wand and Cloak of Invisibility, Harry Potter; and so on. And for Gavin, the sacred books of coon-craft and animal-lore, in this case mostly random scraps of Tallwalker books like *The Tales of Arthro* and *The Hollow Bubble*, are learned from the lessons of his father and uncle. Gavin's perilous journey (Gutteridge's chosen title) is episodically structured: the racoons awake to find their world in ruin, one after another they meet and collect the creatures who will form their Troupe (Adderly, Hubert de Cottontail, Quiver, and the rest), then the journey to find home begins, and, almost immediately, the encounter with the dangerous Tallwalker who shoots at them, then the descent to the Valley of Lost Hope, the discovery of the Tallwalker cabin and corpse, the construction of Noab's Arkle, the journey across Heartbreak Channel, arrival at Castelot with a shift into Arthurian lore, and so on, one event after another. Gutteridge writes action and suspense with a palpable flair, infusing the story with exciting chases and precipitous pursuits, dangerous conflict and the wrenching doubts of characters, particularly the leader Gavin, eerie foreshadowing and chapters with cliff-hanger endings, continuing mysteries and imbedded clues. And humour in the tale acts as comic relief, both easing the tension and ratcheting it up, as comic relief always does, like those jokes told before an exam or in a eulogy. In particular, the malapropisms of Quiver the Porcupine comically infuse every statement he makes— "hypodermical" for hypothetical (96), "Comprehend" for apprehend (155), "expectorate" for expire (203), "obtrusion" for intrusion (234), "detergent" for deterrent (270), "subconscious" for unconscious (316), and so on and on— droll to the point, almost, of being bathetically overused. Humorous also, in the same manner, the mole-poet Dante and her comically bad verse awkwardly abusing the heroic couplet:

> Although you may think me an amateur
>
> Who prates in iambic pentameter
>
> I was born with a second inward-sight
>
> And predestined our future to recite... (185)

Somewhere Pope and Dryden are wincing. However, all of this provides a nice illustration of Gutteridge's varied skill at his craft—a good example, Chapter Ten (*Treachery*) offers a compelling sequence as the bedraggled, exhausted Troupe struggles just to cross the next hill as both Renée's pregnancy and Wylee's treachery near fruition. The entire passage is skillfully written, using short, clipped paragraphs, blunt description and quick snips of dialogue, all rapidly building suspense and an atmosphere of tension as the chapter and its characters crawl toward the gory birth scene, Wylee's flight and the disheartening realization that they are trapped on an island.

Along the journey, sometimes at the last moment to save the day, each member of the Troupe demonstrates the varied abilities she or he possesses (the beavers cut down trees for the raft, the porcupine sacrifices quills to serve as bindings, the racoons dig a trench, the rabbits use their powerful hind-legs to guide the logs) and Gavin, time and again, resorts to his intellectual skills to guide and to save the company, always genuine but sometimes with a bit of performance added:

> There was a collective sigh of relief among the animals when they spotted Gavin coming out of the Tallwalker's brambled abode and walking meditatively over the waste-ground toward them. He's been consulting the sacred *Book*, was the general but unspoken opinion, and a comforting one it was. Gollah had spared them for a reason, and only Gavin had the means and heart to discover it. See how the gravity of such a responsibility even now weighed heavily upon him, making the fine racoon-brow droop and the naturally nimble racoon-step laboured and ordinary! (145)

And so, partly truth and partly fiction, Gavin becomes an effective leader. He always seems able to use his knowledge adroitly, coming up with the perfect pieces of advice at the perfect time; for example, early on in the adventure he outlines the necessary rules for their survival: "First: we stay together no matter what happens. Two: we fully support one another, whatever our personal feelings might be. Three, we suspend Gollah's laws of nature until we have found Earthwood again..." (82). Gavin outmanoeuvres the treachery of Wylee the Fox by replacing the sacred texts in his satchel with stones ("...there is a difference between cunning and wisdom, opportunism and foresight," (157) observes Gavin) and in combat, bravely and instinctively, he defeats the cougar-beast with the swordstick (273-274). Like Mark Antony quiescing the mob, or like the sermon from the mount, Gavin skillfully preaches to his following:

Friends, do not trouble to open your eyes…but I beg of you to listen to what I have to say, and then make up your own minds whether or not it seems worthwhile to raise your heads and look once again at the world out there…I have been studying one of the most ancient chapters of the good book … It tells about another momentous and world-ruinous flood visited upon earth's creatures… (164-165)

And so he teaches his Troupe how to escape Deadwood Island by building a "huge raft," an "arkle" in the manner of Noab. He truly becomes, as Cuyler exclaims, "Gavin the Great" (247). Most important of all, throughout the perilous journey, Gavin continues to refine his reading skills:

On one page he saw what he took to be letters in the Gibberish tongue. He stared hard at them, as he had done with those that had risen up and brought the story of Noab to life. But no words grew together out of those squiggles. … Again, he stared hard at the strange markings, blocking out all competing thoughts in his head as RA-Mosah and Papa had taught him whenever he attempted to interpret runes and lexical enchantments of *The Book of Coon-Craft*. Suddenly his mind emptied, and the blood-thump of his heart faded away. Soon a gauzy, mesmerizing mist began to swim across the path of his vision—between it and the scratchings on the page. Then without warning, it started to lift itself, and shred, and vanish as silently as it had arisen. And in a single, blinding flash, he knew what he was looking at.

It was a diagram, what RA-Mosah had called a map… (250)

Accordingly, Gavin discovers a path across Serpentine Ridge toward Earthwood that will lead his Troupe to home and to safety.

About halfway through the novel, Gavin uses his recollection of the *Tales of Arthro* as a means to raise hope and spirits among his followers. He names the delipidated outpost at which they are sheltering, Castelot, the swordstick (a hunting knife) becomes Hex-Calibre, their meeting place is nicknamed the Round Tablet and, as he re-identifies his Knaves, Gavin explains to them:

> You cannot *be* those mighty heroes of old, but you can by assuming their duties, gather unto yourselves, by gradual degrees, the wisdom they employed to make the world work. Like you I can only, and most humbly, take on the role of one of Arthro's knaves. I shall be Sir Gavum, and sit at the Round Tablet where the great Athro would have seated himself. But I will not be your king, only your elected leader and only that as long as I may prove worthy of your confidence (264-265).

At this point, all of the characters are newly "daubed" as the Knaves of the Round Tablet, Gavin becomes Sir Gavum, Cuyler, Sir Kayla, Quiver, Sir Quivelot, Hubert, Sir Percibert, and so on (192-193). There is certainly some wit and whimsy here, and the motif of the animals never quite getting their human-translations accurate is clever and carried throughout the book, an ongoing source of humour. At times, though, the novel begins to become a hodgepodge of layered and skewed allusions, Gollah and Jovah and Zeebub from Hebrew tradition, Arthur and the Grail legend from Celtic mythology and Minervah (the Owl) from Greek and Roman lore. Beyond naming and planning to search for their own "Golden Quail," the narrative never really develops or examines the Arthurian patina it has laid out. There is no Lady of the Lake or tragic romantic tryst that brings about the fall of Castelot only the betrayal of Jocko who is never actually one of the Knaves anyway (having disappeared from the raft before their arrival at Castelot). Basically, the animals go about their adventures; at one point, the narrative even tries to re-explain the names (294) and then, in its final pages, seems to give up entirely and returns its characters to the identities we know. And for contemporary readers, at least of the adolescent variety, referencing the Arthurian legends would mostly just obscure the story anyway—*Minecraft* and *Mortal Kombat*, maybe, or *Harry Potter* and *Game of Thrones*, but probably not Arthur and his Camelot. (By 2010, when this novel is published, long gone are the halcyon days of JFK or even the popular Broadway musical and its catchy, albeit hokey, tunes:

...there's simply not
A more congenial spot
For happily-ever-aftering than here
In Camelot.
        (Lerner/Lowe *Camelot* 1960)

(In retrospect, one wonders if a myth or a text in which the goal of the quest is to get home might not have been a better template (*The Odyssey*, perhaps, or *Pilgrim's Progress,* or even *The Wizard of Oz,* to which the book actually makes allusion when Jocko is revealed by Gnash: "He's over there behind that curtain. You may see for yourself" (386). Pay no attention to that man (or rabbit) behind the curtain, indeed!)

At the end of the journey, Gavin takes on his greatest foe, the onomatopoetically named Lord Gnash, "a mad Tallwalker who wants to be king of the world" (360). Gnash controls an army of orc-like Squeezels who protect him inside his hideout. Gavin's plan is one of action and cleverness, diverting a stream to scatter the Squeezel army, setting fire to a stubble-field, distracting the inner chamber guards by having them chase the rabbits and then, "the most perilous part of Gavin's carefully sequenced scheme" (373), to enter Gnash's sanctum for a final attack. The action scenes are compelling as is the description Gutteridge uses to flesh out the appearance of Gnash and augment the sinister atmosphere:

> Lord Gnash was indeed a squat Tallwalker, no taller than a bear-cub but twice as fat. His bevelled paunch pushed against the edge of the desk and strained at the cloth covering trying to contain its girth—testimony to a glutinous and greedy life. Most of him was hidden behind ludicrously (and needlessly) coloured humanoid-garments, but the backs of his hands were hairy, and his face sprouted whiskers everywhere except around his eyes, which lurked unseen behind dark glasses (noted often on Tallwalkers in bright sunlight). Upon his head he wore a metal ring, or crown (as *Tales of Arthro* called such a decoration) (375).

Lord Gnash happens to be the long-lost Uncle Sylva who, it turns out, survived the doomsmobile-crash that killed Gavin's mother; Sylva was nursed back to health and, Pygmalion-like, trained by Tallwalkers to walk and do tricks and write like one of them, all for a bet. But the crafty uncle plays their game, reads their books and, just before the Great Burning, seeks refuge in their remote mountain summer-home. He then trains the itinerant Squeezels and makes plans to take over Earthwood, "not as RA but as its lord and master" (383). The arrival of the flood alters his plan, of course; now he decides, as his "grand scheme ... to make myself Lord of Everdark and then Earthwood and then whatever's left of the Tallwalker world" (385). Like an oligarchic Noah, he captures pairs of animals, giving what he "does not need," as he puts it, as enticements to the Squeezels. But, having forgotten much of animal craft and cunning, Gnash realizes that he needs *The Book*; thus he coaxes Jocko ("one of us forever lost" (205) in Dante's verse) to betray the Troupe (promising him his lady fair—Sprightleg) and sends the Squeezels to raid Castelot and take the satchel that supposedly has the prize; but that, of course, containing "but a useless Tallwalker book of childish adventure stories and a fragment of their *Holy Bible*" (386), does not give him what he thinks he needs—ironically, of course, that is exactly what has sustained Gavin and his fellows.

The final battle is aborted when Gavin and Gnash have a long discussion, mostly filling in Sylva's life and plans, and Gnash then dies suicidally of the poison he has consumed (in fear of a Squeezel uprising). Because Uncle Sylva seems like such a minor character with almost no previous appearances in the book, this conclusion is not quite as dramatic as it might be. Gnash somewhat anticlimactically dies; Gavin packs up all the books and papers he finds in Gnash's chamber and, learning how to work the key taken from his dead uncle's grasp, opens the dungeon cell, releasing its pairs of prisoners, among them, his beloved Tee-Jenn (although she has apparently put on a few pounds). Gavin heroically declares: "I am Gavin the Great ... I have come to lead you all back to Earthwood" (392).

And so the novel and the perilous journey arrive at their conclusion; the Troupe descends from Serpentine Ridge, resilient Earthwood is alive, grass and trees are growing, birds are singing and fish are in the streams. As Trisbert says, recovering from his wounds of battle, "We've found the Golden Quail" (396).

And in the cautionary tradition of the fable, there are morals to be learned. In part, the novel speaks directly to contemporary concerns about environmental catastrophe, about what will ensue if global warming and reckless neglect and unabated pollution continue. The great firestorm in Everdark precipitates the flood and tsunami in Earthwood; the soil is saturated, trees levelled, vegetation drowned and most wildlife destroyed. This is global warming in an instant. And as the novel progresses, we learn that one dire side effect of that fire is the universal mutation of the species that resided in Everdark. And not only are those beings physically and mentally distorted into rabid cougar-beasts and ever-marauding squeezals and pig-owl creatures like Barbar, but they are also made sterile—reproduction is impossible, and so, extinction is inevitable. So too, it seems for the humans who live nearby; these so-called Tallwalkers (who, from what Gnash suggests, probably caused the Great Burning) seem doomed to a fate of desperation and starvation. The Great Burning, whatever its origin, seems to have been some kind of radiation-infused scourge that has stripped and reshaped the land into a grotesque and toxic resemblance of whatever it might have been (it is referred to as "Zeebub's evil plan" (353).) From human to animal to environment, all pay the price. That is one of the moral lessons of *The Perilous Journey of Gavin the Great: a fable*.

But not the only one. In the end, Gavin's nostrils note: "Something green was growing somewhere; its pungent aroma was unmistakeable" (396). As the racoon pulls away a nearby branch, he discovers green grass and the new sprouts of trees—the earth is alive again. Life prevails. Fire and flood may have brought on erratic change and a devastating degree of destruction, but the earth renews itself. Life emerges. Hope survives. And so also for the generations. Just as they are about to conclude their journey, Gavin and his troupe discover Lord Gnash's pairs of Earthwood prisoners and, like the ark of Noah, there are just enough animals to repopulate their world. So as one generation passes, Gavin and his brothers and their troupe will be able to create their animal world anew. In many ways that is the ultimate success of Gavin's quest for the Golden Quail, unlocking, discovering the resiliency of Nature. (As various environmental studies have noted recently, during the years of Covid lockdown with many factories shuttered and people staying home away from the highways, while the cost in human life was high, water and air pollution decreased by 20 to 40 percent and the ozone layer rapidly continued to heal. The earth truly can be resilient (see articles at: https://www.medicalnewstoday .com/articles/how-covid-19-has-changed-the-face-of-the-natura-world).

The illimitable value of friendship, fellowship and family is another of the abiding themes of *The Perilous Journey of Gavin the Great: a fable*. Throughout the book, the brother racoons time and again come to the rescue of one another and sustain one another. The only way the Troupe as a whole manages to survive is to work together as a team, literally leaning on one another as they travel and taking turns sharing their individual talents to build their raft, defend Castelot and make their quests into the wilderness. It is as a collective that they defeat Lord Gnash and his forces and find their way home. The inherent and eternal value of fellowship and family and love resurrects and sustains life itself.

Near the beginning of their journey, Gavin comments: "I suddenly have the strangest feeling that we're here entirely on our own" (128). The relationship with the divine, having some degree of belief or faith in a greater power, may, or may not, be a moral of this fable. Be they Gollah or Jovah or Zeebub or Owl, gods of the animal and Tallwalker world do seem to exist in the minds of the creatures, and many commandments exist. As leader, to appease his followers, Gavin often strives to find just the proper adage at just the proper time: at one point, he reasons "In *The Book* Gollah commands that no creature should die without good reason" (80) and at another time, "In the book, Gollah says, 'When the spirit fails, look death in the eye.'" (123). Gavin realizes "[i]f he were to tell them the truth—that *The Book* had been lost in the flood—they would abandon all hope, whatever clever plan their leader might produce. What then, to do?" (249). Allusion to entering Dante's 'gates of hell,' aside, often Gavin's search is a difficult task: "He was wondering ... where Gollah was hiding—and why, so far, it had been the corrupted things of the demon Tallwalkers that time and again had saved them all from certain death..." (247). Any easy faith in these divine forces generally seems quite tenuous; and Gavin has reservations: "Was Jovah not really Zeebub, then, in one of his many seductive poses?" (207) Divine doubt seems ingrown in the fabric of the perilous journey. As their raft is swamped in Heartbreak Channel, and Gavin frantically swims ashore, he is unsure who to worship:

> In a very short time he would have to jettison the knapsack that was now becoming a deadly burden: the very text that had promised salvation would itself have to be sacrificed. Already he suspected that the pages inside might be drenched and warped beyond repair, or use. He was about to undo one of the straps when a forepaw struck sand. A following wave lifted him up and away, but when it settled again, all four of his feet hit bottom. He scrambled and clawed his way the final few paces up onto the shore: the dry, hot sand of Everdark's beach. Should he thank Gollah or Jovah? (219-220)

This is ostensibly a novel aimed at the child or adolescent reader so this problematic theme of divine existence (or relevance) is understandably not one pursued overtly but an uneasiness in this regard does persist in the book. Gollah is frequently called upon—"Gollah be praised!" (129)—but never seems to answer. Along with *The Book*, one wonders if Gollah, too, has been lost in the flood—the salvation Gavin the Great finds has more to do with his own courage and with his faith in himself and his fellows than with anything else.

Another challenge to many child and adolescent readers might be the length and textual density of the book—in just a few pages, for example, consider this esoteric diction: penumbra (164), quixotic (166), caches (167), vindictiveness (169), alacrity (202), leagues, sallied (205), tyro (207), stoat (223), vexatiously (226). Several scenes of death and gore, in some of the fight sequences and the stillborn childbirth scene (162-154), might also be a bit heavy for some young readers.

Early in the journey, Gavin addresses his Troupe in an attempt to raise their morale:

> Gavin undid one of the straps on the leather pouch. He suddenly recalled one of Papa's sayings—whether it had come from *The Book of Coon-Craft* or the shrivelled pages of the Tallwalker's *Tales of Arthro* he did not know. "Gollah tells us," he intoned, "that stories are a kind of sustenance, as necessary

to us as flesh or fodder. We may well starve to death before another night is come; we may find ourselves eaten by fiends on two feet: these matters are in Gollah's hands. But we will not be starved of the stories we are destined to tell" (112).

Like Chaucer's pilgrims on the way to Canterbury, each member of the Troupe tells her or his tale as the journey unfolds and stories, themselves, become a central theme of the book. Stories deepen the bond that develops among the members of the Troupe and, at the very least, help them take their minds off their troubles, help them suspend their disbelief. As Gavin realizes then, fiction, itself, exists in a genuinely functional way: "So, although he did not feel in any way that he deserved to be hailed as Gavin the Great, he realized that it was necessary to continue the fiction that he was invincible and was being guided by the magical words upon the pages tucked in his knapsack" (249). Fiction, itself—magic words on the page—is the foundation for their survival. In some sense, their story is the story. Just before she dies, Minervah gives Gavin the restorative information about those pairs of Earthwood creatures who still survive, and she says: "Take my last tail-feather, please. ...Someone must write the past and the future" (310).

In a didactic passage near the end of the novel, the reader is told:

> Gavin and his fellow survivors on Deadwood had stayed alive and prospered in their efforts to return home not because they were guided by *The Book* alone (only fragments of which Gavin had been privy to), but because of the parables and examples—the wisdom, if you will—of the Tallwalker texts: *The Hollow Babble* remnant and *Tales of Arthro*" (397).

As he is scrambling to leave the chamber of the dead Lord Gnash in Everdark, one of Gavin's final acts is to take all the paper, books and ink that he can find. These are his Uncle Sylva's final gift—a sylvan legacy, if you will. At the end of the journey, Gavin peruses what he has collected: "The Gibberlish titles leapt vividly into his head: *The Arabian Lights, Gullivah Travelling, Mobile Dick, The Tempester*. He would read them all for their wisdom and their sacrilege alike. Knowledge, he now realized, could not be stopped once it was loosed to the free air" (399).

And so Gavin, in his own way, will come to meet Scheherazade and Sinbad, Gulliver and the Houyhnhnms, Ishmael and Ahab and the grand, hooded phantom, itself, Prospero and Caliban, too. In the end, books, reading, literature, stories, and writing, too, all sit at the centre of *The Perilous Journey of Gavin the Great: a fable* for that is the essence of the perilous journey. It is a story made of stories to be shared by all. And it is those stories, told and written, that will ignite and sustain the imagination—for therein exists the true 'Golden Quail.' And so, as his Troupe spreads out and begins to re-populate Earthwood, Gavin reads the last Tallwalker's journal, dips Minervah's tail-feather into Sylva's ink and begins to write the world anew.

Coleridge, Samuel T. *Biographia Literaria.* 1817. New York: Dutton, 1965.

Frye, Northrop. *Anatomy of Criticism.* Princeton: Princeton U. P., 1957.

—Brian T. W. Way (excerpt from *Perilous Journey in the Prose Fiction of Don Gutteridge*)

Don Gutteridge was born in Sarnia and raised in the nearby village of Point Edward. He taught High School English for seven years, later becoming a Professor in the Faculty of Education at Western University, where he is now Professor Emeritus. He is the author of more than seventy books: poetry, fiction and scholarly works in pedagogical theory and practice. He has published twenty-two novels, including the twelve-volume Marc Edwards mystery series, and forty-nine books of poetry, one of which, Coppermine, was short-listed for the 1973 Governor-General's Award. In 1970 he won the UWO President's Medal for the best periodical poem of that year, "Death at Quebec." Don lives in London, Ontario.

Email: gutteridgedonald@gmail.com.